The King of Avalon

The Hound Who Hunts Nightmares
Book Three

Caractacus Plume

SILVATICI

A catalogue record for this book
is available from the British Library.

ISBN 978-0-9935105-2-6

Published by Silvatici.
silvatici@outlook.com

For Jason

With thanks to:
Dr H
George
Kate
Kit
Louise
Olivier De Beventine
Percival

PROLOGUE
The Black Flower

The good ship *Black Flower* sliced purposefully through the chopping iron waves like an oiled porpoise (one might be tempted to say *porpoisefully*, but that might be pushing it a tad too far – unless, of course, one happened to be born and raised in the New York borough of the Bronx during the *Great Depression*) – sleek, black and silent. Following in her wake (surrounded by a clasping grey mist that swirled like an assassin's cloak) a small flotilla of similar vessels surged tenaciously onwards, barely making a sound as they cut through the treacherous waters of the Irish Sea.

At the prow of the proud *Black Flower*, leading his people, as he had done for over seven score years and ten, stood her captain, Danny Blackflower* – Lord of the *Astrai*, *High Captain* of the elusive Sea Elves, the fabled *Red Clan*.

Danny Blackflower was in a foul, foul mood, and had been for over two months now.

'Bad business,' he muttered to himself. Bad business all round. He could see nothing but trouble ahead. Nothing but trouble.

Danny Blackflower didn't like trouble.

There was a rhythmical scuttle of bare feet behind him and he turned his head to see his uncle, Black Jack Blackflower, scurrying towards him on limbs that looked like they'd been fashioned out of ancient driftwood. Black Jack was the oldest of the Astrai (not that there were many of them left these days – barely nine families struggling to crew their nine remaining ships) and if he wasn't the sharpest tool in the box, then no Elf knew the coastal waters better than Black Jack; for, in his long (and accident-prone) life, he'd reputedly hit every rock, reef and sandbank that there was to be found in and around the British Isles (and a fair few that shouldn't have been!).

'Our *guest* is awake, Danny,' wheezed the old Sea Elf, in a voice like a cormorant spitting out cornflakes.

'Is they now,' growled Danny, refusing to take his eyes from the horizon, as though if he looked hard enough he might just find a beacon of hope to lead them through this dreadful mess. 'Looks like they'll pull through then, does it?' he asked, dismally failing to mask his disappointment, as his heart lurched with dismay into his ankles.

'I reckons so. Asked what there was for breakfast and then *demanded* to see you at the first opportunity,' sniggered Black Jack, his face creasing into a weather-beaten mesh of amused wrinkles.

Danny Blackflower leaned to one side and spat leisurely into the waves.

(* As a point of note, all Sea Elves carry the name of the ship that they were born on.)

5

Their unexpected, uninvited and, quite frankly, unwanted guest had flapped onto their decks just over eight weeks ago, arriving like an evil curse unwittingly summoned on a bright summer's morning; an old ship-mate, looking like badly-mauled shark-bait and in obvious need of assistance; an old and trusted companion who brought with them nothing but a gobful of bad news and a fistful of trouble.

Danny Blackflower didn't like trouble.

But, oh well, as Black Jack had said at the time – *a friend in need is a pain in the arse.*

He'd half-hoped that their old comrade would have died from their dreadful wounds (which, if they'd had any decency, they should have done) and then he could have hauled the ill-fortuned, inconsiderate, miserable bastard overboard, along with their awful cargo and hateful news. *Was it still too late,* he wondered? Stop the rot, before they were all drowned in an ocean of despair?

Danny Blackflower pitched another mouthful of phlegm over the side of the ship and turned to face his uncle.

'Bollocks,' he grimaced.

Black Jack gave a cackle like dry twigs being snapped in a tin bucket. 'Still not too late to ... you know ... give 'em the old *heave-ho,* if you catch my drift,' he wheezed helpfully. 'Might be for the best, Danny. Dark waters ahead of us, I'll tell you that for nothing, son. Dark waters.'

'Wish that we could, Uncle. Wish that we could. But we can't. You know that. Don't you?'

The ancient mariner worried a lonesome tooth with his tongue, tugged at the golden hoop in his ear, screwed up his thirty-thrice broken nose, and nodded.

Danny ruefully shook his head, and then slapped the old fellow on the shoulder.

'Best go and see what all this is about then, I suppose,' he muttered, resigned to his fate, as he knew he had been all along. 'Even though I reckon that what you say is true, Uncle – *dark waters ahead,* and no mistake about it. Don't know rightly what it is, mind, but whatever it is, trouble is on the wind.'

Danny Blackflower didn't like trouble.

The King of Avalon

ONE
State Of Play

'Yes, that was smashing. I'll 'ave that please, son,' beamed Professor Cornelius Lyons, kindly, as he delicately dabbed his splendid whiskers with a paper napkin.

The waiter, a young Brightonian with a headful of blond dreadlocks and an armful of tribal tattoos, looked down his long, pierced nose at the tweed-encased old nuisance and submitted a quizzical, nonplussed twitch of the lips.

'I think that *that* was it, Professor,' suggested Inspector Jones, hesitantly, whilst shooting a haunted look in the direction of the bemused young man.

Cornelius gave his friend a blank stare, eyed the waiter suspiciously and then gazed in mournful horror at the empty plate in front of him.

'You're 'aving a laugh?' he gasped. ''Ere, Jonesy, call the police, I've just been mugged. I thought that that were a taster – like in them posh restaurants where they let you sample the wine before buying the bottle.'

Inspector Jones gave a sorrowful little shake of his head, and then aimed a smile at the waiter that had "*deepest sympathy*" written all over it.

Cornelius wiggled his moustache and sniffed.

The tattooed young man made to leave.

'Four pounds fifty,' muttered Cornelius, in genuine dismay. 'Four pounds fifty!' he growled, making the waiter jump and look around in indignant annoyance. 'Four *Maggies* an' *Johnny-boy Major* for 'alf an avocado mashed over a slice of pygmy toast!'

'Hey, it's organic, chap,' retorted the waiter, firing a condescending look down his extensive hooter. 'And *locally* sourced,' he stated, as if that solved the whole matter.

Cornelius shot him a baleful glare and snarled.

'Don't take it personally,' smiled the young man, humourlessly. 'Calm down, dude.'

'Did you just call me a *dude*, son?'

Inspector Jones, seeing Cornelius' knuckles twitch towards a dessert fork, shot out a pacifying hand and laid it gently on the old fellow's forearm.

'Can we have two more coffees please ... and maybe a couple of slices of that walnut cake?' he smiled, with a friendly wink at the hapless young waiter. 'Better make it three slices. My shout, Professor.'

'Do they do 'ire purchase?'

The waiter fired one last withering sneer at Cornelius and nodded, before sauntering off with his piqued and punctured conk lifted high in a smugly superior fashion.

'Come on, Professor, give the lad a break.'

'It makes me seethe, Jonesy. It makes me seethe,' seethed Cornelius. 'Why every Tom, Dick an' 'Enrietta think that they can sprinkle a spoonful of caster-sugar over a blackberry-buttered crumpet an' consider themselves some kind of culinary genius 'oo can charge a small fortune for the privilege, is beyond me. Whatever 'appened to simple food served at a reasonable price?'

Mordecai Jones shrugged and then chuckled.

'It's good to see you again, Professor.'

Cornelius sighed, relaxed his shoulders and then beamed back at his old friend.

'An' it's good to see you too, Jonesy, it truly is. 'Ow was it over on the Continent?'

Inspector Mordecai Jones of the Sussex Police's *Department of Special Cases* (D.S.C.) had been away for the last two months working in Europe at the request of IPISS (the *International Paranormal Investigation Security Sector*) applying his considerable talents (not only was Inspector Jones a first-rate detective he was also a first-rate medium and spirit-talker) into trying to get to the bottom of the hushed rumours regarding the truly terrifying prospect of the possible outbreak in hostilities between the two powerful vampire *Families* who controlled the supernatural underworld of Northern and Western Europe (to wit – the *Nachzehrers* and the *Della Mortes*).

'Remarkably quiet, Professor,' replied Inspector Jones, with another haunted shrug, 'worryingly so, I'd say. On the surface, at least, it appears that nothing is happening, but word has it that both sides are drawing breath and collecting their forces for an all-out war. Feels like the lull before the hurricane. It's going to blow, ain't no escaping it, Professor, and when it does ... well, let's just say that all hell is going to break loose.'

Professor Lyons thoughtfully nibbled the ends of his moustache.

'I don't suppose that Mr Hound has changed his mind about ... *matters* ... has he?' asked Mordecai, with a hint of forlorn hope hanging in his voice.

'I suppose that by "*matters*" you mean – telling the *powers that be* that it were the vile an' villainous vampire, Lord Manfred de Warrenne (last bloodsucker left standing of the odious, exiled an' renegade 'Ouse of Alexios) 'oo instigated the whole bloomin' brouhaha in the first place?'

'That'd be it,' winced Mordecai with a troubled smile. 'It might help to get things sorted a whole lot quicker, and with a lot less bloodshed, if he did choose to pass on that particular nugget of information.'

Cornelius snorted. 'Ain't going to 'appen, Jonesy. The way 'Is Nibbs sees it is that it's 'is responsibility. What's 'appened with de Warrenne 'as become personal. There's no way, in this world or the next, that 'e's going to risk some clod-footed copper (no offense, Jonesy) or government agency ballsing things up an' taking away what 'e (The 'Ound) sees as 'is divine duty to deliver justice for Alberich an' the Pharisees – not forgetting for 'is own long-lost brother, Bors, for that matter. Add to that the fact that 'e is of the firm opinion that if the Della Mortes an' the Nachzehrers do go to war then we'll 'ave a few less bloodsuckers to worry about – an' that can't be nothing but a good thing, wouldn't you say so, Jonesy? An', if they do 'appen to wipe each other out an' let some supposed "*new order*" take their place, well, is that such a bad thing, I ask you? Is it really better the devil we know? 'Oo can say, Jonesy, 'oo can say? But what I do know for certain is that there are one or two European governments 'oo 'ave become just a little too cosy an' *complicit* with *The Families*; so shaking things up a little ain't necessarily such a bad thing. An' whatever we might think about 'Is Nibb's opinions (an' I tend find myself agreeing with 'em), I say we owe it to The 'Ound to respect 'is decision on this one an' stand firm be'ind 'im. I may not know much, Jonesy, but one thing I do know is that I've learnt to trust 'is instincts in matters like this. An' I've no doubt that you've come to feel the same way too.'

Inspector Jones anxiously gnawed the inside of his lip and tentatively nodded his head in agreement.

The dreadlocked waiter returned with the coffees and walnut cake (engaging with Cornelius in a silent duel of sneering civility) and placed them, with a petulant flourish of over-politeness, on the table.

'So what about things here?' asked Jones, as he slid two plates of walnut cake towards Cornelius' quivering hooter. 'What's been happening? Any developments that I should know about?'

'Best that I can say,' replied the old duffer, wiggling his sausage-like fingers in anticipation and eagerly tucking a fresh napkin into his collar, 'is that at least it's bloomin' stopped snowing – an' that's one 'ell of a blessing, let me tell you, Jonesy. Now it's just day after day of damp, drizzling skies an' sodden, soggy pavements. Miserable weather we've 'ad, an' no two ways about it,' he sniffed, as he plunged his dessert fork into the first slice of cake with all the skill and finesse of a cannibal turned Harley Street heart surgeon.

'No *new* news then? No more updates on the *Crowns of Albion*?' enquired Inspector Jones, optimistically.

'Not a dicky bird, Jonesy. Nought. Zilch. Nada.'

The Inspector sipped his coffee and watched in rapture as the old fellow demolished the first slice of walnut cake.

Cornelius looked up and raised a beetling eyebrow at the Inspector. 'We're at a loss, Jonesy,' he croaked, cake-crumbs decorating the fringe of his enormous moustache like damp confetti. 'The trail's gone stale. Until something moves ... we're stuck.'

'And how's young Tom holding up?'

'The boy's doing fine,' clucked the old codger, eyeing the second slice of cake like a constipated goat contemplating an over-ripe prune. 'I 'ope,' he added.

'He's not been affected too much by ... recent *affairs* then?' asked Mordecai, as delicately as he could.

'By "*recent affairs*" I suppose you mean – 'aving to chop the 'ead off 'is dear old dad?' considered Cornelius, briefly pausing to wipe his wondrous whiskers before launching himself onto *cake slice number two* like a famished osprey. 'Nah. There's more than a little touch of the Adamsbane about that one, let me tell you. Seems to be 'olding 'imself up all right, as far as I can tell.'

The Inspector wanted very much to ask Cornelius how *he* was holding up (considering that Tom's "dear old dad" had also been the Professor's estranged, and *cursed,* son) but, knowing his old friend as he did, he regretfully thought better of it.

'And Abigail?' he offered instead.

'Finally managed to persuade 'er to take that 'oliday. I think that she's more upset by events than anyone – as she's got every right to be. She's staying with some old friends in New Zealand. Now that Johnny is well an' truly out of the picture, it's well past time that she got on with 'er life without 'aving to look over 'er shoulder at every toss an' turn. New start for 'er, if she'll allow it.'

'Let's hope she does. Ms Dearlove deserves all the good luck in the world, if you ask me.'

Cornelius nodded his agreement as he stacked the second empty cake plate on top of the first and took a swig of coffee.

'So, as far as we know, the state of play remains very much the same as when I left, then?' considered Inspector Jones. '*The Society of the Wild Hunt* still holds both *The Winter Crown* and *The Summer Crown; the Carnival of Curiosities* is still in possession of *The Autumn Crown*. And *The Crown of Spring* is still ... where exactly?'

''Oo knows, Jonesy. 'Oo knows? Ned an' Archie 'ave been scouring the 'ills an' valleys, retracing Johnny's steps in the vain 'ope that 'e might 'ave stashed it somewhere, or dropped it as 'e trounced along on 'is merry way, wreaking murder, may'em an' 'avoc as 'e went. But, so far ... well, let's just say that it ain't been found.'

'And the rest of the Pharisees?'

'Still in France.'

'Crow?'

'Still with us at One Punch Cottage. Lovely girl. Grown very fond of 'er, I must say. Must say that young Tom seems to 'ave grown more than a little fond of 'er too,' chuckled Cornelius wryly. ''Ere – do you want that slice of cake, or what?' he asked hopefully.

Mordecai sighed and gently pushed the walnut cake towards his friend. 'You have it, Professor. I had breakfast travelling back on the Eurostar this morning.'

Cornelius shot him a grateful (and possibly slightly sympathetic) smile.

'The 'Ound is still a bit wary of 'er, though.'

'Of Crow?'

'Don't think that 'e fully trusts anyone 'oo is so closely connected with the Arch-prat.'

'Sinjon Sin-John?'

'Gesundheit.'

'Well, I suppose that you can't blame him there. Not quite sure what MI Unseen are about these days. I think we've all grown to be a little nervous of them. But Crow, well, she seems to be well and truly on our side, wouldn't you say?'

'I 'ope so, Jonesy. Believe me I do.'

'So, no word on de Warrenne?'

'Nope.'

'Dr Chow?'

'None.'

'What about Prince Edric?'

'Hhmmm,' hhmmm-ed Cornelius, tapping his cake fork against the tip of his nose and scowling at the remaining slice of walnut cake like a walrus with worms. 'Rumour 'as it that more an' more flock to 'is banner daily. The gossip from *under the 'ills* is it that 'e's set 'imself up as some sort of *champion* of the Fae World, 'oo 'as sworn to defend an' protect the Elbi in their darkest 'our.'

'Has he indeed? Interesting,' mused Inspector Jones.

'Fart-faced little twerp.'

'Bess all right?' asked Mordecai.

''Appy as a summer's day,' beamed the old fellow.

'What about Mr Rawhead-and-Bloody-Bones?'

'Ah,' replied Cornelius between munches and a stout slurp of coffee. 'Tommy 'as returned to *The 'Idden Realm* for a little while. What with all this nonsense with Edric, the 'ole of Avalon 'as been in a right old pickle, let me tell you. So, Tommy 'as *gone below* to try an' settle things down a little. An' fingers crossed on that front, 'cause the last thing that we need right now is for the sour little turd – better known to us all as Prince Edric Bloodstone Adamsbane – to be gaining too much support an' starting a flamin' civil war among the Aelfradi. 'Aving said that, mind, Missus Dobbs is more than a little upset at 'is departure. 'Er an' old Tommy seem to 'ave taken quite a shine to one another,' chortled the tweedy old codger in delight. ''Oo'd 'ave seen that coming?'

Mordecai raised an eyebrow of startled wonderment.

'Been quite the little love nest, 'as One Punch Cottage, what with them two an' young Tom an' Crow.'

'And how is young Tom's training going?' asked Mordecai, with hopeful concern (and desperately trying not to imagine Missus Dobbs and Bloody-Bones in the act of ... well ... you know!).

'As good as it can be, I suppose,' replied Cornelius, though not sounding thoroughly convinced. 'Which reminds me, I'd better start 'eading back to One Punch Cottage. Old Bobby Goodfellow 'as taken on the task of being Tom's tutor (much to Tom's annoyance, but, well, what with Tom 'opefully becoming the King of Avalon someday soon, 'e'd better start getting 'imself educated in what's what an' 'oo's 'oo, if you follow me). Promised Bob that I'd bring 'im back some writing paper, ink, a bag of gingerbread-men, a couple of dead chickens an' a brace of celeriacs before Tom starts 'is afternoon session.'

Cornelius rose from his seat, drained his coffee cup dry and gave his spectacular *Newgate-Knocker* a final wipe. 'Drop by this afternoon when you've signed yourself back in at the station, Jonesy, I know that everybody'll be delighted to see you. An' ta very much for the cake an' all,' he said kindly, whilst shooting a look of courteous disdain in the direction of the scowling waiter (who, in turn, was hovering in the background with feigned politeness, ready to pounce and clear them from their table at the first hint of an opportunity). 'Very much appreciated.'

'My pleasure, Professor,' replied Inspector Jones, eyeing the scene of cake carnage in front of him with a sense of awe.

'An' I do 'ope that you'll be able to claim it all back on expenses … or you'll be flippin' bankrupt!' growled Cornelius, tipping his hat (along a wide, toothy and humourless grin) towards the sniffy young waiter, as he reached for the café door.

TWO
Lessons To Be Learned

'Very good, young Tom,' smiled The Hound, with a graceful salute of his blade (a light touch to the forehead and then the heart, followed by a majestic sweep towards the ground). 'Very good indeed. Try to focus on keeping the correct positions during all of your actions; covering in your *offence* and threatening in your *defence*. Do not be hasty in your methods – you must *hunt* rather than *fight*. *Respect your opponent, but fear them not.*'

Tom wiped the sweat from his forehead with the back of his padded sleeve and returned the were-hound's salute with a barely-concealed self-satisfied grin. He felt that he was finally beginning to make sense of The Hound's (once unfathomable) instructions in the art of swordsmanship. Perhaps the irredeemable git (Prince Edric Bloodstone Adamsbane, that is, not The Hound) would rue the very day that he had to cross swords with Prince Tomas Spiritweather-Adamsbane-Dearlove (*ha-ha!*). Deep within, Tom felt the slow growth of a steely confidence that he might just be able to pulverise his demented, psychopathic and (unnecessarily) hateful cousin (once removed) if they did ever actually have to meet in their proposed "Death-Match" – a delightful little contest to decide who was going to be the new *Pook of Avalon* (not that Tom had any desire to be the king of a bunch of sour-faced subterranean faeries who were the sworn enemies of all things human – or, in fact, of any kind of faeries whatsoever, no matter what their political views happened to be – but, there you go: as his ~~uncle~~ grandfather was overly fond of telling him ... "*You can't always choose what you get*").

Crow shot him a beaming smile (brimming with heartfelt admiration) and broke into a rousing burst of applause.

'That was great, Tom!' she enthused. 'You're looking brilliant!'

Tom gave her a modest shrug of the shoulders, accompanied with a nonchalant (and possibly regal) wave of the hand.

'Thanks, Crow,' he replied, sounding as humble as he could, but feeling like he could conquer the world – and certainly smite the despicable shite (Edric) for all that he was worth. 'There's still a long way to go, but I think I'm getting the hang of it.'

'Run along now, Tom,' growled The Hound, oozing in his appreciation of Tom's undoubtedly remarkable martial aptitude and talent. 'A quick shower followed by a spot of lunch and then you best be ready for Puck Goodfellow's afternoon lesson. You are a *person of responsibilities* now, dear boy: a prince of Avalon. The hopes of a nation rest upon your young shoulders. Listen to what old Bob has to say to you, for his wisdom is legendary and his knowledge of the Elbi – their history, customs and expectations – is unsurpassed. If anyone can steer you into becoming the prince that *The Two Albions* not only desires but deserves, then it is he. We'll continue with your fencing lessons first thing tomorrow morning, dear boy.'

'Yes, Mr Hound,' replied Tom, trying to sound as enthusiastic as he could in regards to Bob Goodfellow's upcoming lecture – but really not at all interested in the idea of having to return to anything resembling a "normal" education.

'And very well done again, Tom. You've all the makings of a fine swordsman.'

Tom could barely keep the smile from his face as he jauntily skipped up the steps and towards the shower room.

The Hound busied himself with wiping the training blades clean and placing them back on their stand.

'He hasn't got a fricking hope in Hell, has he?' winced Crow, as the winning smile on her face evaporated like a gambler's lucky streak.

The Hound's ears momentarily wilted to the side of his head.

'Well, he's no *Bodalaine*, it is true, but he is showing ... *signs* of improvement,' offered the were-hound, desperately trying to sound optimistic. 'We have a couple of years yet to work on him and, who knows, perhaps he will ... bloom.'

'He'll need a blooming miracle if you ask me,' muttered Crow. 'Unless he's somehow able to morph himself back into his *Grendel-monster-self* for the big occasion – he's toast! Isn't there anything we can do to sort this mess out before it happens?'

'What would you have me do, Crow?' sighed The Hound. 'Cornelius, Ned and I are doing all that we can to prepare Tom for his ... *ordeal*. But becoming an expert swordsman takes time – rather like becoming a concert pianist. Short of finding some way to assassinate Edric, we must work with what opportunity *The Fates* have chosen to provide us with. We have time, not as much as we would have liked, granted, but I'm sure that things will work out for the best. And if *The Crown of Spring* remains lost, then there will be no need for Tom and Edric to even contest for the succession ... I say, where are you off to, young lady?'

Crow was striding determinedly across the Muse-asium floor, head down and lost in thought.

'Oh, I'm sorry, Mr H,' she replied, turning round to face the were-wolf-wolfhound. 'I didn't mean to be rude, I was just ... preoccupied. I can't stop thinking about Tom and this dreadful duel with Edric. I'm so worried about him. It will be all right, won't it? Won't it, Mr Hound?'

'I will do everything in my powers to make it so, Crow,' replied the were-hound, solemnly. 'I give you my word.'

Crow bowled a grateful but unconvinced smile in his direction.

'Thank you, Mr H,' she said softly. 'By the way, what's a *Bodalaine*?'

'Bodalaine was a famous swordsman. Some say the finest warrior of his age, some say of any age; though of course such talk is nonsensical.'

'Did you know him?'

'No, not really, though I met him once, when I was but a young hound, before my *transformation*. (It's a little bit of a blur, truth be told, but one does like to cling onto the coat-tail of celebrity when it brushes by, however tenuously.) He and his companions (a rather unsavoury lot, I seem to recall, but what can one expect of hired killers?) were employed, briefly, by my dear master, Henry.'

'I see. What happened to him?' asked Crow. 'Bodalaine, that is,' she added hastily, seeing the beginnings of a tear well up in the corner of the were-hound's eye (as was often the case whenever the name of Henry Percy, 9th Earl of Northumberland – The Hound's long-dead master – was brought up in conversation).

'Alas,' sighed The Hound, 'his story followed the same old path as all men who pay their way with violence. As I heard tell, he and his comrades fell foul of the then Pope, Clement VII, and were never heard of again.'

'Oh,' pouted Crow, rather distractedly. 'If it's all right with you, Mr H, might I go to my room now?' she sniffed, sounding as depressed as only a thirteen-year-old girl (contemplating the unavoidable fact that her newfound best friend is going to be legally, and systematically, murdered before his peers [and before too long!] by a bloodthirsty and unhinged, sword-wielding Elven prince) can.

'Of course, Crow. Run along and get some rest. I'll drop by to see you later. And believe me, everything will work out just fine, you'll see.'

'Thanks, Mr H,' replied Crow with the saddest of smiles. 'I'll catch you in a bit.'

The Hound offered a confidence-inspiring wiggle of his dagger-like digits as the young Half-Elf moseyed from the Mym and to her room.

When he was sure that she had gone The Hound hung his head and his tail drooped despondently to the floor. *Whatever was to be done? Crow was right – Tom wouldn't stand a chance against Edric. There was nothing for it,* he thought miserably, as he eyed the gleaming weapons that hung from the wall of the Muse-asium like a cult of over-eager assassins all edging for a promotion, *he was somehow going to have to remove Prince Edric himself.*

Crow flopped onto her bed and stared unflinchingly at the ceiling. Within moments her mind was made up. Why hadn't she thought of it before? It was only when The Hound had unwittingly said it that the obvious line of action had revealed itself to her.

Her train of thought was momentarily broken by a frantic scrabbling from outside the door. Crow rose from her bed to let in the eager and tail-lashing Bess. During her stay at One Punch Cottage she and the wolfhound had become firm friends, and Bess had chosen to make Crow's bedroom one of her favoured resting places for her many well-earned daily kips.

The giant dog nosed her way into the room with a loon-like grin plastered on her long face, edged her way towards the bed and somehow managed to seep onto it like a grey mist of homing-glue before Crow had even had a chance to try and think about reclaiming her space. With a resigned sigh she managed to squeeze herself next to the sprawling oil slick of a hound and ran her fingers through the great beast's coarse and wiry hair.

Bess nuzzled her hand with her nose and looked into Crow's eyes with a disapproving gaze.

Sometimes, thought Crow, it was as if Bess could read her mind.

'Well someone's got to do it. Don't they?' she whispered.

The wolfhound tilted her head to one side and cocked an ear in Crow's direction, seemingly hanging on her every word.

'I've never actually assassinated anyone before, of course, but ... how hard can it be? He's only an Aelfradi prince, champion Exhibition Skirmisher of Avalon, and captain of the murderous goblin war-society known as the *Redcaps* – no doubt surrounded and guarded by a hoard of vicious, homicidal supernatural nasties, all devoted to his cause and ready to lay down their lives for him at the first whiff of trouble. Piece of cake, really. And,' she added, as if it were Bess she were trying to convince, 'not only is he going to try to kill Tom at some point in the very near future, but everybody says that he's a thoroughly unpleasant tosser who needs taking down before he causes any more unnecessary harm.'

Bess looked terminally unimpressed, and Crow found herself wishing for the umpteenth time that Sparrow (her MI Unseen – Achilles Project IX co-agent and only other friend) were here to talk to. He always knew just *what* to do and *how* to do it. But he was far away (somewhere) having thrilling adventures on some exciting mission, knee-deep in conspiracy and counter-intelligence, no doubt daringly embroiled in the upcoming vampire conflict in Europe. Not that she would have swapped places with him – she had enjoyed her stay at One Punch Cottage, no doubt about it, but, well, it was growing a little tedious (no matter how fond she had become of them all, and no matter what her orders from Colonel Sinjon Sin-John had been [and she felt more and more uneasy about having to spy on the trusting occupants of One Punch Cottage with each passing day]). She was, she suddenly realised, in desperate need of some excitement – and here was her opportunity. Not only could she escape the stifling surroundings of her problematic predicament, but she could also pit her (not inconsiderable) skills and test her (not inconsiderable) mettle against a truly unpleasant and worthy adversary (Edric Blood*stain* Adam's-*pain* – ho-ho) and thus save the life of her new and dear friend (and she was, she was very surprised to have to admit to herself, growing more than a little fond of Tomas Dearlove – awkward, pompous, misguided, endearingly humble, sword-fumbling twit that he was). Then, when the grisly job was done, she could finally set all of her (not inconsiderable) resources into tracking down and winning back *The Winter Crown* and thereby, not only bring about an end to The Gentry's self-imposed exile – thus restoring the reputation of her family (the failed and shamed guardians of said *Winter Crown*) and honouring the blessed memory of her dearly-missed and deeply-mourned Nanny Nannie (the sea-witch, Cutty Sark [horribly murdered {eaten} by the foul monster Johnny Grendel {Tom's estranged and lunatic father – now, thankfully, deceased}]) – but also wrap up this whole "Crowns of Albion" debacle once and for all.

Crow quickly arose (moving hastily away from the unlikely [and quite frankly questionable] collection of brackets) and began to collect all of the carefully-hidden hi-tech MIU gadgetry that she'd expertly concealed about her room.

Bess offered a doubtful, mournful and cautionary whine.

Somewhere, deep down inside, Crow felt a heart-breaking twang of remorse for her intended course of action, but she quickly stifled that unnecessary and unprofessional feeling of regret. She had a mission to perform. And if there was one thing that could be said about Crow (MI Unseen Agent AP9-15) it was this – she was simply born to perform.

'Well done again, Prince Tomas,' crooned Bob Goodfellow, as he spat out the chewed-off chicken head and gently put aside the corpse of the unplucked poultry. 'Very well done indeed.'

Tom watched in horrified fascination as the chicken's head looped skywards (with an expression of eternal surprise starched onto its hapless visage), arched gracefully, and landed with a meaty "plop" into the wicker wastepaper basket that waited expectantly by the side of the writing-desk in The Study of One Punch Cottage. Tom dragged his perturbed gaze back to the terrifying old lunatic (Bob Goodfellow, that is – though One Punch Cottage did seem to be becoming some kind of haven for them [terrifying old lunatics]) and tried to keep the grimace of disgust that was sprouting on to his face to a minimum.

Bob Goodfellow's methods of teaching were, to say the least, *unorthodox*, but Tom had to admit that the rancid old scarecrow certainly knew how to hold a pupil's attention.

Tom had always been a little bit wary of Bob – his one-time neighbour (now revealed to be *High Puck* [Grand Wizard] of *The Two Albions* and, until the recent death of Tom's father, the guardian of both Tom and Tom's mother, Abigail) – and it wasn't just the smell.

The ancient warlock stared at him with fierce, slanting blue eyes that pierced through his grimy, unwashed face like sunshine cutting through smog. He was dressed, as Tom had always remembered him being dressed, in a grubby granddad-shirt, that practically writhed under an even grubbier knitted tank-top (that was more hole than knitwear), with tattered brown corduroy trousers held up with string. (*These*, Tom reflected humorously to himself, as he burst into silent song, *were a few of Bob's favourite things*.)

'So,' growled Bob (immediately deflating all comical musical thoughts as he lanced Tom with a look like an *operatic-Austrian-nun* hunter's harpoon), 'that was the grisly end of the royal line of *Grimtooth*. Now, let us move forward to the noble house of *Adamsbane*.'

The wizard cleared his throat and peered at Tom from under bushy eyebrows (plastered like a pair of pissed caterpillars across his soiled forehead). 'As we have just discerned – Grizler Grimtooth, last of the Grimtooth dynasty, was killed by …?' he asked expectantly.

'Was killed by Ashdread *Corpse-hand* Adamsbane – also known as *The Puck-Pook*,' replied Tom, watching in uneasy fascination as Bob Goodfellow plucked a gingerbread-man from a paper bag.

Nipper and Snapper, Bob's two scruffy (naturally) and savage-looking Airedale terriers (allegedly) – who sat as patiently as Death on either side of the desk, like a set of psychotic bookends – eyed the gingerbread-man hungrily and broke into Pavlovian crocodilian grins (revealing several sets of ragged, snaggle-toothed chompers that would have made a veterinary surgeon weep and an *attack dog* trainer rub his hands with glee).

'Indeed. *The White*-Wyrm *Wizard-King*,' rumbled Goodfellow, with a look of inward disapproval. 'Who had been …?'

'Grizler Grimtooth's chief-advisor.'

'And?'

'And the *Puck of Avalon*.'

'Good. Go on.'

'Who took the crown from King Grizler because he felt that he – Grizler, that is – was letting the Aelfradi side down.'

'And so what did *The White-Wyrm* do?' demanded Bob, chomping his unsightly gnashers rhythmically.

'He transformed himself into a giant bear and, as King Grizler went walking through the forests of Avalon – collecting posies of his favourite flowers – attacked the old Pook and killed him by biting his head clean off,' finished Tom, with a grimacing glance towards the wicker wastepaper basket.

'Indeed he did,' muttered the dishevelled old lunatic, running his tongue thoughtfully across his unsightly black choppers. 'Ashdread Adamsbane. *Corpse-hand. The Puck-Pook. The White-Wyrm*. The founder of the Adamsbane dynasty, and the longest ruling monarch in Elven history. King Corpse-hand was succeeded by …?'

'Er … His only son – *Urhur the Unpleasant*.'

Bob Goodfellow jubilantly waggled the gingerbread-man in Tom's direction expectantly. Nipper and Snapper's stumpy tails waggled in jubilant expectation. 'Who …?'

'Who,' continued Tom, biting his tongue in concentration and squinting with strained intelligence, '… killed his father by … uhm … by … er … turning him into a biscuit and dunking him in a vat of poisonous tea?' he suggested, rather hopefully, eyeing the Puck's empty mug of tea (expertly prepared by the infamous, gurning and apple-cheeked old tea-poisoner herself, Missus Dobbs).

'No, Prince Tomas, no he did not,' chastised Bob, trying not to sound disappointed. 'The White-Wyrm's death remains a *mystery*,' he rumbled mysteriously, passing a grimy, black-nailed hand over the gingerbread-man and making it mysteriously disappear – much to Tom's astonishment and Nipper and Snapper's disappointment. 'Urhur succeeded the throne peacefully, the only child of the line of Adamsbane to ever do so,' he concluded, with a pleasant and comforting black-toothed smile.

Tom offered a pleasant beam of his own back at the callous bastard, and let that particularly delightful nugget of information sink in (as a wave of bowel-squeaking shivers ran up and down his spine, and a chorus of spine-rumbling squeaks sought to musically *express* themselves to the world at large). However you looked at it, none of this was ever going to work out well for him, even if, by some absolute miracle, he did make it to the throne of Avalon unscathed.

'And what can you tell me about Pook *Urhur the Unpleasant*?' pressed the malodorous old Puck.

'He was ... unpleasant?' offered Tom, expecting to be reprimanded for his facetiousness.

'Indeed he was, Prince Tomas. Oh, indeed he was,' muttered the Puck, nodding his head sagely. 'But not as unpleasant as his nephew ...?' continued the immortally unwashed wizard expectantly.

'You mean ... *Wulfstryde Woe-betide* – who succeeded the throne by ... er? ... by ... ?'

Goodfellow plucked another gingerbread-man from the bag and savagely slammed it head-first into the tabletop with alarming ferocity.

The gingerbread-man's head exploded in a violent cloud of crumbs.

'Ah yes, now I remember. By surreptitiously replacing Urhur's golden-earrings with anvils and then pushing him down a dry well.'

'Correct,' replied Bob, with a throaty chortle (obviously delighted at the thought of a job well done), brushing gingerbread crumbs from his hands and watching Tom intently as he broke the crippled remains of the headless gingerbread-man's corpse in half and tossed one each to the eagerly waiting Nipper and Snapper. 'And Wulfstryde Woe-betide was in turn followed by ...?'

'*Balin the Bastard*!' screeched Tom, possibly over eagerly.

'Indeed. And Balin was known as "the Bastard!" because?'

'Uhm? ... He was illegitimate?' offered Tom, hesitantly.

Bob Goodfellow sighed. 'No, Prince Tomas. No. Balin was known as "the Bastard!" because he was a right cun–'

'More tea, Duckies?' enquired Missus Dobbs, sticking her head around The Study door and gurning like a moonstruck ferret at the two of them.

'Oh how splendid, Missus Dobbs,' beamed the Puck, with a smile like a decaying cesspit sprawling across his grimy visage.

'How about you, Ducky?' she asked Tom, hopefully.

'Not for me, Missus Dobbs,' replied Tom with steely-lipped surety.

The House-Faery gave him a slightly disappointed gurn and then lurched away towards the kitchen, closing the door noiselessly behind her.

'Oh, she does know how to brew a splendid cup of cha,' chuckled old Bob. 'There are not many that know how to make a proper brew these days, let me tell you, young prince. What a treasure she is.'

'Indeed,' reflected Tom uncertainly, looking at the hare-brained cretin before him with newfound horror. 'But back to *Balin*? He was called "the Bastard!" because ...?'

'Because he was a right cunning so-and-so, that's why. Now, Tom, what did Pook Balin do to win the throne of Avalon?' continued Bob, fishing a new gingerbread-man from the bag and turning it to face Tom.

Tom sucked on his teeth and tried to look bright.

The shabby wizard plucked off a leg from the poor gingerbread-man and tossed it artfully to the smug-looking Snapper.

'Ah, yes. He cut off Wulfstryde Woe-betide's arms and legs and threw him into the river Adur.'

'Correct,' replied the pongy Puck, tossing another gingerbread limb towards the patiently waiting Nipper. 'Which started the brief war between the Aelfradi and the Pharisees – known as ...?

'The War of the Puckered Pook.'

'Indeed. Very well done, Prince Tomas. A conflict that was ended when the Pharisee king, *Aelflock the Wise,* proved without doubt that it was indeed Balin who had murdered Wulfstryde in the first place, and thus averted further bloodshed between the two tribes. This terrible act has left poor Pook Wulfstryde Woe-betide remembered to history as ...?'

'Bob?' tried Tom.

'No, Prince Tomas, not Bob,' muttered Goodfellow, with strains of exasperation beginning to be heard in his musical voice. The Puck glowered at Tom and then proceeded to pluck the remaining limbs from the unfortunate gingerbread-man.

'The Floater?'

'NO!' barked Bob, instantly curbing his irritation. 'He is remembered as *The Drowned King*. The Drowned King.'

'Ah yes, of course. *The Drowned King*. How foolish of me.'

'And Balin's punishment for falsely starting this terrible war was ...?' asked Bob as he rose from the desk, taking with him the last of the gingerbread-men.

This, concluded Tom, was the old moron's most elaborate *aide-memoire*, and not one that was easily forgotten.

'He was,' answered Tom, in assured fascination, as he watched the ragged loon attach two lengths of mangy-looking twine to the poor biscuit-man's limbs (and who might have had a perfect expression of horror iced onto his face – but perhaps Tom was projecting), which in turn were fastened to the collars of the happy-to-help Nipper and Snapper, 'tied to wild horses and ripped in half,' winced Tom, as the *Airedales* trotted in opposite directions (with the nearest thing to a giggle that a brace of biscuit-tugging Airedale terriers can manage) tearing said gingerbread-man asunder.

'And then?'

'His remains were fed to the Aelfradi Yeth hounds.'

'Indeed they were,' frowned Bob, as he fed the two halves to the ecstatic Airedales. 'Which unfortunate act depleted the stock of *Wish Hounds* to near extinction; for Balin Adamsbane's blood was poison to the very last drop (and which is why he is so fondly remembered and revered by the Aelfradi to this very day).'

Tom watched in disgust as the two dogs snaffled their prize, licked their lips and then looked expectantly over towards him as if eyeing the main course.

What wonderful fate awaited him, he wondered, should he ever actually reach kinghood that is? Perhaps he would he be found with a shovel embedded in his skull? And thus be remembered to history as *Doug*. (Ha ha). Or, if the shovel was removed, *Douglas*? (Ho ho.) But seriously, how would he be known? What title should he adopt? *King Dearlove the Thoroughly Decent,* had a lovely ring to it. *Pook Tomas died peacefully asleep in his own bed after a long and uneventful life filled with happiness and cracking good fortune,* sounded even better. Or how about Dearlove the –'

'DOOMED!' boomed Goodfellow, thunderously slamming the palm of his hand onto the desk-top.

'You what?!' meeped Tom, unpleasantly jolted from his pleasant daydream.

'Doomed is the Elf who would dare become *The Pook of Shadows!*' snarled the rancid old warlock, menacingly. 'And so, with the execution of Balin, the crown of *The Hidden Realm* eventually passed to your great-grandmother, *Titania the Terrible* – harridan queen of the Aelfradi; the second-longest serving monarch in Avalon's dark and spite-filled history. Hers was a long life, full of bitterness and bile, teeming with cruelty and cunning – and she was loved and feted by her people for it as no other had ever been before her. But even she,' soliloquised the insensitive honking old hobo, producing a brain-like celeriac from under the desk and holding it up before him like some homespun Hamlet, 'met her end before her days had run their natural course; for she was *murdered* by her grandson ...' he roared, suddenly clutching the root vegetable in both hands, squeezing his blackened thumbnails into it and sending vegetable-matter splattering in all directions, as the *turnip-rooted celery* (or *knob-celery* as it is sometimes appetisingly known) exploded like a ... well like a brain crushed between the homicidal hands of a murderous ten-foot tall monster, 'Johnny Spiritweather! Better known to us all as ...'

'Dad.'

'... Grendel!'

Missus Dobbs returned with a huge mug of tea and placed it down on the writing-desk.

'Mr Hound and the Professor have requested toasted cheese-and-onion sandwiches for lunch,' she gurned, with heartfelt excitement. 'Will that be all right for the two of you?'

'Splendid, Missus Dobbs. Prince Tomas and I are almost done for the day.'

Missus Dobbs looked almost overcome with delight, and she bimbled from the room muttering to herself about the untold wonders and wizardry of the Breville sandwich-toaster.

'So ...' asked Tom nonchalantly, finally finding the right moment to pop a question that had been pressing him somewhat urgently, 'did any of the other Pooks of Avalon have to ... fight a ... *Death-Match*?'

Old Bob scrutinized him for a short eternity (as if someone had asked him what toothpaste he used). An oppressive silence settled in The Study. Something scurried noiselessly through the unwashed warlock's filth-encrusted beard

'Indeed they did, Prince Tomas,' he sighed at last. 'Wulfstryde had to contest The Crown with his brothers, Wulfgewif and Wulffetch. And when Balin's rule was ended, Queen Titania famously battled against her step-uncle, two sisters, a brother, three cousins and one niece.'

'But why?' enquired Tom, trying to sound stoically indifferent. 'I don't get it. None of the other Elbi tribes keep up the practise of ritually murdering their nearest and dearest. And, what with Elf numbers declining and everything, why deliberately reduce their ... *our* population with a totally unnecessary (and needlessly barbaric) tradition? Why don't they just get together, have a nice chat and a lovely cup of tea, and then take a vote, or play Monopoly or something equally morally despicable?' suggested Tom, helpfully, and trying not to sound as if he was in any way against the wonderful idea of ceremonial family homicide.

'The Aelfradi are the largest and most powerful of all the tribes of the Fae Folk; their numbers account for almost half of all the Elbi in *The Two Albions*,' replied Bob Goodfellow, eyeing Tom like an owl who has just crash-landed into a pigsty. 'Perchance it is because they have preserved their attachment to the *old ways* that they have retained their strength. Who can say? Perhaps if they had cast aside the ancient traditions their power would have waned, as has the strength of the tribes of Upper Albion. It is, as you rightly say, Prince Tomas, a *barbaric* ritual, but kingship in itself is a barbarous thing. All kings are, to be quite frank, imbeciles – and yet they are dangerous imbeciles. Desire makes even the wise foolish. Who would trust the ambitions of those who seek to wear a crown? Just look at the pickle that we are in today because of the vaulted ambitions of those who would hold sway over *The Crowns of Albion*.'

'Hmm. And what about this *Crown of Albion* malarkey?' asked Tom. 'Will it really work? I mean, if someone actually does manage to collect all of The Crowns, will they really have power over all of supernatural Britain? And if so – are there even enough "*supernaturals*" left to make it worthwhile?'

The unwashed warlock harpooned Tom with an all-knowing stare and slowly smiled, revealing the full wonder of his revolting set of blackened and fetid tomb-like gnashers.

'Oh yes, Prince Tomas. Oh yes. Whosoever managed to reassemble the fabled *Crown of Albion* would indeed have dominion over all of the Fae Folk of these lands. And yes, though it is true that the *Children of Magic* are fading from the world, do not underestimate their power. Dragons still slumber beneath the green hills of Albion –'

'Dragons! Really?' gasped Tom in surprised delight, momentarily dragging his horrified gaze from the sight of Puck Goodfellow's distressing and disgustingly decaying gob.

'Indeed. At last count these isles still held three Drakes, nine Wyrms and nigh on two dozen Knuckers.'

'No way! Wow!' Even with all that he'd seen Tom wasn't expecting that. Would he, he wondered, ever get to actually see a dragon? Coo-el!!!

'Add to that the power of the Elbi and the Sidhe, Goblins, Brownies, and all of the other numerous families of *The Children of Light*. Then, there still remains at least one clan of Giants hidden high in the remotest mountains. A few Trolls continue to walk beneath the skies of Albion, as well as: Ogres; Gillytrots; Shucks and Dandy-dogs; Werewolves; Witches; Ghosts; Revenants; Wights; Sprites and Zombies; Kelpies and Eachys; Curse-ed Men –'

'*Curse-ed Men?*' enquired Tom, dramatically. 'Who the flipping heck are they?'

'Men who are cursed,' replied the rancid ragamuffin, helpfully. 'Oath-breakers; spell-locked and forced to wander the world for all eternity, until somehow released from their terrible bonds. And there are many other strange and wondrous folk that would make a new-crowned High King a most powerful and dangerous creature; one to be feared and reckoned with. However, there is something that has been – quite amusingly really, if you stop to think about it (though of course they never do) – overlooked ... Ah Missus Dobbs, is it time already? What modern magic is this? How thoroughly splendid!'

'Lunch is ready, Duckies,' gurned the googly-eyed House-Fairy excitedly.

And with that, class was dismissed and Tom, Bob Goodfellow and his faithful hounds, Nipper and Snapper, hastily made their way to the kitchen for a round or two of cheese-and-onion toasties.

THREE
Letters & Lonely Hearts

After lunch, Tom found himself relaxing in The Study with the rest of the ~~inmates~~ housemates of One Punch Cottage: The Hound lounged artistically in his giant armchair, his pointy snout buried excitedly within the pages of a new hardback novel, entitled "The Last Werewolf"; opposite him sat Cornelius, polishing his favourite set of silver-coated knuckledusters, and quietly humming one of his favourite Music Hall ditties to himself (a rather charming little number [made popular by his long-time, and dearly-missed, chum – the one-time boxer, keep-fit-enthusiast and star of the Edwardian Music Halls – Alexander {Alec} Hurley] that went by the catchy title of "'*Arry, 'Arry, 'Arry*"); Bob Goodfellow was idly perusing the bookcase, occasionally plucking a hefty tome from the shelves and flicking through its pages, as he thoughtfully scratched his frowzy beard – and sent the *strange things that lay within* scuttling, in fear of being unhomed; Bess was sprawled across the sofa like a felled ox, while Nipper and Snapper *snoozed* in front of the fireplace (Bess and the *Airedale*s had mastered the art of ignoring each other's presence while remaining on a permanent state of nonchalant vigilance); and Crow perched on the tatty footstool, clasping her knees to her chest and surreptitiously watching everybody in the room with a strange, haunted expression etched onto her pale and lightly-freckled face.

Tom sat at the writing-desk pretending to read G. Gillespie Livermore's (riveting) "*The Rise & Decline of the Great Troll Dynasties of Western Europe: 910 – 1463*", but in actual fact daydreaming about his potential lifestyle should he ever become *Pook of The Hidden Realms*, whilst abstractedly fondling the small kingfisher pendant that he wore around his neck (an heirloom of the royal house of Adamsbane that had once belonged to his grandmother, Princess, Spiritweather, and had been given to him by the Aelfradi goblin – and one-time infamous child-murderer [reformed] – Tommy Rawhead-and-Bloody-Bones).

He looked up and caught Crow's eye. The Half-Elf smiled shyly at him and then quickly looked away. Tom grinned inwardly. *Who could blame her?* he thought to himself, modestly. He was, after all, quite a catch – a prince of Avalon, a valued member of a firm of paranormal investigators of international repute, and a swordsman of extraordinary potential. *What girl wouldn't be enthralled?* he mused, bubbling with self-effacement. Funny how life had changed. A little more than six months ago he had been the absolute definition of an AWK (*Avoided Weird Kid)* – friendless, ignored and excluded by his peers, and most positively invisible (to say the very least) to any girl of his (limited) acquaintance.

Inspector Jones had briefly dropped by during ~~The South Lanes Cheese-Toastie Massacre~~ lunch to catch up on any news (of which there was none) and to fill The Hound in on the state of play between feuding vampire families, the

Nachzehrers and the Della Mortes. In his short visit the Inspector had been quite shocked at how much Tom had grown during his absence. Tom (to his absolute delight) couldn't help but notice that he was almost as tall as the D.S.C. detective. His joy was rather shattered however when Missus Dobbs started eyeing him up like an undertaker in a hospice and then excitedly wittering about how she must buy him a new set of clothes. Tom, still deeply traumatised by the memory of his bright-blue plastic/lino funeral-suit, had hastily avoided eye contact with the interfering old Brownie (most probably on the run, and in perpetual hiding, from the Fashion Police) and made the vain attempt to shorten his arms and make it look as if the sleeves of his jumper actually did meet his wrists after all.

'Tom, Crow,' said The Hound, suddenly lifting his great snout from his book and attempting a reassuring smile at the two children, whilst absentmindedly watching old Bob, 'before I forget, I have a small task for the two of you.'

Tom looked up sleepily from his own *enthralling* read.

'What is it, Mr H?' asked Crow, seemingly happy to have something to distract her from her private thoughts.

'During the unfortunate ... *incident* of a few months ago,' continued the were-hound, shooting Tom a sympathetic glance, 'many of the books were rather violently ejected from their homes, and, whilst Missus Dobbs has done her very best to return them to their correct location, well, shall we say that literacy isn't perhaps the strongest of her talents. I wondered, therefore, if you wouldn't mind re-alphabetising the library for me? Perhaps tomorrow, after your morning lesson, Tom?'

'Urhh!' groaned Tom, with a truculent teenage huff, as he tried to suppress the disturbing image of his monster-father rampaging up and down The Study, sweeping priceless books from the shelves like a delinquent and illiterate, uncouth and uncultured, malformed and badly-shaved gorilla with a giant chip on its shoulder.

'Of course, Mr H. Be delighted,' replied Crow, with a warm and eager-to-please smile.

Before Tom could attempt an equally enthusiastic beam of his own (positively unfelt), Missus Dobbs burst through the door of The Study like a carbonated whirlwind of insouciant excitement.

'Post has arrived!' she buzzed, with barely suppressed enthusiasm, as she skipped over and placed two envelopes on the arm of The Hound's armchair and then sauntered over to Cornelius and forcefully handed him an A4-sized manila packet.

(Tom had wondered how the post actually did arrive at One Punch Cottage – what with the mysterious old house being hidden and protected by all types of charms and spells? Did Missus Dobbs lie in wait [poised like a geriatric ninja] for the poor unsuspecting postman/woman/person to saunter merrily along Black Lion Lane in order to violently assault the hapless chap/chapess/person-of-non-specific-gender with a sharp little jab of her gnarled, chipolata-like digit to their unseeing eye? But no: he was reliably informed that all mail was delivered by H-

MADS (*Hermoth's Mail and Deliveries Service*) – courier extraordinaire to the Nine Realms. *Of course*, thought Tom, what had he been expecting – owls?)

'Ta very much, Missus Dobbs,' replied Cornelius, breaking off mid-hum and barely glancing up from his work.

Missus Dobbs loitered expectantly around the old fellow's armchair, rubbing the toe of a hefty hobnailed boot on the back of her spindly, crinkled and gravy-coloured stocking-encased calf.

'Er? ... Everything all right there, Missus Dobbs?' asked Cornelius, looking up at the gently fizzing House-Fairy; who seemed to be on the verge of erupting with barely-restrained anticipation.

'Yes thank you, Ducky,' she replied in a failed attempt at indifference, whilst eyeing the A4 manila envelope like a toddler ogling an opened bag of Jelly Babies.

Cornelius carefully followed the direction of her googly gape.

'That'll be my weekly copy of the "*Nag an' Gillytrot*" (that's the "*Faery 'Orse an' 'Ound*" to you), nothing to get excited about, Missus Dobbs.'

The Hound looked up from his book and watched the fidgeting Brownie with curiosity.

'You wouldn't mind if I ... if I ... well, if I ... er ...' floundered the tiny tea-poisoner, hopping restlessly from one foot to the other.

'... *borrowed it*?' offered Cornelius, hesitantly.

Missus Dobbs gurned in awkward appreciation.

'Errr? ... Well, no ... No, of course not, Missus Dobbs. 'Elp yourself,' smiled the kindly old codger, slightly bewildered as he offered the packet to Missus Dobbs' expectant and outstretched mitt.

'Ta very much, Ducky,' she cooed, snatching the envelope from Cornelius' hand and bimbling at a ferocious and ecstatic full tilt towards The Study door. 'Tea anyone?'

'NO THANK YOU, MISSUS DOBBS!' [chorus]

'What do you think all that's about?' frowned The Hound, having watched the House-Fairy all but sprint from the room, and then waited for the door to stop rattling on its hinges.

'You don't think she's developed an 'abit for the gee-gees do you, 'Aitch?' hissed Cornelius in bemused wonder, rubber-necking between the were-hound and the quivering Study door.

The Hound licked his teeth and pursed his lips. 'No,' he growled softly. 'Surely not? ... Preposterous.'

Cornelius chewed the tips of his moustache anxiously and then fastened his attention to the letters on the arm of The Hound's giant armchair. 'So, what 'ave you got there then, 'Aitch?'

'Ah, yes. Let me see.'

The were-wolf-wolfhound adjusted his red silk dressing robe, plucked up the first envelope and carefully examined it. 'Greek postmark,' he observed, slicing it open with a graceful flick of his lethal little finger and delicately extracting the letter.

'Extraordinary!' he exclaimed under his breath.

'What is it, 'Aitch? What is it?'

'A letter from The Pan.'

'The who?' asked Tom.

'Goat-men, son,' replied Cornelius, curtly.

'Yes of course, how foolish of me. *Goat-men*.'

'Fierce warriors, they is. Guardians of the mountain forests. Secretive folk. Whatever do they want, 'Aitch?'

'It appears that they are in need of some assistance in their ongoing and gallant crusade against the aggressive and unethical explorations into their homeland by unscrupulous and unprincipled oil companies,' sighed the were-hound, scanning through the letter with a regretful shake of his massive head. 'A cause that I wish I could commit my full resources to, but alas, what with the current situation here at home, I must unfortunately decline their noble plea until matters here have been resolved.'

'What about the other one?'

The Hound carefully lifted the second envelope and ran his nose along it.

It looked, to Tom's inexpert eye, like the most expensive envelope that the world had ever seen.

'Intriguing,' pondered The Hound. 'Posted from Morocco, a little over a week ago.'

He carefully opened the envelope and drew out and unfolded a luxurious-looking sheet of *writing paper*.

'Parchment,' mumbled the were-hound, lightly dabbing the top of the page with the tip of his enormous tongue. 'Astonishing.' He then set about reading the short message that was handwritten in the most exquisite of scripts.

'Absolutely fascinating,' he muttered, to no one in particular, as he read and re-read the letter again.

'What does it say, 'Aitch? What does it say?'

The Hound looked up at Cornelius.

'Forgive me, Dandy. How rude of me. It reads:

To The Hound Who Hunts Nightmares.

Dear Sir,

Fortune directs me towards the fabled shores of Albion – on a quest that is of imperative importance and the utmost urgency. I have heard, through a most devoted and capable associate, that you have had recent contact with one whom it is my greatest desire and duty to discover.

I shall visit your home, the legendary One Blow Bungalow, at my first possible convenience. Once there, I candidly request of you any information that you may be able to offer regarding this most delicate and difficult of affairs.

Until that time, I am your humble servant,

Prince Maffdetti-A-Su

'Prince Maff Eddie a 'oo?' asked Cornelius, with a badger-like twitch of his whiskers.

'Maffdetti-A-Su,' replied The Hound with a Gallic shrug of his thin black lips.

"Oo's 'e then, when 'e's at 'ome?'

'I have absolutely no idea, Dandy. Though it would seem that we are destined to find out in the not too distant future.'

At that moment Missus Dobbs surged through The Study door in a state of high agitation.

'Whatever is the matter, Missus Dobbs?' asked The Hound, laying the intriguing letter to one side.

'Well, Ducky,' she began, tentatively, 'it's this ...'

She thrust the opened copy of Cornelius' *Faery Horse and Hound* under the were-hound's startled hooter.

'And what *exactly* am I looking at, Missus Dobbs?' he enquired, gently relieving the House-Fairy of the periodical and squinting down his long muzzle at the open page.

'Well, for the last few weeks ... me and To– ... I mean ... Mr Rawhead-and-Bloody-Bones and I ... have been ... well, we've been keeping in touch through the small ads pages of this here magazine ...' she began, her eyes brimming with secretive delight.

'Yes ... yes I ... see,' replied The Hound apprehensively. '"*Roochy-Hoochy-Boo-Boo misses Missus Doochy-Oochy-Doos – XX*" ... That would be a message from ... Mr Bloody-Bones, I presume?' he asked tactfully, while Crow made a silent gasp and Tom stifled a gag.

Missus Dobbs reddened a little and then quickly composed herself and straightened her pinny.

'Yes it would, Mr Hound.' she gurned gleefully.

'Well that is ... *lovely,* Missus Dobbs. I can't begin to tell you how ... *happy* I am for you both.'

'Ooh, thank you, Ducks, most kind. But that's not what I wanted to show you, Mr Hound.'

'It isn't?' replied the were-wolf-wolfhound, with noticeable relief.

'Ooh no, Ducky. You see, as I was scanning through the pages for Tommy's message, I came across this,' she scowled, jabbing a gnarled little digit like a javelin onto the page, and making The Hound jump from his seat in alarm as her chipolata-like finger almost speared him in the conk.

The were-hound peered in concentration to where Missus Dobbs' digit had lanced the page, and his eyes lit up like fiery coals.

'What is it, 'Aitch? What is it?' demanded Cornelius, for he knew that look of old – and it could only mean that something of paramount importance had been discovered.

'Two paragraphs above Mr Rawhead-and-Bloody-Bones' ... *delightful* ... message to Missus Dobbs,' replied the were-hound, 'is another communiqué: it reads – "*My dear Lord dW, Regarding the recent meeting of our two associates – I find that everything is most agreeable. I await communication regarding the final logistics. Yours, Dr C.*"'

The Hound looked up, his eyes smouldering with excitement. 'By George,' he snarled, 'the game is afoot!'

'It is?' asked Cornelius, bursting with bemused attentiveness. 'So what, exactly, is all that about, then?'

'You don't think that "*Lord dW*" could be Lord de Warrenne?' cried Crow, breathlessly.

'Without a doubt!' growled The Hound, with the ravenous smile of the hunter catching the scent of his quarry. 'Without a doubt. And therefore "*Dr C*" can be none other but the devilishly mysterious –'

'Dr Chow!' cried Tom.

'Crikey!' yelped Cornelius. 'But what does it all ... mean?'

'It means, my friend, that the two rapscallions are, for whatever reason, in discussion about something and, therefore, we must conclude that they have entered into some sort of nefarious cahoots.'

'What do you think they can be up to, Mr H?' asked Crow, unfolding herself from the tatty footstool and purposefully striding over to look over the were-wolfhound's shoulder at the intriguing message.

'What indeed, young Crow? That is the question.'

'Well, take a look at this then, Duckies,' croaked Missus Dobbs, dramatically producing a crumpled back issue of the *Faery Horse and Hound* from within her pinafore and placing it, opened to the relevant page, on the writing-desk.

The Hound, Bob Goodfellow, Tom, Crow, Uncle Cornelius and all, crowded around the desk in a hushed excitement, scrutinising the magazine.

'Good God!' spluttered The Hound.

'That is without doubt a most inventive and descriptive use of Tommy's last name,' muttered Bob, somewhat aghast.

Missus Dobbs slammed her palm over the offending script, blushed, flashed a truly disturbing and embarrassed smile, and hastily pointed to the intended entry. It read:

> My dearest Lord dW,
> Suspecting that you might be an avid reader of this venerable publication, and having no other means by which to contact you, I have placed this unworthy

entry, in the small hope that it will come to your attention.

Both of us being enthusiastic *philatelists,* and both being in the hunt for the most rare and precious of collections, I would like to propose a simple and swift resolution to our unfortunate, yet sadly unavoidable, confrontation: A contest – champion to champion – with each of us placing one piece of the aforementioned *collection* as a stake.

Should your worthy champion defeat mine, then not only would I pass over to you what is in my possession but I would also immediately vacate this revered and enchanted isle, and, in so doing, leave you, free from any hindrance on my part, to pursue your cause. However, if my champion were to prevail, then, of course, I would receive half of what is in your possession (I suggest that we begin with Summer?); however, with you still in ownership of the third piece, I would insist that we play a second match (and so on), until the unseemly matter is finally resolved.

Yours humbly, Dr C.

'What's a flaturist?' asked Tom.

'A philatelist, Tom, is –' began Cornelius.

'A stamp collector,' finished Crow.

Tom smiled, but inwardly cursed. How come she knew so much ... stuff? It was rather annoying at times, but also oddly endearing.

'So why are they collecting stamps?' wondered Tom, thoroughly confused.

Crow regarded him with a look of amazement.

'Oh!' gasped Tom. 'Oh! I see. Yes. Yes of course! It's a cover. A code for *The Crowns of Albion!'*

Crow smiled at him, but all but slapped her forehead.

'And then there's this one, Ducks,' said Missus Dobbs, triumphantly producing another well-thumbed edition of the *Faery Horse and Hound.*

It read:

My dear Dr C,

What a delightful surprise. And what a thoroughly swell idea too! Top drawer, old chap, top drawer! I concur wholeheartedly. As you must be aware, I would stop at nothing to complete the *collection.*

I suggest a meeting, my dear fellow, in order to discuss matters in more detail. I will send a party to represent my interests, and request that you do the

36

same. My man will be waiting for yours by the mast
at the top of Whitehawk Hill at sundown on the
evening of next week's publication day.
TTFN, Lord dW.

'So what sort of contest do you think that it will be, Mr H?' asked Crow, with the businesslike expression of an MI Unseen secret agent reviewing a cracking clue settling onto her face. 'Some sort of hunt perhaps?'

'Nah,' sniffed Cornelius, with a beam of unbridled delight blossoming over his whiskery visage. 'Sounds to me like a good old-fashioned prize-fight. Just like it were back in the day;' he chirped, 'outwitting the Peelers, baffling the Beaks; the world an' 'is auntie's 'ound 'olding their breath, as The Fancy waited for last-minute word as to where an' when the mill would be 'eld.'

'This is the just very lead that we've been waiting for!' snapped The Hound excitedly, grinding his humongous right fist into his colossal left palm. 'Well done, Missus Dobbs, well done indeed!' he cried, suddenly clasping the surprised-looking House-Fairy's head between his knife-rack-like hands and planting a slobbery kiss on her forehead.

Missus Dobbs blushed, gave off a high-pitched giggle (that could have been embarrassed delight or pure terror) and then made a dizzy curtsey

'So,' growled The Hound, bristling with a resolute vigour, 'the arch-rotter, de Warrenne, and the mysterious cad, Chow, are going to gamble their ill-gotten gains (to wit – the *Crowns of the Elven Kings*) in a winner-takes-all contest. Well, we'll just see about that. All we need do is to find out where the malicious rascals plan to hold this illicit set-to. Any ideas, Dandy?'

'Well, if it's the word on a prize-fight that you're after, then there's only one chap to ask,' replied Cornelius, still grinning to himself as if he'd just discovered that Christmas had come round early.

'And just who would that be?' enquired The Hound, keenly.

'Whelky,' replied the old duffer, wisely.

'Whelk-face?' gasped the were-hound, incredulously.

'Whelk-faced Willie,' nodded Cornelius, sagely.

'Whelk-faced *Willie the Wheeze*?'

'Whelk-faced *Willie the Wheeze* Willikins.'

'The south-side snotter?'

'The mollusc-mouthed mucous muncher.'

'The lisping Lothario of the Lowland Ladies? I thought he was dead,' sniffed The Hound. 'Didn't he fall foul of Billy Kimber and the Brummagem Boys back in the early Twenties? Got shoved off a bridge, or so I heard?'

'Per'aps 'e did, 'Aitch,' replied Cornelius, with a rueful shake of his head. 'But good old Whelky is very much alive an' dripping, let me tell you. Runs a *drum* up near Kemptown.'

'A tavern? Really? Where abouts, Dandy?'

'Errrrmm …' replied the tweedy old codger, the smile uncertainly fading from his face. ' … Up near … Brighton College … if memory serves me right …'

'Indeed? Which one?' asked The Hound, a hint of suspicion creeping into his voice. 'The Cuthbert? The Bute? The Sutherland, perhaps?'

'No – that particular rumness 'as long since gone, 'Aitch – thank the Lord,' chuckled Cornelius. 'It's called *The Round Georges* these days, much more upmarket an' family-friendly … well, friendly full-stop, if you ask me.'

'Do you mean to tell me that Whelk-faced Willie the Wheeze is running a family-friendly pub?' spluttered the were-hound in astonishment.

'No … no, not … exactly,' wriggled Cornelius, looking decidedly uncomfortable.

'Then what?' enquired The Hound, with a tolerant yet quizzically piercing smile.

"E's *mine 'ost* of a little establishment up on … er … Canning Street … if I recollect correctly, that is, by the name of … erm, what was it, now? Hhmmm? *The Concealed Arms* … I think?' replied Cornelius, sounding doubtful, and looking like he was about to break out in a cold sweat.

'Extraordinary! *The Concealed Arms,* you say? I can't say that I've ever heard of it. How … *interesting.*'

'Ah, well, I do 'ear tell that it's a … sort of … private members' club,' gulped the old fellow.

'Oh it is, is it?' sniffed the were-hound, eyeing his old friend with a look of barely-concealed misgiving. 'Well, I suppose there's no point in hanging about, is there, Dandy? If you'd be so good as to prepare Old Nancy, we'll head off to … *The Concealed Arms* … directly.'

'Ooh, you don't want to trouble yourself with that, 'Aitch,' grinned the wily old tweedster. 'Why don't I pop over by myself an' have a … *chat* with old Whelky while you stay here an' –'

'Oh no, Dandy, I insist,' replied The Hound, jauntily. 'In fact, I think that we should *all* go and visit this *celebrated* institution.'

'Cool!' cried Tom, delighted to get out of this madhouse at any opportunity (plus he'd never actually been inside a pub before and was, quite naturally, fascinated).

Cornelius gnawed the tips of his Newgate Knocker for an instant whilst wearing an expression that could best be described as *"uncomfortable"*, before replacing it (somewhat stoically) with one of grim determination.

'All right,' he muttered, though sounding none too happy about it.

'I think I'll give it a miss, lads, if you don't mind,' said Bob, plucking something from his beard and examining it intently. 'I've got a fancy to take the dogs for a walk. Was thinking about heading along the Undercliff Path to Rottingdean, pay my respects to an old friend.'

Nipper, Snapper and Bess wagged their tails vigorously at the mention of the word "walk".

'Would you mind if I went along with Mr Goodfellow and the dogs?' cut in Crow. 'I could really do with some fresh air. If that's all right, I mean,' she asked, with irresistible charm.

That's a bit weird, thought Tom. So far Crow had avoided Bob's company wherever possible – whilst bombarding Tom with a constant stream of complaints about the old Puck's wizardly whiff. But, oh well, maybe she was warming to the nitty old ragamuffin, or at least becoming immune to the eye-watering stench. A long country hike supported by a strong sea-breeze should make the old lunatic's company bearable at least.

'Not at all, Crow,' smiled The Hound. 'I'm sure that Bess will be delighted to have you along.'

Bess rapidly beat her tail against the back of the sofa in heartfelt agreement.

'Now come along, Dandy, Tom. No time for delay. Chop-chop and off we trot,' beamed The Hound, evidently enjoying himself immensely.

Cornelius smiled uneasily back at him (noticeably enjoying himself rather less immensely) and headed for the door and towards the underground beach-side lock-up where the newly-repaired and souped-up old crock, Old Nancy, awaited them.

FOUR
The Concealed Arms

It was a rather silent, possibly frosty, and thankfully short drive to the quiet and unpretentiously pretty little road that is Canning Street – which nestles unassumingly (like a shy little brother) behind and betwixt the grandiose playing fields of Brighton College and the prosperous surrounding streets, stacked with highly-desirable and highly-priced houses. The Hound sat in the back seat of Old Nancy, nose pressed to the small crack in the opened window, seemingly lost in his own thoughts, while Cornelius grimly focused his concentration on steering the old crock through the bewildering one-way system of Kemptown (the vibrant and trendy area of Brighton that slumps, with over-practised decadency, towards the city's eastern flank).

On finding a parking space (no easy matter, and a task that took more than a couple of circuits around the block), Tom, Cornelius and The Hound – (dressed in his enormous grey duffle coat, with the hood pulled up and over his head to disguise his appearance – not that there was anything remotely suspicious about a seven-and-a-half foot tall *entity* wandering around the community with a nose like a blackened light-bulb protruding from the hood of his coat, nor the sabre-like wire-haired tail jutting from beneath its hem, nor indeed the gigantic and monstrously-clawed paw-like feet elegantly trotting along the pavement with the softest of clicks like a soft-shoe shuffle. *What the hell*, thought Tom, *it is Brighton after all!* And so, to be honest, the sight of a giant duffle coat-[or more correctly a *duffel* coat – after its place of origin]-encased cynanthrope sauntering jauntily through the local boulevards was nothing compared to some of the "wonders" that the residents of Kemptown had been subjected to over the years. *Besides,* he concluded, *it was raining and there was absolutely no one to be seen on the streets anyway*) – seeped from the car and took stock of their surroundings.

A relentless drizzle of rain greeted their arrival. Cornelius pulled down the brim of his coachman's bowler, turned up the collar of his knee-length tweed coat, and grimaced to himself as he marched over and fed a small handful of coins into the nearest parking meter.

'Well?' asked The Hound, looking up and down the street. 'Are you quite sure that it's here? I can see no sign of it.'

The bewhiskered old duffer, having made a deliberate show of carefully placing the parking voucher on Old Nancy's dashboard, stole a vigilant glance about him and then ambled across the road and over to an old-fashioned lamppost – on whose embossed and black-painted column he rhythmically rapped seven times.

There was a slight *shuffle* in reality (as if someone were slowly cranking up speed whilst perusing through a flip book) and suddenly, where there had been nothing but a short row of two-up two-down terrace cottages, there now appeared a spiralling iron staircase that led down from street level to what could only be described as an old-school basement saloon (that seemed to run the entire length of said row of houses) with an ancient wooden signpost hanging above it, on which was written (in a large, whirling and barely-legible scrawl) the legend – *The Concealed Arms.*

The Hound raised an eyebrow and looked at Cornelius like a disappointed headmaster about to confront a Head Boy who has just been caught flogging chewing-tobacco to the First Years.

Cornelius returned a humourless pout and loitered uneasily at the top of the steps.

'Oh, do lead on, old chap,' insisted The Hound. 'No point in us all getting soaked through, is there now?'

Cornelius sniffed stoically, re-set his hat, and led them down the twisting staircase and through a large, heavy wooden door, that looked like it hadn't seen a new lick of paint since Queen Victoria's dour days of mourning.

They found themselves in an expansive, dimly-lit room, scattered with hefty wooden tables (stained with centuries of spilt beer and candle-wax) and a floor covered with sawdust (and probably spit, but Tom didn't fancy looking too hard). It smelled strongly of stale ale, cheap cigars and shattered dreams. The smoky air hung about them like a net-curtain weaved from lung-glue. Seated at various tables were various shifty and nefarious-looking characters of *enchanted* origins, who suspiciously whipped around their heads like a posse of guilty desperadoes waiting for the replacement sheriff to turn up, and eyed the three new-comers like threatened cobras.

An out-of-tune piano abruptly halted mid tinkle.

The Hound threw back his hood and watched with a contemptuously curling lip as the tavern's occupants hastily fled the room faster than a posse of guilty desperadoes finding out that the newly-arrived replacement sheriff was in fact a seven-and-a-half foot tall were-wolf.

'Dandy!' cried a voice like a goblet of phlegm sliding down the inside wall of a damp prison cell. And from the piano-stool, up stood Whelk-faced Willie the Wheeze Willikins himself – arms outstretched in heartfelt welcome. 'What are you doing here, old thun?' he lisped. 'Wathn't exthpecting you till nextht Thurthday.'

'Good morning ... *Mr* Willikins,' sniffed Cornelius, in a rather unconvincing attempt at unfamiliarity.

Whelk-faced Willie the Wheeze was a short, lightly-built Goblin, of indiscernible age, dressed like a Victorian book-maker down on his luck. He had the complexion of a badly-wrung flannel – his grey and pallid countenance covered with a rather unsettling sheen of sweat – and an expression like a falsely-accused mollusc. His most distinguished feature, his rather disturbing and unsightly nose, snuggled to his perpetually perspiring visage like an arthritic slug – with a globule of snot hanging in a permanent state of readiness to descend at a moment's notice.

'And who ith thith I thee before me!' he cried in delight, palms upturned in a display of unbridled joy. 'Mithter Hound! Ath I live and breathe. What an unexthpected pleathure, thir. It ith, indeed. Indeed it ith.'

He grasped hold of The Hound's *paw* with both hands and shook it vigorously. The were-hound did his best not to look revolted, and surreptitiously wiped his mitt against his coat when the Goblin's attention was turned.

'And you, young thir? Who might you be?' wheezed Willie, turning to Tom and appraising him like an out of work pawnbroker. 'Could it be young Marthter Dearlove, of whom I have heard tho much about from my dear friend Profethor Lyonth?'

Tom retuned an unyielding and uncertain smile, watching in (he hoped) concealed horror as Whelk-faced Willie's slimy mitt slithered its way towards him in an attempt to ruffle his hair. Tom politely took a side-step and ducked his head out of the way (silently thankful for all of Cornelius' lessons in the art of pugilism).

'A pleathure, young thir. A pleathure indeed,' smiled Willie warmly, ignoring Tom's defensive flinch of revulsion. 'Welcome to my humble ethtablithment – The Conthealed Armth. Welcome.'

A long and awkward silence followed: The Hound looking sternly at Whelk-faced Willie; Uncle Cornelius looking uncomfortably at anything that wasn't Whelk-faced Willie; Tom looking at his surroundings in disgust – determined, at all costs, not to touch anything, and silently praying that there were no holes in the soles of his shoes; and Whelk-faced Willie looking as welcoming as he possibly could, but obviously straining under the threat that one of many wrongdoings was just about to be outed.

'... Well ...' began Whelk-faced Willie, finally breaking the fraught pause, 'thith is ... *nithe*. And jutht how ith it that I can be of athithtanthe?' he asked, shooting a worried grimace in Cornelius' direction.

Cornelius dodged eye contact.

'Am I to athume then, that thith little vithit ith buthineth and not pleathure?' he enquired, the smile slipping from his face like a widow's tear.

'I suppose you could call it both,' replied The Hound, a friendly air etched into his precisely clipped tones. 'However, Willie, I wasn't aware that you and Professor Lyons were such firm acquaintances.'

Whelk-faced Willie shot another hesitant glance at Cornelius.

'Well ...' he began, uneasily.

'We're 'ere on a case, *Mr* Willikins,' cut in Cornelius.

'A cathe!' replied Willie, managing to sound both alarmed and offended.

'Indeed,' growled The Hound, picking up a bag of pork scratchings from the bar and carefully examining it. 'A case of the highest importance and most deadly consequences ... Good God, man! These went out of date in 1975!'

'That'th how thome of my clientele like them, *Mithter* Hound,' snapped Whelk-faced Willie in annoyance, huffily grabbing the packet from the astonished were-wolfhound's grasp. 'They can't all have your refined and cultivated palate, thir, can they?'

'Do accept my apologies, Willie,' replied The Hound, with a frosty smile to Cornelius. 'I am so sorry, you were about to tell us more about your association with my dear friend, Professor Dandy Lyons.'

The smile re-rose on Willie's face like snot to a runny nostril after a deep sniff.

'Oh yeth, Mithter Hound, me and Corneliuth go way back. Mutht be ... ooh ... almotht an hundred yearth by now; ithn't that right, Dandy?'

Uncle Cornelius twitched his nose and readjusted his hat.

'Oh do go on, Willie,' pleaded the were-hound. 'Cornelius is so ... *reluctant* to talk about himself. It's an absolute pleasure to find out what the old *fellow* actually gets up to on his days off.'

'Now come on, 'Aitch, Willie's got a business to run an' we've got a case to crack an' no time to be standing around chewing the fat –'

'Well, ath you can thee, Dandy, it appearth to me that all of my trade theemth to have been ... thcared off!' smiled Whelk-faced Willie, with a face of happiness and a voice of barely-suppressed displeasure.

'Yes, come now, Dandy, all things in good time. Do go on, Willie.'

'Well, Mithter Hound, it will be my pleathure. Drinkth anyone?'

'I'll 'ave a pint of –'

'Tea would be marvellous,' replied The Hound, curtly.

Whelk-faced Willie smiled warmly at the were-hound.

'MAVITH!' he bellowed over his shoulder.

'WHAT?' croaked a voice like a rheumatic fart.

'FOUR TEATH, PLEATHE! AND UNWRAP A PACKET OF DIGETHTIVE BITHCUITTH! THE NEWETHT ONETH. I'VE GOT ... *GUETHTTH*!'

'So,' enquired The Hound, amiably, as they all sat around one of the hefty wooden tables (everybody armed with a steaming mug of tea and a plate of almost crisp Digestives), 'how *did* you and Dandy get to know one another?'

Tom, elbows propped up on beer mats so that he didn't have to touch the table top, looked over at his grandfather and took a moment to delight in watching the old duffer squirm like a tweed-encased whiskery old worm on a hook.

'Well, Mithter Hound, I firtht met young Dandy, here, way back when he wath nothing more than a fine young prothpect, though I doubt that he rememberth it. But we to be were reunited and properly introduthed, thhall we thay, in Brighton, when we were both prethent at an exthhibition between the wily old ex-champion, the great Jem Mathe, and young Dick Burge back in ... oh when wath it, Dandy, 1895 perhapth? Well, I'm thure that you don't need me to tell you of the Profethor'th boxing pedigree, Mithter Hound, but I too have a long and dithtinguithed career in the ring mythelf.'

'You were a boxer?' snorted Tom in amazement, looking at the Goblin's underdeveloped frame and unhealthy disposition.

'No, no, young thir,' chuckled Whelk-faced Willie. 'Nothing tho vulgar – if you'll forgive me, Profethor. For while Nature hath not provided me with the motht robutht of frameth, Thhe hath theen fit to furnith me with an intellect ath wide ath the Golden Mile on the Great Wetht Way, ath they thay. I wath a fixer, young Marthter Tom. A match-maker. Oh, I've rubbed thhoulderth with all the greatth in my day, from Daniel Mendotha to Tom Thayerth himthelf, yeth I did, indeed I did, thir. I did indeed.'

'And you've remained firm friends ever since. Well, yes, I can see why the two of you would have hit it off so soundly,' said The Hound, smiling at Cornelius with something like warmth.

Cornelius smiled back at his furry companion with a look that bloomed with the relief of one being let off the hook.

'And tho it wath that we thet about thetting up *The Bridge Club*,' continued Whelk-faced Willie.

The smile on Cornelius' face starched.

'*Bridge Club*?' enquired The Hound, a little surprised. 'You're a member of Dandy's bridge club? How extraordinary. I wouldn't have had you down as a player of *Russian Whist*, Willie.'

Willie chortled to himself, while Uncle Cornelius tried to wilt into the lapels of his tweed jacket.

'Very funny, Mithter Hound. Motht amuthing. Ath you mutht be only too well aware, *The Bridge Club* ith a fighting thothiety, where we, the enthuthiathtth of the Noble Art, thet up matcheth for the entertainment and enjoyment of our friendth.'

'Is it?' cooed The Hound, eyeing Cornelius like a betrayed spouse. 'Is it indeed? How ... *edifying*.'

'Why yeth, Mithter Hound,' blathered Willie, oblivious to the stoic tears that were beginning to appear in the steely eyes of his drooping friend beside him. 'Oh, we've had thome rare old nightth, ithn't that right, Dandy. Thome rare old ding-dongth, let me tell you.'

'Oh, please do!'

'Though I do doubt that any could top that rare and wonderful evening when Dandy, here, won One Punch Cottage, in one of the motht famouth fitht fightth of them all.'

A vapour of tea sprayed from the were-hound's lips.

'I beg your pardon!' he choked, looking shocked and somewhat appalled. 'Cornelius!' hissed The Hound, accusingly. 'You told me that you acquired One Punch Cottage in a game of cards!'

'No I didn't,' sniffed the tweedy old codger, defensively. 'I said I won it at *The Bridge Club*.'

'But ... But?' floundered the Hound, flabbergasted.

'What happened?' asked Tom, partly because he was fascinated to find out and partly because he was beginning to feel a little sorry for the cornered old git.

'Well, young Marthter Tom, back in the day there wath thith nathty big fellow called Luther Longboneth. Wicked he wath, mark my wordth, young Marthter Tom, wicked to the core of hith twithted heart!'

'Luther Longbones! The Giant?' rasped The Hound in amazement.

''Alf Giant,' muttered Cornelius. ''Is old man was an Ogre. Nasty combination, an' a nasty piece of work 'e were too.'

'Indeed,' rumbled the were-hound. 'I remember the stories. A very bad sort of the very worst kind. Rumour had it that he'd killed over twenty men in assorted brawls and brouhahas.'

'And the retht, Mithter Hound. And the retht. Anyhow, thome thay killed, thome thay murdered, take it ath you will.'

'Indeed,' indeeded The Hound. 'Please continue, Willie.'

'Well, on hearing of the opening of *The Bridge Club*, Big Luther turnth up one day and demandth a match. Prepothterouth, thayth I. For to be honetht, Mithter Hound, who would have dared fathe him?'

Tom listened eagerly.

'But he wath not to be put athide, no he wathn't, and he wath cauthing all and thundry *much* conthern, let me tell you, when young Dandy, here, turnth up and acceptth hith challenge.'

'Did he indeed?' smiled the thin lipped were-wolfhound, humourlessly.

'Indeed he did, thir, indeed he did. But no ordinary match. Oh no, Mithter Hound. For Big Luther demanded a *Thir Gawain*.'

'A Thir Gawain? What's a Thir Gawain?' asked Tom.

'A Sir Gawain, son. Sir Gawain – you know, like in King Arthur.'

'How fascinating, Willie. Do tell more,' insisted The Hound, with a withering glance in Cornelius' direction.

'A *Thir Gawain* ith when the two contethtantth agree to take it in turnth to deliver blowth to the head, until one of them is no longer able to ... continue, thall we thay. In thith cathe, Dandy, here, had the firtht thtrike, him being the challenged party, and if Big Luther wath thtill thtanding then it wath hith turn to deliver the nextht blow to Dandy'th noggin. And tho on and tho on.'

'Were you out of your whiskery little mind?!!' snapped the were-hound. 'You were ready to trade blows with a Giant/Ogre? What the devil were you thinking of, man? You could have been killed!'

'But I wasn't, was I?' grinned Cornelius. 'Best punch I ever threw. 'Ad to be. If old Luther 'ad 'ave got up, then you're right, 'Aitch, it would 'ave been curtains for me, an' no two ways about it.'

'And then of courthe there wath the thtake, Mithter Hound. The thtake. Oh, what a lovely home you do live in. Very jealouth I am, I mutht thay. Alwayth have been. Beautiful property. Motht dethireable'

'One Punch Cottage,' beamed Cornelius, kissing his right fist. 'What a beauty!'

The Hound stared at him in drop-jawed astonishment.

'But enough about me, Whelky,' sniffed the old duffer. 'Let's get down to business, shall we? If that's all right with you, that is, 'Aitch? I mean, unless there's anything *else* that you might like to enquire about? he enquired, tetchily.

The Hound, for once lost for words, waved him on.

'Whelky, we need your 'elp, old son.'

Now it was Whelk-faced Willie's turn to look uncomfortable.

'We're after information, Whelky. We've 'eard tell that there's to be a big underground ding-dong going on in the very near future. Most probably a *full mooner*. Supernaturals: vampires versus were-cats. Now, is there anything that you've 'eard on the matter that might be of interest to us?'

'No-oo. Not a dicky, Dandy. Thorry. Withh that I could help but –'

'Hey! What's this?' cried Tom, with a feeling of uncontrollable anger suddenly welling up inside. For, as he had lifted his elbow from the table, a beer mat had become stuck to it, and, as he gingerly peeled it off, he noticed that pasted to the underside of said beer mat was a business card – a business card that read:

UP THE STAKES!
Professor Marvin K. MacFee
Professional Vampire Hunter
(& teacher of Theatrical Studies)
Free Consultancy – Sustainable Solutions
Contact: profmacfee@h-mads.com

The Hound snatched the card from Tom and then hurriedly passed it over to Cornelius.

Whelk-faced Willie the Wheeze Willikins shrugged his shoulders in a perfect display of nonplussed innocence, and broke out in to a profuse sweat.

'How thould I know?' he managed to say (sounding less than convincing), before a claw like a butcher's hook was thrust under his chin.

'Start talking, Willie, before I lose patience,' growled The Hound.

'Mithter Hound! Mithter Hound!' wheezed Willie. 'I can't thay nothing! They'll kill me! I thwaer it by all the Godth! On my mother'th life!'

'And what makes you think that *I* won't?' snarled the were-hound, sounding thoroughly reasonable and thoroughly convincing.

'Becauthe we've had tea and bithcuitth together?' squeaked Willie, hopefully; his eyes squelching from his face like a brace of firmly-squeezed slugs, as The Hound gently increased pressure.

'Willie, listen to me,' sighed Cornelius, gently pushing aside The Hound's murderous claw. 'Terrible things are afoot. The safety of all of *The Two Albions* is at stake. If you know anything about this prize-fight then you've got to tell us or we'll all be up the creek without a paddle an' no bloomin' canoe. You've 'eard tell of *The Crowns of Albion*, right?'

Willie frowned, massaged his throat and nodded his head. 'Courthe I have, Dandy. Where do you think I grew up, in a thlug-pit?"

'An' you know the legend that says that should they ever be reunited again then all of the Fae Folk of Britain would be under the 'eel of some power-crazed maniac, right?'

'Jutht what are you thaying, Profethor?'

'Well there are two rival gangs 'oo 'ave their wicked 'earts set on doing that very thing,' explained Cornelius. 'An' between them they 'ave in their possession almost all of the pieces of that fabled Crown. An', to decide just 'oo will be 'Igh King of supernatural Britain, they've agreed to battle it out – champion to champion – so that one of the despicable so-an'-sos will end up with all of the pieces that they do 'old in their villainous 'ands, an' thus take one step closer to being crowned the *King of all the Magic Folk*. So you can choose, Willie; do you want to be lorded-over by some nasty Norman aristocratic vampire (an' Christ 'elp us, but 'aven't we 'ad enough of that already!) or be subject to some mysterious Chinese sorcerer-cum-were-cat-fancier – tied to their every whim, an' slave to their every desire? Or do you want to 'elp us stop them in their tracks before it goes too far, an' remain at liberty to enjoy the lifestyle that you've avoided working so 'ard for all your life? It's up to you, Whelky, old son.'

Willie rubbed his neck and swallowed hard. A globule of snot dribbled lethargically from his nose and came to rest, dangling from his chin like a moth's cocoon. He looked in turn at the pleading Cornelius, the menacing and scowling were-hound, the dry-retching boy, and slowly nodded his head.

'All right,' he whimpered forlornly, hanging his head, wiping his nose on the back of his finger and flicking snot onto the sawdust. 'What do you want to know?'

'So, let me get this straight,' growled the were-hound, pointing a claw like a cleaver at the wilting Whelk-faced Willie. 'Two men, two *human* men (one of whom we can safely assume, by the misplaced business-card and your detailed description – *short, pudgy, pock-faced American, with an over-loud voice and dressed like a Wild West undertaker* – was none other than our old friend, the rotten bounder and backstabbing swine, "Professor" Marvin K. MacFee) were here two weeks ago discussing details about this proposed match?'

'That'th right, Mithter Hound. They were thitting at thith very table.'

'An' what did the other bloke look like, Willie?'

'Upper-clathh. Thounded very ... *Englithh*. Very pothh. Tall, lanky. Dreththed like an Oxthbridge Don.'

'So if MacFee (the treacherous cad!) was representing de Warrenne and his despicable *Society of the Wild Hunt*, then this university-type must be working for Chow and his loathsome *Carnival of Curiosities*. Does this thin chap ring any bells with you, Tom?' asked The Hound.

Tom shook his head.

'And did they approach you or did you approach them, Willie?' asked the were-hound.

Whelk-faced Willie the Wheeze smiled.

'Mithter Hound,' he sighed, sympathetically. 'Everyone who ith anyone knowth that if there'th an illithit fight to be arranged then there'th only one plathe to go to. No one cometh here for no reathon, Mithter Hound. Paththing trade ith not my throngetht point, thall we thay.'

'So what do they want from you, Willie?' asked Cornelius.

'They want me to find a thuitable venue for the fight to take plathe, of courthe.'

'Ha!' The Hound clapped his hands excitedly.

'An' 'ave you found 'em one, Whelky?' asked Cornelius.

'Not yet. No.'

'Excellent,' cried the were-hound. 'Then please allow us to find one for you.'

Whelk-faced Willie looked on aghast.

'When is the fight set to 'appen, Whelky?'

'Nextht full moon, ath you tho rightly guethed, Profethor.'

'Then we have little over three weeks to get everything into place,' considered The Hound.

'Spectators?' enquired Cornelius.

'Why yeth, I do believe that there may be ticketth for a ... thelect few.'

'And from whom you'll no doubt be hoping to line your pockets handsomely?' sneered the were-hound.

'A man'th got to make a living, Mithter Hound,' squelched Willie, with an attempt at an endearing smile.

'You unscrupulous scoundrel!' snorted The Hound.

'Very hurtful, Mithter Hound, I mutht thay. Very hurtful.'

'So, what type of a fight is it to be, Whelky?'

'Unarmed, initially, I'm happy to thay. No roundth. No ruleth. A *finithher*,' replied Whelk-faced Willie the Wheeze, with a pleasant grin aimed at Cornelius. 'Then a thecond match, if needed, with weaponth. And after that – the manner of combat wath to be dethided by the flick of a coin.'

'Intriguing. And how are you to contact them?' asked The Hound.

Willie scrutinized the were-hound with an affronted glare and then shook his head. 'I don't. They thaid that they'll be coming back here next Tuethday.'

'So we have five days to find a suitable venue for their illicit game. Not much time at all,' mused The Hound. 'Anything else, Willie?'

Whelk-faced Willie shook his head glumly and sniffed tearfully.

'Come along, Tom, Dandy, time to get on. Much to do. If you do hear anything more then you must inform us immediately, Willie. And Willie ...'

'Yeth, Mithter Hound?'

'... if you play us false on this, I swear by all that is good that I shall have you closed down, do you understand me? You do, I hope, have a licence? I think that the D.S.C. would be more than delighted to hear about your charming little establishment, don't you? And I seem to remember that MI Unseen is still most eager to haul you in for an interrogation; something to do with their investigations into that unseemly and unsolved episode regarding the Bank of Liverpool forgeries. When was it now ... 1896? ... 97? Where exactly were you at the time, Willie? I know that you were on their list of prime suspects, but they were just never able to catch up with you, were they? And as for IPISS –'

Whelk-faced Willie hastily stood up from the table.

'Enough, Mithter Hound!' he wheezed, placing his slimy hand over his slimy heart, his eyes watering with earnest loyalty and heartfelt duty. 'Enough! Trutht me, thir. I thall not let you down, I thwear it, on my mother'th life, I do indeed. I thwear it, thir. Indeed I do.'

FIVE
The Nachzehrer

Before heading back to One Punch Cottage, The Hound had insisted on taking a long walk, explaining that he needed to have some time and space to think things through. Cornelius had unenthusiastically eyed the drizzling grey sky and waited stoically for the were-hound to morph into dog-form, before leading them down Canning Street and a couple of turns upwards onto Bute Street, where, at the end of the cul-de-sac, stood a small flight of steps leading up to the little-known and beautiful woodland that is Craven Wood. They marched up Whitehawk Hill, along the Racecourse, and then over into Sheepcote Valley.

Tom had buried his head into the collars of his coat (his beloved plain, army-style, khaki-green combat jacket) and strolled purposefully after the quietly grumbling Cornelius, as they gingerly picked their way through the sodden, muddy landscape of Sheepcote Valley, under a sky the colour of soured milk, and followed after The Hound (as the were-hound gambolled merrily across the green fields, occasionally pausing to tumble playfully in the patches of long, wet grass) with grim determination. Watching him rolling about like a demented maniac (The Hound, that is, not Cornelius), Tom couldn't help but think how strange it was that the were-hound always seemed so much happier and at ease with the world when in dog-form. *Was it*, he wondered to himself, *such an uncomfortable burden for The Hound to be transformed into his strange and supernatural "other self"? And if so, how did he manage to bear it?*

By the time they began to head back towards One Punch Cottage the sun was starting to go down – sulkily disappearing from view as if it had finally given up the ghost on any chance of brightening up the dreary day, and couldn't be bothered anymore anyway.

As Old Nancy pottered her way steadily homewards, the chilly silence between the were-wolfhound and the tweedy old codger (both radiating their own singularly individual eye-watering bouquet of musky dampness) was near palpable.

'So,' began Tom, in an attempt to lighten the mood and get the two conniving old rascals talking to one another again, 'thinking about it, I'd say that The Mighty HASS has to be Dr Chow's champion, don't you?'

'Hhmm,' replied The Hound, absentmindedly. 'Unless, of course, Chow chooses to contest himself – which I doubt. No, I suspect that you are correct, Tom.'

'Would a were-jaguar beat a vampire in a fight?' he asked, genuinely intrigued.

'Possibly,' said Cornelius, chancing a quick glance at the were-hound in his driving mirror, 'if it's 'and-to-'and, that is. 'Owever if it's a weapons fight then I'd put my money on the bloodsucker.'

'So for the second match they'll probably send out one of the Caracal Brothers (probably Bruce),' mused Tom. 'It's got to be Ajit Singh for *The Wild Hunt*, I'd say ... hasn't it? Who's your money on, Uncle?' he asked, keenly.

'The problem is, Tom,' interrupted The Hound, with an uneasy tone to his voice. 'I very much doubt that de Warrenne will be sending one of his beloved *children-of-darkness* into the arena for the first contest. It is my unhappy belief that the arch-cad has a very unpleasant surprise in stall for Dr Chow, and an even worse one for The Mighty HASS; one that will wrap things up in de Warrenne's favour in one fell swoop.'

'And what's that?' asked Tom.

'I believe that de Warrenne's champion will be my poor, long-lost brother, Bors.'

'Really! Cool! Er, I mean ... oh. So ... were-jaguar versus were-wolf-wolfhound, that'll be ... *interesting*.'

'For as long as it lasts,' muttered Cornelius. 'It'll be a bloody massacre, if you ask me; if Bors is anything like 'Is Nibbs back there, that is,' he said with a tilt of his head in The Hound's direction. 'Believe me, son, I've seen a thing or two in my day an' there ain't a lot in this world, supernatural or otherwise, that would stand much of an 'ope in 'Ell against 'im.'

'Really, Cornelius, I think you're over-exaggerating matters a little,' sniffed The Hound, trying to sound stern, but with a hint of delighted appreciation sneaking into his voice.

Well, that was progress, thought Tom; at least The Hound had managed to speak to Cornelius in a vaguely civil manner – one that didn't sound mortally disappointed.

'Credit where credit's due,' replied Cornelius, holding were-hound's eye in the mirror. 'I'm only saying what we all know to be true.'

'Well that is most kind of you, Dandy,' smiled The Hound with a short but rapid wag of his tail. 'Most kind.'

Cornelius grinned back.

'And let me just say, for the record, Tom, that your grandfather is no slouch himself. Possibly the finest human exponent of the art of unarmed combat that I have ever had the privilege to see.'

Cornelius' whiskers bristled with pride.

'I say, old chap, why did you never invite me to join you at The Concealed Arms?'

Cornelius looked a little taken aback. 'Well, 'Aitch, it's not really your sort of ... establishment, is it? I mean, I'd 'ave thought it a bit ... lowbrow for your taste.'

'Quite the contrary. I am, as you must very well know, a veritable Prince Hal – as equally at home with the common fellow as I am with a peer of the realm.'

Cornelius chuckled silently into his whiskers. 'If you say so, 'Aitch, if you say so.'

The Hound rolled down the window a fraction and took a deep and satisfied snort.

'Do you know, I think that matters have just begun to take a swing firmly in our favour,' he mused, jauntily drumming his talons against the leather seat. 'I do indeed. Indeed I do,' he chortled, making an impressive impersonation of Whelk-faced Willie the Wheeze.

Cornelius and Tom both laughed.

'Let's bloomin' well 'ope so, 'Aitch. What's the plan?'

'Obvious, I would have thought. Tom, what would you do?'

'Well,' smiled Tom, for he had, of course, thought of little else during their long and soggy hike, 'now that we can dictate *where* the fight is to take place, we can set everything to our advantage and then swoop down and capture both de Warrenne and *The Wild Hunt*, and Dr Chow and his feline cronies as well,' he grinned.

'An' rescue *The Summer*, *Autumn* an' *Winter Crowns* to boot!' chirped Cornelius. 'Though we might need to drum ourselves up a bit of 'elp on that front,' he added, a hint of doubt creeping into his words.

'One step at a time, old chum,' grinned The Hound. 'First things first. We'll cross that bridge when we come to it. Let us just enjoy the fact that for the very first time in this whole abominable performance we're the ones in the driving seat. And best of all, the wicked devils don't even know that we're onto them.'

Tom clapped his hands in glee and restrained a whoop.

'I'll drink to that, old son,' chuckled Cornelius. 'In fact, what say we park up Old Nancy an' then trundle off to get some fish 'n' chips for supper? My shout.'

'What a capital idea, Dandy. What a capital idea indeed,' cooed The Hound, his tail thrashing against the leather seats in delight.

And though the air within the rattling old crock was still somewhat musty, the mood had decidedly lifted.

They turned into the easterly entrance of Black Lion Lane – The Hound trotting elegantly along in dog-form, followed by Tom, and with Cornelius bringing up the rear (with a white plastic carrier bag containing half a ton of cod and chips clasped lovingly to his chest). Suddenly the hackles on the back of The Hound's neck bristled in outrage, swiftly followed by a five-second cacophony of crackling pops as the wolfhound exploded into were-from, alert and snarling through his murderous teeth. Cornelius pulled Tom behind him, thrust the piping-hot plastic bag into his arms, and produced a hefty-looking cosh from the inside of his jacket.

A tall, gaunt figure slowly seeped from the shadows of the lane.

The Hound growled menacingly.

'Vampire!' hissed Cornelius.

Tom gingerly peered around his grandfather's cast-iron bulk and, with eyes on alarmed stalks, observed the stranger.

The vampire's face looked like somebody had described what a human's features should look like to a blind alien sculptor. His cheekbones stuck out like numbed razors and his eye-sockets were like pitiless black pools of despair. Despite the wet weather his thick blonde hair was waxed to an upright position, making him look even taller and thinner.

'Goot evening, Herr Hund,' smiled the vampire, in a voice as unassumingly chilling as an assassin's blade.

'Victor Bertrand!' snarled The Hound, ready to pounce on the skeletal bloodsucker at the first uncertain movement that the grisly nightmare might make.

Tom silently gasped. Victor Bertrand was one of two assassins from the notorious Nachzehrer clan (one of the twelve vampire *Families* that controlled most of the supernatural underworld) who had been involved in de Warrenne's recent hunt of The Hound in Hollingbury Park. (The other was Baron Rudolf Von Bathory, who had been calculatingly murdered by *The Wild Hunt* – a fact that was unknown to Victor Bertrand and the Nachzehrers [who had been led to believe, via the vile and devilish machination of Manfred de Warrenne, that *The Clockwork Baron* had been executed by the Della Morte clan] and an act that was at the very heart of the current burgeoning hostilities between the two powerful *Families*.)

'I mean you no harm, I assure you,' declared the vampire, politely clicking his heels together in formal welcome, and keeping his hands firmly wedged in the pockets of his long leather coat (presumably in a [much-needed] sign of goodwill). 'In fact I have come to ask for your assistance. If I may be so presumptuous as to request an invitation to your vunderful home, zhen I hope zhat we can put our differences to vun side for zhe moment undt talk, civilly, about matters zhat might just be to our mutual benefit.'

'Well? Get on with it!' growled The Hound, donning his red silk dressing-gown, eyeing the gangly vampire suspiciously, and indicating a chair that the unexpected visitor could sit on with an impatient wave of his lethal paw. 'What is it that you want?'

Victor Bertrand took his time to retrieve the wooden chair from under the writing-desk and place it at a safe distance from The Hound's ginormous armchair (and ginormous reach). He shot an uncomfortable glance at the were-hound and then slowly sat down, deliberately folding one long leg over the knee of the other.

'It is my belief zhat you have information zhat is of zhe utmost importance to my ... family,' he began.

'I'm sure that I do!' snorted The Hound, making himself comfortable and throwing a barely-concealed look of disdain in the Nachzehrer's direction. 'But that doesn't mean for one second that you're going to get it.'

The vampire smiled, sadly, revealing the tips of his elongated canine teeth.

'Ve have many reasons to mistrust vun another, it is true,' he nodded grimly, 'but I ask you, for vun moment, to put old hatreds aside.'

'Whatever for?' scoffed The Hound, with contemptuous astonishment.

'I'm going to get some logs for the fire, 'Aitch,' announced Cornelius. 'Be back in a mo.'

The sturdy old duffer flitted gracefully from The Study.

The vampire watched his exit with a look of concerned misgiving, briefly scrutinised Tom (which, Tom found, was a blood-chilling experience – however, he was unfortunately becoming something of an expert in being the object of various vampire's analytical examinations) and then returned his undivided attention to the enormous were-beast, and legendary vampire-slayer, sitting before him.

Missus Dobbs burst through the door and looked their new guest up and down with an anxious gurn.

'I've put the fish and chips in the oven to keep them warm, Mr Hound, until Crow and Mr Goodfellow have returned,' she smiled. 'Tea anyone?' she asked hopefully.

'Not for me, Missus Dobbs,' replied The Hound gently, steadily holding the vampire's pitiless stare. 'Though perhaps our visitor would like one … before he leaves?'

Victor Bertrand kept his blood-red eyes fixed on the were-hound. 'No, zhank you,' he replied softly.

'How about some soup then, Ducky?' insisted the kindly old House-Fairy (who hated the thought of any visitor to One Punch Cottage – however distasteful she might find them – being without food or victuals). 'Freshly made this afternoon,' she said proudly. 'Garlic.'

'NO! I mean … no. Most kind, but no. Danke.'

Missus Dobbs looked at the vampire with something approaching disappointment. 'Suit yourself, then,' she mumbled as she turned and bimbled from the room, pausing to prop open the door for Cornelius, who was returning with an armful of logs and kindling.

'Well how about something more substantial then, Ducks?' she asked doggedly, suddenly sticking her head around the door again, having decided that the gaunt and pasty-looking visitor was obviously in need of a good meal. 'I've got some lovely thick steaks?'

The vampire eyed the lovely thick logs in Cornelius' arms, shuddered and then shook his head.

The House-Fairy vanished with a disheartened gurn.

'I thought you might be partial to a good stake,' chuckled Cornelius, placing the wood by the fireplace and then sitting down in his armchair. 'I know I am.'

Victor Bertrand raised an eyebrow and then returned his attention to the were-hound. He was, however, beginning to look increasingly uncomfortable with each passing moment.

'Please, understand zhat it is no easy zhing for me to be here.'

'And *why*, exactly, *are* you?' asked The Hound, with a terrifying scowl. 'Here, that is,' he added, on noticing the expression of confusion fluttering over the vampire's waxen face.

'*Zhe Vild Hunt*,' replied Victor.

It was The Hound's turn to raise an eyebrow.

'Please, Herr Hund, vhat do you know about zhese fellows?'

'Hah!' snorted the were-hound, with amusement. 'I would have thought that it was *you* who should be telling *me* what you know regarding the despicable swine. Was it not your odious clan who answered their deplorable advertisement and paid an undoubted fortune for the privilege to hunt me when I was their captive?'

The vampire shrugged his shoulders.

'So you undt my family have history, Herr Hund, vhat of it? If it vere you who had been offered zhe chance to destroy vun of your most implacable enemies, vould you have not leapt at zhe chance? Zhere is no need to pretend, for ve both know zhe answer.'

'I have worked tirelessly for the protection of the weak and innocent, as a force for justice,' snarled The Hound, witheringly.

'As have I, Herr Hund. As have I.'

Both the were-hound and the tweedy old duffer (currently reclining in the armchair opposite him and opening up a large penknife) scoffed in amused disbelief.

The vampire looked at them like vermin.

'Laugh if you vant to,' he sneered in return. 'You look at me undt you see only a monster; vell shame on you! Do you zhink zhat I wanted zhis?' he cried, his ashen, razor-sharp features suddenly becoming animated. 'Do you zhink zhat I did not try everyzhing zhat I could to put an end to zhis curse? You vould be very surprised, Herr Hund, Professor.

'Vhen I vas in my *first life* I was, let me tell you, a miserable excuse for a man. A hateful undt loathsome creature; a worse monster zhan zhe vun zhat you see before you now. Undt how I paid for zhat life, Herr Hund. I vas turned by a *Rogue*, a houseless undt nameless *Child of zhe Night*, undt left abandoned to zhe horror of zhis unbearable existence. Hunded undt persecuted, I fled from vun place to zhe next; alone, scared, friendless – terrified by vhat I had become. Vas it, I vondered, some sort of divine retribution for my vicked, vicked vays? But I was saved, Herr Hund. For the very first time in my *unglucklich* existance I vas shown freundlichkeit ... excuse me, how do you say? ... ah yes ... *kindness*. I vas rescued, Herr Hund, by another of my kind – by a vampire.

'You knew him vell, Herr Hund, for he vas an old associate of yours.'

The Hound twitched an ear in interest.

'His name was Baron Rudolf Von Bathory.'

'The Heartless Hussar!' sneered The Hound.

'The Clockwork Baron!' squeaked Tom.

'The Wind-up Wampyre!' sniggered Cornelius.

'He took me in, showed me zhe ropes, if you vill, undt, in time, he brought me into zhe unbeating bosom of vhat vas to become my new family – zhe Nachzehrers.'

'Most touching,' sighed The Hound, wearily.

'Zhe point iz zhis, Herr *Jagdhund*: my family is in danger undt I vill stop at nothing to save zhem from zhat danger. Nothing!

'It is my suspicion zhat zhis mysterious *Society of zhe Vild Hunt* may have had more to do with zhe tragic circumstances of zhat terrible night on Hollingbury Hill zhan was previously zhought. Zhey have, shall ve say, been most noticeable by zheir absence since zhe murder of Zhe Baron. In fact, Herr Hund, zhey have vanished, undt who undt vhat zhey are remains a mystery.'

'Then your masters know nothing about them?'

'Richtig, Herr Hund. Correct. It is suspicious, vould you not say? Ve are invited to exterminate an old undt (pardon me for saying) irritating foe (undt are charged a quite extortionate fee for zhe privilege!), undt in the process vun of our number is murdered. *Zhe Elders* believe zhat *Zhe Vild Hunt* is nothing but a ruse, a deception by zhe backstabbing Della Mortes. But I have my doubts, Herr Hund. Perhaps I am wrong, but before zhere is var I mean to track *Zhe Vild Hunt* down undt eliminate zhem from my enquiries ... or perhaps I vill just eliminate zhem, ve shall see.'

'Well, I wish that I could be of some assistance,' smiled The Hound, humourlessly, 'but alas I have nothing to say on the matter that could help you in any way. Good day. Cornelius, would you be so kind as to show our visitor the way out.'

'Be delighted 'Aitch.'

'Vun moment, if you please. No doubt you zhink zhat a var between zhe Nachzehrers undt zhe Delle Mortes is a goot zhing. Perhaps you feel that if ve vipe each uzzer from zhe face of zhe Earth zhen it can only be for zhe best. You vould be mistaken, Herr Hund. May I remind you of Yellowstone Park?'

'I beg your pardon?' spluttered the were-hound, arching an eyebrow.

'I vould have zhought zhat it vas a matter close to your heart, Mister Volfhund. Zhe volf (who rightfully sits at zhe top of zhe food-chain) is hunted to extinction in zhe area, undt so ... a new order arises. Zhe coyote, a lesser, undt less capable, hunter, takes on zhe role of the apex predator. Zhe herds of deer undt bison (vithout a predator vorthy to hunt zhem) grow in number, undt zhe vegetation undt landscape are adversely affected. Because of zhiz, other, smaller creatures suffer, as their habitat is destroyed undt zheir place in the order of zhe vorld is assaulted.

'But vhen zhe vulf is eventually reintroduced, vhen zhis wrong is righted, vithin zhe passing of a few years zhe whole ecosystem is once more in balance. Zhe herds are pruned to a sustainable size; zhe over-ambitious coyote is put in its place; zhe beaver returns to the rivers undt, in so doing, creates, once more, zhe necessary habitat for flowers undt insects to survive undt to prosper ... undt so on, undt so on, undt so on. You get my point, Herr Hund? If we are ... *eliminated*

56

zhen zhe whole vorld vill suffer–VHAT IN ZHE NAME OF DER TEUFEL ARE YOU DOING!!!'

Cornelius looked up from his work.

'Just whittling some logs, mate,' he replied innocently, waving the large piece of firewood that he'd been working on (which he'd managed to shape one end of to an extremely sharp and stakey-looking point) in the vampire's direction. ''Elps me relax.'

'Vould you be so kind as to desist,' pleaded Bertrand, his voice sounding suddenly hoarse and timid. 'It is most ... off-putting.'

Cornelius shrugged and leaned the stake against the side of his chair.

The Hound regarded the gently-perspiring vampire with a stern and thoughtful face.

'If I *were* to find out anything regarding *The Wild Hunt* that I thought might be of use to you, how do I contact you?'

The vampire slowly stood up, pulled a small card from the inside pocket of his long leather coat and placed it on the writing-desk.

'I may be reached on zhis number,' he answered. 'Undt once more, I beg of you, Herr Hund, zhis var must be avoided .... at all costs.'

'I'll keep it in mind,' replied The Hound, picking up his copy of "The Last Werewolf" and eagerly finding his place. 'Good day.'

And with that the meeting was concluded, and the vampire was unceremoniously dismissed. Cornelius arose and escorted Victor Bertrand from premises.

Cornelius had just returned to The Study, to discuss the extraordinary episode, when Bob Goodfellow burst in the room looking even more dishevelled than usual.

'Whatever's the matter, Bob?' cried Cornelius in some alarm, for the Puck was not the sort to look flustered without good reason.

Bess and the two Airedales bounced into the room (Bess heading straight for the sofa like the old pro that she was).

'It's Crow!' wheezed the whiffy old wizard. 'She's gone!'

The Hound threw down this book and leapt up. Cornelius looked like he'd been punched in the stomach. Tom felt his heart lurch into his kneecaps.

'How?' demanded The Hound, who'd grown very fond of the Half-Elf in their brief acquaintance.

'We were in Rottingdean, when she said that she wanted to have a look in one of the charity shops near the seafront. I thought nothing of it, and, as someone had to stay with the dogs, I waited for her outside.'

'And?' screeched Tom, his mind whirling with terrible thoughts of terrible possibilities – what if she had been abducted by *The Bucca* again, or by the *Carnival of Curiosities*, or de Warrenne and *The Wild Hunt*? It didn't bear thinking about.

'Well, she never came back out, that's what. I was waiting a good twenty minutes before I had an inkling that anything might be amiss,' grimaced The Puck. 'When I finally tied the dogs up and went inside, none of the shop-workers could recall ever having seen her. And then I found these ...' he muttered, thrusting a filth-encrusted hand into a filth-encrusted pocket of his filth-encrusted jacket and pulling out two wrinkled envelopes.

'Don't know how she managed to sneak them in there without me noticing. Just what exactly *do* you call the opposite of pickpocketing?' he asked.

The Hound snatched the two envelopes from The Puck's grimy mitt. One was addressed to he (The Hound) and Professor Cornelius, while the other was addressed to Tom.

The were-hound gently passed one letter over to Tom, and then carefully opened his and Cornelius' note. The old man shuffled over and stood next to him, and together they read the short letter that was written within.

> *Dear Mr H and Professor Lyons,*
>
> *I hope you don't think me too rude, but I had to go. Important things to do. (MI Unseen and all that). Sorry that it had to be done like this but if I'd have asked you'd have never let me go. Please don't try to follow me (not that you'd ever be able to find me anyway – ha-ha).*
>
> *Don't blame Mr Goodfellow, there's nothing he could have done to have stopped me. (I've left a bottle of shower-gel and a bottle of shampoo in my room as compensation for any distress that I might have caused him. PLEASE MAKE SURE HE GETS THEM!!!)*
>
> *Also, please say goodbye to Missus Dobbs for me. And Alfie and Ned and Maggs and Dame Ginty and Inspector Jones and all at the D.S.C. And to Bess – especially to Bess! And please, please look after Tom.*
>
> *Miss you all,*
>
> # Crow *xx*

Later that night, Tom lay on his bed and tried to get some sleep. It was useless. No matter how tired he felt, he just couldn't stop thinking about Crow.

How could she do it? he kept asking himself. *Why did she do it?* If she'd have told him what she was up to then he could have talked her out of it, or gone with her and looked after her (he was, after all, a pugilist and swordsman of quite extraordinary potential).

In his hand he held her letter to him, already crumpled and worn from over-reading. It read:

Dear Tom,

I hope that you can forgive me for going away so suddenly. I wanted to get the chance to say goodbye properly, but it just never came. Just as well really as I'm crap at goodbyes.

Whatever happens I want you to know that I'll always be your friend and that I'll only ever want what's best for you. Be strong, Tom, and brave. It's a really tough path that you have to follow, but I'll be with you all the way (somewhere, somehow).

Look after the old rascals won't you. And look after Bess.

Love

CROW XXX

So that was it? So long, see ya and *"thanks for all the fish"*. His best friend (well, his only friend, if truth be told) had buggered off and left him – just like that. How could that happen? What sort of world was this? Why did anyone even bother?

He turned his face towards the window and listened to the quiet, rhythmical pitter-patter of the rain.

His throat and his heart felt like they'd been slowly pumped full of lead.

SIX
The Cat's Cradle

Sunrise saw Tom escorting The Hound and Bess on another damp and dreary walk across Brighton Racecourse and over into Sheepcote Valley, while Cornelius paid a second visit to Whelk-faced Willie in order to collect a few more details concerning the necessary requirements for the intended fight-site (it was agreed that another call to The Concealed Arms by The Hound might arouse suspicion – should anyone be watching out for such things – whereas Cornelius' appearance, being a well-known and regular member of *The Bridge Club*, wouldn't).

The mood that morning was decidedly glum. On the short drive to the Racecourse no one had said a word about Crow – which was just fine with Tom (who was in no mood to talk to anyone about anything – especially Crow!), instead Cornelius and The Hound had discussed possibly locations for the upcoming contest: Stanmer Park? (Too popular); Hollingbury Park? (Already compromised by de Warrenne and *The Society of the Wild Hunt,* and therefore unlikely to get the green light from Dr Chow); Sheepcote Valley? (Too exposed). What was needed was an open-air venue (*Children of the Moon*, and most other *supernatural types*, preferring to "perform" under the stars, as it were – plus Cornelius' insistence that it was traditional for *proper* prize-fights to be held outdoors), hidden from the prying eyes of the uninitiated but not too difficult to get to and from, and with enough cover for the *One Punch Cottage Crew* to lay their trap without it being spotted by either *The Carnival* or *The Wild Hunt*.

Tom mooched after the two wolfhounds, lost in his own self-pitying and miserable thoughts, as the giant dogs romped merrily together (seemingly without a care in the world) along the mist-coated racecourse (which, if not for the blanket of morning fog, would have offered Tom a truly stunning panoramic view of Brighton), past shed-laden allotments (where squadrons of slugs and snails hurled themselves towards the flimsy wire-fence defences like a horde of determined barbarian raiders, hell-bent on the ransack and plunder of this edible El-Dorado) and onto the rolling hills of Sheepcote Valley, where kestrels hovered like kites over the long-grassed meadows as they hunted by the sun's early light, and skylarks jittered across the sky, their bellies flashing like flipped golden coins.

On returning to One Punch Cottage, Tom had managed to drag himself through the motions of his morning training session and then had sat in numbed indifference as Old Bob croaked endlessly on – for what seemed like slow-roasted hours – about the history of *The Council of the Pooks* and the *rise and decline of the Oberons (The High Pooks* of *All Albion)*. And then, oh joy of joys, The Hound had asked him if he would be so kind as to re-alphabetise the library (as previously requested). Tom had groaned at the thought, but being distracted by such a mundane and mind-absorbing chore actually proved to be a mild comfort.

Tom had deliberately left the shelves that homed the books concerning the supernatural until last – these being, of course, by far the most interesting (and fast becoming his chosen subject of expertise). He randomly plucked out a rather small and pristine-looking tome by the rather dry and dull-sounding *Dr Hyslip-Campbell*.

Is that filed under "H" or "C"? he wondered to himself.

He flipped the book over and examined its cover; it read – "*In Search of Ailuranthropes*".

'Mr Hound?' he asked.

The were-hound, who was poring over several maps of the Sussex and Kent countryside, in an attempt to locate the perfect spot for the upcoming fight (Cornelius was currently in the Mym sullenly battering the bejesus out of the punch-bags, and The Puck was out walking Nipper and Snapper), twitched an ear in his direction.

'Yes, Tom?' he replied distractedly, not looking up from his task.

'What's an *Ailuranthrope*?'

The Hound raised an eyebrow, but still didn't look up.

'I would have thought that you of all people, Tom, would know the answer to that,' he rumbled. 'An Ailuranthrope is a therian of the feline persuasion; a were-cat: from the Greek – *ailouros*, meaning *cat*, and *anthropinos*, meaning *human*.'

Tom let out a dour chuckle. 'Yes, I suppose I should have known that,' he replied.

Bess hauled her head from the sofa and cocked an ear.

There was a sudden knock at the front door.

BOOM! BOOM! BA-BOOM!'

'I'll get it!' cried Missus Dobbs from afar.

Tom looked back down at the neat little book in his hands. Something was gnawing away at him, just on the edge of his reasoning. What was it?

He absentmindedly flicked open the leather cover.

IN SEARCH OF AILURANTHROPES
BY
DR WALTER OCTAVIUS HYSLIP-CAMPBELL
DOCTOR OF ORIENTAL STUDIES – BALLIOL COLLEGE, OXFORD.
LONDON:
THOMAS HURST, 5, ST. PAUL'S CHURCHYARD;
MACHIN AND CO. DUBLIN;
SOLD BY WILLIAM F. ORR, AND CO. PATERNOSTER ROW;
AND J. THOMAS, FINCH LANE, CORNHILL.

———

1866.

'Hhhhhmmmm? Walter Octavius Hyslip-Campbell,' he mused. 'Doctor ...'

He snapped the book shut and decided to file in under "H", when it suddenly hit him like one of Missus Dobbs' suet puddings dropped from a second-storey window.

'Good grief!!!' he gasped.

Unfortunately his *eureka moment* was in perfect timing with Missus Dobbs noisily opening The Study door and ushering in three visitors, and was therefore, rather frustratingly, lost in the moment.

The Hound looked up from his maps and examined the new arrivals (Tom pushed his jaw shut and did the same). Three humans; one male (a sturdy-looking, dark-skinned African, with a shaved head, and shoulders like a bison on steroids) and two females (one – tall and slender, with long dark curly locks and the creamy complexion and bearing of an Afghan princess; the other – much shorter, and covered from head to foot in a flowing and exquisitely patterned sky-blue burqa, complete with a tightly-meshed and impenetrable veil).

'May I introduce Prince Maffdetti A-Su and his ...er ... *friends*(?),' gurned Missus Dobbs, in a voice like the Queen Mum choking on a creamed scone, and almost toppling over face-first into the carpet as she made an elaborate and wobbly curtsy.

The Hound re-tightened his red silk dressing robe, rounded the writing-desk and offered a welcoming hand (well, as welcoming as the hand of a seven-and-a-half foot tall were-wolf-wolfhound's dagger-like mitt can be) to the burly bald chap.

'Prince Maffdetti,' he said, oozing cordiality, 'what an absolute pleasure it is to ...'

The Hound faltered (his hairy mitt left dangling uncertainly in the air).

The brawny African glowered up at him with hostile, tawny-coloured eyes and snarled ominously under his breath.

The were-hound looked over to the regal-looking Afghani – currently clenching and unclenching her fists and looking decidedly (and dangerously) on edge.

Bess seeped from the sofa, stood next to The Hound and bared her teeth; her hackles raised like a bed of nails and her ears flattened to the side of her head.

Tom swallowed hard and surreptitiously shuffled over to rest his free hand on the haft of the fire-poker.

'Tea anyone?' offered Missus Dobbs, hopefully, glancing nervously around the room like the proprietor of a newly refurbished Wild West frontier saloon on Friday night payday.

'That would be a most welcome and blessed relief,' chuckled a soft, musical (and quite clearly amused) voice.

Tom looked over to the speaker – the one calm figure in the room (well, Tom had the feeling that she was calm, but it was, truth be told, a little hard to tell – what with her being dressed, as she was, in a full-length burqa). And then his jaw bounced off his kneecaps and onto the carpet (where it might have danced a little fox-trot for all he knew), for, as the speaker slowly removed said burqa, it was revealed that *she* was in fact a *he*, and that the *he* was not entirely *human*.

He was dressed like a fugitive from the Arabian Nights: huge baggy trousers (gathered at the *ankles* with tightly-wound golden thread, and wrapped at the hip with a thick band of silk); near naked from the waist up – save for a small and exquisitely embroidered waistcoat (opened); a collection of golden and bejewelled arm-bracelets; and a sky-blue scarf wrapped tightly around the top of his head like a swashbuckling pirate prince. However, more impressive than the pantomime get-up was the unavoidable fact that the recently unveiled visitor was, undeniably, a were-cat.

'Please forgive the subterfuge,' purred the man-cat, 'but, as you must know only too well, my dear friend, it can be so ... shall we say ... *awkward* ... to walk the streets of the *talking apes* without being molested. May I introduce myself – *I* am Maffdetti A-Su, so-called *"The Magnificent"*; a prince of the Naravirala, and Captain of the legendary Temple Guard of *The Forbidden City*. I trust that you received my communication informing you of my arrival?'

The Hound managed to snap shut his gaping jaw and nodded.

The prince gave a curt little bow to The Hound and then turned and smiled pleasantly at Tom.

Prince Maffdetti A-Su must have stood a little over five-and-a-half foot tall, with a slender, lithe and sinewy human-like body. He had a head somewhat similar to a leopard, with soft, thick fur covering his face and torso – which bore markings somewhat akin to those of a cheetah.

'It is indeed an honour to receive you in our humble house,' smiled The Hound, swiftly recovering his composure. 'Please, my dear Prince, make yourself at home,' he said, offering the were-cat Cornelius' chair.

Maffdetti *the Magnificent* smiled courteously, bowed again, gracefully settled himself in the armchair, and proceeded to wrap his dexterous, spotty, and tufted tail elegantly across his lap. With an imperial roll of his bejewelled and regal hand, the were-cat prince indicated to the were-hound that he should take a seat.

The Hound found himself dutifully obeying the prince's request and, a little uncertainly, and somewhat stiffly, seated himself in his enormous armchair. Bess came and positioned herself at the were-wolfhound's side, head high, ears pricked, and on a state of high alert.

'Missus Dobbs, would you be so kind as to go and ask Professor Lyons to come and join us,' said the were-hound, in a calm and gentle voice – as he quickly marked the position of the two other visitors (currently stationed either side of The Study door like a brace of over-enthusiastic nightclub bouncers out to make a Saturday-night reputation).

The House-Fairy nodded.

'Will you still be wanting that tea then, Ducks?' she gawked.

'Perhaps you could ask Cornelius to prepare a pot? You know how he prides himself on matters like these.'

'Of course,' replied the Brownie, though possibly a little sniffily. 'But perhaps they don't want tea, Mister Hound?' she added thoughtfully, turning and gurning kindly up at the beefy African. 'Anyone for a saucer of milk?'

The big man growled menacingly.

'Jelani!' purred Prince Maffdetti, reproachfully, a glint of anger flashing across his emerald eyes.

Jelani bowed submissively, but warily glowered at the Brownie as she sidled past him (with a menacing growl of her own – and with a glint in her eye that suggested that she was very well prepared to hoof the discourteous visitor in the shin if there were to be any more exhibitions of unnecessary rudeness) and headed towards the kitchen.

The Hound (with a look of relief) refocused his attention upon the majestic man-cat before him.

The prince reclined in the armchair and smiled warmly at the were-hound, revealing, in the process, a set of thick, white, and decidedly pointy teeth.

'It is indeed an honour to actually meet the legendary *Hound Who Hunts Nightmares*,' grinned Maffdetti. 'We have heard such *interesting* tales of your *adventures*.'

'Well, may *I* say, in return, that it is an honour for me to meet one of the fabled *Naravirala*,' replied the were-hound courteously (and with genuine intrigue). 'An experience beyond my wildest expectations; for it is commonly believed that your people had long-since vanished from the world.'

'Ah, Mr Hound, it is true that we have indeed become a reclusive and secretive folk. The world has changed much since our great days of glory (when we were worshipped and adored by all of the lesser creatures of the world) – and the change, shall we say, has not been to our liking. Thus, my dear friend, we have chosen to remove ourselves from the affairs of the *modern age* and make ourselves .... unknowable.'

'Fascinating,' huffed The Hound. 'I do hope that you might allow me, at some point, the privilege of interviewing you regarding the history of your renowned race.'

'It would be my pleasure,' purred Prince Maffdetti, regarding the were-hound like a cat watching an overgrown rat. 'However, I have travelled far, my dear friend; far from our secret homelands high in the Himalayas, over vast deserts and across wide oceans. I do not like the seas, Mr Hound, but it has been a most necessary discomfort.'

'Then you *must* tell me how I can be of assistance.'

'Good,' beamed Maffdetti, clapping his clawed fingers lightly together in a show of pleasure. 'Straight to business. I like that. How very ... *English*.'

The Hound crinkled his lips in the semblance of a smile.

'As captain of the Temple Guard,' continued Maffdetti, unfalteringly holding the were-hound's eye, 'it is my duty to preserve the customs of my people; to defend the city and uphold our laws. A terrible crime has been committed, my dear friend, and it has come to my understanding that the culprit is currently residing in this ... *fabled* isle.'

'Then of course I will give you every assistance that I can regarding the matter. May I be so bold as to ask just who this villain is? And what, indeed, is their heinous crime?'

'For you to understand the situation correctly, my friend, I must start at the beginning of a long and arduous tale. Perhaps we should wait for the refreshment to arrive? ... Ah! And this must be the famous Professor Lyons, I presume?'

Cornelius had just rolled into the room – still dressed in his training togs (black vest, tights and boxing boots, with rolled-down white socks, and with a pristine white towel draped around his chiselled shoulders). In his hands he carefully carried a large silver tea-tray, on which was balanced One Punch Cottage's very finest bone china tea set.

'That's me all right,' replied Cornelius, eyeing the seated were-cat with a slight arching of a beetling eyebrow (though, having led the life he had, it took more than the sight of a spotted cat-man dressed up like Sinbad the Sailor lounging regally in his beloved armchair to make him react with anything other than mild surprise). The old duffer nodded a courteous hello to the hulking Jelani (sizing the big fellow up – heavyweight to heavyweight) and then smiled pleasantly at the silent and beautiful *"Afghani"*. 'Missus Dobbs said we 'ad visitors but she didn't say 'oo they were ... exactly. An' just 'oo might you be then, sir?'

'Dandy, this is Prince Maffdetti A-Su,' explained The Hound.

'Well 'ow do you do, Your 'Ighness,' he replied welcomingly, as he placed the tray carefully on the table.

'The pleasure is mine, my dear sir,' purred Maffdetti. 'Please, you may call me *"Your Magnificence"*.'

'May I indeed? 'Ow very kind.'

'Your reputation as a *pugilist* is well known to all, Professor; even in my far-away and fabled city. Such an entertaining (if barbarous and technically limited) form, is it not?'

Cornelius (who wasn't exactly what you'd call a royalist) prickled a little. 'You fancy testing that *technically limited form* some time, Tiddles?'

'Cornelius!'

'That is quite all right, Mr Hound,' smiled the mottled were-cat, with a voice dripping with supreme confidence. 'It would be my absolute delight, Professor.'

'Cracking,' beamed the old duffer. ''Oo's for tea then?'

With The Hound nestled attentively in his enormous seat, Tom perched on the tatty footstool, Cornelius propped against the writing-desk, and Jelani and his equally silent companion stationed by the doorway like a couple of Grenadier Guards on sentry duty, Maffdetti A-Su reclined elegantly into Cornelius' armchair and took his time in savouring Cornelius' fine brew before beginning his extraordinary tale.

'Many, many years ago, when I was little more than a cub, a strange incidence occurred in the great city of the Naravirala; a thing that we had thought all but impossible. An outsider, a talking-ape, a murder-monkey, a … *human* … actually found its way to the centre of our fabled homeland. Remarkable!'

'Astonishing!' agreed The Hound.

'You see, my dear friend, not only are our lands hidden, inaccessible and remote, but outsiders are strictly forbidden. Our borders are jealously guarded by *The Chosen Ones*.'

'*Chosen Ones?*' enquired The Hound, with fascination.

Maffdetti smiled. 'For millennia we have been *served* by a small community of humans; humans whose ancestors were fortunate enough to be permitted to bask in the splendour of our company. They serve our needs and attend to our every whim and requirement.'

'I think that the word you're looking for, *Your 'Ighness,* is "*slaves*",' sneered Cornelius, unable to mask his disgust.

Maffdetti smiled at him like he was an irksome guinea-pig, and twitched his tail in annoyance. 'We prefer to use the term – "*companions*",' he purred. 'They are no more … *slaves* … than is this magnificent creature before us,' he smirked, pointing a slender, clawed and bejewelled, finger towards Bess. 'I have heard tell of the mighty wolfhound, but I must confess I did not expect them to be so …. impressive.'

Bess (vain old tart that she was) wagged her tail and offered her noble profile to the aristocratic were-cat.

'Please continue with your tale, Prince Maffdetti,' said The Hound, shooting a reproachful wither in Cornelius' direction.

Cornelius curled his lip and sipped his tea.

'In return for their loyal service, some of our *companions*, if they prove themselves worthy, are blessed with the greatest of all gifts.'

'That being?' sniffed Cornelius, delicately placing his cup and saucer on the writing-desk.

'We bestow upon them certain cat-like qualities,' grinned the prince, his emerald eyes shining with delight, 'so that they may (when the need is requisite) protect our borders and guard our flocks and, when necessary, enter into the world of the *ape-who-kills-with-no-understanding* … forgive me, I mean *humans.*'

Cornelius let out a long, slow and overly loud sigh.

'My two cohorts, Jelani and Fauzia, are both *Chosen*,' he churred, beaming proudly in their direction. 'Jelani has the great fortune of being a were-lion.'

'In the anthropomorphic form?' enquired The Hound, taking one last sip of tea and eyeing the big fellow with newfound interest.

'Quite so,' smiled Maffdetti.

'Remarkable!' remarked The Hound, carefully and deliberately placing his cup and saucer to the side of his armchair and surreptitiously calculating how far away the fire-poker was from his grasp.

'While my dear Fauzia,' continued the Prince, indicating the stately and silent woman with a regal wave of his hand, 'is a were-leopardess.'

'How *extraordinary*!'

'If I may be permitted to return to my tale, my friend, for time is, as always, of the essence. As I have told you, an *ape-who-kills-without-reason* was brought to our holiest of temples. A heinous crime indeed, for the one who carried him there was one of *The Blessed* – a *Chosen One;* a were-lynx by the name of Oyunbileg (who, as punishment for her scandalous misdemeanour, and as our ancient laws dictate, was blinded). The *muttering-monkey* was near to death with fatigue and disease, but we are a kind people, Mr Hound, and so we refused to let him die. We nursed him back to health with the thought that he could be introduced among our *companions* and so *complement* their stock.

'But a strange thing happened, my friend: this new ape, this ... *outsider*, was blessed with such an intellect and an enquiring mind that he became a favourite at the court; a curiosity, a pampered pet – indulged and encouraged to pursue his amusing interest into our history and customs. Even stranger still was that this bizarre creature seemed to possess a modicum of magic within him.

'However, the ungrateful wretch betrayed the kindness and goodwill that we had shown to him, for slowly, deviously, year by year he wormed his way ever closer and closer towards the great secrets of our noble race; feigning devotion and loyalty, when the truth was that his heart was filled with nothing but deceit and treachery. What can I say, Mr Hound: he stole from us not only our trust and goodwill but also knowledge and power – knowledge that was never his to possess, and powers that are not for him to wield.'

'What sort of *powers*?' asked The Hound.

'Many things, Mr Hound, many things. But perhaps most importantly, he stole from us the ability to pass on our greatest gift – the secret enchantment to turn a man into a higher being; into a were-cat.'

'Astounding!' exclaimed the were-hound.

'It is a power that he has no right to use. Just think how this magic might be abused. Imagine how he might reduce the quality of our kind. On top of this, my dear friend, envisage what dire consequences would befall us if he chose, or was somehow forced, to reveal the whereabouts of the secret homeland of the Naravirala – *The Forbidden City* itself? It would be, dare I say, a cat-astrophe.'

'And what was the name of this vile villain?' asked The Hound.

'What his true name is was never revealed to us and remains, to this day, a mystery,' sighed Maffdetti. 'When with us he simply chose to call himself ... Chow.'

'Chow!' snarled The Hound.

'The mysterious sorcerer 'oo fronts *The Carnival of Curiosities*!' gasped Cornelius.

'I know who he is!' bubbled Tom, near bursting with excitement.

'Of course you do, my dear boy,' smiled The Hound, sympathetically.

'No! I mean I know wh–'

'Not now, son,' whispered Cornelius, with an understanding nod and a wink.

'Then you do know of him?' purred Maffdetti, excitedly.

'Indeed we do, Prince Maffdetti, indeed we do,' growled The Hound. 'He is currently a prime perpetrator in a most peculiar case that we are presently pursuing.'

'And do you know where he is to be found?' asked the were-cat, his tail beginning to lash about him quite alarmingly.

'Alas no. Until now we had very little information about the scoundrel. We can give you the names of his associates, but little else, I'm afraid to say.'

'Of Chow's associates we already know,' hissed Maffdetti. 'The so-called Caracal Brothers – deserters from *The Chosen Ones;* mere kittens fooled into following this ... how did you so admirably describe him, my friend? ... ah yes ... *vile villain*, as is the disgraced Oyunbileg.'

'Lady-Lynx!' cried Tom.

'Indeed, that is, I believe, how she chooses to call herself these days. We suspect that it was she who aided Chow in his escape from the fabled city of the Naravirala. The misguided fool! The others are of Chow's own making – let us say that he has not been ... wise.'

'What about HASS?' asked Tom.

'Ah yes, the man-jaguar? Truly, he is a most intriguing specimen. I am most curious to study his peculiar mutation. Long have we wondered about the origins of our Olmec *brethren*,' purred Maffdetti, in a manner that Tom thought didn't bode well for the were-jaguar at all, were he ever to be captured by Maffdetti and the Naravirala.

'So what is it that you plan to do?' enquired The Hound, studying the were-cat thoughtfully through a steeple of rippling fingers.

'Chow must be captured and brought to trial for his crimes against us,' snarled Maffdetti. 'This is not open to debate. I will have him, Mr Hound, and I assure you that I will stop at nothing to bring him to justice.'

'An' just what do you intend to do with 'im once you 'ave caught 'im?' asked Cornelius, doubtfully. 'Chop 'is 'ands off or cut out 'is tongue?'

'The sacred laws of the Naravirala are not for you to pass judgement on, Professor,' purred Maffdetti the Magnificent, coldly (and with an irritated swish of his tail). 'Though I fear that you do us a great disservice, Professor. Ours is a kind and liberal society: we are the givers of law; the architects of justice; the cradle of civilised thought.'

'Tom!' hissed The Hound, in annoyance. 'Will you please be still, dear chap! This is a very important discussion. Whatever it is you have to say, can you please wait until our visitors have finished.'

'There is no need to reprimand the cub,' smiled the prince. 'Such matters are of little interest to the minds of children. I have taken up more than enough of your time, my dear friends, and we are all weary from our travels. We will be staying at the Grand Hotel. Please do not hesitate to contact me if you discover any further information that you think might be of assistance.'

68

'Of course, Prince Maffdetti,' said The Hound, rising from his chair to take the were-cat's offered hand (and admiring the Prince's enormous trousers in the process – just as the Naravirala, in turn, was sizing up the were-hound's voluminous plunderhosen with an appreciative glance). 'I sincerely hope that we might be in a position to be of enormous benefit to one another in our mutual endeavours. I shall be in touch at the very first hint of a development, you have my word.'

When the trio of remarkable visitors had left, The Hound and Cornelius swapped an excited glance.
'What an astonishing turn of events,' chortled the were-hound, rubbing his murderous mitts together in glee. 'Things just keep on getting better and better. Do you know what, chaps, I do believe that I just may have the beginnings of a quite brilliant (if I may so bold as to say so) plan.'
'Well I do believe that I may just have made a *quite brilliant* (if I may be so bold as to say so) discovery!' huffed Tom, with the puff-cheeked and righteous gurn of the hitherto unlistened-to. 'If you'd be so good as to pay me a little respect, that is, and stop treating me like a fricking child!'
'Ooooo! Get 'im!'
'Whatever is it, Tom?' sighed The Hound impatiently. 'You've been fidgeting about as if you've had ants in your pants for half the morning; most distracting, let me tell you – and in front of such distinguished guests. I would really have hoped for better from you.'
'Well I'd have hoped that you'd have learned to trust me a little bit more by now,' withered Tom, close to screaming but managing to keep his voice close to calm. 'For I think that I know who Dr Chow really is!' he announced.
'An' just 'ow do you know that then, son?' asked Cornelius, eyeing his grandson like an over-stuffed owl.
'Because I've been holding his fricking book in my hands for the last fricking hour!' he cried, waving the neat little leather-bound tome at the two infuriating old rogues.
'Whatever do you mean Tom?'
'I believe that Dr Chow,' he declared dramatically, 'is none other than ... *Dr Walter Octavius Hyslip-Campbell!*'
'And just what makes you think that, dear boy?'
'*"In Search of Ailuranthropes"*. Ring any alarm bells? No? Were-cats!' he sighed, in near-exasperation, jabbing his finger theatrically against the book's leather-bound cover.
The Hound and Cornelius swapped a nonplussed and befuddled glance.
'By Dr ... Walter – "*W*"; Octavius – "*O*"; Hyslip – "*H*"; Campbell – "*C*".
'Fascinating, my dear boy, but what has this got to do with anything?'
'Oh, for Christ's sake!' Tom was beginning to develop the sneaking suspicion that the two prehistoric lunatics, currently gaping at him like a brace of discombobulated stoats, weren't particularly good at being detectives at all – they

were just particularly good at beating things up. 'W – O – H – C; which, if you spell it backwards reads – "CHOW"!'

There was a slight pause before The Hound snatched the little volume from Tom's righteous grasp.

'By George,' he gasped. 'I do believe he's got it!'

SEVEN
Where Are You Now Dr Chow?

'It was here, right under our very noses, all this time!' chuckled The Hound, as he closely scrutinised Dr Hyslip-Campbell's neat little volume. 'Well, I must offer you my sincerest apologies for not listening to you sooner, Tom. And my congratulations. What an absolutely top-drawer piece of detective work, dear boy. Very well done indeed, Tom. You're *the bee's knees*, old chap.'

'*The snake's 'ips*, an' no mistake about it,' beamed Cornelius, as he slapped Tom heartily on the back.

'Dare one say,' tittered the were-hound, '*the cat's whiskers*?'

''Ow about – *the cat's pyjamas*,' chuckled the tweedy old duffer.

'Indeed. *The monkey's eyebrows*.'

'*The kipper's knickers*.'

'*The canary's tusks*.'

'*The badger's nadgers*,'

Tom, caught up in the moment, couldn't help but join in with the *elephant in the room* (so to speak).

'*The dog's bollo–*'

'Now then, Tom! There's no need for that sort of vulgarity, son,' hissed Cornelius, with a reprimanding scowl.

'Sorry.'

'I have to admit that I know very little about the *dear Doctor*,' mused the chortling cynanthrope. 'How about you, Dandy?'

'Naff all, 'Aitch.'

'Well let's just see if we can remedy that, shall we?' he purred, with a wink to Tom, as he bounced over to the bookcase and began to peruse the shelves intently.

'Ah-ha!' he declared after a short hunt. 'There you are, my little beauty.'

The were-hound teased a hefty tome from the shelf and carried it eagerly over to the writing-desk. It read:

Who's Who of Nineteenth-Century British Occult Society

'Now then, let me see ...' he huffed keenly, as he flicked through the crisp, thin leaves of the musty-smelling book. 'Ha-ha. Got you, you scoundrel!' he suddenly snapped, stabbing a poniard-like claw onto the page in elation.

Tom and Cornelius eagerly perched themselves at his shoulders and peered anxiously at the book. It read:

Hyslip-Campbell, Walter Octavius
31 July 1831 – 1868(?)

Occultist; ceremonial magician; doctor of Oriental Studies; co-founder of the Oxford Oriental Cat Club; field-agent for *The Unseen League;* member of *The Golden Order Of Theosophy;* High Priest of *The Brotherhood Of The Secret Scrolls*.

Dr Walter Hyslip-Campbell's promising career as a lecturer at Baliol College was cut short when his old school friend, **Captain John Henry Phelps**, recruited him to *The Unseen League.*

Hyslip-Campbell served with distinction during the early years of the British Empire's secret war against the powerful *Jia Family* [see *"The War against the Opium Vampires of South East China – 1861-65"*: J. H. Phelps; Cambridge – 1880].

In the early summer of 1863, while heading a scouting mission for *The League*, in the north-eastern Chinese province of Shanxi, Hyslip-Campbell & his unit were (allegedly) attacked by a band of marauding *were-cats*. The sole survivor, Hyslip-Campbell returned to base, where his report of the incident was received with scepticism & suspicion by his superiors. Relations between Hyslip-Campbell & his commanding officers rapidly deteriorated, resulting in his dishonourable discharge from *The League*.

With his reputation in tatters, Hyslip-Campbell travelled through China in an attempt to track down his *ailuranthropic* attackers & clear his name.

In 1865 Hyslip-Campbell briefly returned to England to resume his career in academia. In 1866 he published a small work recounting his adventures in China (*"In search of Ailuranthropes"*; London – 1866). However his career at Oxford quickly faltered as he became increasingly obsessed with discovering the mythical kingdom of the *Naravirala* – a legendary race of cat-headed men, whom Hyslip-Campbell believed to be survivors of the Lemurian race (see **Helena Blavatsky** – *"The Secret Doctrine". V2:* 1888).

In 1867, having finally secured sponsorship for his endeavours from *The Golden Order Of Theosophy*, Hyslip-Campbell set sail to find the fabled domain of the Naravirala. The expedition, however, was doomed to failure. He was last sighted in the late spring of 1868 in Bhutan, at the *Taktsang*

Goemba Monastery ("The Tiger's Nest"), but was never heard of, or seen, again.

'Fascinating,' rumbled The Hound, as he gently drummed a short, sharp rhythmical tattoo on the page with his talons.

He glanced up at the Grandfather clock (ticking softly with an unerring and rather comfortingly resonant precision) in the corner of the room.

'Good Lord!' he exclaimed. 'Is that the time? Our friends will be with us at any moment.'

'Friends?' asked Tom, with a reasonably justified feeling of apprehension. 'What's going on?'

'You've not forgotten, have you, old chap? Tonight the whole of the *One Punch Cottage Crew* will dine together. With the pieces of this deplorable puzzle finally beginning to fall nicely into place, we can take the opportunity to lay out our plan of action and put this wicked case to bed, once and for all.'

That evening saw the kitchen table of One Punch Cottage fully-booked, as Missus Dobbs served up a supper of her famous venison-stew – (oh yes, dear reader, have no fear, the were-hound, Cornelius and Bess had not been idle in their illicit activities – Tom had of course been invited to join them in their nocturnal [*most definitely not poaching*] excursions, but the mere mention of *Petworth Park* was enough to bring him out in a quivering rash) – to The Hound, Cornelius, Tom, Bob Goodfellow and their most welcome guests: to wit – Inspector Jones, Sergeant Hettie Clem and Constable Tuggnutter of the Sussex Police's *Department of Special Cases;* the witches – Old Maggs and Dame Ginty Parsons; and the Pharisees Elves – Archie Swapper and his cousin, Ned Leppelin.

'So,' said Inspector Jones, munching away manfully on a hunk of broiled meat, 'you believe that de Warrenne and Chow are arranging a prize-fight to gamble their ill-gotten gains on, and so decide who has the right to pursue the final piece of *The Crown of Albion* (wherever that might be)?'

'Correct, Inspector,' rumbled The Hound, as he devoured another of Missus Dobbs' delicious dumplings.

'And *we*, I suppose, are the ones who are going to be stopping them in the act?' asked Hettie Clem, looking, it must be noted, a tad concerned.

'Correct again,' smiled the were-hound, licking his lips with a satisfied grin. 'Once we've located a suitable site for their despicable contest to unfold, we'll lay our trap and see the whole parcel of rogues behind bars before the night is through,' he declared confidently.

'So let me get this right, Mr Hound,' enquired the Inspector, with a pained and haunted stoop of his neck, 'the ... eleven ... of us are going to arrest all of them ... in one go?'

'Exactly!' purred The Hound emphatically.

'Won't we be a little ... outnumbered?' offered Hettie, doing her very best not to sound in any way unenthusiastic.

Tom mentally did the numbers: one were-wolf-wolfhound (expert in unarmed and armed combat and ... well ... a were-wolf-wolfhound); one nigh-on two-hundred year old tweedy, badger-whiskered Regency bare-knuckle pugilist and first-rate lunatic; one rancid Elven Wizard (High Puck of *The Two Albions*); three police detectives (one spirit talker, one psychic and one half-troll – who was built, it must be noted, like the proverbial brick-shithouse); two witches (Old Maggs and Dame Ginty Parsons); two 'fighting' Elves (one of whom, Alfie Swapper, was the Pook-in-waiting for the [currently self-expatriated] tribe of the Pharisees [and in actual fact not an Elf at all, but rather a human, nabbed as a baby and raised by the Sussex Fair-Folk], the other, Ned Leppelin, being the current *Exhibition Skirmishing Champion of All Albion* – known and celebrated throughout the Fae world as *The Smack Faery*); and finally, himself (Tom) – a prince of the Aelfradi (the subterranean tribe of human-hating Elves), and swordsman of quite extraordinary potential, who (of note) had once (when his immortal soul was in peril) transformed into a "monster" and apparently thumped the unliving daylights (*apparently* – because he had absolutely no recollection of it) out of a vampire.

Up against them were:

1. *The Society of the Wild Hunt* – including, as it did: four vampires; one witch; one were-wolf-wolfhound (Bors – The Hound's homicidally-deranged and long-lost brother); at least three highly-trained henchman; and one 'theatrical' *vampire-hunter*/backstabbing traitor.

And:

2. Dr Chow's *Carnival of Curiosities* – consisting of: one sorcerer (capable of shape-shifting into the terrifying form of a mythical Manticore); three martial arts expert and acrobatic were-caracals; one blind fortune-telling were-lynx; two tone-deaf Siamese-were-cats; and one wrestler/strongman/borderline alcoholic were-jaguar.

Putting it mildly, thought Tom, as he pushed a chunk of diced venison pessimistically around his plate with his fork, *it was a task that could perhaps be best described as ... "fricking daunting"*!

And, judging by the expressions on the faces of the rest of the evening's guests, it looked like they'd been making the same calculations and come to the same rather unsettling conclusion.

Cornelius broke the nervy silence with an *excuse-me-but-I've-got-something-to-add-that-might-be-of-importance* cough.

'Ah yes,' beamed The Hound, 'I do believe that Cornelius has something to contribute to proceedings.'

'Well, yes. Ha-ha!' blustered the kindly old codger, pausing to take a hefty gulp of tea. 'When I last saw old Whelky –'

'Whelky?' spluttered Ned in astonishment.

'Not Whelk-face?' snorted Archie in disbelief.

'You don't mean Whelk-faced Willie?' chuckled Old Maggs, incredulously.

'Whelk-faced *Willie the Wheeze*?' snickered Dame Ginty, with a curious pout of her perfect lips.

'Whelk-faced *Willie the Wheeze* Willikins?' scoffed Old Bob, with a scowl of disapproval.

'The zouth-zide znotter?' tittered Ned.

Constable Tuggnutter sniggered something unintelligible.

'The lisping Lothario of the Lowland Ladies?' cackled Old Maggs.

'I thought he had long since shuffled of this mortal coil,' mused Ginty, with some surprise.

'That'z right, I 'eard that 'e got 'iz throat cut by Charlie McDonald an' the Elephant Boyz, zome time back in the Twentiez?' stated Ned, thoughtfully.

'Nah! I'm very 'appy to inform you all that dear old Whelky is very much alive an' dripping,' chortled Cornelius, as he dabbed his wondrous whiskers with a napkin.

'Though perhaps the years have not been ... shall we say ... kind, to *dear old Whelky*,' offered The Hound, possibly a little harshly.

'Well, as a wise man once told me, 'Aitch,' replied Cornelius, '*Time wounds all 'eels*'. Any'ow, that's beside the point, as I was saying – when I saw Whelky this morning, 'e let slip that most of the ticket sales for said prize-fight seem to 'ave been purchased by known members an' associates of *The Bucca*.'

Hettie Clem thoughtfully tugged at one of her lip-rings. 'You mean the Goblin Mafia,' she asked, with an air of Gothy misgiving, 'whose newly-elected *Gobfather* is none other than Madame Buckleberry, the powerful witch and right-hand hag to de Warrenne and *The Society of the Wild Hunt*?.

'The very same, 'Ettie,' winked Cornelius, jovially twirling the ends of his moustache.

'Which implies,' chuckled The Hound, with a jaunty and contemptuous curl of this thin black lips, 'that no matter what happens, de Warrenne is planning to play Chow a double-cross.'

''Ow many of theze *Bucca-men* do you think there might be then, Dandy?' asked Archie Swapper.

''Oo knows, Archie? Anywhere from twenty to fifty would be my guess.'

'Is there any chance that Picktree Bragg and the Oakmen might be persuaded to help us out?' asked Old Maggs, hopefully.

'From what we've 'eard, Maggz,' replied Ned, with a rueful shake of his golden locks, 'Picktree Bragg an' mozt of the Oakmen 'ave gone over to Prince Edric Bloodstone'z cauze.'

'How about any assistance from the Sussex Police Department?' tried Dame Ginty, optimistically.

'Not a snowball's hope in Hell,' muttered Hettie Clem.

Constable Tuggnutter mumbled something unintelligible in agreement.

'MI Unseen?' suggested Maggs, hopefully.

Cornelius offered an amused chortle of whispery tuts, and shook his head.

'What about this Nachzehrer fellow, Victor Bertrand?' asked Inspector Jones, slightly tentatively.

'No. I'd rather not,' scowled The Hound, with a disapproving smile.

'Not that I'm wishing to question your judgement in any way, Mr Hound,' pressed the D.S.C. Inspector, cautiously, 'but, it seems to me that we could do with all the help that we can get on this one. Plus,' he added, with a look of forlorn hope, 'wouldn't it be something of an idea to get *The Families* involved in some sort of way, and perhaps stop this war in Europe before it properly kicks off and causes all kinds of mayhem?'

'When the arch-swine de Warrenne has been brought to brook,' rumbled the were-hound, sternly, and leaving all in no doubt that they shouldn't try to push the subject any further, 'I will divulge what information I have on the matter to the relevant authorities – and not beforehand. Lord Manfred de Warrenne is mine, do I make myself clear? Mine, and mine alone.'

'Well, not wishing to sound anything less than enthusiastic about the whole affair, Percival, but it does seems to me that the odds are well and truly stacked against us,' offered Dame Ginty, as she distractedly picked at her (home-made) organic and moon-grown raw cabbage, seaweed and beetroot salad. (Dame Ginty being a devout vegan had, as always when invited to dine at One Punch Cottage, brought her own supper – Missus Dobbs' range of vegan cuisine didn't really get much beyond beans-on-toast).

'Not at all, Dame Ginty,' chirped The Hound cheerfully. 'For not only will we have the element of surprise, but it is my sincerest belief that we will be aided in our efforts by the considerable might of Prince Maffdetti A-Su and his companions; to wit, Jelani (a were-lion of the anthropomorphic kind – a most unusual and intriguing state of metamorphosis) and the were-leopardess, Fauzia. I have no doubt that our newly-acquired Naravirala friends will be chomping at the bit to join us in this extraordinary brouhaha.

'However,' he continued, examining the sea of rather unconvinced faces gathered around the table, 'my hope is that we can tilt proceedings even further in our favour with some sound detective work and a whopping slice of good fortune.'

'An' 'ow'z that, Mr 'Ound?' asked Archie Swapper, artfully lancing a suet-dumpling with his fork.

'Having recently discovered – thanks to the excellent work of young Tom, here – that this ... this ... this ...'

'*Scoundrel?*' offered Cornelius.

'(Thank you, Dandy.) ... that this scoundrel, Dr Chow, is no Chinese sorcerer at all but rather an Oxbridge-educated Englishman.'

''Oo, in my experience, are very often the very worst sort of scoundrel imaginable,' muttered Cornelius.

'(Thank you, Dandy.) I therefore propose that we put together a criminal-profile of the swine (Chow/Hyslip-Campbell, that is), with the expressed intent of apprehending him before the contest even takes place.'

'So you mean that we'd only have to take on *The Society of the Wild Hunt* and *The Bucca*?' stated Inspector Jones with nervous scepticism.

'Indeed.'

The Hound reclined in his chair, licked the tips of his messer-like canines, and smiled with barely-suppressed satisfaction at the congregated collection of misfits currently gawking at him in uncertain anticipation. 'If we can remove Hyslip-Campbell and his feline cronies from the picture, not only will we be balancing the odds quite firmly in our favour,' he grinned,' but we can also put into place quite a nasty little surprise for the nefarious swine Lord Manfred de Warrenne – and, in so doing, settle this ghastly matter once and for all.'

There was a hushed silence as everyone looked at The Hound expectantly.

'Well go on then, 'Aitch, just what is it that you've got up your sleeve?'

The Hound all but chuckled. 'With Chow out of the way, and thus, hopefully, with *The Autumn Crown* firmly in our possession, we can still delude de Warrenne into continuing with this vile and odious recreation, with ne'er a thought that anything is amiss, because, the *Carnival of Curiosities'* place, for all intents and purposes, will be taken by Prince Maffdetti and his companions. De Warrenne will never even think to suspect that there is any subterfuge, never even question that the Naravirala aren't members of Chow's despicable retinue (a were-cat is a were-cat is a were-cat, after all) and thus we can keep proceedings going in a more than convincing manner. Once the details are set in place, in we swoop – bish-bosh-bang! – and Bob's your Auntie's husband.'

There was a short (and possibly unimpressed) silence.

'So what should we do now then, Mr Hound?' asked Inspector Jones, tentatively.

'Well, I say we spend a little time enjoying the splendour of Missus Dobbs' exquisite Sussex Pond Pudding,' he beamed (to the aghast gastric groans of his gathered guests), 'and then, in the morning, we act!

'Dandy, if you, Maggs, Ned and Archie would be so good as to accompany me for an early morning stroll, first thing on the morrow, there's a little spot that I'd like to check out as a possible site for this contemptible contest to take place in.'

'Where's that then, 'Aitch?'

'On the very edge of the Castle Hill Nature Reserve there stands an abandoned farmstead. I think that it might just offer us the perfect location to arrange the prize-fight and lay our trap.'

'You meanz the old barnz 'tween Woodingdean an' Kingzton?' said Ned, looking excitedly over towards his cousin Archie. 'Cloze to the lozt 'amlet of Balzdean?'

'The very same,' growled The Hound, keenly. 'Inspector, I want you Hettie and Constable Tuggnutter working on that criminal-profile of Chow/Hyslip-Campbell. Find out anything that might give us a handle on how to second-guess the contemptible scallywag's movements; any old haunts that he might be inclined to visit, or old associates who might still be alive. If we can find him before the fight takes place then our task will become considerably easier.'

'We'll do our very best, Mr Hound,' replied the inspector.

'I have no doubt of it, my friend. If it proves to be of no avail then we shall have lost absolutely nothing, and will just revert to our original plan. But come what may, the rotters will rue the very day.'

'What about me?' asked Tom.

'Ah yes, Tom. I have a small errand that I would like you and Dame Ginty to perform for me. Would you both be so kind as to make a visit to Lewes, first thing tomorrow morning, and pick up a most rare – and hopefully enlightening – book (one that I've been hunting for, for quite some time now) from the antiquarian book merchant *Yallery Brown?* One that, by considerable effort on his part, he has finally managed to track down: a little-known and extremely rare volume entitled – *"Behind the Dark Curtain: A history of the rise of the Twelve, and the fall of the House of Alexios"*, by the necromancer Kristofer F. H. Hey.'

'Our pleasure, Percival,' smiled Ginty, and somewhere in the world hedgehogs contentedly sighed and snuggled comfortingly together under dry, warm compost heaps.

And with that, the meeting was concluded and pudding was served.

EIGHT
Yallery Brown's

Tom readjusted the hood of his brand new coat to shield his face from the incessant hammering of the morning rain. It was a little after nine o'clock and here he was, standing in front of Brighton Pier, waiting for the glamour witch, Dame Ginty Parsons, to pick him up so that they could head off to the nearby town of Lewes and collect the recently tracked-down antiquarian book that The Hound was so eager to get his hairy mitts on (an extremely rare and mysterious little volume recounting the arcane and blood-drenched history of the powerful *Vampire Families*, written by the infamous [apparently] necromancer Kristofer F. H. Hey, and rather intriguingly entitled – "*Behind the Dark Curtain*").

The weather had shown no signs of relenting and so Tom, much to his dismay, had been forced to wear said new coat; which, in their all-too-long association, he honestly considered to be the most poisoned of gifts.

It had been presented to him earlier that morning by Missus Dobbs (of course!) just as he had been about to pluck his much-loved old jacket from the coat stand (the plain, military-style khaki-green combat-jacket that he had had for years, and that was worn to the point of being like a comforting second-skin: an old companion that had accompanied him on many an adventure, and had, on one memorable occasion [whilst being chased by *The Society of the Wild Hunt's* terrifying *Tumbler* vampires during the *Battle of Hollingbury Hill*], actually saved his life, if not his very soul).

As his hand had purposefully reached for his cherished old coat, the tiny tea-poisoner had suddenly appeared at his side (as if by magic), tugging persistently at his sleeve.

'Hello, Missus Dobbs,' he had said, innocently unaware of the horror that was about to befall him.

The House-Fairy had gurned at him like an over-protective shrew with a squint watching one of her young *shrewlets* about to leave the den for the very first time. "I've got something for you, Ducky," she had announced proudly.

Tom hadn't given it a second thought, and had turned to face the Brownie with a smile. 'Oh? Thanks. What is it?'

It was then that she whipped from behind her back what Tom had first mistaken for a carefully-folded Arctic sleeping-bag, designed for an adventurous Girl Guide with a passion for all things *Barbie*.

'A lovely new jacket!' beamed Missus Dobbs triumphantly, offering a gleeful smile and letting said garment unfurl to reveal its full *splendour*.

'Good God!' he had cried, raising a clenched fist to his gaping maw and shielding his eyes like a distressed heroine from a Victorian melodrama.

'Isn't it a beauty?' she had gurned, excitedly. 'Should last you for a little while, at any roads, Ducky, what with you getting taller by the hour,' she croaked, whilst giving him an affectionate and scrutinising once-over.

Tom looked on appalled. The coat was so large that even with Missus Dobbs holding it up at full-stretch, at least a quarter of its length was still scrunched-up on the floor (Constable Tuggnutter and his twin [if such a thing existed – though thankfully, to Tom's knowledge, it didn't] could quite easily have fitted into the damned thing); around the rim of its bulbous hood was a fringe of fake (he hoped) fur, that looked like it had been woven from hairballs hacked up by a Persian cat with a nasty chest infection, but much more distressing than that was the unavoidable fact that said coat was constructed of the most vomit-inducing shade of fluorescent purple that Tom had ever had the misfortune to see.

'You've got to be fricking joking!' he had managed to hoot, with a nervous laugh, as his heart sank to the pit of his jittering stomach like a shipwreck's anchor. But even as the words had seeped from his wibbling lips, the vicious little crone had wedged the tent-like garment firmly into his horrified hands, snatched his beloved old jacket from its peg and was inspecting it with a look of dismissive destruction glinting in her googly eyeballs.

'Why, this old thing won't even do for dust-rags,' she cackled, as she joyously ripped a sleeve asunder.

Tom gasped! But the mackintosh-murdering midget was in full-flow and, with never a by or leave – and in less time than it takes to tell – had proceeded to shred his precious old parka into a plethora of pieces faster that an over-bored Staffie let loose on a child's favourite fluffy-toy.

'NOOOOOOOOOOOOOOOOOOOOOOOOOOOOOOOOOOOO!!!!' he had howled; but it was too late, the hateful old harridan was already bimbling towards the kitchen without a care in the world. 'I've put some sandwiches in one of the pockets,' she croaked merrily over her shoulder (obviously choosing to ignore, or not even noticing, the tears currently welling in the corners of Tom's quivering eye-sockets), 'along with a few other *bits and pieces*,' she guffawed. 'Now off you go. No, there's no need to thank me. Ah, you are such a sweet and sensitive boy, Tomas. Have a lovely time with Dame Parsons. And make sure that you follow Mr Hound's instructions to the letter. TTFN then, Ducky, and I'll see you at lunch-time.'

And so it came to pass that now he waited, his back wedged against the whipping wind and the wailing rain, hunched in his hideous new apparel like a disconsolate purple penguin, as passers-by either sniggered into their brollies or gave him cruelly sympathetic smiles.

The coat (more tent than coat, really) hung from his shoulders like an overly-ambitious wigwam draped over an undersized frame; if he stretched his arms out, his finger-tips could almost reach the cuffs of the sleeves; the hem waggled inches above the ground like one half of a pair of repulsing magnets. All in all, with the hood up, he looked like a portly caricature of Death (minus the sickle) who was high on drugs and going through a psychedelic phase. Missus Dobbs was right about one thing – the frickin' thing would last him a lifetime!

How is Dame Ginty ever going to recognise me? he briefly wondered, before suddenly realising, with a despairing sigh, that she would have to be frickin' blind to miss him!

Soon after that cheer-inspiring thought (but nowhere near soon enough), a pastel-green Nissan Figaro (resplendent with white vinyl roof) trundled into view, pulled up at the curb and honked twice. Tom waddled over and peered through the window to see the glamorous Ginty sitting at the wheel, dressed like a dazzling 1950s movie star – elegantly attired in an exquisitely tasteful white (and perfectly fitting) rain-coat and with a brightly-coloured silk-scarf wrapped stylishly around her head.

'Morning, Tom,' she beamed as she opened the door for him (desperately trying to mask the look of revulsion that leapt in horror onto her gorgeous face as she took in the full effect of his ghastly appearance). 'You look ... nice ... and dry,' she managed, kindly (though Tom had the distinct feeling that she was somewhat distressed by the horrendous colour-clash that he was, through no fault of his own, guilty of creating).

'So, Tom,' began Ginty, as the little Figaro chugged determinedly through the rain and along the A27 (to the determined *musical* accompaniment of its overworked and chugging windscreen wipers), 'how's things? I mean, I hope you don't mind me saying so, but you seem a little ... *glum*?'

Tom sighed. 'Fine' he replied, somewhat unconvincingly. 'Thanks for asking.'

'A lot has happened to you in quite a short space of time, dear. It would be no surprise to anybody if you were feeling a little *overwhelmed*.'

'No. Really. I'm OK.'

'Everything all right at home?'

'You mean One Punch Cottage?'

'Of course, dear.'

'Yeah, it's a *blast*.'

'And how's your Mum? You must be missing her awfully?'

'A bit, I suppose ... when I get the chance. But I'm glad that she's been able to get away. After all she's been through I think that she deserves a nice long holiday.'

'That's very kind of you, Tom,' smiled Dame Ginty, and somewhere in the world bees hummed joyfully around a blossoming honeysuckle. 'She's very proud of you, you know. And rightly so. As are we all.'

Tom smiled humourlessly.

'So,' pressed Ginty, with animated interest, 'how are you feeling about potentially becoming the king of an Elven realm? That's quite exciting, isn't it?'

'Well it's a little difficult to get past the *potential* of being mortally skewered by my dear cousin (once removed),' replied Tom, doing his very best not to sound too sarcastic. 'I do find that the impending thought of being murdered by a newfound family member in front of an appreciative audience somehow overshadows the joy of possible sovereignty.'

Dame Ginty giggled.

'Oh, I wouldn't worry too much about that, Tom. A lot of things can happen along the way. I very much doubt that this *Death-Match* will even take place,' she said.

And somehow Tom, despite his own misgivings, couldn't help but feel a little less anxious.

'And how are you feeling about the events surrounding your ... father?'

'You mean having to chop his head off?'

'Hhhhmmm? Well, yes ... I suppose I do. It must be very hard on you, Tom.'

'Not really. It's not as if I knew him, is it? I only met him twice; once when he was an inert but still living skeleton – staked through the ribcage and wedged under a millstone, and the other (this time in the flesh, I'm unhappy to say) when he had me pinned by the throat and was gleefully trying to throttle me, whilst contemplating whether or not to gnaw my head from my shoulders. I can't say that the two of us ever became that attached really.'

'And what about Crow?'

Tom suddenly felt like he'd been kicked in the stomach by an irate giraffe with hobnail boots on.

He looked disconsolately out of the window, though he couldn't see much through the rain-splattered pane apart from his own purple-tinted reflection.

The sound of the rhythmically squeaking windscreen wipers suddenly filled the small car.

'Oh, who knows what's going on there, Tom,' said Ginty at last, giving him an affectionate pat on the knee. 'The best that we can hope is that she's safe and sound. I wouldn't worry; she's a very capable young lady. And besides, I've got a very strong feeling that we'll be seeing her again before too long, don't you fret.'

Tom shrugged his mouth into the shape of a smile.

'I tell you what, before we pick up young Percival's book, what say you and I stop off for some tea and cake? I know just the very spot: *Bill's* – it's one of my all-time favourites.'

'Yeah, why not? That'll be great,' replied Tom in a 3/10 attempt at enthusiasm.

And on plunged the plucky little car, through the torrid rain and on towards the historic town of Lewes, where the promise of hot teas and Sicilian Lemon Drizzle Cake awaited them.

Tom had left Dame Ginty browsing in one of Lewes' many antique/bric-a-brac shops (a chore that Tom considered to be among the very worst fates imaginable) and headed up Lewes High Street, following the carefully given directions that would lead him to Yallery Brown's – the antiquarian and secondhand book shop where The Hound's precious, and recently discovered, volume waited for collection.

The Hound had assured Tom that he had already phoned ahead and that the proprietor (Mr Yallery Brown himself) was expecting him. All Tom had to do was to introduce himself as *Mr Dearlove, the courier for Mr Percival Percy's newly-acquired book,* (with the bizarre but sternly-delivered warning that he was not to thank Mr Brown under any circumstances) and then off he could trot, back home to the dry, warm haven that was One Punch Cottage.

It just so happened that the Yallery Brown's Bookshop turned out to be a most thoroughly yellow affair: yellow tiles, yellow door, yellow window frames and a large brown sign with (unsurprisingly) the words *Yallery Brown* written on it in large yellow letters. The sprawling script on the warped and old-fashioned shop window proudly proclaimed the promise of *"antiquarian & second-hand books"* and the secret wisdom of *"specialists in the esoteric and the occult"*. All in all, it looked just about as inviting and intriguing as one would hope that an independent and specialist bookshop, dealing with the esoteric and the occult, would look.

Tom peered through the window. The small, dimly-lit space was abound with over-packed shelves and higgledy-piggledy piles of stimulating-looking volumes and exotically titled tomes – all carefully stacked with just about the right amount of haphazardness to offer the inquisitive customer the hope that, not only were there were some truly remarkable treasures to be found buried within, but also that the proprietor knew very well what he was about.

Tom pushed opened the stiff yellow door, entered into the small and tightly-packed shop, and took a deep breath. He liked the smell of bookshops. There was something extremely comforting about them. They filled him with an air of expectant excitement – a multitude of discourses to discover, a thousand tall tales to thrill and take you into hitherto-unexplored realms of unimaginable delight and adventure.

'Can I help you?' barked a stern and rather unwelcoming voice.

Tom looked over towards the owner of the severe tones – to see a small, sharply-dressed fellow, with skin the colour of dark mustard and a laughably optimistic comb-over, peering suspiciously at him from behind the book-strewn counter.

It suddenly dawned on Tom that the misguided bookseller might very well have mistaken him for a shoplifter, what with his enormous padded coat with enormous pockets (though, he considered, what self-respecting shoplifter would draw such attention towards themselves by dressing in a fluorescent purple parka? Unless of course it was a double-bluff – for what self-respecting shoplifter would draw such attention towards themselves by dressing in a fluorescent purple parka?).

Tom pulled back the fur-lined hood of his preposterous jacket and dazzled the shopkeeper with his most endearing smile.

The shopkeeper looked on, thoroughly unimpressed, and continued to scrutinise Tom with an expression that oozed suspicion.

'Er ... Hello,' smiled Tom, slowly approaching the counter. 'Mr Yallery Brown?' he enquired.

'That's me. What do you want?'

'Enchanted. My name is Mr Dearlove,' he said rather woodenly, 'the courier for Mr Percival Percy's newly-acquired book.'

Yallery Brown's grimace of distrust instantly evaporated and was replaced by a smile that wouldn't have been amiss on the face of a mother being reunited with a long-lost child.

'Why didn't you say so, young sir!' he cried in delight, vaulting over the counter and heartily pumping Tom's hand. 'Mr Percy is one of my very best and most valued customers. What a pleasure it is to meet you, Mr Wellbeloved.'

'Dearlove.'

'Dearlove, yes of course, forgive me. Wait right there, sir, I have Mr Percy's purchase ready and waiting.'

The strange little bookseller vanished under the counter.

'What an extraordinary turn of events it is, Mr Dearpup,' he gurgled excitedly from beneath the desk.

'Dearlove.'

'This little volume,' he cried, suddenly popping back up from beneath the counter like a demented jack-in-the-box, his comb-over fluttering alarmingly to one side and flapping up and down like a dying turtle's flipper, 'is one of the rarest books that I know of.'

In his hands he carefully cradled a small, unimpressive-looking leather-bound tome and placed it tenderly on the desk-top as gently as if it were a clutch of phoenix eggs.

'Only five copies were ever produced,' he half-whispered, as he curled his comb-over back into place with a deft sweep of his hand.

His fingers returned to the strange little volume and he lightly stroked its cover with the tips of his fingers, as if it was a dying pet.

'Handwritten,' he hissed softly, 'some say ... *in blood*.' He shot an ominous squint in Tom's direction. 'Leather-bound,' he grinned, a ghoulish glint flashing across his mustardy visage, 'some whisper ... *in human skin*. I have heard tell that within its pages are scattered a dark and troubled magic, and hidden within the text there lies a truly horrible secret. And as to the author, you ask?' he whistled conspiratorially. 'Well, some say,' he looked over his shoulder and scanned the room, as if he was frightened of being overheard, 'some say ... some say ... Oh, but you haven't come here to hear tall tales like that, have you, young sir? I'm sure that Mr Percy would be most displeased if I was to give you nightmares. But you'll never guess what, Mr Dearlump?'

'Love.'

'Yes, Pudding?'

'My name is *Dearlove*.'

Yallery Brown regarded Tom quizzically for a moment, as if he couldn't quite believe what he'd just heard, and then shook his head.

'Well, would you believe it, but this is the *second* copy of this most rare and, some say "disturbing", little tome, that I've managed to track down for a customer this week? Extraordinary!'

'Really?'

'Why yes, Mr Dearhump. Most unusual.'

'And who ordered the other one, may I ask?'

'You may indeed, young sir, you may indeed.'

There was a long and pregnant pause.

'Well?' probed Tom. 'Who?'

'Oh yes ... A Dr Campbell.'

'Campbell!'

'That's right. I do believe that he should be in to pick it up today, at some point. Now isn't that the strangest of coincidences?' gurgled the mustardy little shopkeeper excitedly.

'Why yes it is,' replied Tom, as steadily as he could, but with his heart hammering like a riddle-drum. He cast a furtive and nervous glance towards the door. 'Mr Brown, I wonder if you would do me a great favour?'

'Just name it, Mr Dearchump.'

'Love.'

'Yes, Petal?'

'You wouldn't be so kind as to have Dr Cho... I mean ... Dr Campbell's address, would you? I just know that Mr Percy would be delighted to be able to swap ... notes with him ... on the book, that is ... as it were.'

'Oh. Let me see now,' hummed Yallery Brown, helpfully, as he flipped through a large and dusty order book. 'Do you know what, young Mr Deadchimp? I seem to have mislaid Dr Campbell's details. How very strange.'

'But you think that he'll be in to collect it today?'

'Oh yes. Most emphatically, yes! He was as keen as mustard when I told him over the phone that I'd finally managed to acquire the book for him.'

'So you have his telephone number?'

'Afraid not, Mr Deadgimp. Dr Campbell is in the habit of phoning me.'

Tom's brain was whirring frantically.

'Not to worry,' he smiled, as pleasantly as he knew how to.

'I'll put this in a bag for you, shall I?' asked Yallery Brown, kindly, with a nod towards the book.

'Yes please, that would be lovely. Thank you.'

'DON'T THANK ME!' snarled Yallery Brown suddenly, a look of bloodshot and indignant malice flashing into his alarmingly bulging eyeballs, as the whole room trembled violently, the windows rattled and a couple of books dropped from the shelves.

'Aarghh!' meeped Tom, taking a startled leap backwards. 'Oh ... er ... I'm ... *sorry* ...(?)'

'Don't be,' said the bookseller, all smiles again, as he handed Tom a plain plastic bag with Professor Hey's dark and mysterious tome in it. 'I just don't like being thanked, that's all.'

Tom smiled as normally as he could manage at the demented little lunatic, hastily plucked the bag from the shopkeeper's outstretched fingers and turned to go.

'Oh, one more thing, Mr Brown?' he asked (in time-honoured Columbo fashion).

'Name it, Mr Eargimp.'

'Would you be so kind as not to say a word to Dr Campbell about Mr Percy's purchase?' he said, hoisting the bag skyward with a little wiggle. 'Or about my being here ... especially about my being here. You see, I believe that Mr Percy and Dr Campbell are old colleagues, and I'm very sure that Mr Percy will want to surprise his old friend.'

'Consider it done, Mr Earlump,' smiled Yallery Brown.

'Not a word then ... to anyone.'

'I give you my promise, young sir. No words shall pass my lips.'

'Thankgggg...I'll be off then,' beamed Tom, quickly correcting himself before he got another withering blast from the balding little weirdo.

Pulling up his hood, he headed steadily towards the door, although his breath was beginning to stick in his throat with nervous excitement. This was it! The breakthrough that they'd been hoping for – and it was he, Tomas Dearlove, paranormal detective extraordinaire, who had solved it, once again. He'd most probably be made a partner: *Lyons, Hound & Dearlove*; didn't that just have a lovely ring to it. Hang on, maybe it should be *Dearlove, Lyons & Hound?* He was royalty after all. All he had to do was to go and find Dame Ginty, then they could wait and keep a watch on the bookshop until Dr Campbell aka Walter Octavius Hyslip-Campbell aka Dr Chow turned up, expertly follow him to wherever it was that he was holed up these days, and then, as The Hound might have said, William is your cousin's grandma's daughter's brother.

Just as Tom was about to reach for the doorknob, a tall and willowy figure appeared on the other side of the door, shook dry a leopard-print umbrella and prepared to enter the shop.

Tom, being the polite young lad that he was, and being all of a sudden in the very best of moods, opened the door and gestured for the rain-soaked old gentleman (who was dressed rather nattily in a long grey raincoat and with a trilby hat perched on top of his head at a peculiarly perilous angle) to enter.

'Most kind,' smiled the new arrival, distractedly, as he shuffled his way into the tiny shop.

Whether it was the enormous hood, or the fact that his attention was captivated by the rather distracting volume of purple undulating before him, or simply the sad fact that old people rarely seem to properly communicate with young people these days, but the tall, thin, kindly-looking and well-dressed new arrival didn't seem to take any note of Tom's features. Which was, to put it extremely mildly, a blessing. For Tom had certainly surveyed the old gent's soggy visage and, in a blood-chilling flash, had gone from thinking that the old fellow looked somehow vaguely familiar to the heart-stopping realisation that he (Tom) was currently holding open the door for his one-time captor and tormentor (currently attired in Western dress and without the, now quite obviously, pantomime disguise) – the sinister sorcerer, shape-shifting Manticore, tea-drugging cat-fancier and impresario of the *Carnival of Curiosities* .... Dr Chow!

NINE
The Delicate Art Of Tailing
An Evil Shape-Shifting Sorcerer
Whilst Wearing A Bright Purple Parka
In The Pouring Rain

Tom's heart quailed like a flightless chick's on seeing a hungry tabby prowl past its badly-concealed nest. He stole a worried glance from under the furball-lined hood of his hideous coat and towards Yallery Brown, offering a silent prayer that the eccentric old fruitcake would be as good as his word, as Dr Chow/Hyslip-Campbell picked his way towards the counter and the eagerly waiting bookseller.

'A very good morning to you, Dr Campbell,' oozed Yallery Brown, in joyous greeting. 'I have your order right here, sir.'

'How thoroughly   splendid,' purred Dr Chow/Hyslip-Campbell.

Tom chanced a little attention-grabbing wave at the bizarre little bookseller, put a finger to his pursed lips and then pointed dramatically to the plastic bag in his hand – in a silent gesture that (he hoped) urgently pleaded for Yallery Brown to stay true to his promise.

Yallery Brown returned an exaggerated wink, in an appalling attempt at a secretive reply: a gesture that, unsurprisingly, did not go unnoticed by Chow, for the wily sorcerer slowly turned his head and looked in Tom's direction.

Tom hastily shrunk is head down so that the hood flopped over his face.

'Aye'll be de-livering that booek for ye nai then, *Uncle*,' he growled, in the very worst of Scottish accents. 'Be back as sooen as I can.' And then, to his utter dismay, he couldn't help himself from adding a falteringly and feeble-sounding – 'Och aye the noo.'

Dr Chow raised a quizzical eyebrow and then turned back to regard the strange little shopkeeper with cat-like curiosity.

'Right your are Mr Earglu...er I mean ... er ... N*ephew*,' replied the ham-tongued imbecile. 'And don't worry about the ... *thing* ... that we discussed earlier. It will all be just as I promised you it would be,' he smiled.

Yallery Brown returned his undivided attention to Dr Chow. 'My nephew,' he explained. 'Over from ... *India* (?) ... for his holidays. He's helping me out for a bit ... while he's here.'

Tom was out of the door in a flash. He stumbled down the road on spaghetti legs, and, when out of view of the shop window, flattened himself against the wall to catch his breath and try to stop his knees from knocking together.

What was he to do? Should he go and search for Dame Ginty? That would be the sensible thing. But what if Chow left the shop and disappeared before he found her and they'd made their way back up the hill? He couldn't take the risk. No, he would have to conquer his (justifiable) fears and take control of the situation himself. Dr Chow needed to be stopped and it looked like it was down to him to do it.

He looked about at his surroundings. There was a bus stop just a little further along the road. He could wait there and watch the bookshop without looking in any way suspicious – and, with any luck, Dame Ginty would soon make her way up the hill to find out what was keeping him so long, and then they could tail the odious Dr Chow all the way to his odious hideaway.

Tom slunk to the bus stop, positioned himself in his very best attempt at nonchalant normality, and kept his eyes surreptitiously but firmly pinned to the door of Yallery Brown's bookshop.

His heart missed a beat, and took the opportunity to lurch itself into his throat and perform a quick-paced *malagueña*, as the shop's door suddenly opened and out stepped Dr Chow with a plain plastic bag in hand. The evil old warlock collected and erected his leopard-print umbrella, and then hurriedly made his way down the street and straight towards the bus stop ... and Tom!

'You wouldn't happen to know what time the next bus is?' he asked with pleasant cheerfulness, as he came to a halt beside Tom, showing the tips of his impressive canines as he smiled, and bent forward to study the timetable.

'Hoots mon, no-o,' meeped Tom (Scottishly?), dropping his chin like a pelican with an anvil trapped in its gular. 'Och, excuse me,' he managed to rasp through the fearful feeling of nausea that was in danger of overwhelming him, as he watched the razor-like talon of Dr Chow's forefinger skim down the list of bus times. 'I've just realised that I've forgotten something. I'd forgert my own heed if it were nay screwed on, d'ye ken, mon,' he blithered idiotically, hastily surging past the terrifying swine and insouciantly bolting towards the first shop door that presented itself.

As luck would have it, said shop door happened to belong to a newsagent's. Tom blustered through the door like a purple storm and took a moment to try and swallow the bile that was suddenly stuck in his throat. He couldn't help but notice that he had broken out into a profuse sweat, and that his teeth were violently rattling.

'Can I help you?' barked an unfriendly female voice

Tom looked up to see a middle-aged woman with her hair pulled into such a tight ponytail that it gave her features the effect of a severe and unfortunately-executed facelift. She attempted to scowl at him suspiciously. It suddenly dawned on Tom that she might very well think he was some sort of a shoplifting drug-addict – what with the psychedelic purple parka, his chattering teeth, the hacking cough, and his, undoubtedly, pallid and clammy complexion.

'Shave the flippin' monkey!' she snorted. 'That's one hell of a coat you've got there, Sonny Jim. Did you lose a bet or something?'

Tom threw a queasy sneer at the callous cow (though thankfully his bulbous hood masked his disparaging expression).

'What can I get for you then?' Or have you just popped in to step out of the rain?' she sneered, with an unpleasant and accusing tone to her voice.

Tom patted his pockets like a Bavarian folk dancer, in the vain hope that he might find some money in them – while the shopkeeper glowered mistrustfully at him like a starched fart. Tom tenaciously tugged a large brick-shaped and tinfoil-wrapped package from his pocket (undoubtedly Missus Dobbs' latest attempt at sandwiches). But wait, what was this? Oh, wonder of wonders! Sticking out of the corner of said brick-shaped tin-foiled parcel, slightly smeared with what Tom hoped was pickle, was (bless you forever you wonderful little cha-poisoning, destroyer of favourite garments, eye-poking, apple-cheeked and hobnail-booted gurner) a crumpled £10 note!

This changed everything! If he purchased himself a small piece of confectionery, he would have ample change to buy a bus ticket (you try getting on a Brighton – and surrounding district – bus without anything resembling the correct coinage and see how far it gets you!), catch whatever bus the despicable Chow was waiting for, and then see just where it took him.

The newsagent puckered an ill-disposed and under-formed frown at him, as he picked up a bar of Toblerone and then offered his pickle-coated tenner to her un-eagerly waiting hand. She tentatively snatched the note from his fingers, as if it was a sheet of used toilet-paper, hastily thrust it in the till, and then prodded a £5 note and some coins onto the counter. Tom pocketed the change and then pretended to look at the comics on the shelf while watching Dr Chow from the window.

The number 28 bus (double-decked and resplendent in red and milky-yellow) rumbled into view and juddered to a shuddering halt. Tom watched as Dr Chow shook the excess rain from his brolly, neatly furled it, hopped onto the bus, waved a ticket at the driver, and then began to make his way up the steps to the top deck.

As Chow's head disappeared from view, Tom dashed out of the newsagent's (to the accompaniment of "It's not a library, you know!") and sprinted to the doors of the bus, just as the driver closed them.

Tom banged frantically on the doors.

'Hurry it up then,' muttered the driver tetchily (a balding, chubby and world-weary sounding fellow) as he begrudgingly opened the doors for Tom. 'Flippin' heck, son!' he gawked, his eyes suddenly widening in grumpy hilarity. 'That's one mother of a coat you've got there, mate! Did you lose a bet or something?' he chuckled sourly.

Tom chose to ignore the crabby and insensitive cad, and proffered some coins.

'Where do you want to go to, exactly?' asked the bus driver.

'Where, exactly, do you go to?'

'Churchill Square.'

'Then I'll have a single to Churchill Square, please.'

'You got a *Young Person's Travel Card*?'

'I'm afraid not, no.'

The driver huffed a surly sigh and pumped Tom some change.

Tom pulled his ticket from the ticket machine and then hastily lurched and stumbled his way towards the back of the vehicle, as the cantankerous git of a driver started up the engine and set off with an expert display of *uphill stop-start slalom charabanc racing* (known to bus drivers the world over [*amusingly*] as *Passenger Skittles*).

The bus was all but empty, and so Tom artfully positioned himself at the rear window seat – from where he would be able to see Chow get off, without Chow being able to see him (unless, of course, the cunning swine chose to look around!).

As the bus chugged drearily on its halting way, Tom found himself cursing the fact that he didn't have a mobile phone. He really should talk to The Hound about that. Just think how easy (and safe!) life would be if all he'd had to do was to press a few digits and then announce dramatically to his impressed, grateful and comfortingly dangerous colleagues, that he'd found Dr Chow, and that they'd better get themselves over here asap – instead of having to sneak about on public transport, with his bowels increasingly loosening with each jittering jolt and heart-stopping halt (scheduled and unscheduled) that the bus made. What the hell had he been thinking! Oh well, there was nothing for it now but to wait and see where this, the very worst of magical mystery tours, might lead him.

With nothing better to do, Tom pulled Missus Dobbs' brick of foil-wrapped door-stopper sandwiches from his pocket (the Toblerone would be left for later – ho-ho!) and gingerly opened it, to find (to his eternal relief) a small platoon of hefty slices of freshly-baked bread, lightly dusted with half a ton of butter and layered with slabs of cheese as thick as roofing-tiles and strips of lightly-fried venison, topped with sun-blushed tomatoes (all generously dowsed in an ocean of dark-brown pickle). How wonderful! He was suddenly starving. Funny how coming face-to-face with an old nemesis – a shape-shifting mythical man-eating Manticore and evil sorcerer, who has, in the not-too-distant past, had you trussed, drugged and imprisoned in a cage and then openly mused about the pros and cons of (a) transforming you into a were-cat or (b) having your still-beating heart ripped from your chest and devoured before your dying eyes by a trusted minion (and unequivocally deciding that option (b) was simply the very best idea imaginable) – coupled with an unexpected solo trip into the realms of wind-inducing terror, did absolute wonders for working up an appetite.

The bus pitched to a halt outside Falmer Station.

Over the grumble of the dying engine, Tom heard a light cat-like tread of footsteps from the deck above.

Chow!

He ducked down – so that he was hidden from view – and peered through the gap between the handrail and the back of the seat in front of him.

Dr Chow slowly appeared from the stairwell and made his way to the doors.

'Thank you, Driver,' he rumbled pleasantly, with a spry tip of his hat. And then he sprang from the bus, squinted up at the sky, unfurled his umbrella and sauntered his way past the long queue of impatiently waiting people, desperate to get on the bus and out of the rain.

Tom left it as long as he dared and then made a dash towards the door, one hand clasping his billowing hood to his head and the other clutching the plain plastic bag that contained The Hound's precious and recently purchased antique book. However, his progress was hampered by the barrage of damp students who were now seeping onto the bus like a badly-dressed virus. He put his head down and apologetically battled his way forward (to the accompaniment of – "Here, watch it, mate!" and "Whoa! Will you look at that coat! I'm having flashbacks to the weekend, man!" and "What happened, chap? Did you lose a bet or something?") until, like a pulsating purple salmon pushing against the tide, he finally managed to burst his way off the bus.

Tom looked nervously about him. There was no sign of the evil swine (Chow). He cautiously peered over the railings and saw the top of a leopard-print umbrella lightly bouncing its way jauntily down the long flight of stairs that lead towards the subway between Falmer Station and Sussex University.

Tom readjusted his hood and stealthily pressed after his unsuspecting quarry, contemplating, all the while, the delicate art of tailing an evil shape-shifting sorcerer whilst wearing a bright purple parka in the pouring rain.

With his heart pounding in his teeth, Tom merged into the surroundings as best he could – putting as much distance (and the bodies of as many students) between himself and Chow as he dared – and followed the malicious swine through the subway and towards the entrance of Sussex University. As the students surged their way onto the campus, Chow veered to the left to take a narrow path that ran parallel to the motorway and that headed towards Stanmer Park – the rambling spread of open land and woodlands that homed the small and delightful village of Stanmer (unsurprisingly) and the beautiful and decadent *country pile* known as *Stanmer House* (once home to the prestigious Pelham family [the one-time Earls of Chichester] and now a rather splendid restaurant and popular wedding venue).

Tom stopped. What was he to do? If he followed after him, and Dr Chow happened to turn around, there would be no place for him to hide – and there would be no way that the evil bastard could fail to recognise his appalling attire and become (homicidally) suspicious.

As Tom watched the leopard-print umbrella receding along the path, he thrust the plain plastic bag containing the recently-purchased mysterious little tome into his (now) sandwich-free pocket, and pondered on just what the hell he was going to do next. What he needed, he decided (rather brilliantly), was a stroke of blinding good luck – some piece of whopping good fortune to enable him to pursue the dangerous blighter without sticking out like a Belisha beacon (or indeed like the junior member of a well-known firm of paranormal investigators following a prime supernatural suspect whilst disconcertingly camouflaged in a parka of a somewhat eye-catching and vomit-inducing shade of purple).

A gaggle of voices suddenly hummed around him, and Tom found – to his utter surprise – that he was suddenly engulfed by a small shoal of chattering teenagers, all wrapped up neatly against the dour English weather in a collection of vividly (and rather loudly) coloured anoraks. Their leader – a thin, animated and nervous-looking young blonde woman – was holding a bright green brolly high into the air and urging her wayward wards forwards in a somewhat high-pitched and increasingly exasperated voice.

'Come along! Please hurry. The sooner we get to Stanmer House the sooner we can all get out of the rain and have some lunch. *Camine is mas rapido, por favor,*' she pleaded, with good-natured and tightening gusto.

Her brightly-coloured and nattering flock quickened their step without seeming to draw breath or pause in their conversations.

English language students, thought Tom to himself. *Spaniards, by the sound of it. What a stroke of luck!*

He saw Dr Chow turn his neck, glance around the brim of his umbrella, and cast a fang-filled smile at the raucous and brightly-coloured swarm. Tom hastily tucked himself onto the end of the herd, stuck his head down, tried not to puke in terror, and *blended in* for all he was worth.

They surged along the narrow path like a flock of psychedelic and gabbling geese; Chow a hundred yards ahead of them, and increasing his lead with every stride of his long legs. The old sorcerer suddenly veered to his right and hopped through a gap in the fence of a small car park with cat-like grace. The students marched past the gap and onwards along the path. Tom, bringing up the rear, ventured a quick peek into said car park to see Dr Chow making his way across a large field, with several dejected-looking football-pitches mapped upon it, and towards Stony Mere Way (the long and winding road that leads in from the main entrance, dissects the park in two, and eventually takes you to *Stanmer House* and then on to Stanmer Village). Tom rapidly calculated that if the group of students were heading to *Stanmer House* then they would soon join onto the very same road that his despicable quarry was now heading towards. He made the quick decision to stick with them and hope that Chow wouldn't somehow disappear from sight by the time that they had rounded the corner.

Stanmer Park is a large, open, and stunningly beautiful park and nature reserve (bookended by some truly sumptuous woods – to wit: the *Great Wood* to the south and *Millbank Wood* and *Highpark Wood* to the north) that Tom knew very well indeed, due to the many walks that he had been forced to endure whilst accompanying The Hound and Cornelius on their early morning hikes. It was also here, (somewhere in Millbank Wood. he thought, though he wasn't exactly sure) where Tom had been imprisoned by the chilling bounder Chow and his hateful *Carnival of Curiosities* during the lead-up to *The Society of the Wild Hunt's* pursuit of The Hound in Hollingbury Wood earlier that year. In the ensuing weeks after their respective escapes, The Hound, Cornelius, and Tom had tried to find the site where the *Carnival of Curiosities* had camped, but had been unable to pinpoint its exact location with any certainty. Was it possible that Chow and his pride of evil were-felons were once again hiding out in Stanmer Park?

A chill ran down Tom's spine that had nothing to do with the weather.

As the gaggle of students hit the main entrance of the park and began to head along Stony Mere Way, the rain began to ease a little. Tom could make out the sprightly figure of Dr Chow now striding purposefully away to Tom's left and heading straight towards the tree line of the Great Wood. Before them lay a long and open stretch of grassland leading to the woods that, woefully, offered Tom no cover if he chose to follow; but there was nothing for it but to head after the terrifying and hateful bastard, for he dared not risk losing sight of him.

Tom mooched to a halt until he was left far to the rear of the chattering throng of students. No one seemed to notice that he had lagged behind, but then no one had seemed to notice that he had been there in the first place. Chow was now halfway along the field and Tom knew that he couldn't afford to leave it any longer. With a deep breath, and with his heart hammering in his chest, he pulled his billowing, hair-barfed hood closer to his head and set off in a direct line behind Dr Chow/Hyslip-Campbell. If the evil swine turned around and spotted him he could only pray that he would have enough of a head start to make it back to safety (to the group of students, the university, or the train station) before the murderous lunatic could catch up with him – unless, of course, the sorcerer turned himself into a Manticore. Tom didn't think that he could outrun such a mythical beast, but he doubted that Chow would dare risk changing shape in broad daylight and in open country ... or so he tried to convince himself.

Dr Chow came to the tree line, pulled his umbrella down and gave it a vigorous shake. Tom hurled himself to the ground, just in time, it turned out, for the murderous were-cat-fancying evil-hearted-enchanter and one-time Oxford Don cast a wary glance over his shoulder before slipping into the Great Wood via a neat and darkly arching opening in the otherwise near-impregnable wall of green foliage.

When he was definitely out of view, Tom leapt up and ran as fast as he could towards the entrance of the woods, determined not to lose sight of the scoundrel. He reached the trees, steadied his nerve and gingerly entered into the gloom of the forest.

Before him was a round, shrub-filled dell with two paths circling steeply upwards on either side.

No sign of Chow.

Tom pulled back his hood a little and looked carefully around. Both pathways seemed to eventually head in the same direction; in fact, it looked like they converged at the top of the basin. He decided to take the less steep of the two (mainly because it looked less slippery). At the top of the bowl he was soon faced with a narrow and muddy little track that picked its way through the trees.

No sign of Chow.

Tom hastily looked about him and tried not to panic.

Inside the woods the noise of the traffic from the A27 was spookily hushed. The only sound was the gentle and strangely comforting patter of the rain fizzing against the thick covering of leaves above him.

Think, Tom, think! What would The Hound have done?

He could almost hear the clipped and plummy tones of the were-hound – *"Look up, Tom, look around and then ... look down."*

Tom squatted to the floor and examined the muddy path before him.

There! The slight, freshly-scuffed imprint of a shoe ... and then another and another, made by someone with a wide stride, a light tread and an exceptionally large shoe size.

Tom swallowed the bile that was rising in his gorge and followed the tracks.

The path snaked its way through closely-packed woodland comprised of tall and slender trees – that reached up high (thirty, maybe forty feet) into the rain-lashed sky. A crooked line of yew trees ranked against the path's lower side, like a row of dark and alien sentries. Tom found yews a little spooky, if truth be told; they looked like the strange survivors of a long-lost time when trees were ... *different* – but he remembered that Alberich Albi had once told him that yew trees were the earth's messengers; ancient and wise, friends to be trusted in times of trouble. Tom hoped that Alberich was right, and then found himself missing the old Elf King.

Onwards along the path he crept, his eyes casting about in a state of alert terror as the rain pattered above him. He recalled another thing that The Hound had once said to him – *"that there was no greater delight than a long walk through an English wood in a gentle rain and a light breeze"*. At this particular moment in time Tom found himself somewhat in disagreement, as he tiptoed forward with wobbly knees and in constant dread that his bowels might suddenly betray him and trumpet his approach like an overzealous herald.

Chow's tracks suddenly stopped.

Tom looked worriedly up and down the path. Nothing. He doubled back and rechecked the ground. The light (and fast fading) footprints seemingly vanished before a narrow piece of open woodland. And then he saw it – the slightest of trails where someone might have recently walked, smudged like a damp graze through the ankle-deep carpet of green before him, weaving its way purposefully through the trees.

Tom took a deep breath and followed it.

After a few minutes he was convinced that he must have made a mistake. It was probably just an old fox path that he'd been trailing. What an idiot. He'd lost Chow!

But, just as he was about to turn back and retrace his steps, he saw him, strolling sprightly through the trees as if he didn't have a care in the world, his folded leopard-print umbrella elegantly resting over his shoulder.

Tom almost squealed in shock and instantly ducked down, holding his breath and offering a silent prayer that (a) the sound of the rain had muffled his steps and that (b) the deranged and murderous lunatic wouldn't look around.

The sly old sorcerer briefly paused to examine a flower, and then carried on. Tom slowly rose and tiptoed after him, darting from all-too-thin tree trunk to all-too-thin tree trunk, as Dr Chow strolled blithely onwards, passing through a group of trees with their trunks painted blue (which Tom thought a little weird) – Tom flitting behind him like a billowing purple phantom.

Chow veered to his right and vanished from view. Tom stealthily crept forward, desperately calculating how close he dared get to the murderous swine. He finally came onto a wide and well-used pathway and hastily looked up and down it. Dr Chow had disappeared!

To the left of the track was a small area of woodland dominated by the remains of three enormous and moss-covered tree stumps. Tom cautiously picked his way through the undergrowth and walked around the first of the stumps.

The sound of the world around him popped into silence. The rain seemed to stop and the wind died, as if someone had flicked a switch.

It was then that he scented something strangely out of place. What was it? It smelled like … stale alcohol … ?

Suddenly he was violently jerked backwards by the hood of his coat and heaved into the air like a rag doll. He landed in a painful heap on the moss-covered floor with the breath bludgeoned out of him.

Dr Chow/Walter Octavius Hyslip-Campbell stood before him, smiling like the Cheshire Cat's evil twin brother, and regarding Tom like a raptor eyeing a brightly-coloured field mouse unexpectedly caught sunbathing in the Mushroom Forest.

'Good afternoon,   Mister Tom,' he purred, oozing sinister curiosity, and prodding Tom's foot with the tip of his umbrella as if he were inspecting the downed rodent for signs of life. 'What an   unexpected,   but   delightful, surprise.'

Tom managed to draw himself into a sitting position, struggling to take a breath as his heart quailed in terror and Chow scrutinised him with his peculiar and chilling lion-like gaze.

A pair of huge and mottled hands seized Tom by the shoulders and hoisted him to his feet as if he were a bag of rumpled feathers.

Tom was almost overpowered by the stench of stale booze.

'Hello, Little Cub,' growled a voice like thunder rolling down dark mountains.

He managed to turn his head and caught a glimpse of The Mighty HASS's granite-like jaw.

And then the world went black.

TEN
An Unexpected Friend

Tom was bound hand and foot, stretched and suspended on a rack – in the classic *prisoner star-shape* – in the middle of a circus-ring. Gathered before him the whole of the deplorable cast of the *Carnival of Curiosities* prowled restlessly, surveying him with forbidding feline rapture. Oh, all his old chums were present: his cannibalistic dining buddy, the alcoholic, pant-staining, organ-chomping were-jaguar, known to fight fans the world over as The Mighty HASS; the tone-deaf little darlings that were Mae and Lu (Siamese were-cats, and a source of constant comfort during Tom's various dark days of imprisonment); the vicious and deadly brotherly trio of *kung-mew* experts that were the were-caracals – Bruce, Chuck and Jackie; Lady Lynx – the blind fortune-telling were-lynx who had once delighted in telling Tom that his future, like his past, was bathed in blood (callus old bitch that she was – all the more galling because it looked like she might be right!); the revolting and moth-eaten Mr Tickles skulked spitefully to and fro, like Frankenstein's moggy badly reanimated for one last withering grimace at the world; and last, but by no means least, the terrifying, hateful old hat-balancer and shape-shifting sorcerer, the third-rate Fu Manchu impersonator and opium-tea guzzling complete and utter cad himself – Dr Chow/Walter Octavius Hyslip-Campbell.

'You'll not get a word out of me, you devilish swine!' snarled Tom, in a show of heroic defiance that he didn't feel completely committed to.

'Really?' purred Dr Chow, whilst distractedly examining the exquisite floral pattern on his priceless china teacup. 'Mae? Lu? How would you feel about a new *member* for your   act? I do so love the sound of   a   soprano,   don't you, Master Tom? The castrato voice is   so   *pure.*'

'I'LL TELL YOU ANYTHING YOU WANT TO KNOW! JUST PLEASE DON'T TOUCH ME!' wailed Tom, valiantly.

'Much better,' smiled Chow. 'So tell me,   what were you   doing?'

'Following you.'

'Yes,   I know that. But   why?'

'Because ... uhm ... I wanted to see where you were going?'

'Of course you wanted to see where I was going, otherwise you wouldn't have been following me, you dolt!' snapped Dr Chow, a tone of ominous exasperation creeping into his voice.

Tom whimpered manfully.

Dr Chow took a sip of tea and then carefully returned the cup to its saucer (resting elegantly in the palm of his other hand). The despicable brute was still in Western dress: smart grey flannel trousers, a pristine white shirt (opened at the collar and with the sleeves rolled up just below the elbows) and a trilby hat perched jauntily on the side of his head at perilously impossible angle – all in all (bar the polished fingernails and the mien of a psychotic anteater with a personality disorder), he could have been a close-to-retirement 1950s accountant on his tea-break.

'You intrigue me, Master Tom,' smiled Chow humourlessly. 'Where once I thought you *worthless* I now know that you are, in fact, a person of *interest*. Where once you were nothing but an expendable pawn, I have since discovered ...' he shot a grateful smile over to Lu (who bristled with pride under the golden gaze of Chow's appreciation), 'that you are, in fact, a king. A Goblin king, to be exact.'

'An Elven prince, actually,' interrupted Tom against his better judgement, and sounding, to his utter horror, like a proper little smart-arse.

'Indeed? I stand corrected, educated and enlightened,' chuckled Chow, horribly. 'Truly fascinating. And here you are again? Once more within my power. I shall have to be far more careful, Master Tom, for this time I shall not lose you.

'Now, tell me, why you have followed me? No doubt you were sent by the illustrious *Hound Who Hunts Nightmares* (such a descriptive appellation, don't you think?) and his friend, your venerable uncle, Professor Lyons.'

'No I wasn't!' cried Tom, and to be fair it was the truth – and probably just about as close to it as he intended to come it, if he could help it.

'No?' purred Chow, with menacing inquisitiveness. 'Then what?'

'I was sent to pick up a book and ... er ... and ...'

'Ah yes, *the book*. Intriguing. Quite the coincidence, don't you think, that both The Hound and I have desired, and succeeded, in procuring a copy of the very same, extremely rare and dangerous volume? (I presume it was *he* who sent you on that particular errand, for I fear that the "Professor" barely gets much further than the sports pages.) What exactly does he want with it?'

'Presumably the same as you,' wheezed Tom, wriggling his fingers to try and get some blood back into them.

'And that is ...?'

'To help him find some way to defeat the vampire, Lord Manfred de Warrenne ... I would imagine.'

'Indeed,' smirked Chow, slyly. 'However, as our dear friend Mr Brown has just recently informed me, the book has other, more interesting possibilities. But enough of this. If you were not *ordered* to find me, then why follow me?'

Tom had half-formed his plan – it was a long shot but it was the best that he could come up with under the circumstances (and you try coming up with something better when helplessly trussed up like a Guinea-pig's carcass before a troupe of salivating were-cats) – his only hope lay in trying to sound as convincing as possible.

'Because I hate them!' he snarled.

Chow managed to curl an eyebrow and almost look surprised.

'They're always making me do things that I don't want to. *"Tom, do this!"* *"Tom, fetch that!"* They treat me like I'm a slave! It's appalling, really. I made up my mind to run away a long time ago but was always too scared to try. And then I saw you. Or I thought it was you. The truth is, Dr Chow, is that I hoped that it was you.'

'*Hoped*?' snorted Dr Chow in amusement, sipping tea and scrutinising Tom like a viper.

Tom managed a carefree laugh. 'Yes, I couldn't believe my luck.'

'*Luck*?' echoed Chow, placing cup to saucer with a delicate clink of china.

Tom took a deep breath and held it for a moment for added effect. 'There's something that I want to ask you, Dr Chow. A favour. A *gift* really. The greatest gift imaginable.'

'*Gift*?'

'Yes. I want ... more than anything in the world ... to be ...' he made his eyes go moist (it wasn't hard) in an effort to look like a recently-orphaned toddler asking for a kitten for Christmas, '... to be turned into ... into ... a were-cat (but one with all its *bits* intact, if you follow me),' he added hastily.

'You do?' asked Chow, somewhat incredulously.

The old sorcerer briefly turned to look at the company of surprised feline faces about him and then turned his attention back to Tom. 'Why?' he asked, as he raised his cup to his lips again.

'Why! Are you serious? Look at you all! I mean ... wow! Just look at you, you're ... you're all so ... amazing!'

'We are?' queried Dr Chow, his teacup (and arm, of course) suspended in mid-air and his head tilted to one side as if he couldn't quite believe what he was hearing. Tom found himself wondering, once again, how it was that the old bastard's hat didn't fall off?

'Why yes!' exclaimed Tom, bursting with feigned excitement. 'And then ... and then I saw ... *him* ... and I just knew. I just knew that it was what I wanted, more than anything I've ever, ever wanted in my whole life!'

'*Him*?' enquired Dr Chow, his teacup still poised.

The collected *Carnival of Curiosities* seemed to lean in closer, with – dare one say? – carnivorous curiosity, enthralled to hear what Tom had to say.

'Why, the Prince of course!'

'*Prince*? What prince?' hissed Chow, his voice a barely audible whisper.

'Prince Maffdetti A-Su, that's who!' announced Tom, his voice brimming with as much of a hero-worshipping tone as he could muster (being one of Nature's cynics it wasn't easy but, well, under the circumstances ...).

The tent went silent ... save for the sound of Dr Chow's teacup and saucer shattering on the floor. And then there was a terrible yowling from the collected audience. Tails lashed. Fangs were bared. Worried glances were swapped. And Tom took the greatest of delight in seeing something that he never dared hope to see – for he looked over at Dr Chow and saw fear in his eyes.

Dr Chow sprang forward and grasped Tom by the throat.

'How do you know that name?' he rasped, his face a mask of stricken terror. 'HOW DO YOU KNOW THAT NAME?!'

'Well,' wheezed Tom, as matter of factly as he could (which was a tad of a struggle – but then it's a tad awkward to sound nonchalant when an evil sorcerer who is suddenly in mortal fear of his life [and who sees you as the possible source of his woes], and who, it should be noted, has talons that would shame a b*rown-throated sloth*, has you grasped around the neck while you're helplessly strung up like the Count of Monte Cristo), 'he came round One Punch Cottage for tea and crumpets the other day.'

'You mean to say   Maffdetti is here   in England?' gasped Chow softly, though looking like he was close to screaming.

'Oh yes,' continued Tom, trying to prattle away nonchalantly, while his voice was steadily squeezed up the register, 'he's over here visiting with some of his friends. Perhaps you know them. The Naravirala. Lovely ... cat ... people. Well, that Jelani is a bit of a grouch; you've got to wonder what he's so angry about? But Fauzia seems quite lovely, though I do suppose that you wouldn't really want to get on the wrong side of her ...'

Dr Chow let go of Tom's throat and staggered back as if he'd been stabbed in the heart.

'What do they want?' he asked, kitten-like.

'Oh, I don't know, wasn't really listening. But it sounded to me like they're chasing after somebody. The Prince seemed very angry with someone. I certainly wouldn't like to be in their shoes, let me tell you. Something about them stealing something that they shouldn't have; betrayal, ungratefulness, retribution, punishment, you know, that sort of thing. Mainly punishment though, if memory serves me right.'

'HOW COULD HE KNOW THAT I WAS HERE?!' screeched Chow, to no one in particular.

'You old fool!' growled The Mighty HASS. 'You've killed us all! The Naravirala will track us down, each and every one, and slaughter us!'

'Whatever shall we do, Master?' cried Bruce.

Jackie and Chuck flanked their brother, their fur standing up on end and their eyes as wide as worried saucers.

Mae and Lu hugged on to each other, weeping hysterically and looking very small.

Mr Tickles fled from the tent like an electrocuted feather duster.

Tom tried to mask his delight.

'SILENCE!' roared a voice.

Everybody blubbered to a halt.

Tom looked over to see Lady Lynx tottering over to collect the quivering Dr Chow by his trembling hand.

'Chuck, Jackie,' she commanded, 'take the boy and cage him. We will decide what to with him later. Bruce and HASS – go and scout the area. See that the child has not been followed.'

'What about us?' sobbed Mae and Lu in panicked chorus.

'You will stop mewling like kittens – immediately!' snapped the were-lynx, turning her sightless white eyes towards the trembling lady-boys. 'Go and prepare some food or something. Make yourselves useful, and then perhaps we will all live to see our old age.'

The legendary lady-boys of Siam shimmied from the tent at an alarmed full tilt.

As Tom was being untied by Chuck and Jackie he overheard the were-lynx comforting Dr Chow as she ushered him from the tent.

'Come now, Walter,' she soothed. 'We have seen darker days than this, you and I, and still we live to tell the tale. Calm yourself, my love. The Naravirala are not yet on our doorstep. We will out-think them, again. As we did before. As we will always do.'

Tom sat with his back against the bars of the cage (the very same cage that he had been imprisoned in before). In all his dark thoughts and worst nightmares (and believe me, he'd had some absolute beauties) he'd never imagined for one minute that he would ever find himself back here. What sort of world was this that he was now embroiled in? He seemed doomed to spend several sleepless nights a year imprisoned at the will and whim of some demented supernatural villain. This was the third occasion that he'd had to spend time behind bars, and the experience was in no danger of becoming any more comfortable. Perhaps he should change his job description to that of "*professional hostage*"?

*W*ant to place someone in the clutches
of a
horrible homicidal monster?
Why not call
TOMAS DEARLOVE!
Experienced detainee *available at knock-down rates!*
No **cage** *too small. No situation too* **perilous**.
No **lunatic** *too unhinged for*
TOM – THE MIRACLE HOSTAGE.
Free quote & consultation.
Discount available for first time customers.
Terms & conditions apply
You must be able to pay all ransom demands on time.
Failure to do so could result in the dismemberment of limbs, removal of digits, or, in extreme cases, lose of life.

The light had gone and it was beginning to get cold. Apart from a thin covering of straw on the cage floor, there was nothing to try to warm himself with. Tom wrapped his arms about him (taking a moment to delight in the fact that he had now regained the feeling in his hands) and listened, in dejected misery, to the sound of rain lightly falling against the canvas of the tent that his prison was housed within. It offered little comfort, and he found himself wishing for something that he never would have imagined that he would ever wish for. He wished he had been allowed to keep his purple parka.

There was a sodden thump as something soft and heavy landed in a heap in the corner of his cage. Tom buttock-jumped into the air, bashed his head against the roof of the cage, howled with a strange mixture of pain and surprise, and almost soiled himself with fright.

'Sssshh!' hissed a deep voice.

'Who's there?' meeped Tom.

A pair of emerald eyes suddenly appeared out of the darkness and peered through the bars.

'I have brought you something, Little Cub,' growled The Mighty HASS in a fierce whisper, his face suddenly coming into focus as he pressed his mottled features between the bars, 'to keep you from the cold.'

Tom clutched both hands defensively over his heart and shrunk as far away from the murderous swine as he could.

The were-jaguar gestured towards the dark shiny lump in the corner of the cage and Tom suddenly realised that it was his purple parka.

'What happened?' whispered the man-cat, in earnest curiosity. 'Did you lose a bet?'

'Naff off!' snapped Tom.

'Do not fear me, child,' whispered HASS, in what might have been an attempt at a comforting smile.

'Oh, really?' snorted Tom in disbelief. 'How do I know that you haven't just popped down here for a midnight snack?'

'What? ... Oh, that. He-he-he,' the man-cat chortled good-humouredly, as if it was of no consequence at all that he had once promised to rip Tom's still-beating heart from his chest and devour it before his dying eyes. 'Do not concern yourself with that small matter. Think on it as a ... *cultural difference*. It was nothing personal, Little Cub, believe me.'

'Nothing personal!' snorted Tom, as bravely as he dared. 'Are you fricking drunk?'

The were-jaguar shrugged his massive shoulders and sighed deeply (an act which, it must be noted, made Tom's eyes water a little).

'Probably,' said the man-cat, sadly. 'No, why lie? Always. How else could I live with myself, Little Cub? I do not blame you for mistrusting me, child, but I will prove you wrong, my friend. I am here to help you.'

'Oh you are, are you?'

'Tell me, is it true?' asked HASS, pressing his lantern-like jaw further into the cage and grasping the bars with his humongous hands.

'Is what true?'

'The Naravirala; they are here? In England?'

'Yes they are.'

HASS looked dejectedly at the floor of Tom's cage.

'I hate this country,' he sighed forlornly. 'It is so damp, Little Cub. It chills my bones. It chills me.'

The were-jaguar pulled his head from the bars and quickly glanced over his shoulder.

'When the time comes,' he growled in a low and menacing snarl, 'I will help you. I will kill Chow with my own hands. I will tear his throat out and feast upon his sinful heart. I swear it. Remember it, Little Cub. Remember that I, Hector Antonio Sanchez Silvio, known to fight fans the world over as *The Mighty HASS*, was, at the very end, your friend.'

And with that he slowly backed away from the cage and disappeared into the gloom like a vapour.

'Remember,' he hissed, his voice like a spear thrust into the darkness. 'Remember me to your friends.'

Tom reached for his coat and hastily pulled it on.

'Stupid drunken poltroon!' he whispered out loud (but not too loud – just in case the dangerous bastard was still in earshot).

Not that he had any doubt that HASS hated Dr Chow with a vengeance, it was just that he found it a little difficult to forgive the murderous tosser for dragging him through the woods all those months ago, terrifying the living crap out of him, and then topping it all off by promising to inflict the most horrendous of deaths imaginable upon him. Maybe he should be a more forgiving person, but deep down Tom suspected that the were-jaguar was terrified of Prince Maffdetti and the Naravirala and was just trying to curry favour with Tom should the worst happen.

He curled his bright purple parka tighter around him and waited for some warmth to return to his body.

As he sat silently in the dark, the very picture of wretchedness, he suddenly had the quite brilliant and liberating thought that he should really try and escape. What had Crow said about her brief imprisonment with the Carnival of Curiosities? Ah yes – "Really? *How they think that those ridiculous antique prisons are supposed to hold anyone with half a brain for more than a minute is beyond me!*" ... or something very much like that.

Suddenly he was filled with a sad and heavy longing for his friend, that hit him so hard that it felt like it physically hurt. He hoped that she was all right, wherever she might be. And he wished, for the thousandth time, that she hadn't left.

Well, if she could do it (escape from this prison, that is) then why not he?

He stood up as much as he could (either this cage had shrunk since his last visit or he had grown quite considerably) and shuffled over to the bars.

Maybe there was a weakness in one of them?

No. No there wasn't.

Perhaps he could squeeze himself through one of the gaps?

No, he most definitely could not.

Perchance there was a trapdoor in the ceiling?

Nope.

Mayhap he could try and pick the lock on the door?

But, of course, he had nothing to pick a lock with.

.... Unless ...

He hastily checked the pockets of his coat and soon found, to his utter amazement, an old-fashioned hairpin. Incredible! He was beginning to suspect that Missus Dobbs might just have given him some sort of magic purple parka; bless her googly-eyed and apple-cheeked visage.

He'd never actually picked a lock before, but how hard could it be?

Tom was at the door of the cage in a flash and fumbling with the lock. He'd seen the films – who hasn't? – the hero expertly thrusts a pin into a padlock or locked door and artfully wiggles said pin around for a few moments before – hey presto! – the door/vault/cage magically flies open.

After a few exasperating minutes, Tom had to admit that it was a lot harder than it looked.

There was a soft shuffle in the darkness. Tom stifled a meep, silently leapt away from the cage door, and positioned himself in the centre of his cell, trying to look as innocent and obligingly resigned to his fate as he possibly could.

'Hello, Mister Tom,' mewed a soft and pitiful voice that Tom knew only too well, for it was that of his old tormentor and one-time jail-mate (whilst they had both been briefly [and terrifyingly] incarcerated in the house of the Bucca-Boo, waiting to be interrogated by the newly-crowned *Gobfather* – who, as it turned out, was none other than the dastardly witch and *Society of the Wild Hunt* stalwart Madame Buckleberry), the conniving, deplorable, joint-worst interpreter of the works of Shirley Bassey known to history, the worm-tongued and bitter-hearted lady-boy, the untrustworthy rogue of a Siamese-were-cat, known and loathed the world over as Lu.

'Piss off, Lu,' snapped Tom, for he was in no mood for the were-cat's company.

'Well that's no way to treat a friend,' pouted Lu, shaking his head with queenly regret.

'You're not exactly what I'd call a friend.'

'So misunderstood,' sighed the were-cat. 'It is true that we have not got off to the very best of starts, Mister Tom, but I hope that we can put all of our *unfortunate* history behind us and work towards a more meaningful future. Tell me something, Mister Tom.'

'Yes,' sighed Tom, with his best tone of bored irritation, 'the Naravirala *are* in England, and they *are* most definitely looking for Dr Chow.'

'Oh?' cried Lu, in danger of cracking the thick layer of make-up that was plastered over his face. 'That is terrible news indeed. But I was going to ask you if you'd lost a bet or something, Mister Tom? That coat, well it's ... well it is quite ghastly is what it is!'

'Thanks, Lu. Now be a good chap and bugger off.'

The were-cat regarded Tom for a while and offered his best attempt at a friendly smile through his trowelled veneer of foundation.

'It is the thing that Chow has always feared the most,' he continued at last, 'that one day the Naravirala would find him and punish him for his misdeeds. As you know, Mister Tom, we (Mae and I) have no love for Dr Chow. He has used us most awfully, Mister Tom. But we will have our revenge, I swear it. Perhaps you are the means for us to extract that vengeance? I will do whatever I can to help you and your newfound friends, Mister Tom. I give you my word.'

'That's very *kind* of you, Lu, but if you don't mind I'm trying to get some sleep – and even if I wasn't, I think that you're about the last person on earth that I'd trust.'

'Do not misunderstand me, Mister Tom, it is not for you that I will betray Chow,' said Lu, in a voice that was soft, harsh and deadly serious, 'but for Mae. I will do everything that I can to make sure that he is safe from harm. He is my rock, Mister Tom. It is only because of him that I have been able to endure these long and terrible years. I love him, Mister Tom, it is that simple.'

'Well that's very touching but –'

'I am not a fool, Mister Tom, I know that the Naravirala have come to kill us. But I have also heard that they are a just people. Perhaps they will take pity on us. Mae and I, after all, are merely victims of Dr Chow's atrocious crimes. Maffdetti can have no grievance with us. '

'Maybe,' sulked Tom. Though he hated to agree with Lu, he did, somewhere deep inside, feel a little sorry for him and Mae. 'Why don't you show me how much you want to help by helping me to get out of here?'

Lu regarded him for an agonising moment.

'The time is not yet right, Mister Tom. We must plan your escape most meticulously. I will do all that I can to save you, Mister Tom, I promise.'

Tom snorted disdainfully and looked away.

'One day, Mister Tom, we will look back on these dark days and laugh. One day you will be a king, Mister Tom. A king needs trusted courtiers, does he not? And Mae and I can be so true, Mister Tom, so loyal, so ... *useful*. Do not forget us in our hour of need, for we, Mister Tom, will not forget you.'

Tom turned and held the were-cat's glistening eyes.

'I'll think about it,' he muttered, though he already had and there was no way in hell that he would ever trust either of the creepy little cretins, even if they did help him escape, and even if he did somehow miraculously manage to survive all of the hellish ordeals that no doubt awaited him and somehow make it to kinghood. 'But only if you get me out of here. And soon!'

'Be patient, my friend, and all will be well and good. We will look after you,' beamed Lu (as much as he was able). 'And when the time comes, do not forget to put in a good word for us to Prince Maffdetti and your new friends.'

Lu pushed his hand through the bars and reached out to Tom in a gesture that oozed sympathetic support, offered a little overwhelmed but stoically understated sob (accompanied with a top-notch display of tortured lip-chewing), before dramatically sweeping away (like a tragically hard-done-by heroine from a 1920s silent movie, dragged against her will from her mother-in-law's dying dog) and disappearing into the gloom of the night.

Tom didn't know whether to laugh or cry. But one thing was for certain: the "brotherhood" that was the *Carnival of Curiosities* was about as solid as a chocolate teapot.

Hhhmmm ... chocolate.

Tom suddenly realised that he was famished. It had been hours since he'd finished Missus Dobbs' delicious sandwiches. But – wait a minute! He should still have his bar of Toblerone. Ha ha! Oh joy of joys.

He frantically searched the pockets of his purple parka.

He frantically searched them again.

Nothing! Would you believe it? Some irredeemable tosser must have swiped it! What was the world coming to? What kind of cruel and callous wanker would steal a rare and treasured treat from a young kidnapped (catnapped?) lad, as he lay helplessly confined in prison? Was nobody to be trusted these days? He could just imagine the whole despicable pride of feline unpleasantnesses arrogantly sitting around and hatching evil plots over a pot of opium-laced tea whilst sharing out rich chocolatey triangles bursting with golden crunchy nuggets of nougat. What a bunch of complete and utter –

'Tom!' whispered a voice behind him.

Oh for Christ's sake! thought Tom. *Who is it now? The Ghost Of Christmas Yet To Frickin' Come?*

'Who's there?' he rasped, getting a little bored with all the interruptions.

'Do not turn around,' the voice urged, urgently. 'It is better for both of us if you do not see my face.'

'Oh? And why's that?' asked Tom suspiciously.

'If you do not know who I am then you cannot tell Chow my identity if he should torture you.'

With that delightful thought to keep his spirits up, Tom reflected how things just kept on getting better and better.

'Is it true?' hissed the mysterious new arrival.

'No,' huffed Tom. 'It isn't.'

'What do you mean?' squeaked the speaker, as if they'd been whacked in the goolies with a splintered mallet.

'I didn't lose a bet. It was a gift from Missus Dobbs.'

There was a hefty pause.

'I wasn't asking about the coat. I was asking about Prince Maffdetti and the Naravirala.'

'Oh. Then yes, it is true.'

'And they are in Brighton, now?'

'Yes they are,' smirked Tom.

There was a long, and Tom felt rather relieved, sigh.

'Then my charge is almost at an end. Praise be.'

'What do you mean?'

'I am an agent for the Naravirala, a loyal and true servant of Prince Maffdetti the Magnificent.'

Tom instantly recalled Maffdetti's letter to The Hound, in which the prince had spoken of a "most devoted and capable associate". Of course! It all made sense! One of the members of the *Carnival of Curiosities* was working for the Naravirala, and had been all along. But just who was it? Clearly not HASS, nor Lu, but from the whispered voice it was impossible to tell just who it might be.

'How long would it take you to get word to the Prince and lead him here?' asked the stranger.

'Err?' Tom calculated as fast as he could. There was a phone box in Stanmer Village and one at Falmer Station. At most twenty minutes to either one – if, that is, he wasn't too far from the spot where he had been abducted (though, thinking about it, the station seemed by far the safer option, as there was more likelihood of people being around) – a quick phone call to One Punch Cottage, then the gathering of troops (surely the Naravirala would be on a state of high alert and be ready to roar into action in a jiffy). One Punch Cottage was a fifteen minute drive away, traffic permitting … so … 'About an hour before I could get him here … maybe?'

'Excellent. Chow plans to strike camp with the first light of the rising sun. That gives us a little over two hours.'

'You're going to help me escape?' gasped Tom, his heart suddenly swelling with hope.

'Yes. Sweep back the wafer-thin covering of straw on the floor of your cage and you will find a trap-door that opens from the inside.'

Damn it! thought Tom, as he face-palmed himself with a gentle slap. *Why hadn't he thought of that*?

'Hurry, Tom, there is no time for useless theatrical gestures. We must be swift.'

Tom hurriedly brushed away the wafer-thin layer straw and, searching in the gloom with the tips of his fingers, found the outline of a trap-door. In less time than it takes to tell it he had located the latch and was wriggling through a small hole in the antique prison's floor and onto the dirt flooring of the outer tent.

A furred and cat-like hand reached out and all but dragged him from under the cage. Tom found himself facing a short, hooded figure whose features were lost in shadow, but who, Tom instantly knew, must be one of the Caracal Brothers. But which one could it be?

His cloaked and hooded liberator hurriedly steered him across the circus-ring and to a corner of the tent. With practised stealth he silently flipped up a corner of the tent's wall and gracefully dipped through the gap. Tom followed, rather less gracefully, managing to get the hood of his coat caught on a peg and almost garrotting himself in the process.

'Kkkkkkth!' kkkkkthed Tom

'Ssshhhh!' ssshhhed the were-cat, leaping a startled ten feet into the air with fright and then hurtling back noiselessly to free Tom's coat from its snagging.

Tom was suddenly struck by the horrifying realisation that his newfound rescuer seemed to be even more terrified than he was. This was a new and rare situation, and one that Tom had to admit he wasn't particularly enamoured by.

He quickly clambered to his feet. Through the inky gloom around him he could just make out the dark outline of tall and slender trees, yet somehow they seemed to shimmy and shudder – as if their image were being projected onto a rippling screen.

Tom's mysterious saviour prowled warily forward, clearly ready to bolt at the slightest sound. Suddenly coming to a halt, the were-cat anxiously cocked his head, listening intently for any sign of danger. After a brief and bowel-loosening moment, Tom was frantically beckoned to follow.

In the darkness, Tom tiptoed forward as stealthily as he possibly could – though, to everybody's absolute delight, his new coat burst forth with an animated anthem of noisy swishes like an orchestra of 1970s funk guitarists warming up for the big event. The were-cat brought up a panicked finger to his lips like a stricken railway signal, his nerviness all but rippling through every fibre of his cloak.

As Tom reached him, the *Caracal Brother* leant down and lifted a *veil in the reality of the world*. Through the gap (that was no gap but somehow... was[?]) Tom could still see the trees – they were still plunged in darkness but they no longer shimmied and swayed like a projected image.

The were-cat gently pushed Tom's head down and shoved him through the opening.

'Fly!' he hissed, pointing in the direction that he should follow.

Tom staggered forward into the open air, stumbled over a root and almost lost his balance, but somehow managed to steady himself without falling to the ground. He turned just in time to see the flap fall shut. Amazingly, there was now nothing but trees and woodland in front of him.

For all intents and purposes, the *Carnival of Curiosities* had disappeared!

Tom pulled his hood up to protect against the rain and, with his bottom twitching like a rabbit's nose (and expecting to be caught at any moment and with every trembling step that he took), made his way forward – with as much stealth and speed as he knew how – through the woods and over the sapling-covered ground and towards the muddy pathway that lay somewhere before him with its promise of sanctuary.

ELEVEN
Cats & Dogs

Tom slipped and stumbled as noiselessly as he could along the gently meandering, but treacherously sodden, pathway. The tall, lanky trees seemed to dip downwards to snatch and claw at him as he lurched past them; their wind-blown and rain-blasted leaves hummed and drummed a rhythmical and perfidious mantra – *"There he goes! Here he is! There he goes! Here he is!"* they whispered accusingly, as he weaved, slithered and skidded his way between them in his breathless and squeaking bid for freedom.

By the time he was nearing the edge of the woods, Tom was distressingly convinced that he was being followed. He could hear an occasional rustle of movement from the undergrowth behind him that was chillingly out of sync with the rest of woodland's nocturnal music, and he could feel the suffocating presence of something large and menacing closing in on him.

He caught a sudden blur of movement out of the corner of his eye and suppressed a meep. There was no doubt about it – something long, shadowy, and very big was stalking him! Tom instantly decided to give up on his effort of stealth. He put his head down and sprinted as fast as he could along the slippery and mud-splattering track.

If the enormous billowing hood of his purple parka hadn't acted like a drogue parachute, Tom would have liked to have thought that he might just have gotten away, but within a couple of strides he was slammed to the floor as if he'd been hit by a small truck.

He crashed face-down into the mud, the mouthful of slimy earth being the only thing that stifled the scream of horror that tried to escape from his frozen lips. The *thing* was upon him, pawing frantically at his shoulders and back! Instinctively, Tom curled up into a tight ball.

This was it! This was the end! The bards of Avalon (and, no doubt, the callous old swine, Bob Goodfellow) would gleefully sing of the death of young Prince Dearlove; ripped into a thousand pieces whilst trying to escape a peeved pack of were-cats on a sodden and miserable night; murdered before he'd even had the chance to properly live. (Sob!)

Cursing himself for ever having been so stupid as to follow Dr Chow on his own, he wrapped his arms tighter around his head, but his attacker relentlessly tore and clawed at him ... nuzzling him with a warm wet nose ... and a tongue like a badly-wrung sponge ...?

Suddenly Tom re-found his voice.

'Uuurgghhh!' he squealed.

He managed to roll over.

Bess!

The giant wolfhound took a step back, gave him an almighty grin and then sprang back in and smothered Tom's face with another revolting cuddle of her flannel-like tongue. Tom threw his arms around her neck and let go a muffled howl of relief into her short, wiry fur. And then from out of the trees stepped the heart-warming sight of Cornelius and Sergeant Hettie Clem.

Ten minutes later, Tom was sitting in the back seat of Old Nancy (who was elegantly parked next to the D.S.C.'s sleek, grey Alfa Romeo in one of the lay-bys that run off Stony Mere Way) with a flask of hot sweet tea and a packet of ginger creams, explaining his adventures to the gathered (and delighted to see him) search party – to wit: The Hound, Cornelius, Bob Goodfellow (with, as always, the ever-attentive Nipper and Snapper stationed with portentous readiness at his side), Dame Ginty, Archie Swapper, Ned Leppelin, Inspector Jones and Sergeant Hettie Clem (Constable Tuggnutter and Old Maggs were both at One Punch Cottage, manning the fort [so to speak] with the indomitable Missus Dobbs) and, of course, Bess (though she seemed more intent on mournfully following the plight of the ginger creams than on hearing of Tom's amazing adventures – mind you, to his credit, Cornelius was giving her a damned good run for her money on that front).

'So you saw the scoundrel, Chow, at Yallery Brown's and decided to follow him,' chuckled The Hound, as he rubbed his hands together joyfully. 'Good work, Tom. What a stroke of luck. Quite the breakthrough, I'd say, old chap. Very well done indeed.'

'I do wish that you'd waited for me though, Tom,' pouted Dame Ginty, with gentle concern.

'I wish that I could have,' replied Tom, doing his best to sound heroically practical, 'but there just wasn't time.'

'Of course there weren't, son,' croaked Cornelius, through a mouthful of biscuit crumbs. 'You did what you 'ad to do. Well done, son. Proud of you. 'Ere, any of that tea left, lad?'

'How did you know I was here, in Stanmer Park, I mean?' Tom asked, as he handed Cornelius the flask.

'Missus Dobbs sewed a *finding-charm* or two into the lining of that … *lovely* new coat of yours, dear,' soothed Ginty, eyeing Tom's purple parka with a disdainful pucker.

Tom sighed and smiled to himself. He owed the little old tea-poisoner big time. Oh, how he owed her!

'So,' clucked Inspector Jones, looking up from his notepad as he finished jotting down Tom's tale, and casting a haunted glance over towards the dark and ominous wall of trees behind them, 'Dr Chow and his cronies are holed up in the Great Wood, are they?'

'Yes, but not for long. They plan to break camp at sunrise,' replied Tom, 'if my mysterious rescuer is to be believed, that is.'

'Well there's no need to doubt 'im that I can see (though it won't 'urt to maintain an 'ealthy dose of scepticism, I suppose). An' you reckon that 'e was one of them there Caracal Brothers?' asked Cornelius, snapping the last ginger cream in two and tossing one half to the appreciatively waiting Bess.

'Yes, I think so. But as to which one it was, I've no idea.'

'Car coming!' called out Archie.

The Hound pulled up the hood of his duffle coat and ducked his head down.

'That *should* be Prince Maffdetti,' he grinned, his teeth flashing in the shadows of his hood as he was suddenly raked by the double beams of the new arrival's headlights, 'but we can't be too careful.'

And into the lay-by pulled a large, impeccably polished, and brand spanking new, bronze-coloured Bentley.

The front passenger's door slowly swung open and, like a miffed genie summoned from a multi-millionaire's motor, the Naravirala *Chosen One*, Jelani, appeared. He scowled a possible attempt at a welcome in their direction and then stood by the bonnet of the enormous car with his enormous arms folded menacingly across his enormous chest. Fauzia elegantly seeped from the driver's side, took a couple of backward steps, whilst erecting a large umbrella, and opened the rear door. Out stepped Prince Maffdetti A-Su *the Magnificent*, resplendent in a long blue raincoat and matching headscarf.

Nipper and Snapper pinned back their ears and gave a low and warning growl, their hackles raised and bristling like a pair of electrocuted porcupines.

Jelani glared at the two dogs with a disdainful curl of his lip. Bob Goodfellow bent down and whispered something to the two Airedales that made them reluctantly stop their snarling, but they still huffed a little, and met Jelani's challenging scowl with one of their own, that dared him to *try it*.

'Ah, my dear friends,' grinned the Naravirala prince, as he stalked forward to greet the gathered throng and bless them all with the countenance of his regal smile. Fauzia trotted stoically by his side holding the umbrella for her prince and sheltering him from the rain, though getting uncomfortably drenched herself in the process. (*One of the many joys*, considered Tom, as he observed the miserable expression on poor Fauzia's rain-soaked visage, *of hanging out with royalty*). 'What a *beautiful* night for a hunt,' chuckled Maffdetti, a hint of sarcasm in his voice as he eyed the dripping sky with a regretful grimace.

'Prince Maffdetti,' replied The Hound in greeting, pushing back the hood of his duffle coat. 'Thank you for your speedy arrival.'

'It is I who must thank you, my friend, for your help in this matter. It shall not be forgotten.'

The Prince pulled off his long blue (and near-priceless) raincoat and tossed it carelessly to Fauzia (safe in the certain knowledge that she would be there to catch it for him). He plucked the umbrella from her hand and she hurriedly trailed back to the Bentley and carefully placed the prince's jacket on a coat-hanger in the back of the car. Standing hand on hip, Prince Maffdetti the Magnificent looked about at the crowd of expectant faces before him, his brilliantly-tailored baggy trousers billowing heroically in the night's gentle breeze. 'The hour has come, my friends,' he purred, widening his emerald-coloured eyes and tapping the jewelled hilt of the wide-bladed scimitar that swung valiantly from his hip, 'when we will at last bring this ungrateful wretch, Chow, to justice.'

The Hound removed his thick, grey (and sopping) duffle coat and casually chucked it onto the back seat of Old Nancy. He stood before the prince, his own rather magnificent scarlet and black slashed plunderhosen (worn especially for the occasion – for he was determined not to be *out-trousered* by a were-cat, be he prince or no) fluttering majestically in the night's gentle wind.

'It is my belief, Your Highness, that we can bring this rogue to brook in a more *diplomatic* manner,' he said, as the two faced each other, both eyeing the other's ostentatious display of gentleman's outfitting with a chary appreciation. 'It would appear that the *Carnival of Curiosities* is on the edge of disarray. My hope is that this matter can be ended peacefully – with the right tactics.'

Maffdetti scrutinised the were-hound intently for a moment, and Tom was convinced that *His Highness* was going to lose his temper and have a *right royal paddy,* but the prince simply laughed and nodded his handsome leopard-like head with a resigned joviality.

'We are in your country, my friend, so I will *consider* your request. As long as Chow and his wretched parcel of rogues are successfully captured, we can decide what fate awaits them later. I thank you once again, my friends, but we, the Naravirala, will take control of proceedings from here.'

'With all due respect, Prince Maffdetti,' replied The Hound, bowling the man-cat a courteous, yet slightly stiff, smile, 'but Chow and his despicable cronies are also of particular interest to us. The swine is in possession of a great and ancient treasure of these islands; one that he stole from its rightful owners. It is my duty to recover that treasure and to make sure that Chow receives the just reward for his heinous crime.'

The prince did his best not to look too put out.

'I see,' he purred pleasantly, but with a hint of annoyance shuddering along his long, hooped and tufted tail. 'And what, pray tell, is your plan?'

'I propose that you and I go and talk to him.'

'Talk?!' guffawed Prince Maffdetti, an air of disbelief in his voice.

'I also feel that it would be of great benefit,' continued The Hound, ignoring Maffdetti's near-apoplectic state, 'if young Tom were to accompany us.'

The prince shot a look over at Tom (who was currently trying not to vomit at the thought of a return visit to the *Carnival,* and contemplating if he could get out of it with a well-timed swoon) and raised an eyebrow.

'Why the cub?' he asked.

'Tom knows these rascals better than any one of us, having spent more time in their company than he would, no doubt, have cared to. Significantly, he has also been approached by several members of Chow's retinue who have each offered their help in our endeavours to bring the *dear Doctor* to justice. On top of this, he is a prince of the Aelfradi nation and his presence will add great significance to the act of reclaiming a fabled treasure of the Elbi people.'

Prince Maffdetti A-Su regarded Tom with new interest, scratched the royal whiskers and slowly nodded his head in acceptance.

'All well and good, my friend,' smiled the regal were-cat, 'but these are violent criminals, and so I suggest, in turn, that it would not be prudent to seek them out unarmed, even when we have such an advantage of numbers.'

'I completely concur,' agreed The Hound. 'Therefore may I also suggest that Cornelius, Inspector Jones and Bob Goodfellow (and of course Nipper and Snapper) along with your own people (Jelani and Fauzia) stand ready, in reserve, and within sight – just in case things do go ... *amiss*.

'Bob? Would you be able to detect and destroy any magical barriers that might present themselves?'

'Of that you can have no doubt, Percival,' grinned the filthy old lunatic.

'Splendid,' replied The Hound. 'And Tom, do you think that you could lead us to your point of exit from the *Carnival's* concealed camp?'

'Yes,' replied Tom, with a long hard swallow, 'I think so.'

'Capital,' beamed the were-hound. 'Ned, Archie, Sergeant Clem, Dame Ginty and Bess, would you be so kind as to circle behind their camp and make ready, should any of this *parcel of rogues* (as you so imaginatively put it, Your Majesty) make a break for it?'

'Right you are, Mizter 'Ound.'

Prince Maffdetti clapped his hands in delight.

'Oh, it is a fine plan, my friend,' he declared, full of vim and brimming with gusto. 'Good, good. To arms, my friends, to arms, and we shall win the day!'

And with that, he turned to Jelani and Fauzia and gave the slightest of nods. Maffdetti's companions stepped back a little and offered a displeased glance at the gently bucketing sky before removing their coats. And then, to everyone's delight/amazement, they morphed and writhed, pulsing and popping like a pair of unset clay figurines squeezed by a sculptor's irate fist ... until they stood before their enraptured audience in full ailuranthrope magnificence; the fabled guardians of the Naravirala – *The Chosen Ones*.

They were, Tom noted, more human-like than their prince, and he was instantly reminded of The Mighty HASS.

Nipper, Snapper and Bess bounced on the spot, stiff-legged; their hackles raised and warning growls set deep within their throats.

Fauzia prowled, panther-like; lithe and sinewy like the deadliest of dancers; her light skin mottled with tightly-packed rosettes. In turn, Jelani, four-hundred-and-fifty pounds of bristling muscle and ill-intent, snarled menacingly at the startled posse of One Punch Cottage.

The were-leopardess then glided to the boot of the bronze Bentley and armed herself with a long-bladed spear. She tossed a hefty, short-hafted iron-headed mace to Jelani, who caught it effortlessly in one great hand and tested its weight in the palm of the other.

Not to be outdone Cornelius unfastened the boot of Old Nancy and opened up the secret compartment where their own travelling armoury was stored.

The tweedy old duffer armed himself with a lethal-looking heavy wooden cane (in the Pierre Vigny style) and a set of silver knuckle-dusters; The Hound drew out a huge Renaissance *war-rapier*, long and thick-bladed, with a vicious point and a simple half-hilt of blued steel; Tom, to his surprise and delight, was handed a partizan (essentially a short sword on a long stick); Archie and Ned were already equipped with their beloved battle-putters and spears; Dame Ginty produced her favourite blunderbuss from her tiny handbag, whilst Inspector Jones and Sergeant Clem unholstered their D.S.C. regulation Glock 26 pistols.

'I'll zignal you az zoon az we'z in position,' said Archie with a wink, as he, Ned, Ginty, Hettie and the mighty Bess headed to the Great Wood, to station themselves behind the *Carnival's* concealed camp and thereby cut off any attempt at escape.

The rest of them waited in a state of nervous excitement. Well, Tom was certainly in a state, one that was both excited and more than a little nervous; however, one look around him quenched most of the fears that he had.

And so it was that he, along with one Francis Drake impersonating were-wolf-wolfhound and one aristocratic were-cat, dressed up like Ali Baba after a second lottery win, waited to head off and have a little chat with the despicable swine, and deplorable Fu Manchu impersonator, known as Dr Chow. And if that wasn't enough to calm Tom's nerves, in reserve there stood: one were-lion, one were-leopardess, one police detective, the most powerful wizard in the realm (along with his pair of psychotic terriers) and, not to forget, the lethal tweed-suited-bulk-of-whiskery-destruction, the Regency-trained, monster-battling, bare-knuckle pugilistic wonder – the one-time leading contender for the Championship of all England (when that actually meant something) – that was his dearest grandpapa.

They paced back and forth with ever-growing anticipation, as the rain fell like a murmuring prayer in the darkness. And then, in the distance, there suddenly came the soft yip-yap-yapping of a *fox*.

The Hound looked up at the sky and smiled.

'Lead on, Tom,' he said softly.

And in silence they pressed forward, with Prince Maffdetti at their side.

Bob, Jelani, Fauzia, Cornelius, Inspector Jones and the Airedales followed slowly after them.

'You are not armed, my friend,' whispered Maffdetti, as he turned to look at Bob with a curious tilt of his head. 'Is that wise?'

The rancid old Puck smiled at the Naravirala prince with a grin like a bubbling tar pit.

'My weapons lie all around me, young sir,' he replied, with a sweep of his fingerless and grime-smudged mittens. 'But if it makes you feel any happier ...'

The faery wizard bent down and whispered something to a tall blade of wild grass, before gently plucking it from the soil by the root and then striding purposefully forward with the blade of grass carried in his filthy mitt like a spear.

Maffdetti shrugged his shoulders, wrinkled his nose, and strode onwards, catching up with The Hound and Tom. And in silence, they marched across the open field that led to the Great Wood and to the hidden camp of Dr Chow and his *Carnival of Curiosities*.

TWELVE
The Siege Of The Great Wood

After a few false turns, Tom led the unlikely posse to the spot that he was convinced was his point of exit from the *Carnival of Curiosities'* encampment.

Old Bob sniffed the air and gurned a liquorice smile.

'Magic lies before us,' he grinned. 'Here they be, behind this here cloak of invisibility.'

The Hound nodded grimly.

Bob padded back to join the waiting reinforcements, who stood, spread out and in a state of readiness, some twenty paces behind Tom, the were-wolfhound detective and the were-cat prince.

The Hound took a step forwards and rested a hand upon the giant pommel of the great sword that hung by his side.

'Chow!' he roared, his voice sounding both authoritative and reasonable as it bounced between the trees like a cannonball. 'You are surrounded. Give yourself up and I give you my word that no harm shall come to you or your people.'

There was a long and empty silence, save for the gentle fizz of the drizzling sky.

Prince Maffdetti twitched edgily, his fingers drumming impatiently along the hilt of his lethal-looking scimitar.

Suddenly there was a ripple in the fabric of reality and before them stood the short, slender and noticeably quivering human form of Tom's old pal, the Siamese-were-cat and torch song torturer, Lu.

Lu offered a small and troubled smile at the two glowering were-creatures before him, and then wiggled his fingers in welcome at Tom.

'Hello, Mister Tom. How lovely to see you again ... and so ... soon,' he said, an uncertain smile starched across his face, and looking like he was suffering from a terrible bout of stage-fright.

'Is this Chow?' whispered The Hound hurriedly to Tom.

'Oh no, Mister Hound,' replied Lu, before Tom had a chance to correct the were-hound, 'I am simply a humble messenger. Dr Chow has sent me to [gulp] *negotiate.*'

'There will be no negotiations with criminals!' snarled Prince Maffdetti. 'Surrender now or you will all lose your lives!'

Lu looked at the Naravirala Prince and tried not to quail.

'Dr Chow is only too happy to surrender,' he squeaked uneasily, swallowing hard and offering an elaborate and wobbly curtsey in the prince's direction, 'but he has some ... ah ... conditions.'

'Conditions?' blasted Maffdetti. 'Conditions! Is his life not enough? The unworthy, despicable scoundrel!'

'I think it only reasonable that we at least listen to your master's request,' said The Hound, as reassuringly as he could.

Maffdetti shot The Hound a baleful glower.

Lu attempted a smile at the were-hound but kept his eyes firmly glued on the volcano-on-the-edge-of-eruption that was Prince Maffdetti.

'Dr Chow, he say that he will gladly yield and return *The Crown of Autumn* ... but only ... but only ... if ...'

'Only if what, Lu?' asked Tom, and despite all that had happened between them he couldn't help but feel a little sorry for the wretched little fellow.

Lu looked at Tom as if he were a life-line thrown to a drowning moggy.

'Only if he is ... if he is put under the protection of Mister Hound and tried in a British court of law.'

Prince Maffdetti guffawed and snorted loudly in derision.

'Accepted,' replied The Hound, with a sharp wag of his sabre-like tail.

'DENIED!' roared the were-cat, looking at The Hound in disbelief, his tail bristling and swatting back and forth as he drew his scimitar an inch from its jewelled and exquisitely-patterned scabbard.

Lu looked in horror from the were-hound to the were-cat, like the last lobster in a seafood restaurant watching two customers arguing over who gets the *house special*.

'Chow is a British citizen and within British territories and will therefore be tried accordingly,' answered The Hound, with unflappable patience and an upper lip of impeccable stiffness.

'Whatever he has done on this miserable, damp and joyless island is of no consequence!' snarled Prince Maffdetti, his tail continuing to twitch like an overworked whip behind him. 'He is a thief and a murderer! An enemy of the Naravirala! Our laws, our justice, reach further and serve a higher cause than yours, you dog!'

'I say, steady on, old chap,' bristled The Hound, eyeing the were-cat like he were in need of a right royal good hiding – and, if he carried on with this current exhibition of inexcusable behaviour, was in grave danger of receiving one.

'Do not dare to challenge my authority, or you shall rue the day, you arrogant cur!' seethed the Naravirala prince.

'Right!' barked The Hound. 'That's it, you insufferable buffoon! Now see here, I will tell you this once and once only: if you cannot hold your tongue, then I must insist that you leave the scene immediately and let us conclude this investigation without your unbearable interference.'

'*Unbearable!*' hissed Maffdetti, stiffening in affronted outrage. He suddenly leapt back, fully-drawing his weapon, and settled into an on-guard position teeming with lethal intent.

The Hound eyed him with disdain, puckered a thin black lip in his direction, and folded his arms contemptuously across his chest.

There was a gabble of snarls and growls behind them and Tom hastily turned to see Jelani and Fauzia beginning to menacingly prowl towards Cornelius,

Inspector Jones, Bob Goodfellow and the *Airedales*. Cornelius was most certainly not going to back down, the bristling Nipper and Snapper looked like they were rather looking forward to the challenge, Inspector Jones already had his pistol steadily trained on the approaching were-cats, and old Bob Goodfellow was watching the two ailuranthropes with a look of grubby-faced serenity, a strange half-smile just visible in the sodden darkness. All in all, Tom couldn't help but think to himself, things were suddenly looking a little ... *fraught*.

Faster than a striking mongoose, Prince Maffdetti lunged forward and aimed a murderous swipe at The Hound. In one action, The Hound pushed Tom to one side (and thus out of harm's way) and voided the cat-man's attack with an angled backwards pass, suddenly springing forward with his left leg and sending the outraged prince tumbling to the floor with a back-heel trip.

Tom landed in a breathless heap, his partizan scattering noisily from his grasp. Maffdetti, however, rolled effortlessly to his feet with an elegance that an Olympic tumbler could only ever dream about. He glared daggers at the were-wolfhound, his scimitar slicing through the air with an ominous chorus of swishes as he weaved the blade skilfully before him – its wide, curving blade flashing back and forth like an underfed guillotine.

'You will die for that, you dog!' he hissed, a vicious smile spreading across his handsome mouth. And his eyes were hard and wild as he edged gracefully forward, inch by deadly inch.

The yap-yip-yapping of a fox suddenly cut through the dark rain-filled night like the wail of a banshee who has just stubbed its toe.

'That's Ned!' cried The Hound. 'Chow must be escaping!' And with a single bound he leapt over the startled were-cat prince and disappeared into the woods in hot pursuit.

Maffdetti turned to follow after him but his progress was somewhat hampered by the fact that Lu had flung himself forward and was currently wrapped around the were-cat's exquisitely-trousered leg.

'Oh my prince, my prince, my prince!' begged Lu, looking up forlornly at the Naravirala. 'Take us with you. Save us from our terrible and horrible ordeal. Rescue us from the villainous Dr Chow. We surrender to you and you alone. Always we have worked against Chow. Oh, he has used us most cruelly, my prince. We are your true and loyal servants, from now until the end of time.'

Maffdetti looked down at the pleading and pitiful little man with a look of vexed bafflement.

There was a sudden flash of movement and Tom looked up to see Lady Lynx hurtling like an unleashed arrow towards the prince and Lu.

'You treacherous coward!' she screeched, her face a contorted mask of blind and white-eyed rage.

Before anyone had time to even think about reacting, the were-lynx was upon them, binding Maffdetti's sword arm in a vice-like lock. With a sudden roll of her hips she twisted and turned, forcing Maffdetti off balance and manipulating the prince's great scimitar downwards like a dropped doodlebug. The point

120

effortlessly pierced through the top of Lu's skull and reappeared through the bottom of his chin, impaling him like a cocktail cherry.

'No!' gasped Tom.

Without a sound Lu slowly slid sideways to lie motionless on the floor, his arms still tenderly encircling Prince Maffdetti's ankles, his head propped up at a strangely theatrical angle by the Naravirala's blade, his eyes opened wide with surprise, his flawlessly made-up mouth a perfect circle of astonishment.

Without a pause the were-lynx wriggled and adjusted her grip, trapping Maffdetti in a rear naked choke.

Tom stumbled to his feet and frantically looked around for his fumbled partizan. But his hands and feet felt like they belonged to someone else and his mind was frozen numb. He couldn't believe what he had just seen! Lu killed before his eyes! It had happened so fast. Throughout their short acquaintance he'd always detested the strange and spiteful little sod, but he'd never wish for this on anybody. It was little over an hour ago that they had been talking together (through the bars of his cage, granted; but then all of their conversations had been through bars, in one way or another) and now he was dead. *Switched off* in the blink of an eye. How fragile is this life. How invincible we all feel and then – BAM! – it's over, and all your hopes and all your dreams, everything that you might have ever wished for, are gone and lost forever.

Tom desperately looked from the trapped Maffdetti (currently gasping for air, his eyes somewhat bulging, and his fingers desperately fumbling to reach the bejewelled hilt of his sword – presently impaled in the head of poor Lu) and towards the clearing where the rest of their happy team-mates where on the edge of tearing each other to pieces, obviously oblivious to what was happening only a few feet away from them. And then he saw old Bob Goodfellow casually sauntering towards them, like a tramp who has just spotted a pair of boots left by the side of a park bench.

'Why couldn't you have left us alone?' hissed Lady Lynx into the choking Maffdetti's ear.

Maffdetti spluttered and pawed uselessly at Lady Lynx's vice-like grip.

Bob casually lifted the long blade of grass that he carried in his hand to his lips and seemed to mumble something to it. Then, drawing back his arm, he hurled the slender stalk forwards like a javelin.

'What harm had we done to you?' yowled the were-lynx. 'What harm? And now, because of your stupid pride and your stupid rules, we will all die. Oh, all of the misery you have caused me in my life, you arrogant fool! My one reward is in knowing that you will see the horrors of Hell before I, and that your death came at my han–'

Lady Lynx slammed backwards like a toppled domino, pinned to the sodden earth with a small spear-like sapling impaled through her skull and sprouting from her forehead. Its branches slowly unfurled and stretched out as if awakening from a mighty slumber, and Tom could hear its roots cracking as they pushed downwards, burrowing themselves deeply into the rich, dark earth beneath them.

Prince Maffdetti staggered forwards gasping for breath, clutching his throat and frantically kicking his exquisitely-tailored legs free from Lu's eternal embrace. He gaped at Bob with an expression of wonder, then turned to Tom, and finally to the prostrate form of Lady Lynx (currently resembling some sort of avant-garde flowerpot).

He looked like he wanted to say something, but couldn't seem to find the words (though Tom thought that a "thank you" to Bob wouldn't have been out of the question), and then he turned and faltered forwards like he was drunk, thought about drawing his sword from poor Lu's head but obviously realised that he didn't have the stomach for it. Unbuckling the sword-belt from his hips and casting the scabbard to the floor, he offered one last uneasy glance at Tom and Bob before sprinting away into the woods.

'Follow after him, Prince Tom,' said Bob, 'while I try and calm down our *comrades,*' he sighed, with an exasperated glance towards the bristling stand-off between the *One Punch Cottage Crew* and Naravirala's *Chosen Ones*. 'Help his Highness find Chow, while we make a search of the *Carnival's* encampment.'

Tom nodded, began to run towards the trees, but then hurriedly turned back to pick up his fumbled weapon. He gripped the shaft of the partizan tightly in his hands, unsuccessfully forced himself not to look at Lu (whose lifeless eyes seemed to follow him wherever he moved, and whose lavish make-up was steadily smearing into a grotesquely patterned death-mask – smudged and sullied as it was by the uncaring and incessant drubbing of the softly seeping night), and followed after the prince and into the silent darkness of the woods.

Tye-Dai Taffy tipped the remnants of his bedtime cup of tea onto the dying embers of his little campfire, before contentedly retreating into the refuge of his one man tent and climbing into the comforting warmth of his sleeping bag. It had been months now since he'd been "*clean*". No drink. No drugs. Here, far away from the temptations of the city centre, the solitude of the forest had helped him get over the worst of his addictions. And best of all – no more "*incidents*": no more bed-wetting visions of *were-wolves* or night-quivering hallucinations of *Edwardian grave-robbers* waking him from his addled slumber. No, he was making a fine recovery. Say what you want about Tye-Dai Taffy (and most people did) but he was on the mend and on the up.

'I'm sure that he came this way, Ned,' said Dame Ginty, stopping to dab away a tiny spot of perspiration from her perfect brow.

The Smack Faery knelt and examined the ground around him. He looked a little puzzled for a second or two and then slowly looked up to the great beech tree before them.

A pair of wide and emerald eyes stared nervously down at them from among the dripping foliage.

Ginty followed Ned's gaze and quickly pointed her blunderbuss-cum-bazooka at the quivering jaguar who was perched precariously above them, clinging to the uppermost branches like a bullied koala who's suddenly lost his head for heights.

'Hello, dear,' smiled Ginty, cocking back a trigger and squinting along the cannon-like barrel. 'How lovely to see you again.'

The Hound heard the low bark of a gunshot ring out from the trees to his left and instantly changed his course to investigate. Part of him wanted to switch into dog-form (so much easier and faster for running through woodland in the dark) but decided against it. It would have meant having to lose the great sword that he wore at his side – not that he had any real intention of using it (he rarely used a sword these days ... well, not if he could help it, and then only when hunting the most powerful of vampires – and, as they were already dead it somehow didn't seem to count) for he had long since come to the point in his *martial education* where, unless necessity directed, he would much rather not use a weapon at all; however, sometimes the show of steel was enough to stop short a possible conflict before it had even begun.

He could hear the blood-racing music of battle; the unmistakable low growl of Bess (the one that she reserved for the rare occasions when she was truly angry – which didn't bode well for somebody) overlaid with the harsh hissing of cat-like ire and distress.

He pinned back his ears and sprinted forward.

Within moments Tom had lost any idea as to which direction Prince Maffdetti might have taken. The man-cat was so much faster than he was that he knew that, even if he'd been able to track him, he had virtually no hope of actually catching up with him. There was a sudden sharp crack of a gunshot to his left, followed by a yelp of surprise to his right. Tom gave a little yelp of his own and stopped dead in his tracks. A speeding flash of brilliant blue flashed through the woodland before him like an exotic bird flitting through the trees, and Tom instantly recognised the magnificent headscarf of Prince Maffdetti, as the cat-man darted gracefully through the woods and towards the direction of the gunfire.

Tom swallowed hard, readjusted his grip on the partizan, and pressed urgently on after the were-cat.

The Hound approached a small clearing with a stealth that could only be described as *supernatural*. Before him was a scene of bustling and bloody activity. Chuck Caracal was clinging for dear life to the top of a slender and dangerously swaying sycamore tree, a slow but steady trickle of blood dripping from his right forearm. At the bottom of said sycamore tree Bess leapt and pawed at the trunk, scrabbling to reach her cornered prey. There was, The Hound reflected with almost parental pride, nothing that brought Bess more joy than a treed cat (though, if truth be told, the wolfhound rarely showed anything that could be described as coming close to a 'killer instinct' and usually just wanted to play with the poor little things). At the base of the wobbling tree trunk lay a lethal-looking Krabi sword. The Hound deduced that Bess must have somehow disarmed the villain and chased the odious swine into the tentative sanctuary of the swaying branches.

The rest of the scene, however, was somewhat less encouraging.

Sergeant Hettie Clem lay sprawled on the ground with a nasty-looking cut opened on her forehead. Lying uselessly a few feet from her worryingly prostrate form lay her D.S.C. regulation Glock 26 pistol.

Behind her, Archie Swapper, his back pressed to the edge of the clearing, was fighting tooth and nail to keep the menacingly lithe and agile forms of Bruce and Jackie Caracal at bay. The were-caracals were lightning fast (as The Hound knew only too well) and armed with curved Krabi swords similar to the one that their brother, Chuck, had just dropped. Archie, armed with his long and silver-bladed cutting-spear, was, with a desperate skill, managing to fend them off. But for how long?

The Hound crept over and knelt by the fallen Hettie Clem, checking for a pulse and making a swift examination of her wound. It was bloody, but not life-threatening. He was almost tempted to pick up her gun, but he knew that his fingers would be far too large to be able to use the damned thing, plus, not only did he detest firearms but he was also one of the worst shots in history, and would probably have placed Archie in more danger than his adversaries were currently managing to do.

He turned, carefully readjusting his crouched position, and sprung high and forward with a mighty leap, targeting the unsuspecting Caracals like a precision bomb. As he landed between them he delivered a hefty hammer-blow to the top of Jackie's skull, which felled the poor lad like a ... well, like he'd been rabbit-punched in the head by a three-hundred-and-seventy-five pound were-wolf-wolfhound dropping on him from a height of fifteen feet at an accelerating velocity. As Jackie crumpled like a felled jelly, The Hound grasped Bruce by the scruff of his neck and hurled him high into the night sky.

To his credit Bruce landed (dare one say – *cat-like*) on his feet and took in the situation with all the speedy thought of the expert martial artist. With barely a break in stride he sprang towards the cover of the trees, but his path was instantly blocked by a raking thrust of Archie's long spear. The were-cat elegantly swerved the blow and spun, launching an immediate and lethal attack towards The Hound with a leaping slash of his deadly blade.

The surprising speed, agility and ferocity of Bruce's attack almost caught The Hound out, but he managed to lean backwards and void the were-caracal's assault (oh the joys of having a two-and-a-half foot height and reach advantage on your opponent!) and then placed a hefty kick (a *coup de bas*) onto the ailuranthrope's ankle. (Many years ago, The Hound had had the great pleasure of training with both *Michel Cassuex* and *Charles Lecour*, two of the pioneers and codifiers of the early form of *Savate* – the French style of *street-fighting* and self-defence that is sometimes referred to as "*fencing with four limbs*"). Bruce howled with pain and began to buckle. In that moment the were-hound was on him; dropping forwards he seized Bruce's weapon by the forte (not the wrist – a seasoned swordsman like Bruce might have easily switched the weapon to his left hand, and left The Hound in all sorts of bother) before landing (like a tornado from Hell) with his full weight behind a corkscrewed right hand punch (delivered, of course, over a falling *trigger-step*) that would have had Jack Dempsey (*The Manassa Mauler* – so called '*The Man-Killer*': the legendary 1920s heavyweight boxing champion and author of one of the finest works on the art of pugilism ever written) reaching for his notebook.

Bruce collapsed like a chopped mast.

Archie rushed over to offer a supporting arm to Hettie as she slowly tried to rise on wobbly legs.

The Hound ambled over to the treed Chuck.

Bess bounced at the bottom of the trunk, stiff-legged, tail wagging furiously, and obviously delighted with herself.

'Chuck, isn't it?' asked The Hound, resting one hand on the pommel of his great sword and looking up at the bristling and petrified were-caracal.

'Call that monster off!' pleaded Chuck, yowling uncontrollably as he momentarily lost his grip.

'Now, I'm taking a hopeful guess,' mused The Hound, as he casually watched poor Chuck sway back and forth like a slowly set metronome. 'that you might be the very chap who's been working for Prince Maffdetti?'

Chuck took a moment off looking terrified and managed to look perplexed.

'Maffdetti? *Me*? Are you mad?' he hissed.

'Oh?' pouted The Hound, looking a tad perplexed himself. 'Then perhaps it must have been one of your brothers.' He turned and looked towards the senseless Bruce and Jackie – who were in the process of being hauled towards and fastened, wrist to wrist, around the trunk of a tall and sturdy-looking beech tree, with several sets of D.S.C. issue handcuff (willingly provided to Archie by Hettie). 'Oh dear. How ... *unfortunate*.'

'What are you blathering on about? I'm bleeding to death up here!' yelped Chuck, gingerly holding up his wounded arm for effect.

'Oh I think that you'll live,' chuckled The Hound, as he gave Bess a congratulatory pat on the head and turned to walk over to Archie and Hettie. 'Do stay there for a moment, there's a good fellow.'

The wound on Hettie's forehead was bloody but not deep. She would have an almighty headache for a couple of days and carry a scar for the rest of her life, but otherwise was going to be fine.

'Are you all right, Hettie?' asked The Hound, gently tilting her chin to one side and looking with kind concern into her eyes.

'I'll be fine, Mr Hound,' she replied, a touch paler than normal, and looking slightly embarrassed by the whole incident. 'I'm sorry that I let everybody down.'

'Don't be daft, lazz!' cried Archie. 'If it weren't for you we'd 'ave all been cat-meat. If you 'ad't fired that warning zhot they'd 'ave been on uz like a doze of meazelz. I reckon it waz you what zaved uz all, an' no miztake about it.'

Archie tenderly took Hettie's hand and gallantly kissed the back of it.

Some semblance of colour flashed into the sergeant's cheeks and she looked away.

The Hound bent over, picked up Hettie's gun and passed it to her.

'So what happened, exactly?' he asked, shooting Archie a curious glance.

'We heard some activity going on, behind the spot where Dame Parsons thought the Carnival's camp was located, and went to investigate,' said Hettie, as she reholstered her gun. 'Ned and Dame Parsons, being the closest to the disturbance, went on ahead.'

'We waz following fazt be'ind 'em,' picked up Archie, 'when, thank the Powerz, 'Ettie 'ere ... oh, I'm zorry, I mean Zergeant Clem ...'

'You can call me *Ettie*, I mean Hettie,' cooed Hettie coyly.

Archie suppressed a shy little smile. 'When Mizz 'Ettie, 'ere, zaw theze two zcoundrelz' (he waved his spear in the direction of Jackie and Bruce) ''eading ztraight for uz with bad intentionz written all over their zorry facez. Mizz 'Ettie fired a zhot that zent them zcurrying backwardz, juzt az that one' (he waved his spear up at Chuck, who sobbed something about his arm) 'pounced out of the treez an' did hiz bezt to take poor Mizz 'Ettie'z pretty 'ead off! You don't mind me calling you pretty do you, Mizz 'Ettie? Not really zure what you'z allowed to zay to a young lady theze dayz without offending 'em.'

'You can call me pretty,' whispered Hettie, demurely, before quickly collecting herself and carrying on in her usual bluff and matter of fact manner. 'If it hadn't been for Bess, I think that he would most probably have succeeded.'

'Aye, Bezz 'ere were on 'im like a flazh. Good girl, Bezz. Clamped onto 'iz arm zo that 'e miztimed 'iz blow. Then she chazed the wicked zo-an'-zo up yonder tree.'

'My arm?' offered Chuck, hopefully.

The Hound looked up at the weeping were-caracal.

'So, my dear chap, where is Chow now?' he demanded.

Chuck looked down at the giant dog-man, down at the massive wolfhound hopefully circling the base of the tree, down at Hettie with her gun, and Archie with his spear and war-putter, and then over to his brothers – bound, trussed and unconscious.

'I don't know,' he sighed with a resigned shake of his head. 'Gone by now, I shouldn't wonder.'

'We'll see about that,' muttered The Hound.

Bess wagged her tail and skittered as far up the tree as she could. Chuck inched his way a little higher.

'That's the ticket, Bess. Good girl,' chuckled The Hound. And, with a nod to Archie and Sergeant Clem, he turned and disappeared into the whispering gloom of the Great Wood.

Tom cursed himself and cluttered to a halt. He had managed to lose sight of Prince Maffdetti – again. He was just about to turn back and retrace his steps when he heard the unmistakable sound of Dr Chow's chilling tones coming from the other side of the clump of trees before him.

'You dare face me unarmed? You pathetic fool, Maffdetti! You should have stayed safe in your mountain palace, protected by you ignorance and your arrogance, for I have grown more powerful than you could ever have dared to imagine!'

Tom began a quick and inward debate as to whether it would be best to simply leave them to it. (Old friends and all that.) Who, after all, was he to interfere? Perhaps he could make his way over to the Stanmer Village café for a sausage roll and a late-night cup of cocoa until all this *unpleasantness* (as The Hound might have tactfully put it) passed over? But, to his horror, his legs (for once) were betraying him, for he found himself stealthily creeping through the undergrowth and *towards* the sound of Chow's terrifying threats and Maffdetti's angry hisses.

In a few short steps he reached the edge of a clearing – the one with the blue-painted trees in it, if he wasn't mistaken, though it was hard to be certain in this light. He pressed his back tightly against the last and thickest of the trees and tentatively wound his head around to take a peek.

In the centre of the clearing stood Dr Chow, tall, proud, and scowling with minacious disdain at Prince Maffdetti, who, in turn, was slowly circling him, scowling back with equally contemptuous menace, teeth bared, tail lashing furiously behind him, and doing his utmost to look like he was the hunter and not the prey.

Not really knowing what (or why) he was doing, Tom pushed himself from the cover of the trees into the clearing, and instantly went flying head-over-heels as he noisily tripped over something that felt remarkably like a tripwire.

He landed face-first on the floor with a dignified and heroic 'Ummphh!', accompanied by the jazz-like drum-roll of his partizan (as it scurried from his hands like an accidentally rolled dice on a craps table) and the cymbal-like "swish" from his beloved purple parka, as he elegantly tumbled into the undergrowth like a harpooned elephant seal.

Chow and Prince Maffdetti both turned and regarded him with mild surprise, like two championship swimmers, vying for the gold medal, who have just noticed a turd floating ahead of them in the pool.

To his dismay, Tom found himself offering an apologetic smile and a jaunty little wave of his hand.

Dr Chow chuckled with sinister delight.

'Good,' he snarled, showing his rather impressive gnashers. 'That has saved me some time. You have troubled me once too often,   Master Dearlove. When I have dealt with this meddling   *oaf,*' he smiled unkindly towards the indignant prince, 'I shall take great delight in   *removing* you from this troublesome equation.'

'OY! Will you just shut it!!!' came a rather exasperated, though reasonable-sounding, voice.

It emanated, Tom realised, from a small tent that was carefully concealed on the very edge of the clearing, and whose guy rope it had been that he had just tripped over.

'Some of us are trying to get some sleep! I don't know what you're up to, and quite frankly – I DON'T CARE! Just take it somewhere else! All right!'

To his credit, the first to recover from the surprise of being admonished by a hitherto unnoticed world-weary tent-dweller was Prince Maffdetti (breeding will out, you know). With a low roar he pounced, hands outstretched like a leopard hurtling towards his prey: that prey was none other than the nefarious Dr Chow.

Say what you like about the Naravirala prince, thought Tom as he heroically crawled back towards the sanctuary of the bushes, *but he's a braver man-cat than I'll ever be (not that I have any plans to be a man-cat, you understand, but – if Dr Chow has his wicked way, and really, it doesn't bear thinking about – who knows?).*

Dr Chow gave an evil laugh as Prince Maffdetti sprang towards him with murderous intent. The Naravirala's menacing snarl however turned into one of perplexed surprise as he crashed into the floor. Maffdetti looked about him, scarcely able to believe his eyes, for Chow had completely disappeared – save for a swirling column of green smoke that was beginning to gently evaporate into the inky blackness of the rain-filled night. Comfortingly, however, Chow's wicked chuckle still echoed around the clearing, bouncing round the trees in disagreeable mirth.

Tom – scared witless and wishing his legs would obey him and remove him, once and for all, from harm's way – found himself unable to force his eyes from the horrible drama that was being played out before him.

Maffdetti quickly rolled to his feet and tentatively prowled forward, his head snapping from side to side as he desperately tried to locate the source of Chow's terrible laughter.

Suddenly Tom saw a billowing curtain of smoke appear behind the Naravirala prince, as if an invisible giant had just exhaled after a long drag on a fat cigar.

'LOOK OUT!' cried Tom.

Maffdetti turned like lightning and instantly sprang backwards, his fur standing on end and his back arched like a threatened alley-cat. For stepping out of the curtain of smoke before him stalked Chow, no longer in his human form but in the deadly guise of a Manticore – four-hundred-and-fifty pounds of muscular lion body, a snapping tail like a scorpion's, and a cruelly smiling human face with all too recognisable features.

'By Apedemak's whiskers, what have you done, you fool!' gasped Maffdetti, as he edged his way backwards.

Chow shuddered his venomous tail from side to side and padded forward with ominous intent.

There was a rustle of movement in the bushes behind Tom. Near to wetting himself, he almost twisted his head off as he rapidly turned round to see a pair of eyes like two dying tea-lights pressed deeply into a face like a roughly slapped scrotum, scowling at him in a rather unsettling display of naked outrage. Tom almost (pardon the expression) had kittens, and squealed in dismay as the horrible visage suddenly raced towards him.

Being the resourceful young chap that he was, Tom was on his feet, through the bushes and tearing across the clearing in a heartbeat, almost weeping with terror, and with a manful refrain emanating from his lips.

The Manticore/Chow/Walter Octavius Hyslip-Campbell (one time Oxford Don turned mythical-beast-shape-shifting-evil-sorcerer) turned to see what the commotion was about, saw Tom flapping about hysterically, instantly dismissed him as no threat and turned his attention back to his cornered quarry.

Instinctively, Tom spun round to see just what it was that was about to kill him, and got the unpleasant eyeful of the revolting Mr Tickles pounding towards him with a look of pure murder dully glowing in his repellent yellow eyeballs. Tom stumbled and fell forwards (almost more terrified by the irate and moth-eaten moggie than he was of Dr Chow) as Mr Tickles pounced towards him, expecting, at any moment, to have his face ripped to shreds by the cantankerous old fleabag's needle-like claws. But the scrawny hairball of doom leapt straight over him, morphing like a squeezed plasticine figure as he flew through the air.

Mr Tickles landed on his feet (his back feet!) and stood up in an undoubtedly anthropomorphic form. Cat-like, yes, and bearing an uncanny resemblance to Prince Maffdetti; save that whereas the prince was cheetah-like in his markings, Mr Tickles was black like a panther.

'My prince!' cried Mr Tickles in a low and sonorous voice, as he launched himself at Chow.

Tom instantly recognised that voice. It was that of his mysterious rescuer – not one of the Caracal Brothers, after all, but a Naravirala agent disguised as Dr Chow's beloved pet pussy!

Chow spun round, speedily side-stepped Mr Tickles' attack, and lanced him in the chest with a rapier-like thrust from his venomous tail.

Mr Tickles hung suspended for a moment in mid-air, until Chow flicked his tail and sent him crumpling to the floor.

'Teffenetti!' cried Maffdetti, as he watched in horror as the old Naravirala tumbled to the ground.

And in that moment Chow was on him, pinning the prince to the floor with his mighty paws.

The Manticore/Chow smiled down at Maffdetti (three sets of shark-like teeth gleaming in the dank and miserable darkness) and brought his deadly tail into position for a killer blow.

'Goodnight, sweet prince,' chuckled Chow. And then, with a look of pure satisfaction, he delivered the mortal strike.

However his look of fulfilment was soon replaced with one of bemusement, because his *coup de grace* never hit its mark, for, clinging on to his deadly tail was none other than young Tomas Dearlove. Or rather, young Tom had flung his *treasured* purple parka around Chow's toxic appendage and was hauling for all he was worth like a windsurfer caught in a squall.

Chow spun like a bucking bronco and swatted Tom away with a contemptuous swipe of his paw. It sent Tom crashing through the sky to land in a painful heap, but it served two rather excellent purposes:

1. It gave Maffdetti the chance to free himself from his perilous position, and
2. It offered Tom a splendid opportunity to finally be free of the fricking fearful garment that Missus Dobbs' had so generously gifted him.

The Manticore/Chow pounced on the purple monstrosity and ripped it asunder like a puppy with a sheet of wrapping paper.

As luck would have it, Tom had landed right next to his fallen partizan. He snatched it up and, like a classical hero of old, hurled the lethal spear with all his might towards the dastardly Chow (who had lost little time in resuming his newfound hobby of pursuing Naravirala aristocracy around woodland clearings on wet rainy nights).

The partizan soared through the drizzling night sky like a shimmering bolt of righteousness, and landed a heroically disappointing two feet from its embarrassed and somewhat unmasculinised-feeling thrower.

Unaware of Tom's epic fail, Chow steadily stalked the backward scurrying prince; Maffdetti never daring to take is eyes off the prowling monster before him. Suddenly the prince lurched backward as he tripped over a guy rope.

There was a bustle of activity from the tent and out rushed the indignant (and somewhat dishevelled) form of Tye-Dai Taffy, saucepan in hand.

'Right! That's it! I've had enough of this!' he bellowed.

Chow stopped dead in his tracks. Maffdetti looked up in surprise at the irate intruder. Tom took a couple of steps backwards (partly to give himself more of a head start if need be, and partly to make it look like his pathetic javelin throw had been of a more impressive proportion).

Tye-Dai looked around and absorbed the unsettling scene before him: lying on the floor was what could best be described as a *were-cat* – who looked like he might once have been the star striker for the *True Blues* in their infamous football match against the *Dirty Yellows [see Walt Disney Productions – Bedknobs and Broomsticks {1971}]* who'd decided on a career change and was now in the middle of a dress rehearsal for *The Prince of Persia II*; standing over him – exuding menace and wicked unpleasantness – was a "lion" ... but with the tail of a scorpion and a human head that wore an expression akin to that of an overly-bookish and somewhat peeved-looking *Antiques Roadshow* presenter who's just been told that he's going to be "let go" because (irony of ironies) he's *too old*; while on the edge of the clearing stood a skinny and awkward-looking adolescent, who bore a disconcerting resemblance to the grave-robber's assistant who had once haunted one of his (Taffy's) very worst nightmares.

Tye-Dai's jaw slowly dropped open, a tear welled in the corner of his eye, and his lower lip began to quiver uncontrollably, as he looked from impossible face to impossible face. His gaze finally settled on Tom, the most "normal" looking of the three apparitions before him (little did he know!).

Tom attempted a comforting and reassuring smile in reply.

Tye-Dai tried to smile back, the effect somewhat ruined by the little sob that accompanied it.

'Help?' offered Tom, with a hopeful tilt of his head and arching of his eyebrows.

Tye-Dai looked back towards Maffdetti and Chow and then down to the saucepan in his hand.

'Leave now or you will die,' snarled Chow, unpleasantly.

'Bugger this,' whispered Tye-Dai Taffy.

Taffy launched himself forwards and belted Chow across the chops with the saucepan with all the force he could muster.

The Manticore staggered back, clutching his swelling hooter between his great paws, and wearing a look of incensed astonishment.

Tom and Prince Maffdetti both lurched forwards and grabbed Tye-Dai by an arm, pulling him backwards and just out of reach of the murderous stroke of Chow's venomous tail. The three of them backed away, arm in arm (all of them meeping softly into the whispering night like a trio of ex-professional champion meepers reunited for a display of world-class meeping at an international meeping convention), as Chow stalked forwards, the cold stare of death smouldering through his streaming eyes.

Tom couldn't help but whisper out loud – 'Toto, I've a feeling we're not in Kansas anymore.' And then he blasted himself for a fool. *With what proud words*, he wondered, *should an Aelfradi prince meet his death?*

And then, just as Chow looked set to pounce and finish them off for good, a spear landed between them. As one, they turned to see the leopard-like form of Fauzia appear like a blessed guardian angel from the trees. Then came the massive figure of the were-lion, Jelani, followed by Cornelius, Inspector Jones, Nipper and Snapper, and, bringing up the rear, like the festering form of wonderful wizardry that he undoubtedly was, came Bob Goodfellow.

Tye-Dai Taffy went limp and swooned to the floor like an Edwardian heroine.

Chow wailed in despair, sunk to his haunches and buried his head in his elbows; for it was clear to see that there was no way out – he was outnumbered, surrounded and, best of all, thought Tom, utterly defeated.

Maffdetti swaggered over to him.

'On your feet, villain!' he cried.

But Chow would not move, just sat with his massive head sunk into his deadly paws with his shoulders heaving up and down.

Old Bob sauntered up to the weeping Manticore and whispered something in his ear … and suddenly the Manticore was gone and in its place sat the tall, lanky and dejected form of the despicable sorcerer, Oxford Don and travelling-circus impresario Dr Chow/Hyslip-Campbell.

Inspector Jones pulled Chow's hands behind his back and handcuffed him.

'You're nicked, mate,' he growled.

Dr Chow looked up at the prince, who was towering over him with bristling rage, and was about to say something when Maffdetti struck him across the face.

Oh you're brave all of a sudden, thought Tom, not out of any sense of moral outrage at the prince's behaviour, but because he was wondering if he could get away with sauntering over and belting the irredeemable old bastard in the chops, now that the terrifying swine was safely trussed up (a thought that he instantly dismissed as he knew that Cornelius would give him a right royal bollocking if he tried anything of the sort).

Chow rolled his head with the blow and looked down at the floor. Maffdetti sneered at him and then turned and ran to the fallen body of Mr Tickles/Teffenetti.

'Teffenetti, my old friend and teacher, how are you?' sobbed the Naravirala prince, cradling the old cat-man's head tenderly in his hands.

Teffenetti opened his eyes, and Tom couldn't help notice that they seemed to be even dimmer than before.

'Oh, my prince,' he whispered. 'It is my joy to see you, one last time.'

'Nonsense, old friend. We'll have you back on your feet in no time. Soon you will be home again, have no fear.'

Teffenetti smiled. 'Oh my prince, you were ever a terrible liar. Here, in these damp woods, will I end my days. It is the truth, do not dare deny it. I wish that I could have seen *The Forbidden City* one last time. How I would have liked to have sat in her great libraries and watched the little cubs at their lessons; how they grow, how they blossom and flower as they unlock the wonders of the world. And I should have liked to have felt the cold sweet breath of the *High Majestic Mountain* upon my cheeks. But no matter. Do not mourn for me, Maffdetti. I die in the service of what I love the most. Who could ask for more? Not I. Protect the City, my prince. Protect our people.'

And then the fading light died in his eyes and a breath like the flap of a small bird's wing escaped his lips … and he was still.

The Hound bounded into the clearing.

'Well, well, well,' he growled, walking up to where Dr Chow sat despondently on the floor. 'Dr Chow, I presume; or should I say – Dr Walter Octavius Hyslip-Campbell, formally of Baliol College.'

Chow looked up at him and smiled.

'The legendary *Hound Who Hunts Nightmares*,' he croaked. 'What an honour it is to finally meet you, sir, though forgive me for wishing the circumstances were somewhat different. The game is up,' he sighed, casting a quick glance over to Maffdetti and *The Chosen Ones*, 'I surrender myself to your authority.'

'Good,' replied The Hound, with quick wag of his tail. 'You've a lot to answer for, my dear Doctor. I shall look forward to interviewing you in person.'

'NO!' roared a voice.

Everyone turned to see Prince Maffdetti stomping towards them, Jelani and Fauzia poised protectively at his shoulder.

'Chow is my prisoner! He will remain in my custody! Hand him over to me – immediately!'

'Now see here,' bristled The Hound, impatiently. 'This man is a British citizen and has been apprehended on British soil.'

'His crimes are against the Naravirala people. It is *we* who will try him.'

'Well I'm sorry to say that I'm just not sufficiently convinced as to what sort of *justice* this fellow will receive at your hands.'

'Hand him over immediately or you will experience *just what sort of justice he can expect to receive,* first-hand!'

''Ere we go again,' sighed Cornelius, as he gave Tom's hair a comforting ruffle before standing shoulder-to-shoulder with The Hound.

Things were looking fraught, with neither side willing to back down and tensions growing tangibly by the second, when Tom suddenly saw Chow lift his head and slowly get to his feet.

'Mae?' whispered the old sorcerer, quizzically.

Tom followed his gaze and saw the tiny and somehow tragically frail figure of the *Carnival of Curiosities* cabaret-singer picking his way slowly towards them.

Everybody stopped their arguing and watched in spellbound silence as the stony-faced and wretched little man staggered through their midst like an animated corpse; head down and with streaks of mascara smudged across his rouged and thickly-powered cheeks – though whether it was from the rain or from his own tears it was impossible to say.

He stopped in front of Chow.

'Lu is dead, Master,' he said, without looking up at the old man, and his voice was the coldest and emptiest sound that Tom had ever heard.

Dr Chow gave him a kindly, almost parental, frown of sympathy.

'I am so sorr–' he began, but stopped mid-sentence.

A strange smile played across Chow's lips as he slowly looked down in wonder at the bone-handled knife that had been plunged into his heart.

He gazed from the knife to Mae, with a questioning look in his lion-like eyes, and then folded like a fallen kite, dead before he hit the ground.

THIRTEEN
Autumn's Blood-Red Tears

If Tom was honest with himself it was a scenario that he had all too often fantasised about: a wonderful role reversal, with members of the *Carnival of Curiosities* powerless and locked safely behind bars while he *lorded* masterfully before them in a perfect picture of justly-deserved revenge. The reality, however, was anything like satisfaction. For here he stood, looking through the bars of One Punch Cottage's dimly-lit basement gaol at the forlorn, broken and all too recently bereaved figure of the Siamese-were-cat known as Mae.

Mae sat huddled in the furthest corner of the prison, staring blankly at the floor. His ruined make-up had fashioned itself into a grotesquely tragic, almost clown-like, mask of smeared and swirling colours. If he had even noticed the tray of food that Tom had placed there a little over an hour ago, then he hadn't touched it.

'You should eat something,' said Tom, not knowing what else he should say, but feeling like he should say something.

Mae ignored him.

'It's nicer than it looks. I'm sure that you're not used to steak 'n' kidney pudding ... but ... it's not bad at all.'

'No thank you, Mister Tom,' whispered Mae. 'I am not hungry.'

Well, that was progress – of sorts.

Tom sat down cross-legged on the floor and leant his forehead against the cold prison bars.

'Have you had a chance to think about The Hound's offer?' he asked, after a long and uncomfortable silence.

Mae continued to stare a hole into the concrete floor and sighed softly, while suppressing a shuddering sob.

When the bloody tragedy had been played out and they had eventually returned to One Punch Cottage, relationships between The Hound and Prince Maffdetti hadn't softened any. The tension between them was almost palpable as they discussed, in tones of subdued and forced civility, what was to be done with the surviving members of the *Carnival of Curiosity*.

The Hound doggedly clung to his view that, as they had been apprehended on British soil, it was the British authorities (i.e. MI Unseen) who should take possession of the vile villains. Meanwhile, Maffdetti was adamant in his unwavering certainty that the survivors were both the prisoners and the property of the Naravirala State.

It had been Tom who had offered a possible solution.

"Why not," he had suggested, "let the prisoners decide where they want to go?"

As Dr Chow and Lady Lynx (who were the main targets of the Naravirala's wrath) were both dead, the surviving members (Mae, HASS and the Caracal Brothers – Bruce, Chuck and Jackie) were of small consequence in the grand scheme of things – bit-part players at best. The Naravirala had got, albeit in the most severe of finalities, the justice that they desired, and The Hound had regained possession of *The Autumn Crown*; which was, undeniably, the most important factor as far as he and the rest of the One Punch Cottage alliance were concerned.

"You have the merciful wisdom of a prince, my friend," Maffdetti had smiled wearily at him.

Truth be told, they were all feeling more than a little jaded. As much as they might not like to admit it, the night's terrible toll had affected everybody.

Four dead bodies.

Four souls rubbed from the circle of the world.

How many more lives would it take before this unseemly mess was sorted out? And, for the umpteenth time, Tom had wondered – was it worth it?

He'd looked around at the roomful of fatigued and haunted faces and decided that it had to be, because if it wasn't, then the consequences didn't bear thinking about.

Strangely, Tom felt himself silently mourning for each of the dead:

Lady Lynx – who had been blinded by the Naravirala for the crime of leading the dying Hyslip-Campbell to the heart of *The Forbidden City*, and then had escaped with him when he had recovered. Perhaps she had felt that it would be a new start for them both? Perhaps she just wanted her revenge on those who had punished her so harshly? Perhaps she had done it all for love – for him, for Dr Chow? Tom would never know, and it was too late to ever ask her. She had once told him that his past and his future were bathed in blood, and he had despised her for it. But now? He hated to think on it, but she might very well have been right.

Lu – cursed and most cruelly mutilated by Chow: a victim as much as anything. Was it any wonder that he and Mae were so spiteful and deviously deranged, with all that they had seen and been put through?

Mr Tickles/Teffenetti – the Naravirala spy and sorcerer; Prince Maffdetti's tutor, mentor and friend – who had spent decades in the service of his prince, disguised as a procession of scrawny domestic cats (faking his own death every fifteen years or so and then managing to get himself "rediscovered" in the fresh form of a newly-found kitten) as he loyally spied on the *Carnival of Curiosities* in order to bring Chow to justice for his crimes against the people that he, Teffenetti, so loved. And his reward for his years of self-sacrificing service? A cruel death a thousand miles from the beloved homeland that he would never see again.

135

And Dr Chow? *Well he*, thought Tom, *could burn in Hell for all eternity for all of the pain and hurt that he'd brought with him into this already wretched world.*

The Hound hadn't been best pleased with Tom's suggestion, but what was there to do but accept it or face the destructive possibilities of a long, drawn-out argument with the Naravirala? – which, in the end, would have served no purpose to anyone.

And so it was that the Caracal Brothers and The Mighty HASS all elected to return with Maffdetti and the Naravirala.

It was then that Tom had collected his courage and asked Maffdetti for a favour.

The prince had loudly proclaimed that he would grant Tom any wish that he desired, for he was indebted to the young *Elven prince* for his life – "For had they not battled heroically together against the monstrous Manticore?" (Well, if that's how the deluded aristocratic lunatic chose to remember their recent "meep-off" then that was just fine with Tom!). And so Tom had requested that the prisoners be treated fairly and be rehabilitated rather than punished for their association with Chow, for it was Tom's belief that they were, in their own way, mere victims of Chow's malefactions.

Maffdetti had slapped his thigh like a swashbuckling pirate and swore it was the finest thing that he had ever heard; that Tom would be a great king when his time came, and that he would be forever welcome in the great halls of *The Forbidden City* if ever he chose to visit. And so, with that princely promise, everybody seemed satisfied and the tension in the room somewhat subsided.

Mae, however, remaining in a near-catatonic state, and refusing to meet anyone's eye, had softly made it known that he had no wish to go with the Naravirala.

When the prisoners had been sent to their respective holding cells (the Caracal Brothers and HASS ordered to shift themselves into animal form before they were caged, crated and transported for safekeeping to Prince Maffdetti's penthouse suite in the Grand Hotel by Jelani and Fauzia; Mae led vacantly away to the muse-asium by Missus Dobbs and Constable Tuggnutter), Bob Goodfellow had produced from a ragged hessian sack the legendary *Autumn Crown*.

It was, Tom decided, the most beautiful object that he had ever seen. Golden leaves of every autumnal shade fashioned to form a spiralling crown of unspeakable glory. Even Maffdetti, who knew a thing or two about expensive gewgaws, was astounded by its splendour and breathlessly asked if anyone knew where he could get one made.

Bob Goodfellow had chuckled ruefully, returned the crown into the sack and handed it over to The Hound for safekeeping, and then muttered something to himself about *Autumn's blood-red tears*.

As Prince Maffdetti had turned to leave, The Hound had urged him to remain in England and help them bring de Warrenne and *The Society of the Wild Hunt* to justice, but the Naravirala prince would not be turned. He longed, he said, to return to his homeland, for he had been away far too long, and had no love for the world of men – nor for how they chose to live their lives. But he wished them luck in their endeavours and extended to them all the hospitality of the Naravirala – if they should ever desire to see its fabled city's walls.

The Hound was suitably annoyed, for his plan had been for the Naravirala to pose as members of the *Carnival of Curiosities* in order to keep up the façade of the upcoming *prize-fight*, and to assist him in the capture of the wretched vampire, de Warrenne, and his devilish crew of the damned.

It was then that Tom had suggested that they convince Mae to help them – in return for a more lenient sentence. The Hound had thought it a capital idea and given Tom the task of persuading the pitiful wretch to join them in their pursuit of justice. Tom had replied that he would do his best, but secretly he didn't hold out for much of a result.

'And what happens if I refuse this offer, Mister Tom?' hissed Mae.

'Er ... I suppose that you'll be taken to The Mound ... that's a high-security prison for supernatural ... criminals.'

'*Criminals*,' sighed Mae. 'I see. And if I should agree?'

'Uhm ... I suppose that you'll still be taken to The Mound ... but get ... er ... more privileges? A nicer room ... and things like that. Maybe your own television set?'

'A nicer room? I see.'

Mae tilted his head a fraction and squinted in Tom's direction out of the corner of his eye.

'Lu ...' he began with a falter, as he stifled a forlorn sniff, 'once told me that you are an Elven prince. Is that true, Mister Tom?'

It was Tom's turn to sigh.

'I'm afraid that it is,' he replied, steadily looking at the strange little were-cat, and suddenly thinking how pathetically fragile he seemed; really he was nothing more than a lost and lonely, deranged and deluded, middle-aged man.

'And that one day,' Mae continued, raising his eyes to meet Tom's with a coy tilt of his head, 'you will be king of all Hidden Albion?'

'Well technically it's *The Hidden Realm* or *Lower Albion*, but yes, it's a remote possibility.'

Mae turned his head back and resumed his determined study of the prison floor.

'So, let me get this straight, Mister Tom;' he continued, after a long and thoughtful pause, 'you want me to act as a front in continuing the charade that Dr Chow is still to participate in the contest with the vampire de Warrenne for *The Crowns of Albion*?'

'Yes. That's right.'

'And if you succeed, then it will help to put you on the throne of *The Lower Realms*?'

'Hhhmm. I suppose it might.'

'It must be very dark below the ground, Mister Tom, in T*he Kingdom Of Hidden Shadows*?'

'Er ... I suppose so. But to be honest I've never even been there.'

Mae closed his eyes, rocked back and forth a little and puckered his smeared and painted lips.

'Very well, Mister Tom. I will do all that you ask of me, but I have a condition.'

'And what's that, Mae?'

'That if you do become the *King of Avalon* you will take me with you to the sunless lands below, and I will live out the rest of my days, unmolested and in solitude, in the gloom of *The Realm of Shadows*.'

It was Tom's turn to look intently at the floor.

He took a long deep breath.

'All right,' he said at last. 'If it ever happens – and I'm warning you now, Mae, that it's unlikely – I give you my word: I'll take you to *The Hidden Realm*, if you still want me to, that is.'

Mae turned and looked directly at him, offering him a grotesque and ghastly smile as he did so.

'Then do with me as you wish, Prince Tom, for I am your servant.'

FOURTEEN
New Beginnings

Tye-Dai Taffy opened his eyes and found himself, much to his bewilderment, lying in an extremely comfortable, if somewhat old-fashioned, single bed. Pristine white sheets and warm woollen blankets encased his aching body, and soft, snow-white pillows supported his pounding cranium. Wondering just how it was that he came to be dressed in a set of sweet-smelling, freshly-washed, blue and white striped flannel pyjamas, he gazed in wonder around the small, cosy room, that looked like it might well have been furnished with the discarded props from a BBC Edwardian drama.

Fussing over a small table in one corner of the room was the diminutive figure of a doddering old lady. She obviously heard him moving in his bed, for she suddenly turned around and beamed a friendly smile at him. As she peered over enquiringly, Tye-Dai instantly decided that she must be just about the sweetest-looking little old lady that he'd ever seen – (My, she was tiny!): two chubby, peachy cheeks gurning under watery eyes as green as a summer-sweet orchard.

'Hello, Ducky,' she croaked kindly, dazzling him with a gurn of unbridled happiness. 'How about a nice cup of tea?'

'Er? Yeah, that would be ... lovely? Ta very much, Missus,' replied Tye-Dai, more than a little disorientated, but charmed by the undeniable warmth of her benevolent bearing, as she bimbled over and offered him a posh-looking china teacup balanced on a matching saucer.

Tye-Dai hoisted himself to a sitting position and delicately took the saucer from the sweet old dear's veiny mitt, suddenly feeling a little awkward to be handling such finery and to be the subject of such unexpected niceties.

'Well go on then, Ducky, before it gets cold,' cooed the strange little biddy, giving him an encouraging nod towards the gently rattling cup and saucer in his hands.

Tye-Dai smiled, bent forward and took a sniff.

He was met with a somewhat strange, almost noxious odour, and concluded that it must be one of those posh, foreign teas that the Brighton middle class mums and trend-minions seemed to be so besotted with these days. With a feeling of comforting warmth welling up in his belly in a "Christmassy" anticipation of this new and exotic delight, he took a tentative sip.

He was out of the bed and hurtling through the door faster that a pin-pricked whippet, spilling and retching "tea" in all conceivable directions.

With his eyes streaming in agony and his throat contorting in uncontrollable spasms, he dashed, half-blinded, along a long hallway and down a steep flight of creaking stairs. Wiping the tears from his face and still gagging violently, he burst through a hefty-looking door and came to an abrupt halt in what looked like an overcrowded Victorian gentlemen's club.

"Ow do, son,' said a lethal-looking pensioner with outlandish facial-furniture – who was dressed like a well-to-do henchman from an episode of Sherlock Holmes, and who looked, all too worryingly, all too familiar. 'Looks to me like you might just 'ave sampled the considerable "delights" of Missus Dobbs' tea-making abilities,' he chortled, kindly. 'Why don't you sit yourself down, son, an' 'ave yourself a proper brew.'

A worryingly large man (who had "copper" written all over him) pressed Tye-Dai into a chair with a hand like a cast-iron shovel, mumbled something unintelligible, and shoved a steaming mug into Taffy's quivering fist.

Tye-Dai folded into the chair and did exactly as he was told.

The tea, it turned out (to his relief and delight), was warm and sweet and marvellous – exactly what tea should be.

With a relieved sigh he looked about at the other occupants of the room (all currently staring at him with varying degrees of encouragement): a stunningly beautiful blonde woman, who looked like a 1950s Vogue cover model; a small, haunted-looking chap with dark skin and a friendly demeanour; a pale young Emo, dressed in black (naturally), with a face full of piercings and a bandage around her forehead; a short, handsome twenty-something who reminded Tye-Dai of a Seventies rock-star, beside him stood a taller and older man who looked like he might have been his roadie; an ageing hippy, with skin the colour of drinking-chocolate and a mass of tight and long raven-coloured curls spilling over her shoulders, squinting thoughtfully at him through her left eye; a gangly, awkward-looking kid, who looked terrifyingly familiar; perhaps the most unkempt and unwashed individual that Tye-Dai had ever seen (and believe me, he'd seen more than his fair share), piercing him with eyes so fiercely blue that they seemed to cut through his grimy face like sunbeams; and three dogs – one the size of a pony, and the other two, scruffy terrier types with the expressions of famished alligators clinging to the edge of sanity.

The one last figure in the room, seated in a truly enormous armchair, and currently masked from view by the opened broadsheet that he was holding in front of him, put down his newspaper and turned to face the new arrival.

'Well hello, my good fellow,' he beamed, in a pleasant and ridiculously deep and plummy voice. 'I do hope that you're feeling suitably recovered from your recent ordeal, dear chap.'

Tye-Dai turned to the big copper who had just given him the mug of tea and said, in a calm and matter of fact manner – 'There's a were-wolf sitting over there, don't you know.'

The big policeman muttered something unintelligible and, with surprising speed for a fellow of such extraordinary stature, managed to pluck the drinking vessel from Tye-Dai's hand before he crumpled to the floor.

Taffy came to (again) with a circle of concerned-looking faces peering down at him, and was gently hoisted to his feet by the tweed-encrusted pensioner with the enormous whiskers.

'You're going to 'ave to try an' get a grip on yourself, son,' he chuckled, 'or we'll be 'ere all bloomin' afternoon.'

'B...b...but ... there's a w...w...were-w...w...wolf s...s...sitting over there d...d... dressed in a r...r...red-s...s...silk d...d...dressing g...g...gown,' blithered Tye-Dai.

'Actually, I think you'll find that the term *cynanthrope* would perhaps be more appropriate,' replied The Hound, 'but even that would, in fact, be an incorrect assessment. A *wolfhound-were-wolf* would be the ticket. However, *'were-wolf'* is an understandable mistake, old chap, so I'll forgive you, just this once,' he added, smiling as pleasantly as he knew how.

Tye-Dai was on the edge of "going" again, when his hand was sharply slapped by the tiny old woman who had tried to poison him earlier.

'Pay attention, Ducky,' she gurned sternly. 'Now, how about another lovely cup of tea, dear?'

Tye-Dai released an involuntary gag and violently shook his head.

'It seems to me, my dear fellow,' continued The Hound, thoughtfully stroking his whiskers, 'that it's way past time that you began to believe in what is *actually* in front of you, rather than what you *want* to believe is there. Time to accept life, rather than deny it, wouldn't you agree?'

Tye-Dai swallowed hard and eagerly nodded his head: who, after all, wants to disagree with a seven-and-a-half foot tall cyna-thingy/were-wolf dressed in a red silk dressing-gown?

'Now, Mr Goodfellow here,' he continued, with a nod towards the reeking little guttersnipe with the unkempt beard and eyes like a cloudless summer sky, 'has a proposition for you. If you've anything about you, young man, then I suggest that you listen to him *very carefully*.'

Tye-Dai nodded enthusiastically.

Bob Goodfellow ambled up to Tye-Dai and looked him squarely in the peepers.

'I've a cottage up yonder,' he began, his beard rustling with small movements that seemed to be independent from the natural movement of his jaw. 'Looks like I'll have to be away from it for the foreseeable future. Seems to me that I could do with someone looking after it in my absence; someone to weed the garden and generally see to its upkeep and maintenance. Now, if you can promise me that you can hold yourself steady, and think that you can be trusted with such a task, then I'd like for you to step up to it. It's in the middle of nowhere, mind, but I'll pay you fairly for your time and drop in to see how you're getting on when I can − and to give what instructions are needed. And if all goes well, then who knows where it might lead? Seems to me a strange and unlikely coincidence that you keep popping up in the middle of so many extraordinary events. Makes me wonder if you haven't got some part to play in this repugnant drama. Who knows? We'll have to see.

'Now, if you accept, then all well and good; I'll take you there this afternoon. And if not, then off you trot and no hard feelings. If you want I can even erase your memories so you may, no doubt, sleep all the easier. But if you're looking for a chance to change things, then here it is. I won't press you though. It's up to you.'

Tye-Dai Taffy held onto Bob Goodfellow's steely gaze.

'You mean all this is ... *real?*' he asked in a confidential whisper.

Bob nodded.

'Then I haven't been going daffy?'

Bob shook his head.

Tye-Dai slumped his chin onto his chest and sighed, then took a deep breath and held it.

'All right!' he declared, looking up and staring around the room at its bizarre occupants. 'All right, I'll do it. I'm your man, Mr Goodfellow. You have my word on it.'

And with that, the matter was decided, and then sealed with a slap-up lunch (consisting of a small mountain of toasted cheese-and-mustard sandwiches). And Tye-Dai Taffy began his courageous and wonderful journey towards a new start and a new beginning.

FIFTEEN
Oh Happy Day!

Tom awoke from a well-earned and long overdue lie in, and sleepily made his way towards the kitchen to pick himself up a spot of brunch. As he made his descent, having already given himself quite a jolt by accidentally stepping on the infamous *creaky step number three* (just to give you some idea of just how tired the poor lad must have been), he noticed that the door of The Study was, unusually, ajar.

'Ah, Tom,' came the low and clipped tones of The Hound. 'Would you be so kind to join us in here for a moment, dear boy? And shut the door after you, there's a good chap.'

Tom, still a little bleary-eyed, did as he was asked and stumbled into The Study.

All was as close to comfortingly *normal* as One Punch Cottage ever got; Bess lay comatose on the sofa, while standing around the writing-desk stood The Hound, Archie Swapper and Ned Leppelin, pouring over a large map laid out on the tabletop.

'What are you up to?' asked Tom, rubbing the sleep from his eyes and stifling a yawn. 'And where's everybody else?'

'About,' answered The Hound mysteriously, giving Tom a keen look and a glowing smile. 'Except for Bob. He's currently escorting Mr Taffy to his new post as caretaker of *Goodfellow Manor*. Ho-ho,' he guffawed mischievously. 'He'll rendezvous with us tomorrow at Ondred's Wood.'

'*Rendezvous*? Woods?' enquired Tom. 'What's going on?'

'Well, while you've been asleep, dear boy, there have been some ... *developments*. We've just had some rather good news.'

'Really? Cool. What is it?'

'Whelk-faced Willie Willikins has just passed word to us that the arch-rotter – de Warrenne – has agreed to "Dr *Chow's*" [ha ha] proposed venue for the "prize-fight"; to wit, the abandoned farmstead over by Castle Hill.'

'He has?' Well, that's brilliant news. So,' asked Tom, drawing a big stretch and collecting himself in the most *businesslike-and-ready-for-action* of manners, 'what's the plan, Mr Hound?'

The were-hound turned his attention back to the map.

'We must lay our trap carefully,' he growled. 'One mistake and the bounder will smell a rat. However, our biggest problem is ...'

'Is what?' asked Tom, innocently.

'Numberz, Tomaz,' clicked Archie.

'Numbers?'

'Indeed,' continued the were-hound, his concentration fixed on marking a spot on the map with his pencil. 'If this little plan of ours is to work, we'll need all the help that we can get. Now, as we've been led to believe, *The Society of the Wild Hunt's* ranks will be bolstered by their newfound associates, *The Bucca* (and God alone knows just what other *lovelies* de Warrenne might have persuaded to support his cause). What with the Naravirala deciding to head back home and leave us to our own devices, things aren't looking quite as rosy as I'd hoped. As it stands, we're outnumbered, by at least five to one. And that, I'm afraid, my fine young fellow, just won't cut the mustard.'

'Hhhmm,' hhhmmed Tom.

'What we'z need, Prince Tom,' frowned Ned, with a hero-like sweep of his golden mane, 'iz alliez.'

'Allies. Yes of course. What about MI Unseen?' suggested Tom, coming to the table and peering at the map like a seasoned old pro (though truth be told he didn't have much of a clue as to what he was looking at).

The Hound sucked his cheeks.

'Even if all of their resources weren't focused on Europe and the possible outbreak in hostilities between the Della Mortes and the Nachzehrers, well, I don't know about you but, what with recent events, I'm not too sure that I'd feel completely comfortable with the likes of Colonel Sinjon Sin-John and his command at my back.'

'Yes, I see,' pouted Tom. 'Any chance that some of the Pharisees might pop back to help out?' he offered hopefully.

Archie tutted ruefully. "Fraid not, Tom,' he sighed. 'Even though old Bob reckonz there'z nothing to fret about, I'm not too zure that we can take that rizk.'

'Oo!' oo-ed Tom, excitedly. 'What about Mr Tregellis and the *were-dog boys* back at The Mound?'

The Hound looked at Tom with an eager glint sparkling in his eyes.

'Oh, Tom,' sighed the were-hound, 'how I long for the day when my brothers will have mastered their *other selves* sufficiently to be able to join us in the fight for righteousness. But alas, I am afraid to say, that that day is not yet with us.'

'Hmmm. Well how about that vampire who came to see us? Victor Bertrand? He seemed only too keen to be of assistance.'

The Hound jotted something down in a notebook and shot the briefest of glances to Tom.

'No, Tom. That bat won't hunt, if you'll forgive me. It's bad enough to have one set of evil vampires to deal with, without embroiling ourselves in a collaboration with another, even worse, set of the bloodsucking blighters. No, Tom, I'm sorry to say that we'll just have to look elsewhere.'

'Yes. Yes, I suppose so. Any ideas?' asked Tom.

'Well ... funny you should ask, old chap,' sniffed the were-hound, still distractedly scribbling notes in his journal. 'But we've just arranged a parley with a most unlikely source. Would never have even crossed my mind, but Bob mentioned it last night, just after you'd gone to bed, old boy, and we received confirmation this morning that he ... they ... were willing to at least listen to what we had to say. Hence (time being against us, and all that) the rendezvous tomorrow. We need you there, Tom, not only as a valued member of the team but also because you are in a unique position to have some sway on the matter.'

'I am? Yes, of course,' replied Tom, the seed of doubt uneasily growing in the pit of his stomach. 'And *who* is it, exactly, that we're going to see?'

The Hound gnawed the top of his pencil and studied his notes.

Ned and Archie developed a sudden fascination with cartography.

'What's that, old chum?' huffed The Hound, absentmindedly.

'*Who*, exactly, are we going to see?'

'Oh, yes, of course,' replied the were-hound, looking up from his notebook, removing the pencil and offering a gnasher-filled grin. 'Prince Edric,' he smiled, awkwardly. 'And his ... chaps.'

'I see,' replied Tom, passively. 'ARE YOU OUT OF YOUR FRICKIN' TINY MIND, YOU INSENSITIVE, WOMBLE-FACED IMBECI–'

Tom's beginnings of an outburst were rather drowned out by the sound of cheering coming from outside the room.

Suddenly, the door of The Study swung open and in sprang Cornelius, Old Maggs, Dame Ginty, the complete collection of the Department of Special Cases and, in the forefront, the kindly old eye-gouger herself – Missus Dobbs – carrying in her arms a giant cake with an assortment of fiery candles, spitting flames like an oil-drilling expedition team-leader's wet-dream.

''Appy Birthday, son,' beamed Cornelius, and then the whole pack of heartless bastards burst into a blistering rendition of "Happy Birthday To You".

Tom turned to face them with the look of petrified fury still starched onto his disbelieving visage, and tried not to weep.

Later that evening, as he lay on his bed, in an absolute frantic state of funk, desperately trying to chase down the uncatchable mare of sleep, Tom wondered just how it was possible that he had forgotten that it was his own birthday. A year ago he would have been counting down the days, but now, it had somehow completely slipped his mind. He supposed that all of the extraordinary events of the last six months, leading up to and including his (re)capture and escape from the sinister Dr Chow, were enough to make anybody forget what day it was. Plus being witness to the murder of four people barely twenty-four hours ago (and, yes, Tom had decided that they were most definitely *people*, even if they weren't entirely human [if at all, in the case of Teffenetti]) was apt to make the more trivial stuff, like remembering birthdays, seem ... well ... unimportant.

To try and take his mind off recent events, and to attempt to avoid thinking about upcoming ones, Tom focused his thoughts on the birthday presents that he had received.

The Hound had given him a hardback volume of the complete plays of Christopher Marlowe, a DVD of a film called "*Dean Spanley*", and a copy of Professor Hey's occult classic "*Behind the Dark Curtain*" (presumably the very tome that had been purchased by Chow – well, the evil swine certainly didn't have any more use for it!), with the choice recommendation that it might prove to be of great benefit if Tom took the chance to read Professor Hey's work before the week was up. Though, to be honest, even touching the ghastly little tome (possibly bound in human flesh, possibly not – depending on who you asked) gave Tom the willies.

Cornelius had presented him with a pair of black leather boxing boots, a set of night-vision goggles, two biographies of the 1920s boxer, Gene Tunney (one titled *"Tunney: Boxing's Brainiest Champ and His Upset of the Great Jack Dempsey"* by Jack Cavanaugh, and the other *"Gene Tunney: the Golden Guy who Licked Jack Dempsey Twice"* [?] by John Jarrett – along with the sound advice that if, by some freak of chance, Tom should ever decide on a career as a prize-fighter, then that is how it should be done), a small knife, and a book about woodcarving entitled *"Whittling The Old Sea Captain"* by Mike Shipley.

Dame Ginty had given him a diary and a set of pens. Inspector Jones had presented him with a box-set of CDs entitled "Genesis – the Gabriel Years". Hettie had given him a black (of course) T-shirt with a picture of a whacky-looking old-school comedian holding up a glove-puppet of a depressed-looking long-necked bird, with the legend *"Rod Hull & Emo"* written under it. Constable Tuggnutter had handed him a Rubik's Cube (puzzlingly). Old Maggs had presented him with a matching set of hat, scarf and gloves that she had knitted herself, whilst Archie and Ned had proudly presented him with a freshly-knapped flint axe head attached to the shaft of a golf-club.

There had been a card from his Mum – with a crisp fifty-pound note inside it. (He had also had an all-too-brief conversation with her on the phone and tried his best to tell her all that had and was about to happen without overly worrying her).

The *piece-de-resistance* belonged, of course, to Missus Dobbs.

The tiny tea-poisoner had staggered over to him with a ginormous parcel in her arms and cheerfully placed it before him, bubbling with a joyous gurn of expectation, as she twitched beside him in anticipation of seeing him open it.

Tom had looked with bewildered excitement from the enormous package to the diminutive Brownie, wondering what it could be.

'It wasn't easy, Ducks,' she purred, 'not at such short notice, but I managed to find another one.'

It was then that the awful truth dawned on him (soon confirmed with the very first tear of the wrapping paper); for beneath the tingling promise of the smartly-wrapped gift-paper glistened the heart-wrenching glimpse of a purple so revolting it offended not only the eye but the very soul.

Tom looked up from the new purple parka to Missus Dobbs with tears in his eyes.

The hateful old harridan choked back her own waterworks of happiness.

'Oo, don't thank me, Tom,' she blubbered, struggling desperately to keep a check on herself, 'just the sight of your face says it all, Ducky.'

And away she dashed, literally spinning with happiness, and began to hack the birthday cake into manageable-sized chunks with a small hammer and a knife like a builder's trowel.

Perhaps an even greater disappointment (if such a thing were possible) was that there was no card from Crow. Not that he really expected one (he tried to convince himself) and she probably didn't even know when his birthday was, but, still, it would have been ... nice.

Fourteen years old, he thought to himself, as he gazed frantically at the ceiling. Fourteen! Another year older ... and another year closer to his sixteenth birthday – when he could be legally murdered by his estranged and psychotic cousin (once removed). That is, if he wasn't done in tomorrow when they went to visit the homicidal brute. Oh, everybody had sworn that it would be fine. Edric wouldn't dare raise a finger against him, not with The Hound and Cornelius and everybody there. And, they had all insisted, they would be protected under the ancient laws of Elbi hospitality. But still, Tom couldn't help but feel more than a little uneasy about the whole adventure. He was, after all, becoming a bit of an expert in the delightful and bloodstained history of the Adamsbane family, and he was only too well aware that if that history proved one thing, it was that they, his delightful clan, were all too prone to a *stab/slash/murder first then apologise profusely* (or not) *after* policy.

Oh happy day!

He forced himself to close his eyes, tightly wrapped his fingers around his kingfisher necklace, and prayed for sleep to come.

SIXTEEN
The Alliance

They reached the outskirts of the remote and barely-accessible Ondred's Wood by mid-morning. Few men even knew of the wood's existence, and fewer still had actually walked beneath its dark and ancient canopy (for it was the secret and scared heart of all that remained of the great Anderida Forest – the mighty woodland which once had covered much of South East England). The whole crew had made the journey, with the exception of Dame Ginty and Sergeant Hettie Clem, who had stayed behind with Missus Dobbs and Bess to help look after One Punch Cottage ... and to keep an eye on Mae.

No sooner had they reached the edge of the sacred woodland than they were greeted by what first appeared to be an animated scarecrow who'd just managed to claw his way out of a pigsty, but soon revealed itself to be Bob Goodfellow. In his grimy and fingerless-glove-encased mitt the mighty Puck held a long staff, whose warped and twisted wood was smoothed and worn to near black through age and handling. With barely a rancid smile of a greeting, Bob ushered them from the rain and into the cover of the murky and cathedral-like trees, with the heart-warming news that Prince Edric and his followers awaited them within.

They were led to the centre of the ancient forest, where stood a small, open-ended circle of standing stones. Each stone stood taller than a man – and somehow evoked (to Tom's mind at least) the picture of a party of deformed and shackled giants. In the heart of the circle awaited Prince Edric Bloodstone Adamsbane himself, dressed, as was his custom, in long boots made of iron and with his long white hair pulled to one side and braided into the complex knot of the Aelfradi warrior of antiquity. Other than the newly-acquired metallic prosthetic hand that protruded from the sleeve of his jacket, he looked very much the same as when Tom had first seen him on the night of the Exhibition Skirmish, when Ned Leppelin had famously won the right to be called *The Smack Faery*.

Around Edric stood the most trusted members of his retinue: the two pale and ghostly Aelfradi warriors who had been with him on that fateful night in the old barn in Falmer (South) – the infamous Elven bogeymen Bad Bobby Bannister and Long Lamkin. Along with them were a small, wizened Goblin with a shifty demeanour and an extremely pointy face, and another Goblin – a huge hulking figure with impossibly long arms and the demeanour of the playground bully. All four were dressed in the iron footwear and blood-red hats of the ferocious and legendary goblin war-society known as the *Redcaps*. Beside them were three more characters: an ancient-looking Goblin, almost bent double with the weight of years (supporting his crooked frame on a sturdy cane), and, to everybody's mild surprise, their old acquaintances, the Oakman spokesman, Picktree Brag, and Dave Sternhammer (the near-aristocratic leader of the Trolls of Britain).

Prince Edric watched the *One Punch Cottage Crew's* arrival with an almost amused arching of a snow-white eyebrow. His *Redcap* buddies eyed them like miffed albino mandrills sucking on lemon-coated cod-liver oil capsules, whilst Picktree wore a slightly embarrassed smile slapped over his squished and battered visage, and Dave offered a friendly little wiggle of his salami-like and oil-stained fingers.

Bob Goodfellow strode between the two groups and glowered at them for a long, heart-stopping moment; his fierce blue eyes scrutinising each and every one of them with a look of rancid suspicion.

'You all know me,' he barked at last, and his words rumbled like thunder-clouds collecting in a blackening sky. '*The Goodfellow*: High Puck of All Albion.

'We meet here, in a place that is sacred to all of the Elbi. Whosoever stands upon this blessed earth must speak the truth – or may his tongue wither in his head!'

He slammed the tip of his staff onto the ground, and sparks spiralled up and down the twisted rod.

'Whosoever stands upon this hallowed hill must cause no bloodshed. For any act of violence will be punished in the severest of manners. Am I understood?'

There was a collective mutter of agreement.

'If there is any among you who has deceit in their hearts then best that they leave now – before that heart stops beating!'

There was a collective staring at the floor as Bob scowled at them all with unwashed sternness oozing from his frowzy features. (Tom, however, did think for a moment about putting his hand up, in the hope that he might be excused and sent to a position of safety – perhaps he could wait in the car until they were all done? – but one look at the faces of The Hound and Cornelius was enough to sink that lovely thought.)

'If there is any here among you who has a weapon upon their person, then now is the time to lay it down – before that weapon burns like fire and turns that hand to ash!'

Again the tip of his staff thudded into the ground, and the air crackled with electricity.

The Goodfellow looked steadily at Cornelius (for some reason) and raised an eyebrow.

Cornelius managed to look a little offended, before returning a shake of the head that assured the Puck that he concealed no weapon.

'I 'ave zhiz canne,' wheezed the ancient and crooked Goblin, speaking with a thick French accent and lifting up his walking stick to show the gathering – and almost toppling over in the process.

'We 'ave no objectionz to that, Grandfather,' replied Archie, respectfully.

'But,' growled Cornelius, suspiciously, 'what about Edric's new 'and? That looks to me like it could do some 'arm.'

Prince Edric smiled and held the old man's eyes with a frosty stare.

'Then what about *his* teeth and claws?' he sneered in a voice like an adder's giggle, indicating The Hound with a tilt of his head. 'If *he* is willing to remove his teeth and talons, then I will gladly lay down my hand,' he grinned.

'Enough of this nonsense,' snarled Bob. 'We have come to talk, so let us talk and not squabble like children, for there are important matters that concern us all. As *Puck of the Albions* I stand here to see that all may have their say and all may be heard. It is therefore my duty to introduce you all to one another, so that no one remains unknown.

'As you have instigated this meeting, Percy, I will start with you.'

The Hound consented with a sharp nod of his massive snout.

Goodfellow cleared his throat and began.

'The Hound Who Hunts Nightmares – a long-time friend to the Fae Folk, and a well-known champion of the weak and the wronged.

'Professor Cornelius Lyons – once a prince of Avalon, who now fights for the protection and justice of us all.

'Maggs – *the ancient one*; older than the rivers, wiser than the seas, deeper than the darkest ocean.

'Archie 'Swapper' Albi – The Silver Spear; the Pook-in-waiting of the Pharisees.

'Ned Leppelin – Pharisee warrior and *The Smack Faery of All Albion*.

'Inspector Mordecai Jones – spirit-talker, and officer of the laws of men.

'Constable ... Tuggnutter – descended from the famous house of Tuggnutter, also an officer of the laws of men.

'And lastly, Prince Tomas Dearlove Adamsbane –' (Tom was convinced that someone sniggered, and he caught a muttered whisper about "losing a bet or something?") '– son of the Grendel, and a prince of the Aelfradi.'

Tom raised his head to see Edric scowling at him with eyes so pale, so cold, that they seemed to be carved from marble.

'Also to this meeting,' continued old Bob, lifting his arm to indicate Edric's party, 'have come:

'Prince Edric Bloodstone Adamsbane – a prince of the Aelfradi; *The Wild Hunter of the Hills*; the Exhibition Skirmish Champion of Lower Albion; captain of the *Redcap* society, and self-styled champion of all the, so-called, *Free-Folk*.

'Bobby Bannyster – known as "The Bad". Aelfradi warrior, *Redcap* and chieftain of Clan Bannyster.

'Long Lamkin – Aelfradi warrior and *Redcap*, who has the blood of ancient heroes coursing through his veins.

'Ek-Boran-Boranaran,' (Bob nodded towards the shifty-looking little Goblin) 'of Clan Portunes. Once the Puck of the Piskie Nation, now the *Redcap Puck*, chief advisor to Prince Edric, and, it should be noted, my former apprentice.

'Koll,' (Bob swept his arm in the direction of the hulking Goblin), 'of the Spriggan. Former member of the Bugganes but now the *Redcap* champion and chief bodyguard to Prince Edric.

'Monsieur Passereaux,' (Bob offered a little bow to the twisted old Goblin almost bent double over his walking stick), 'from our brothers, The Lutin, who has travelled from across the sea to serve Prince Edric's cause.

'Picktree Brag – the designated spokesman of the Oakman communities.

'And Dave Sternhammer – elected *captain* of the Trolls of Albion, and president of the UK lodge of the *Brotherhood Of Trolls, Hill-folk, Ogres & Marsh-people.*'

Bob Goodfellow slowly walked along the inner circumference of the standing stones, then turned and walked back again, carefully retracing his steps. He stabbed his long staff into the ground and deep thunder rolled above their heads. The Puck squinted skyward and then towards the were-hound.

'The scene is set. Percival. It is you who has called this meeting, so choose your words and speak them wisely.'

The Hound stepped forward and into the centre of the stones.

'Prince Edric,' he began. 'I have asked you here to make a request of you.'

'Request away,' smirked the pale and cruelly handsome Aelfradi prince.

'A great peril draws near.'

'*The Children of the Light* have lived with the constant threat of peril for centuries,' cut in Edric, bitterly.

'Beneath our noses a deadly game is being played,' continued the were-hound. 'As you must be only too well aware, Prince Edric, the Crowns of the Elbi Kings are now no longer in the hands of their rightful owners.'

The *Redcaps* hissed and growled beneath their breath in displeasure at the were-wolfhound's words.

'They have been stolen –'

'Or lost through gross incompetence,' sneered Edric, disdainfully.

The Hound held the prince's derisive stare for a moment before continuing.

'Both *The Summer* and *The Winter Crowns* lie in the hands of a rogue vampire by the name of Lord Manfred de Warrenne. De Warrenne seeks to possess the two remaining crowns and thus set himself up as the new High King.'

'Nonsense. This is but gossip,' sneered Edric dismissively. 'I have heard this scurrilous rumour, though I find it hard to believe. For I have met this de Warrenne. Many years ago he feasted in my hall; we have drunk from the cup of friendship together. I see him as no threat. He is a small, worthless and unambitious fellow. I have to say that I found his company quite amusing.'

'Then you have been deceived, Prince Edric. The scoundrel is powerful and ambitious beyond your understanding. For centuries he has secretly fronted an organization known as *The Society of the Wild Hunt.*'

'Are you trying to tell me that Manfred is the mysterious figure known as *The King of the Wild Hunt!*' scoffed Edric in disbelief.

'Indeed he is,' replied The Hound, sternly. 'Whose one goal has been the discovery, theft and possession of the Elbi Crowns. We are all aware of the legend – that whosoever reunites *The Crowns of Albion* will have dominion over all of the supernatural folk of Britain. Well, for centuries de Warrenne has been pursing that very quest.'

'And was it he who stole *The Autumn Crown*?' asked Prince Edric, with a questioning tilt of his head.

'Oh, he tried, Prince Bloodstone, believe me, but he was beaten to the task by another villain with the same dastardly ambitions as he.'

'How ... *fascinating*. And pray tell me – just who this other ... *villain* ... is, exactly?'

'His name was Dr Chow.'

'*Was*?'

'Dr Chow is ... dead.'

'Dead, you say? How *convenient*. And *The Autumn Crown*?'

'*The Autumn Crown* is in my possession.'

'I see,' grinned Edric with a cruel curl of his lip. 'And do the Ellyllon know of this development? I hope that they do, because they should be made aware that your record in the protection of Elbi treasures is – how shall I put it? – deplorable.'

The Hound, with a deep intake of breath, chose to ignore the prince's comment and ploughed on.

'Before his death, Dr Chow and de Warrenne had made plans for a contest, champion to champion; gambling with their ill-gotten gains and using the Elven Crowns in their possession as prizes in a deadly game. A game that was to be played over and over until one of them was victorious and held all three treasures. I have been able to keep up the subterfuge that Chow is still alive and willing to carry on with the tournament. This, as I'm sure you will understand, Prince Edric, gives us an unprecedented opportunity to reclaim the *Crowns of Summer* and *Winter* for *The Children of the Light* and thus return them, along with *The Autumn Crown,* to their rightful owners.'

'And so *you* would be the champion of my people and win back for us what is ours? Oh, how noble. You would risk the treasures of the Elbi and gamble with them as if they were mere trinkets?'

'It is our best chance of tracking down de Warrenne and his crew of the damned,' replied The Hound, somewhat defensively.

'Then perhaps it should befall to *The Children of the Light* to reclaim what is ours. I have champions a-plenty.'

'Do you really believe that you've got anybody 'oo could outfight 'Is Nibbs 'ere?' scoffed Cornelius, eyeing Edric like he was an ill-bred idiot (which, too Cornelius' mind at least, he was).

'The point,' stated The Hound, quickly taking back control of proceedings before they got out of hand, 'is not to actually take part in this uncouth and vulgar tournament at all, but to lead de Warrenne into believing that it will take place. When he turns up to the field of play, it is my plan to lay a trap and capture the irredeemable blighter and so put an end to his despicable machinations once and for all.'

Prince Edric was sullenly silent as he mulled over the were-hound's words.

'That is why I have sought you out, Prince Bloodstone. *The Society of the Wild Hunt* is a small but powerful group, perhaps if they were operating on their own we might have enough firepower to deal with them ourselves, but they are not. They have raised, reunited and rallied to their cause the once-shattered might of the iniquitous *Bucca*. Indeed, one of *The Wild Hunt's* key members has taken on the mantle of the new *Bucca-Boo*.'

'*The Bucca!*' snarled Edric. 'Ever have they been a shameful thorn in the side of my people. I had heard that they were once more daring to raise their villainous heads, but that they are in cahoots with *vampires*? I can scarce believe it. Can it be?'

'How many spears do you carry at your back, Prince Edric?' asked The Hound, earnestly.

'I have the loyalty of the *Redcaps*, the *Boggarts*, *Blue Caps*, and every brigand, from Lands End to John O'Groats, that still drives dread into the hearts of men. Among my followers I have warriors from all of the tribes of Albion – Aelfradi, Ellyllon, Sith and Sidhe, Piskie, Ferrisyn, Oakman, even,' he stated with a proud glint in his strange pale eyes, and a quick glance towards Ned and Archie, 'Pharisees. The swords of The Gentry swell my ranks, disdaining the feeble-hearted commands of their snivelling Council. Goblins from every scattered and outlawed clan. Lutin from across the sea. The cudgels of the Ogres rise at my command. The hammers of the Trolls –'

'So, roughly speaking ...? Ten? Twenty?' asked Cornelius, doing his best to wee on Edric's soliloquy.

'Nigh on a hundred swords have rallied to my banner,' continued the prince, choosing to rise above Cornelius' churlish cut-in, 'and more come every day.'

'Then join us!' insisted The Hound, a fierce light playing in his eyes. 'Join us, and we can smash these rascals, these enemies of Albion, once and for all. And then we can return *The Crowns* to their rightful owners. And then the exiled can return to their homes. And once the deed is done, I swear to you, Prince Edric Bloodstone Adamsbane, that I will not rest one day until we have discovered *The Crown of Spring* and ended the unrest that now threatens the land of Avalon!'

(This last, proud statement was accompanied by a manful squeal, which Tom hastily managed to turn into the semblance of a cough.)

Prince Edric stared hard at the were-wolfhound, turned and looked at Bob Goodfellow, chewed his lip as he examined the rich green grass that carpeted the floor beneath his iron-shod tootsies. He cast a look over his shoulder to the Goblin wizard, Ek-Boran-Boranaran, who returned the slightest and most imperceptible of nods.

'Agreed!' cried Edric at last, throwing his head back and holding The Hound's fierce look with a proud and noble one of his own. 'Until the crowns of Upper Albion are won, until this traitor de Warrenne and his band are destroyed, and *The Bucca* are sent fleeing back to their hovels, the spears of Edric Bloodstone

Adamsbane – *Iron Hand and Iron Lance, The Wild Hunter of the Hills*, the *Defender of the Free-Folk of all the Albions*, stand with you!'

And with that, the uneasiest of alliances was forged.

When such a dramatic and colourful speech is made in film and theatre, there usually follows a curtain-fall or a nifty piece of editing, however, being denied such theatrical devices, the collected gathering of the *One Punch Cottage Posse* and Prince Edric Bloodstone's entourage stood in awkward silence for a moment, not really knowing what to say or what to do (although Tom felt that, if he was given the opportunity, he had a few choice words that he would have liked to have said on the matter).

'Well that's just ... splendid,' said The Hound at last, stepping forward to offer his giant mitt to the *Redcap* prince, who regarded it as if it were ... well, as if it were the murderous paw, full of katana-like talons, belonging to a seven-and-a-half-foot tall were-wolf-wolfhound, before gingerly taking it in his own iron-cast hand (especially designed for him by the Guild of Hobgoblins) and pumping heartily away.

There was a ripple of polite (and possibly untrusting) applause from the assembled gathering (bar one), and Puck Goodfellow slapped the two leading participants on the back as if to seal the bargain.

'We have much to talk about, Prince Edric, and much to plan,' growled The Hound, eagerly, 'for the shameful contest is only but a few nights away.'

Prince Edric looked thoughtfully at the were-hound.

'If I may,' said the Aelfradi prince, a wry smirk playing across his cruel lips, 'I have a request of my own to make.'

'Request away,' chuckled The Hound, with satisfied good-humour.

'I would like to take this opportunity to have a word, in private, with my *cousin*,' he said, smiling like an anaemic tomahawk in Tom's direction. 'So much has happened recently, and I have never had the occasion to get to know the young lad. We are, after all, family.'

Tom suppressed a disdainful sneer, safe in the secure knowledge that there was absolutely no way that either The Hound or Cornelius (nor any of his other dear companions) would ever allow such a preposterous solicitation.

Ha! he thought to himself. *Best of luck with that one, you devious, transparent, odious and conniving, bloodthirsty little turd – 'coz there ain't no way on earth that that's going to be happening, let me tell you right now!*

'What a capital idea,' smiled The Hound, with a jovial wink to Tom.

'What!' meeped Tom, his knees suddenly feeling like they'd been hacked with hockey sticks, and the sour taste of vomit beginning to tap-dance on the edge of his palate.

'Can't think of a better chance for you two to get to know one another,' beamed Cornelius.

What Tom wanted to say was – "ARE YOU FRICKIN' MAD, YOU IRRESPONSIBLE PAIR OF TREACHEROUS TOSSERS?!!!!!", rather than the –

'Oh? Are you sure that's such a good idea?' that seeped from his lips like a damp fart on a warm night.

He frantically looked over to his friends and companions. Surely one of them would put a stop to this madness. But no. Each and every last one of the callous bastards smiled encouragingly at him, as if they were proud parents watching their firstborn child about to stagger through the gates on his first day at *big school*.

'There is a pleasant little clearing, just a few hundred yards over yonder, that would make a wonderful setting for a family get-together,' suggested Bob Goodfellow. 'A beautiful site, and most secluded.'

'How *perfect*,' grinned Edric, looking like a pit-bull who's just swallowed the key to the sausage factory, and who now knows that it's only a matter of time before all of his dreams come true. 'Come along, *Prince* Tomas. *Cousin*. Shall we?'

'Off you trot then, son,' beamed Cornelius, giving Tom a hearty slap on the shoulder. 'We'll see you in a bit. Take your time.'

'But ... but ...'

'But what, son?'

'Do you think that it's safe?' hissed Tom.

'Of course it is, lad. Don't worry. Edric wouldn't dare do anything ... *untoward*.'

'*Untoward!*'

'Not in such a sacred place as this, an' most definitely not with me an' 'Is Nibbs on 'and,' whispered the pitiless old lunatic encouragingly. 'Besides, it would mean sudden death to whosoever dared offer violence, so don't you start getting ideas,' he chuckled.

And so it was that Prince Bloodstone and the young Prince Dearlove, rival heirs to the Aelfradi throne and first cousins (once removed), set off for a much-anticipated Adamsbane family reunion.

SEVENTEEN
The Princes Of Albion

Tom looked over at the pale and cruelly handsome form of his delightfully charming relative (currently perched, in a state of chirpy glee, on a fallen tree trunk a few feet from where Tom himself perched, in a state of quivering purple funk, on a fallen tree trunk of his own). Edric, in turn, was regarding Tom with eyes like polished quartz and a smile like a *Devil's Coachman*.

'I see that you wear the apparel of an Aelfradi prince,' began the *Redcap*, with what he obviously considered was a tried-and-tested ice-breaker (no doubt testing the waters before he got onto the real agenda of breaking Tom's spine). 'That ... extraordinary ... *garment* ... is quite the regal shade of purple. And I see that you bear the ancient sigil of our tribe.'

Tom's hand instinctively went to the kingfisher pendant that hung from his neck.

'It was my grandmother's,' he replied, doing his utmost to keep his voice steady.

'Ah,' sighed Edric, with a chilling little curl of his lips. 'Auntie Spiritweather. How like her to choose the emblem of our people before we hid ourselves within the belly of the earth. She hated *The Hidden Realm,* you know. Always did she dream of the fresh air and the open skies of the land above our kingdom of shadows.

'I was raised in those shadows,' he smiled, possibly a little sadly.'Perhaps that is why I chose the serpent – the newer symbol of our people, in our place of exile.' He gently tapped the adder brooch that he wore upon the label of his jacket with the spidery fingers of his left hand. 'But,' he continued, leaning back, closing his colourless eyes and loudly drawing a deep and joyous breath, 'I too have learned to love the lands of Upper Albion. As an outcast I have walked beneath Her heavens, across Her bosom, along Her thighs. It is a wondrous land. Mother. Sister. Lover. A land worth fighting for, do you not think, Prince Tomas?'

'Uhm ... Yes? Yes I suppose it is.'

'It warms my heart to hear you say so,' grinned Edric, opening his eyes and rolling forward to pierce Tom with his chilling gaze. 'What, then, shall we do to save Her?'

The fight ignited like a spark.

One moment everything was calm, and the next, bloodshed had erupted like a forest fire.

Monsieur Passereaux had innocently asked Archie a question about his origins. Bad Bobby Bannyster had dropped some snide remark about the changeling's parents (both natural and adopted – not a lad to do things in half-measures was Bad Bobby Bannyster). Archie had told him to watch his tongue or there'd be *what for* (or words to that effect). Bad Bobby had responded that he wasn't going to be reprimanded by a *false prince* who had no right to lead a people that he didn't even have any ties of blood to. Archie, using all of the skills of diplomacy that he had learned from his adopted father (Alberich Albi – the recently deceased nineteenth Pook of the Pharisees) had told Bobby to piss off before he slapped some manners into his ill-conceived hide. Bad Bobby had miraculously drawn a lethal-looking short sword from the folds of his jacket and had leapt at Archie with the look of the confirmed homicidal maniac tattooed upon his baboon-like features. Archie, in turn, had produced a short-handled scalping-putter from the sleeve of his coat, parried Bobby Bannyster's murderous blow, and, faster than the flash of a firefly's bottom, had shattered Bobby's knee with one stroke and then embedded the head of said putter in the back of the *Redcap* warrior's skull with another.

'You see,' smiled Edric, leaning even further forwards and resting his chin upon his beautifully-crafted metal hand, 'when I was first *exiled* from Avalon, my one thought was on becoming a *hero*. I dreamt of how I would seek out and battle the enemies of my people. Like a fabled champion of old, I would scour the land of our oppressors until we were once again free. And how – I imagined – how *The People* would rally to me. Oh, I would fight great wars for them and carve a name that would be sung for centuries to come in the halls of *The Children of the Light*. And if I died along the way? Well, what a glorious death it would be! For what is this life without renown and glory, I ask you?'

'What indeed?' agreed Tom, doing his best to sound encouraging whilst hastily scanning the tree line for his best route of escape.

'But then I began to ask myself – *just who would be around to tell those tales? Or even listen to them*? We, as you are no doubt aware, *Prince* Tomas, are a people who are fading from this world.'

Tom gave Edric his most understanding smile, and surreptitiously edged his hand towards the hefty-looking stick that he had noticed was propped against the trunk that he was sitting on.

'Do you know, I almost gave up on the whole *Champion of the Fae World* malarkey when I lost my hand,' sighed Edric, lifting his iron paw before his face and turning it back and forth as he closely examined its intricate design. 'It certainly puts the *consequences of violence* well and truly into perspective, let me tell you. But do you know what, Tomas? You don't mind if I call you Tomas, do you?'

'Hmmm? No. No, not at all,' squeaked Tom, keeping a keen eye on Edric's raised and mace-like mitt.

'It was a new beginning,' he purred, in a voice as chilling as broken glass. 'You see, as I contemplated returning home, with my tail well and truly tucked betwixt my legs, a funny thing happened.'

'Oh? Really? *Funny*, you say? Hhhmmm. Do tell.'

'*The People* – Elves, Goblins, Trolls, all manner of the Enchanted Children – actually did begin to rally to my banner. You see, they *were* looking for someone, anyone, who would step up to the plate (so to speak) and challenge the accepted view that we should walk meekly to our doom without a whimper. They wanted that hero, you see. They needed a beacon of hope; anything or anybody who could make them feel that all was not lost. And, somehow, for many of them, I became that hero.'

'Well, that's absolutely lovely,' beamed Tom, enthusiastically. 'I can't begin to tell you how happy I am for you.'

Edric grinned like a crocodile who's been dreaming of snacking on the zookeeper all morning and has just heard the clock chime for feeding-time.

'And the more I travelled through *Upper Albion*,' he continued, 'and the more I spoke to its inhabitants, the more sure I became. What I saw, what I heard, filled me with such disgust, such outrage for what has been done, for what has been lost, that it changed me, Tomas. And do you know what, *Cousin?*'

'Uhm. No.'

'I re-evaluated my whole life; my very existence. Oh, what a pompous, selfish and arrogant fool I had been, I realised. Truth be told, Tomas, I became more than a little ashamed of myself. And the more I thought about it, the more I came to understand that old Tommy Rawhead-and-Bloody-Bones might just have been right all along.'

'He might?' replied Tom, suddenly perking up – for this didn't sound quite so bad. After all, the deluded old loon (Tommy Rawhead-and-Bloody-Bones, that is) was all for peace, reconciliation and that sort of thing.

'Well, almost,' grinned Edric, holding Tom's hopeful look and crushing it with a smile that would have had the Sheriff of Nottingham reaching for a mirror to practise in. 'For while I am under no illusion that we could hope to defeat the cursed humans in any sort of a war, that does not mean that we should go down without a struggle, does it? In fact, why go down at all? I have come to understand that what is needed is for us to present a united front to the humans – not to challenge them of course, but to make them listen, to be able talk to them from a position of strength; for strength seems to be the only thing that they seem to respect. If we remain divided then they will pick us off, one by one, until our voices and our songs have vanished from the world.'

'What monsters they have become, Prince Tomas, these *humans*. When I was a young Elfling they used to give me nightmares. To let you into a little secret, *Cousin,* they still do. How, and why, in such a short space of time, have they destroyed so much? They are like children, Tomas: arrogant, short-sighted children, puffed-up with their own importance and their own sense of achievement.

'See what they have done to this sacred and bountiful land. Observe their terrifying achievements. Look at the hideous cities that they have built: pouring poison into the sky; venom into the sea; death into the earth. Oh, how their concrete roads score the skin of our Mother like whipping-scars!

'How can we let them do this? How can we let them so wound our Sister? Mutilate our Lover?

'They are blind, Tomas, blind. Take, for example, these ... these *roads*, these *motorways* that they build, with no thought or care for anything other than their own short-sighted needs. When they see that there are too many cars upon them, do they say *"We should have fewer cars"*? No, they say *"We need more roads. Better roads. Bigger roads!"* And so they go on and on and on, foolishly, selfishly, mutilating the world in which they live and depriving every other species the right to life. They have made a hell and call it *Heaven*.

'I have asked myself a thousand times – why have the Old Gods not risen up and destroyed them for their crimes? Why?'

'Often thought that very same thing myself, Edric. You don't mind if I call you Edric, do you?' offered Tom, doing his very best to nurture a feeling of fellowship. Not that it seemed to matter much, for Prince Edric was lost in the swing of things, and it seemed doubtful that he even noticed that Tom had actually spoken.

'And then it came to me. It is *we* who have failed our Mother; for it is *we* who should have stopped them in their tracks in the first place. It is we who are as responsible for this carnage as much the hated *sons of Adam*; for it was our duty to protect our Mother ... and we have failed Her. Why else have we been punished so? We are the *Children of the Dawn*, Her children, just as men are surely the *Children of Sunset*. We should have been like older siblings to them.'

'Siblings? Yes. Yes of course. Good Lord! Is that the time already? Blimey! I suppose they'll be beginning to get worried about us by now –'

'As they bow down to a Father who demands that they *obey*, we still follow a Mother who *inspires* us to be independent and considerate souls. They must be *educated*, Tomas. Saved. They must be halted in their actions before it is too late, for all of us. And it is *we* who must do it.'

'Oh well said, old chap! Now, what say you, we go and talk about this in further detail over a flask of hot tea and a packet of Hobnobs?' I'm pretty sure that Professor Lyons left some in the car –'

'And it is to *I* that this mantle, this great burden – this great honour – has fallen. It is *I* who must unite the *Children of Enchantment*. The old divides must be put aside. Elbi, Sidhe, Goblins, Trolls, Giants, and all who wish to walk beneath the splendour of the sun, must come together as one.'

'Spot on, Edric, old chum. Well, now that that's all cleared up, let's start heading back before the old rascal scoffs all the bickies –'

'So, here I stand, *Cousin,* not only the chosen champion of the Magic Realms but also the heir to the crown of the proud and most noble and warlike nation of the Aelfradi. But,' smiled Edric, standing up and taking a step towards Tom, 'there still remains a rather trifling and irritating little problem to be dealt with.'

'There does?' meeped Tom, scuttling backwards on trembling buttocks, and inwardly cursing as the hefty-looking stick toppled to the floor and away from the clumsy clutches of his fumbling fingers. 'Oh? Heh … and what's that?' he asked innocently, though he had a sphincter-rattling idea of just what it might be.

Edric loomed over him with a face like an esurient ermine cornering a rather rotund rabbit.

'You, *Cousin*,' he grinned. 'You.'

The threat of further bloodshed bubbled on the edge of boiling point.

Archie Swapper suddenly gave a gasp and dropped his battle-putter, as the haft withered to hot ashes in his hand. And then, like a badly rehearsed barbershop choir, a round of gasps, rasps and cries of surprise filled the blood-splattered clearing as, in turn, scorching weapon after scorching weapon was hastily cast to the floor: Ned fumbled his beloved number-three-iron; Inspector Jones' pistol glowed like raked coals; Constable Tuggnutter's truncheon burst into flames; even the sword-length needle and wicker shield that Old Maggs had *magically* produced from her shoulder bag clattered to the floor, billowing smoke. From the other side of the clearing Long Lamkin screeched as the crossbow that he held in his hands erupted into flames, Kroll desperately held onto his smouldering war-club for as long as he could, before dropping it like a hot potato (or red-hot war-club), and Ek-Boran-Boranaran cursed in anguish as his double-ended spear curled like a match lit at both ends and vanished into cinders before his eyes.

Dave Sternhammer and Picktree Bragg (who had both remained *sans weapon* throughout the whole ugly incident) looked on aghast, wondering just what they had gotten themselves into.

But perhaps the most shocked of all (well, perhaps "disappointed" would be a more apt term) was Cornelius Lyons, who looked thoroughly disgusted with himself for being the only member of the *One Punch Cottage Crew* not to have thought of bringing a weapon to the peace conference (bar, of course, The Hound – who was naturally [and quite literally] always armed to the teeth).

'Bugger! Bugger! Bugger! That was supposed to work a lot quicker than it did,' muttered Bob Goodfellow, as he peered from the smouldering remains of the weapons of war scattered around the clearing and over to the pulverised body of Bad Bobby Bannyster.

Cornelius walked up beside him.

'Well if that weren't self-defence,' growled the old fellow, casting a defiant look at the seething *Redcaps*, 'then I'll eat my 'at.'

'No doubt about it in my mind,' muttered Picktree Bragg.

'Mine neither,' said Dave Sternhammer, sternly.

And slowly, one by one, the three remaining *Redcaps* nodded their consent.

The rather awkward silence that followed was suddenly broken by what sounded like an orang-utan getting his todger caught in the fly-zip of his trousers.

'OO-OO-HOO-HOO-O-O-O-O-AAAAAAAAAAAGGGGGHHHHH!!!!!!!!'

'Believe me, Edric, Cousin!' cried Tom, hastily. 'Let me assure you, right away, that I have absolutely no desire whatsoever on becoming the King of Avalon.'

Prince Edric stepped back and tilted his serpent-like head (and, in consequence, his fancy braided barnet) to one side.

'You don't?' he asked, looking somewhat appalled, and sounding more than a little disappointed. 'But I think you'd make a rather excellent Pook.'

'No, no, I don't think you heard me corre- You what?!' spluttered Tom, struggling to believe what he had just heard, and rapidly trying to digest the consequences. 'But ... but I thought, I mean ... I expected ... that you, you know, ... wanted to ... [gulp] kill me; what with me – through no fault of my own whatsoever – being forced – very much against my will, you understand – to be your rival to the Aelfradi Crown.'

Edric slumped back down on the tree trunk and shook his head.

'Whatever gave you that idea, Tomas?'

'Hhhhmmm?' gurned Tom, awkwardly. *Perhaps it could be the fact that everybody says you're a bloodthirsty, grasping little shite who would slit his own mother's throat if you thought it would help you to get closer to putting your slimy hands (sorry – hand [how insensitive of me]), on The Crown of Avalon. Plus the undeniable fact that you're well-known (dare one say, infamous) for being the guiding light behind the resurgence in popularity of the (supposedly outlawed) human-hating goblin war-society known as the Redcaps – a delightful little private-members club, whose favourite pastime, in fact their whole manifesto, would appear to be dyeing their clothes in the freshly-spilled blood of freshly-murdered humans. So, what with me being – as I'm sure that you're only too well aware, Prince Edric, my darling cousin, (and let me just take this opportunity to thank you for being so wonderfully sensitive in not bringing it to anyone's attention) – more human than Elbi, and also the only obstacle to you achieving your lifetime ambition of sovereignty, well, I'm sure that you can imagine my ... concerns.*

'Oh, uhm? I don't know really. It's just the feeling that I got ... about ... *things*,' he managed to say, suddenly feeling a little flabbergasted by this unexpected turnabout in events. (And there was no point in being rude, after all. Especially not to someone who you thought, only a few short, bowel-quivering moments ago, was on the verge of tearing your jugular out with their teeth.)

'Oh. I see,' huffed Edric, looking somewhat offended. 'Well, I'm awfully sorry if I gave you that impression, Tomas. But really, that's been the last thing on my mind.'

'What! Really? But what about this blasted "Death-Match" that we're supposed to have when I'm sixteen? You know ... to decide who is the *rightful* King of the Aelfradi?'

'Oh that. Well, I don't know about you, Cousin, but bugger that for a game of soldiers.'

Tom could feel himself rapidly perking-up. All those restless nights, worrying himself into a state of nervous exhaustion, crying himself to sleep, for, as it turned out (oh happy day indeed), naught.

'But I thought that we have to fight? I mean, isn't it expected of us?'

'Alas, I'm afraid you're right, Tomas, Aelfradi law does demand it.'

Oh God! thought Tom, readying himself for the worst and almost soiling himself in terror. *Here we go.*

'However, I have a plan.'

'You do?'

'There is a way around it.'

'There is?' gasped Tom, now almost sobbing with relief.

'Indeed,' smiled Edric, springing up from his seat and looking like the cat who's about to get the cream with a dollop of sardine sauce on top. 'Ancient law dictates that there *is* a way that there can be two living heirs to the throne of Avalon ... *if* ...'

'Yes! Go on! Go on!'

'If one of them is the Oberon. The High Pook. The King of All Albion,' smiled Edric. 'For you see, Tomas, I've realised that I have a greater path to follow; not just to be the monarch of a dying kingdom, *The Lord of the Land of Shadows.* No. Not just to be the champion and shield of a fading world.

'For I see a vision of the future. I see a hope. And that hope glows like a tiny spark in our hands. And, with care, that spark can be kindled and fanned into a mighty flame! For you are that hope, Prince Tomas! With you by my side – and let me just say that the very fact that you have even been born makes it a whole other ball game entirely, Tomas, believe me – just think what we ca–'

Tom suddenly went blind. It was as if someone had chucked a bucket of lukewarm onion soup in his face.

'Ergh!' he spluttered, somewhat in shock. But his shock was to grow to hitherto unexpected new heights, and he couldn't help but emit a strange and otherworldly cry.

'OO-OO-HOO-HOO-O-O-O-O-AAAAAAAAAAAGGGGGHHHHH!!!!!!!!!!' he wailed; for, as he wiped the "soup" from his eyes (so to speak), he couldn't help but notice that Prince Edric was seeping slowly to the floor, and that half of his head, and half of his beautifully quaffed hair-do, was missing, and what did remain seemed to be pumping a fountain of blood and gore in all conceivable directions.

EIGHTEEN
The Assassin's Creed

'My God, what have you done, Tom?' cried The Hound, as he dashed from the trees and into the clearing where sat Tom (in a state of static trauma, and looking like he'd been dowsed in raspberry porridge), while the still-twitching figure of Prince Edric lay, near-headless, at his feet and well past the point where mouth-to-mouth resuscitation was even the remotest of considerations.

'I didn't do anything!' meeped Tom.

'They'll hang you for this, you fool!' snapped the were-hound in panic, just as the rest of the gathering caught up with The Hound and stumbled to a shocked halt as they took in the ghastly scene before them.

'You have broken the sacred laws of safe-conduct, Prince Dearlove!' hissed Bob Goodfellow, leaning heavily on his twisted staff and eyeing Edric's corpse with rancid horror. 'The punishment for which ... is DEATH!'

'But I didn't touch him!' pleaded Tom. 'You've got to believe me! We were having a ... chat ... and getting on rather well when ...'

'Yes?' demanded the Puck, eyeing him like he was a virus.

'When his head ... suddenly ... exploded!' snivelled Tom.

He sunk his own (unexploded) head into his hands and sobbed.

Cornelius came up and put his arm around Tom.

'I believe you, son. You know that, don't you,' said the old codger, with a comforting squeeze of Tom's shoulder. 'But I do 'ave to say that it doesn't look good, lad.' And then he leant in closer and whispered in his ear. 'Mind you, I couldn't 'ave done a better job of it myself,' he chuckled with a lightning-fast wink.

Tom stormed to his feet and swept the callous old bastard's hand away.

'But I didn't do it!' he cried, weeping at the injustice of it all.

'Kill him!' snarled Long Lamkin, watching Tom with red murder raging in his cold pale eyes.

'The Law demands his death!' howled Ek-Boran-Boranaran, jigging on the spot in outrage.

And then the hulking Goblin, Koll, lumbered forward and chose to eloquently express his feelings on the matter.

'Kill the Grendel's son!' he snorted. 'Kill him! Kill him! Kill him!'

'Now steady on,' growled The Hound, stepping forward to stand at Tom's side. 'Prince Dearlove protests his innocence. Let us first hear what he has to say,' he reasoned, steadfastly staring at each *Redcap* in turn.

'What is there to discuss?' weaseled Ek-Boran, his words as sly and slippery as an oiled stoat. 'Prince Edric is left alone with his one rival to the throne of *The Hidden Realm*, and now he lies dead at that rivals' feet, with his skull shattered and half his brains strewn across the forest floor! It must seem most obvious to all what has occurred here.'

There was a bustle of movement from the edge of the trees and into the clearing waddled the enormous form of Constable Tuggnutter. In one hand he held what could only be described as a long-barrelled, state of the art sniper's rifle, and under his other arm he carried the slender and frantically-struggling form of a lanky teenage boy.

Tuggnutter mumbled something unintelligible and then hurled the kicking and violently cursing figure to the ground.

The boy landed in a sprawled mess and then quickly rolled to a crouched position, his head held down and at a menacing angle, clearly ready to spring at the first one who dared to approach him. He was tall and gangly, dressed in ripped jeans and a leather bomber-jacket that was several sizes too large for him. On his head he wore a grey-and-black-striped beanie hat, beneath which was a thick and short-cut shock of bright yellow hair.

The astounded gathering quickly formed a hostile circle around him.

Slowly, the strange boy looked up at his captors.

Tom's heart skipped a beat; for staring back at him was a pale and freckled face with a long sharp nose and the most beautiful, liquid-brown eyes that he had ever seen.

'Crow!' he gasped.

'Crow?' spluttered The Hound in astonishment, as he stepped forward and plucked the woollen hat from her head. 'What the devil is the meaning of this? Just what are you about?'

She had dyed her hair blonde and cut it short, in a *boyish* style, and Tom couldn't help but think that it suited her; somehow made her look more grown-up. And, ridiculously, he suddenly felt embarrassed. What must he look like? His face covered in blood and gore, and dressed, as he was, in an oversized purple parka that wouldn't look amiss on a toddler.

'You know this boy?' snarled Long Lamkin.

'Girl,' replied The Hound, and for once he seemed to be struggling for words. 'Yes. Yes I do. She ... she ...'

'She is an MI Unseen agent,' growled Bob, regarding Crow with look of uncertain regret.

'MI Unseen!' gasped Picktree Brag. 'Why the flipping heck would they want to kill Prince Edric?'

'Why indeed?' repeated The Hound, suspiciously.

'They haven't got anything to do with me being here,' snapped Crow, contemptuously.

'So you weren't following MI Unseen orders?' quizzed Cornelius.

Crow screwed tight her lips and shook her head.

'Then why, lass?' pleaded the kindly old codger, looking like he might be about to burst into tears.

'Kill her!' hissed Long Lamkin.

'The Law demands it!' screeched Ek-Boran-Boranaran, hopping from one foot to the other in anticipation of a swift and bloody revenge.

'Kill her! Kill her! Kill her!' chanted Koll (quite obviously the captain of the *Redcap's* debating society), eagerly looking over to Bob Goodfellow and expectantly waiting for him to give the command.

'But I didn't do it,' said Crow, calmly.

'Oh, Miss Crow,' sighed Inspector Jones, with a haunted and worried frown. 'I'm afraid that all the evidence would suggest otherwise.'

'No it doesn't,' she replied. 'I *wanted* to do it, believe me. In fact, I *meant* to do it. But, when it came to it, I just *couldn't* do it. So, please, be a good detective, Inspector Jones, and start detecting.'

'But the gun!' shrieked Ek-Boran-Boranaran, pointing rather dramatically at the sniper's rifle in Constable Tuggnutter's hand.

The Hound reached forward, took the rifle from the D.S.C. officer and sniffed the muzzle.

'This weapon has not been fired,' he stated, giving Crow a quizzical look.

Crow stood up and folded her arms triumphantly across her chest.

'Zhen 'ow do you explain zhis?' came a heavily-accented French voice.

They turned as one to see the crooked old Lutin, Monsieur Passereaux, hobbling towards them with surprising agility. He rattled to a halt before the were-hound and looked up at him. Tom couldn't help but notice how his eyes sparkled with a youthful vigour that was somehow as endearing as it was unexpected. The ancient Goblin slowly unfurled his gnarled and twisted fist to reveal a solitary spent cartridge shell in the palm of his hand.

The Hound snatched it up, sniffed it, and then tested it against the ammunition still loaded in the rifle.

It was a perfect match.

'No!' gasped Crow, looking horrified. 'That can't be!'

'The matter is concluded,' smirked Ek-Boran-Boranaran. 'Kill the girl.'

'I didn't do it!'

Koll moved menacingly towards Crow.

'Take another step forward, Koll, and it will be your last,' said the were-hound, gently and softly.

The husky Goblin stopped dead in his tracks.

'There is something amiss about all this,' continued The Hound, addressing Bob Goodfellow, but keeping his eyes firmly fixed on Koll. 'Something that doesn't quite add up. I suggest that, for the meantime, Miss Crow is placed under the custody of Inspector Jones; who will immediately escort her to The Mound for safekeeping until the truth of the matter can be established. Should it be discovered that it was indeed she who committed this heinous crime, then of course she will be handed over to the Aelfradi, according to and under clause *3.17a - paragraph 5* of the *Learmonth Agreement*. If it was not her, then I am sure that her *superiors* will have something to say regarding her conduct.'

'Agreed,' said The Goodfellow.

The *Redcaps* snarled their displeasure, but reluctantly nodded their consent.

'Inspector, if you would be so kind,' said The Hound.

Inspector Jones walked over and gently handcuffed Crow.

'I'll be in touch as soon as everything's sorted, Mr Hound,' he replied. 'This way, Miss Crow,' he said, carefully escorting the young Half-Elf from the scene, with Constable Tuggnutter lumbering in tow.

As she walked past the were-hound, Crow turned and looked up at him.

'Thank you, Mr H,' she said. 'At least somebody's thinking straight.'

And then, as she was being led away, she turned once more, looked Tom squarely in the eyes, and smiled as bravely as she knew how.

NINETEEN
Should All Your Dreams Come True

Tom was heading towards Old Nancy, escorted by Cornelius and Maggs, when he heard Bob Goodfellow call out.

'One moment, if you will, Prince Dearlove.'

If anyone calls me "Prince anything" again, I'm going to smash their frickin' teeth in, he thought to himself.

He turned to see the filthy old scarecrow walking towards him, with the delightful figures of Long Lamkin, Ek-Boran-Boranaran, Koll, Picktree Bragg and Dave Sternhammer following in his wake like the cheese-filled promise of a nightmare

'What is it, Bob?' asked Cornelius, stiffening a little as he saw the collected posse striding purposefully towards them.

'Before you leave, Long Lamkin would have words with the Prince.'

'What do you want?' asked Tom, uneasily regarding the proud and gangling *Redcap* warrior (and legendary Bogeyman, first-class) striding resolutely towards him.

To his own ears his voice sounded flat. His limbs felt numb, his mind was blank, and he didn't know how, or if, he would ever come to terms with what had just happened: the assassination of Prince Edric, right before his very eyes – (he was convinced that he could still taste his cousin's [once-removed] [permanently removed] brains, and was desperately struggling to keep himself from vomiting) – who, it turned out, might actually have been an all right sort of bloke, after all. And then there was Crow. Crow! What had she been thinking? And whatever would become of her?

'Prince Edric is dead,' stated Lamkin, in a voice like a knife plunged into darkness.

'Really?' sneered Tom. 'I hadn't noticed.'

The Aelfradi looked at him for a moment, as if trying to make sense of his words. Tom was worryingly convinced that the infamous old murderer was going to punch him, but the *Redcap* slowly smiled (which was a truly ghastly sight) and then knelt to the floor and bowed his braided head.

'You are the one true Prince of Avalon,' he hissed. '*The Pook of Shadows*. I give to you my sword, my heart and my undying loyalty.

'Long live the Prince!' he cried. 'The Prince of Avalon! Son of the Grendel – Prince Dearlove! Long live *The Adamsbane!*'

And then the rest of the demented cretins took up the chant.

'Long live the Prince!' they roared. '*The Adamsbane! The Adamsbane! The Adamsbane!*'

Well isn't this the perfect end to the perfect day, thought Tom, as Lamkin stretched forward and kissed the back of Tom's hand. *Should all my dreams come true ...*

'What would you have us do, my prince?' asked Long Lamkin, standing up and regarding Tom with a look of moist reverence in his hideous eyes.

'Er ..?'

'You should say something, Tom,' whispered Cornelius in his ear, whilst giving him a gentle nudge of the elbow.

'Erhm ... yes. Yes of course.'

Tom took a moment to collect his thoughts and carefully studied the expectant faces of the nightmarish lunatics gathered before him, hoping that inspiration would come.

'Uhm? So ... what will be done with Edric?' he enquired, partly because it was the first thing that came into his head and partly because he had the feeling that it might be the done thing to ask.

'His body will be carried to *The White Hall of Avalon*,' whispered Bob Goodfellow, solemnly, 'where he will be laid to rest beside the other heroes of his proud name.'

'Good,' sniffed Tom, nodding vigorously and doing his best to sound princely. 'Good.'

'What of us?' asked Long Lamkin.

And then a strange thing happened. Tom had the instant, and quite unexpected, realisation that here was an unprecedented chance to do some good: to honour Edric's dreams; to serve the Elbi people. (He was, after all, an Elven prince, and soon-to-be a king. The King of Avalon. Monarch of the mighty Aelfradi. *The Pook of Shadows – We should really get on with finding that Crown of Spring, you know*.) And suddenly he knew where his duty lay.

'Our first concern must be the protection of all of *The Enchanted Children* of *All* the Albions,' he began, and he knew it to be true. 'The old divides must be put aside,' he stated, desperately trying to remember Edric's words. 'Elbi, Goblins ... er ... Trolls, and all who wish to go on a ... sunny walk, must get together.'

'Truly you are a scion of the house of Adamsbane,' swore Lamkin, his colourless eyes blazing with a righteous fury. 'A champion in our hour of need. It will be done, my prince! The Free-Folk will stand proudly beneath your banner in your quest for justice, you have my word on it.'

'And mine,' grinned Dave, giving Tom a hearty double thumbs-up.

And then the rest of them joined in, promising their allegiance to the cause and swearing that it was the noblest thing that they had ever heard.

Cornelius gave Tom a congratulatory pat on the back and headed for the car, Maggs planted a warm kiss on Tom's cheek and followed after the old codger, and old Bob Goodfellow did his best to mask his pleasure.

'Well that's just ... swell,' Tom managed to say. And despite his misgivings he couldn't help but get caught up in the moment. It was funny, but becoming a prince felt a little like putting on a warm and comfortable coat (unlike the hideous purple monstrosity that he was currently wearing). 'I suppose that the best thing for the moment would be ... urhm ... ah yes, if you worked with The Hound; follow his plans, do as he asks you, that sort of thing. He knows ... my ... er ...wishes on the subject ... For I see a ... vision ... of the future. I see a hope,' he cried, and suddenly his voice warmed and he heard himself beginning to sound like Lawrence Olivier's *Henry V*. 'And that hope glows like a tiny ... sparkler in our hands. With care, that sparkler can be ... wiggled and waved frantically about until it becomes a mighty flame! For we *will* rise again! We few, we happy few, we band of brothers! And we will take our place, somehow, some day ... somewhere ... beneath the blessed stars of Albion! We'll find a new way of living! We'll find a new way of giving! Hold my hand and I'll ... take you there (?) ... No ... ah, no. Wait, hang on ... Long live the Aelfradi! Long live *The Children of the Light*! And long live all of *The Enchanted Folk*! Thank you and goodnight. For I must away now,' [*and wash the remains of Edric's brains from my hair; for I fear that some of it might be beginning to seep through [urgh!], because I'm starting to sound like the pompous old twit!*] 'but we shall soon meet again, don't know where, don't know ... no ... I mean ... we will all meet very soon and ... uhm ... er ... smite(?) ... the enemies of ... us ... we ... *The People* (starting with this odious toad, de Warrenne and his devilish pack of nefariousnesseses) and then–Argghh!'

Old Maggs swung open the rear door of Old Nancy, grabbed Tom by the scruff of his billowing purple hood, and hastily yanked his royal carcass onto the back seat. Cornelius, who'd long since got the engine running, gave a jaunty tug of the forelock to Tom's awed subjects, before putting pedal to the metal and beginning the long drive back home to One Punch Cottage, as Tom waved regally from the window, to cheers that proclaimed him to be the saviour of all *The Magic Realms*.

TWENTY
Friends In Need

'That was close-run thing,' puffed The Hound, as he paused to examine the Stilton, brown sauce, and peanut butter toastie that he cradled in the tips of his claws. 'If not for that quite ... *remarkable* speech that you gave, Tom (and Bob told me just how *extraordinary* it was, in case you're wondering), it's probable that Edric's followers would have disbanded there and then and gone their separate ways – thus leaving us in desperate straits in regard to our plan to capture de Warrenne and regain the lost *Crowns of Albion*.'

Tom offered a smile that he didn't really feel, and contemplated the small mountain of toasties (prepared by Missus Dobbs on their return to One Punch Cottage) which were neatly stacked before him on the kitchen table. Truth be told, he wasn't hungry. All he could see (and, rather unpleasantly, taste) was the image of Edric twitching on the floor with the top of his head missing and his brains dribbling in all directions like the insides of a dropped egg.

That and, of course, Crow.

'When can we go and see Crow?' he asked.

'I've arranged with Governor Butterworth for us to visit her tomorrow morning, Tom. But first we must attend to our strategy for the upcoming vampire-hunt, for we have only a few days left until the arrival of the full moon and with it the chance to finally finish de Warrenne and his contemptible cronies once and for all. As soon as we are done with the preparations, we'll head straight off to The Mound, I promise, Tom,' replied the were-hound, kindly.

'You don't think that she did do it, do you?'

'Well, I have to admit that at first glance things do not look *good*, Tom. *But*, and it's a big *but*, there's something very suspicious about the whole affair. While there can be little doubt that Crow went to Ondred's Wood with the intent of killing Prince Edric, I believe her when she says that when it actually came to performing her misguided task, she was simply unable to pull the trigger. Young Miss Crow may be many things (and not all of them quite savoury) but I do not think that *cold-blooded murderer* is one of them.'

'Then who did kill him?'

'I have my suspicions,' growled The Hound, eyeing the blue cheese toastie suspiciously.

'Go on then, 'Aitch,' scowled Cornelius, teasing a thread of escaped cheese from his moustache.

'When the disagreement between Archie and Bad Bobby Bannyster flared into bloodshed (a fray that was, it should be noted, ignited by the seemingly innocent questions of Monsieur Passereaux), for the life of me I can't remember seeing our Lutin *friend* anywhere in the vicinity. Of course, my attention was absorbed by the mortal combat between *Bad Bobby* and *The Silver Spear*, but the more I think on it, I don't recall seeing Monsieur Passereaux again until he reappeared with the incriminating spent-cartridge shell in his hand.'

'Now that you mention it,' chomped Cornelius, having finally untangled the cheese string from his whiskers and devouring it like a walrus sucking on spaghetti, 'neither do I.'

'Add to that his rapid exit from the scene, after Crow was led away, and I'd say that it all begins to look more than a little dubious.'

'What do we know about this Monsieur Passereaux?' asked Tom.

'Very little. When I asked Long Lamkin what he knew of him, he told me that the old fellow had been with Edric for a little over two months. Not unusual in itself, but he does seem to have worked his way into a position of trust very quickly. I've sent a message over to our dear friend, Monsieur Saterelle, to see what information he can offer in regard to his compatriot.'

'So let me get this right, 'Aitch,' said Cornelius, twirling his mower back into shape, 'you think that when the dust-up broke out between Archie an' Bad Bobby Bannyster, this Passereaux fellow snuck off an' shot Edric?'

'It would appear to be the logical conclusion.'

'But then why return and hand over the bullet?' asked Tom. 'Why not make the kill and get as far away from the scene as quickly as possible?'

'An interesting point, Tom,' nodded The Hound, tapping the toastie against the tip of his snout. 'Let us suppose that Monsieur Passereaux *is* our killer. Let us suppose that he deliberately caused a distraction, thus creating the opportunity for him to carry out his despicable task. He takes his shot, makes his kill and, for whatever reason, hangs around to watch the outcome. It takes a matter of seconds from Tom's warning cry for me to arrive on the scene, followed only a few moments later by the rest of the gathering. Shortly after that, Constable Tuggnutter comes across Crow and drags her to the site of the crime. If Passereaux sees this, he would immediately know that it would offer him an excellent, and hitherto unexpected, cover for his actions.'

'But what about the matching ammunition?' asked Tom, 'And where did he get the gun?'

'Could 'ave 'idden a weapon in the woods before'and,' muttered Cornelius. 'Could very well be that that cane of 'is was some sort of gun-stick.'

'Yes! Yes you're right!' gasped Tom. 'Just like in "*The Day of the Jackal*"!'

'Maybe, son. But what I don't understand is 'ow the bullet that killed Edric was identical in make to those in Crow's rifle. 'Ere? What's up, 'Aitch?'

'Oh dear, oh dear, oh dear,' sighed the were-hound, distractedly gnawing on the crust of his toastie. 'I'm afraid that this is all leading us to a truly terrible conclusion.'

'An' what's that?' asked the old codger, reaching for his teacup.

'Crow's gun was undoubtedly of MI Unseen issue; where else, I ask you, would she have been able to get her hands on such state of the art equipment? Therefore –'

'Good grief!' cried Tom. 'Therefore, Monsieur Passereaux is an MI Unseen assassin!'

Cornelius spluttered tea in all directions.

'If that *is* true,' said The Hound, his eyes filled with a wretched horror, 'then I fear the very worst; not only for the continued freedom of the Fae Folk of *The Two Albions*, but for young Crow's safety.'

Planning the trap for de Warrenne and *The Society of the Wild Hunt* seemed to take forever. Tom did his best to mask his frustrations and appear keenly interested in proceedings, but all he could think about was Crow. The Hound's main concern was how to conceal nigh on a hundred of Edric's *Free Folk* warriors in an area without much natural cover; for if de Warrenne caught even a whiff of anything untoward, then there was no doubt in anybody's mind that he would cancel the whole engagement – and then they would be back to square one in regard of the apprehension and the recovery of the lost crowns of *Winter* and *Summer*.

Also, once a plan of action was finally agreed upon, there remained the problem of getting everything into place without being observed. (The Hound was under no illusion that, having agreed to the site for the *contest* to take place, and hoping to set a trap of his own, de Warrenne would be staking out the venue for his own double-crossing purposes; for there was no doubt that the vampire meant to play Dr Chow false.)

Finally, when all that *could* be done *had* been done to the were-hound's exacting satisfaction, they at last set off to The Mound; Tom and The Hound travelling with Inspector Jones, while Cornelius and the rest of the team stayed put to lay the finishing touches to the final preparations.

On their arrival at The Mound (the secret, Government-funded prison for *supernatural* criminals, political prisoners, refugees, and those who were deemed as being just too dangerous to be allowed to wander the streets freely), they were met by the charming and friendly figure of Agent Fowler, who quickly led them through a labyrinth of clinical-looking and near-identical and soulless corridors, until they came to a large set of doors with the words "Visiting Room" written over them.

'Crow is in there; cubicle number seven,' smiled Agent Fowler, kind-heartedly. 'She's just with another visitor at the moment, so if you'd like to take a seat over in the waiting-room. I'll give you a call when she's ready.

'Mr Hound, could I have a quick word with you?'

'Of course, Agent Fowler,' replied the were-hound. 'Tom, Inspector, take a seat and I'll be with you in one moment.'

Tom and Inspector Jones went to the waiting-room and sat down on the clinically clean, but quite astoundingly uncomfortable, chairs.

Inspector Jones fleetingly picked up the solitary magazine from the low-slung coffee table before them (a copy of *Heat Magazine* from 2002) before standing up and walking over to examine what delights the coffee-machine might have to offer.

Tom watched him with a feeling of nervousness continuing to grow in the pit of his stomach, and wondered just who could be visiting Crow.

'There's someone, a friend, who wants to talk to you, Mr Hound,' whispered Agent Fowler discreetly. 'In an *unofficial* capacity, if you follow me,' she added, not holding the were-wolfhound's inquisitive gaze.

'Is there indeed?'

'If you would be so good as to step this way, Mr Hound, they'll be waiting for you in that room over there.'

She subtly rolled her eyes towards a small blue door at the far end of the corridor.

The Hound looked up and down the hall, half-turned to Agent Fowler with a courteous yet surreptitious nod, and then made his way towards the room and the mysterious "friend" who awaited within.

'Can you remember where the toilets were?' asked Tom, unable to keep still any longer.

Inspector Jones looked around, still halfway through the act of fumbling some change out of his pockets.

'I think they were a few doors up and to our right,' he smiled. 'Don't worry, Tom. Everything'll work out, you'll see. They always have so far, haven't they?'

Tom didn't know whether to laugh or cry at that last remark. Instead he simply nodded and made his exit from the room.

The Hound pushed open the small blue door and tentatively entered in to the room.

It was pitch-black inside but he immediately detected the slight scent of something unsettlingly unpleasant.

Vampire!

The hackles along his spine bristled and his lips pulled back to reveal his lethal fangs.

'Now, now, Percy,' came a soft and musical voice. 'That's no way to greet an old friend, is it?'

Tom washed his hands (mainly because it was something to do) and began to make his way back to the waiting-room.

As he came out onto the corridor he almost bumped into an athletic-looking, and annoyingly handsome, teenager, who had clearly just left the visiting room.

'Watch where you're going, mate,' barked the young man, skilfully dodging Tom's unintended shoulder barge and sneering at him with a look of irate surprise.

'Sorry.'

'Christ! What happened to you? Did you lose a bet or something?' he chuckled, scrutinising Tom's coat with a vigorous sparkle in his eyes, before giving Tom a cheeky (nigh-on patronising) wink, and then hastily strutting his way down the corridor, with what Tom felt was an over-practised and arrogant swagger.

Tom wanted very much to say something witty in response, for the cocky little fellow couldn't have been much older than he was, and was hardly dressed in the height of fashion himself (even to the point of having a dishevelled baseball cap [Ha!] screwed tightly over his long, lank hair, with the hilarious legend of "*MI-?*" written on it).

'Tosser,' muttered Tom under his breath, as he turned and made his way back to the waiting-room.

A lamp suddenly flicked on and The Hound turned to see a young, dark-skinned woman of quite exceptional beauty leaning, cross-legged, against a desk.

'Well, look at you,' she smiled (revealing a pearly set of teeth, including an impressive set of elongated canines). 'You always were such a handsome devil.'

The Hound stared at the smiling bloodsucker, desperately trying to remember where he knew her from, and why she looked so damned familiar. And then it hit him like a train, and his legs almost buckled from beneath him.

'Good God!' he managed to whisper. And he didn't know whether to laugh or cry, for, or so he'd believed, the woman currently sitting in front of him had died over four-hundred-and-twenty years ago!

'I'll wait for you out here, Tom,' said Inspector Jones. 'I'm sure that there's a lot you've got to say to Miss Crow, and I doubt that you want an old fogey like me cramping your style.'

'Thank you,' said Tom, and he really meant it.

He took a deep breath, pushed open the heavy doors of the visiting room and made his way to cubicle number seven in a state of extreme and nervous anticipation.

'Lettice Montague!' gasped The Hound, fumbling for something to support his weight on.

'Percival Percy,' grinned back Lettice, shaking her head as if in disbelief. 'Oh, it is good to see you, old friend. How I miss the old days, before, well, you know, before ... *this* ... happened.'

'But you're ... I mean ... you're a ... a ...'

'A vampire? Oh you noticed, did you?' she chuckled. 'You and that keen nose of yours.'

'But ... how? When? Who?'

Lettice slowly stood up.

'At the very beginning,' she smiled, rather sadly. 'On our very first mission together, in fact. Do you remember? *The Society of the Wild Hunt* caper. Well, that night when Kit and I had infiltrated their headquarters and were in the process of scuppering their evil plans, I was ... *confronted*, shall we say, by *The King of the Wild Hunt* (who, if I remember correctly, had rather improper designs on me), and though he didn't manage to have his wicked way, well, let's just say that he did manage to pass on this rather exceptional "gift".'

'But ... But why didn't you tell anybody?'

'Oh, Percy. Back in the day, no one (well, no one over here) had any real knowledge, or idea, about vampires. By the time my full *affliction* had manifested itself, Sir Francis saw it as nothing but a God-given opportunity to harness my newly-acquired talents for the good of The Realm. So, while you all thought I had given up on my career as a secret agent – What was it that Sir Francis told you all? That I'd run off and married a Transylvanian prince?'

'Yes. Yes he did. I remember that Kit was beside himself for months. Took to the bottle rather heavily, as I remember ... well, perhaps one should say "*even more heavily*".'

'– when in actual fact I was working on the Continent, behind the "Dark Curtain", using my newfound skill set to the best of my ability. Been working for the Government ever since: *The Gentlemen Good Friends*, *The Unseen League*, and now *MI Unseen*.'

'But why did you never come and see me?'

'Oh, you do know that I'm so very fond of you, dear Percy, don't you? I would have liked nothing better, believe me. But by the time I'd made it back to England, you had vanished to the Americas. And when you did return, well, let's just say that your reputation as an implacable vampire-killer was second to none. The legendary *Hound Who Hunts Nightmares*. Ha! Well, I suppose I wasn't too sure what kind of reception would have awaited me had I turned up on your doorstep.'

'But ... But you're one of us, for heaven's sake,' whimpered The Hound.

Lettice laughed. 'Yes, but now I'm also *one of them*.'

'So why look me up now? Is it to do with de Warrenne?'

'De Warrenne?' frowned Lettice, with a surprised arch of an eyebrow. 'You mean that little, lower-league pipsqueak of a vampire? What's he got to do with anything?'

'You mean to tell me that you don't know?' gasped The Hound.

'Don't know what?'

'Lettice, listen to me –'

'No, Percival, you listen to me. We haven't got much time, so I'll keep this brief. As you're no doubt only too well aware, MI Unseen is going through some rather drastic and, dare one say, *distasteful* changes at the moment. Colonel Sinjon Sin-John is taking the whole organisation to hell in a handcart, if you ask me. This whole *Achilles Project XIII* has got everybody looking over their shoulders and wondering what's about to fall. Can't tell you what it is, doubt that anyone outside of *The Project's* inner-circle can, but whatever it is, it isn't going to be pretty.'

'Achilles XIII? And what exactly is this latest ill-conceived nonsense about?'

'No one knows for sure, Percy, but the rumour is ...'

'Yes? Go on.'

'The rumour is that Sinjon Sin-John wants you dead – at any price. So my advice to you is that you should have as little to do with MI Unseen as you possibly can. In fact, I think it might be the very best of ideas if you and Professor Lyons were to take a very long vacation. South America is quite, quite lovely. And I hear that there are parts of Canada that are still unmapped.'

Tom sat down on the hard wooden chair within cubicle number seven and looked through the grille.

There she was – her hair cut short and spiky, and bleached blonde; dressed in a boiler suit of a truly hideous shade of mauve (My God! They almost matched one another!), looking pale, and obviously trying to put a brave face on things – his beautiful friend, Crow.

'Hello, Tom,' she smiled, her face lighting up at the sight of him (though it looked to Tom that she might recently have been crying). 'Or should I say – *Your Highness*?'

'Just *Tom*, please.'

'I was only joking, you pompous ass.'

'Yeah, I know, it's just that it's, you know, a little bit of a sore subject at the moment.'

'Oh. Sorry. I didn't meant to, you know, *embarrass* you or anything,' she snorted.

'How are you doing?' he asked, rather stupidly perhaps under the circumstance, but it was the best he could come up with.

'Yeah, fine. I'll be all right. Don't worry about me.'

'Listen,' said Tom, leaning in closer to the grille between them, 'look me in the eye and tell me that you didn't kill Edric.'

Crow leaned in and pierced him with an unflinching stare.

'I promise you, Tom, it wasn't me. I went there thinking that I *would* kill him, I really did, I admit it, but when it came to it I just couldn't bring myself to pull the trigger. A thief and a spy I may be,' she smiled flatly, 'but I guess that I just ain't no killer. Plus you two seemed to be getting on like a house on fire.'

'Yeah. It turned out he was all right, after all. Turned out that he wanted this "Death-Match" about as much as I did. So why did you do it?'

A flash of colour rose in Crow's freckled cheeks.

'I just told you that I didn't!' she snapped. 'You're as bad as Sparrow.'

'*Sparrow*?'

'Yeah, you know, I told you about him. We were both part of the *Achilles Project IX*. Grew up and trained together at the Academy: surveillance, retrieval of *interesting* items, undercover assignments, you know, all that *super-spy* sort of stuff.'

'Oh, him ... Yes, I seem to remember you mentioning something.' To his annoyance Tom found himself feeling a strange tinge of jealousy. 'So you've seen him, then?'

'He was here. Just before you arrived.'

'Oh,' said Tom, suddenly remembering the annoyingly handsome teenager that he had almost bumped into in the corridor. 'I think that I might have just met him.'

'Oh? What did he say?'

'Not a lot. I think he liked my coat,' smiled Tom.

Crow laughed and her eyes sparkled again. 'I doubt it,' she giggled. 'What happened?' Did you lose –'

'Please don't,' winced Tom. 'Missus Dobbs gave it to me.'

Crow offered a sympathetic and understanding smile.

'Anyway,' said Tom, 'I didn't mean that.'

'What?'

'I was talking about you killing Edric.'

'How many more times! I DIDN'T DO IT!'

'I know. Calm down. I believe you.'

'You do?'

'Yes. I just wanted to know why you wanted to do it, that's all?'

Crow held his eye for a moment and then looked at her fidgeting fingers. 'I don't know,' she mumbled. 'Seemed like a good idea at the time, I suppose.'

'I wish you hadn't.'

'Well, as Nanny Nannie used to say, *if wishes were horses then beggars would ride.*'

'Listen, Crow,' continued Tom, lowering his voice to a hushed tone, 'The Hound thinks he knows who did kill Edric.'

'He does!' hissed Crow, her eyes opening wide with a look of hope. 'Then he can get me out of here! Yeah, sure, I'll probably have to go on some rehabilitation course, or something equally degrading, but so what. After this place; piece of cake, really ... What's up, Tom? 'she said, suddenly looking worried as she saw the expression devoid of hope currently residing on Tom's face.

'The Hound thinks it was MI Unseen who had Edric assassinated.'

'What? Get out of here! No way.'

Tom's face remained stony cold.

'Why would he think that?'

'You remember when Constable Tuggnutter dragged you to the clearing?'

'Of course I do! Not likely to forget it, am I?'

'And you remember the little French Goblin who turned up and showed us the empty cartridge that matched the ones in your gun.'

Crow nodded.

'The Hound thinks it was him. He thinks that maybe you being there provided him with an unexpected and brilliant alibi. So now MI Unseen can just pin the whole thing on you.'

Crow went pale.

'Why would they do that?' she whispered, looking ashen and doubtful.

'I don't know, Crow. Any ideas?'

Tears welled up in her liquid brown eyes, and Tom wished he could reach through the grille and give her a hug.

'No,' she said, and she suddenly sounded very small. 'What's the name of this Lutin, this French Goblin? If he works for MI Unseen, then perhaps I've heard of him.'

'Monsieur Passereaux.'

'*Passereaux!*' hissed Crow. And then she went even paler.

'What is it, Crow? Do you know him?'

'No! It can't be!' she sniffed, tears beginning to roll down her cheeks. 'They wouldn't! He wouldn't!'

'What are you talking about, Crow? Who is it? What is it?'

Crow looked up at Tom.

'*Passereaux* is French for *Sparrow*,' she said coldly.

'And?'

'Oh for Christ sake, Tom, sometimes you're frickin' thick!'

Tom looked blankly at her for a second ... and then it hit him like a truck.

'It's one of the names he uses when he's undercover,' grimaced Crow.

Tom was up from the table and marching towards the door, his face as dark as thunder.

Tom!' she cried. 'What are you doing? Come back! Please don't try to stop him. Not on your own ... he'll kill you!'

TWENTY ONE
Flight Of The Sparrow

As Tom pounded through the heavy doors of the visiting room (skipping around the startled-looking Agent Fowler) he heard Inspector Jones rushing out of the waiting-room.

'Tom!' cried the Inspector. 'What is it?'

'Passereaux!' snarled Tom over his shoulder. And then he put his head down and sprinted down the corridor. *Which way would the arrogant and treacherous little shit have gone?* he wondered.

At the end of the hallway, leaning against a small blue door, stood The Hound, staring at the floor and looking like he'd seen a ghost.

'Mr Hound!' cried Tom, as he approached the were-hound.

'Whatever is it, Tom?' asked The Hound, lifting up his great snout enquiringly.

'Passereaux! Sparrow! He's here! He was walking down this very corridor only a few minutes ago!'

Tom skidded round the corner, dashed past the were-wolfhound, and came to an ungainly and rather embarrassing halt as The Hound grabbed him by the hood of his purple parka.

'What are you doing!' roared Tom.

'Be still, Tom,' said The Hound very calmly, 'and think.'

'But he's here! If we can catch him then Crow will be all right,' he pleaded, struggling to break free from the were-hound's grip, and both infuriated and dumbfounded by the were-wolf-wolfhound's seeming lack of concern.

The Hound put his hands around Tom's shoulders, turned him around and lifted him up, holding him at eye level.

'Not now, Tom,' he whispered.

'BUT HE'S GETTING AWAY!' screeched Tom.

'What would you have us do? Run through the corridors of The Mound (an MI Unseen prison, fortress and stronghold) in pursuit of one of their most valued special agents? Then, if we do catch this fellow and deal out his just reward, shall the three of us then fight our way through the hundred or so heavily-armed guards that are stationed here? And should, by some miracle, we manage to survive that, how do you propose that we cut our way through the twenty-foot-thick steel walls and make our escape? No, Tom, if we are to catch this rascal and help young Crow, then I suggest we find a less conspicuous and suicidal method.'

'But ...' began Tom. And then he went limp in the were-hound's paws, for, though he hated the thought of it, he knew the sense of what he was saying.

'Everything all right, Mr Hound? Tom?' asked Inspector Jones, slightly out of breath after his sprint to catch up with Tom.

The were-hound nodded.

'Tickety-boo,' replied The Hound, gently returning Tom to the floor. 'I think that we've achieved all we can here for the day, so I suggest we make ourselves scarce and head back home. Come along, chop-chop, off we trot. Thank you, Agent Fowler,' he said with a nod towards the MI Unseen warder. And then, with the briefest of glances back towards the small blue door, he ushered Tom and Inspector Jones through the dull and soulless maze of corridors and towards the exit and the sleek grey Alfa Romeo that awaited them outside.

TWENTY TWO
The Tightening Net

'An' you believe 'er?' asked Cornelius with a questioning curl of an eyebrow, as he cracked open a packet of custard creams.

The Hound took a delicate sip of Lapsang Souchong, licked his lips and reclined into his armchair.

'I see no reason to doubt her,' he sighed, with a regretful shake of his head. 'Lettice was always the very best of eggs. Besides, we have to admit that we've had our own growing concerns about Colonel Sinjon Sin-John for quite some time now.'

'Can't argue with that,' muttered Cornelius, reaching over to offer a biscuit to The Hound. 'What about young Crow?'

'Yes, Crow. Oh dear. The more I think on Tom's hypothesis, the more I'm afraid that it all adds up,' replied The Hound, leaning forward to pluck a couple of custard creams from the packet. 'Her *colleague*, this Sparrow fellow, infiltrates the ranks of Edric's followers (expertly disguised as an aged Goblin from a far-distant tribe) with the intent of assassinating the Prince. By sheer chance, Crow turns up with the same intention, and Sparrow/Monsieur Passereaux, along with MI Unseen, are handed an unprecedented alibi for their heinous and, if true, puzzling, actions.'

'By why would MI Unseen want Edric dead?' munched Cornelius.

'Why indeed? The connotations are beginning to look very ominous and very worrying; not only for the Fae World as a whole, but also for Miss Crow's continued safety.'

'So 'ow do we get 'er out of this mess?'

'How indeed? In its long and dubious history, no one has ever managed to escape from The Mound. To make such an audacious attempt would be the height of recklessness. No, we shall have to try and pursue a more diplomatic avenue.'

'So what now, 'Aitch?'

'We carry on regardless,' growled The Hound, pluckily. 'Our first course of duty must be to The Elbi. We have promised that we will return to them their stolen crowns, and so it must be. Once that is done, and de Warrenne and his parcel of rogues are brought to brook, then we can see the lie of the land. There are still many good and true men and women working within MI Unseen. I find it hard to believe that they would *all* stand by and watch while the Colonel and his cronies bring the Agency into disrepute.'

'Excuse me for being a sceptic,' sighed Cornelius, cracking a custard cream in two, 'but it wouldn't be the first time in 'istory that decent folk 'ave stood aside an' done nothing while a pack of madmen brought the world to rack an' ruination.'

'Well, we'll know soon enough, I suppose,' sniffed The Hound. 'In a few short days the net will have tightened around de Warrenne, *The Society of the Wild Hunt* and *The Bucca* – for good.'

Cornelius dunked a halved custard cream into his tea and watched in consternation as it sagged, crumpled, and then slowly sunk without a trace to the bottom of his cup.

'Well let's just bloomin' 'ope that we don't end up getting ensnared in it ourselves,' he croaked.

TWENTY THREE
Beneath My Banner Wild Things Gather

Tom walked down the steps to the Muse-asium and stifled a scream.

'Prince Tomas,' beamed Tommy Rawhead-and-Bloody-Bones, his face lighting up in delight like an albino ferret coming nose to nose with a butcher's tray of chicken livers. 'My heart soars like a hawk to see you again.'

Well, mine curls up like a hibernating hedgehog with toothache at the sight of you, old chum, thought Tom, as he managed to smile at the ghastly old lunatic and legendary child-murderer (reformed).

Tom had been sent to the Muse-asium by Cornelius, with the promise that there was a "*lovely surprise*" waiting there for him. He decided that he needed to have a very long chat with his grandfather regarding the use, understanding and definition of the word "lovely".

Behind the delightful old horror that was Bloody-Bones stood a quite ghastly collection of *The Hidden Realm's* finest; all fidgeting uncomfortably to get a good look at their new, soon-to-be, king. Eleven of the ungodly nightmares in all, and each one, to a homicidal, psychotic and nightmare-inspiring goblin, disturbingly dressed in a luminous purple parka.

Rawhead, misinterpreting the look of appalled dismay on Tom's face, bristled with pride.

'May I present to you, my Pook, your own personal bodyguard. Each one hand-picked, each one ready to lay down their life for you – Prince Grendelson; their king; their lord; The Pook of Shadows. And may I be the first among us to congratulate you on the wonderful news of Prince Edric's *unfortunate* demise.'

'Er ... you may. Thank you.'

'Also, before we go any further, the lads wanted to present you with something, Prince Adamsbane – a gift.'

'Urhm? ...Okay? Cool.'

'THUMB-RACK!,' screeched Rawhead-and-Bloody-Bones, and before Tom could make a dash for the exit, a powerfully built *delight* (with a face like a sun-starved buttock slashed with blunt razor-blades, and, ironically, two hands devoid of any thumbs [and disturbingly few other fingers]) bullied his way forward and grunted his undying loyalty with a short bow.

'If you would be so kind as to show the Prince your *handiwork*,' beamed Rawhead, proudly.

Thumb-Rack smiled, looked a little abashed, and then (after a painfully awkward minute or two, as he clumsily fumbled with his digit-deficient mitts) produced a folded sheet of green silk from within his jacket. With the help of one of his ghastly and grinning colleagues (a poisonous-looking fellow called Inkcap) he managed to unfurl what turned out to be a banner, and proudly held it, outstretched, before their prince.

'It is your sigil, Prince Adamsbane,' growled Tommy, fiercely. 'Beneath this banner wild things will gather. For the whole of Avalon is ready to rally, fight, and, if needs be, die beneath your standard.'

Tom tilted his head and took a moment to try and decipher the image on the flag.

'I spent much time thinking on how best to capture your *essence*, Prince Grendel-Weather,' grinned Rawhead-and-Bloody-Bones, with a smile like a freshly-opened wound. 'I had the opportunity to talk to both The Goodfellow and Long Lamkin, and discuss the merits of your recent martial and noble deeds. See here,' he purred, 'the green background that depicts our bountiful Mother. And here, deep within the belly of that earth, rests *The Crown of Spring*, radiating power. And, striding above that crown, you stand, the Grendel's son – your noble features caught in fearsome battle-cry, sending fierce dread into the hearts of the enemies of our people; majestic in your warlike apparel.'

Having had it explained to him, Tom could begin to see what they'd tried to do. However, the finished effect brought, to Tom's mind at least, the image of a purple gorilla, who looked like he was in the last painful throes of constipation, squatting over a fresh and steaming turd.

Oh good grief, he sighed inwardly. *When do I get anything that looks even remotely cool?*

'Wow. Where do I begin?' began Tom, with a starched grin. 'Tommy. *Lads*. Words fail me.'

'No, don't thank us, Prince Tomas, Lord of Shadows, Pook of Nightmares,' sniffed Tommy, looking like he was close to tears. 'The honour is ours. We stand as one, ready to die at your side. Your enemies shall come to rue the day that they dared to cross us, the chosen spears of the Aelfradi, the crimson swords of the Grendel's son – *The Purple Frighteners*!'

TWENTY FOUR
The Council Of War

'Gentlemen,' growled The Hound, dramatically, 'ladies. We are gathered here for one last meeting before we finally confront the most implacable of enemies.'

He slowly turned and held the eye of each and every one present: Tom; Cornelius; Bob Goodfellow; Archie Swapper; Ned; Old Maggs; Dame Ginty Parsons; Inspector Jones; Tommy Rawhead-and-Bloody-Bones.

Missus Dobbs staggered into the kitchen, almost buckling under the weight of a tray of fairy cakes (of course), followed by Mae, wheeling in a giant and glimmering tea urn. (In the days since Mae's incarceration, the House-Fairy and the were-cat/tone-deaf cabaret-singer had seemed to grow rather attached to one another, and Missus Dobbs had clearly seen fit to take Mae under her protective wing.)

'Ah, thank you, Missus Dobbs,' smiled The Hound, ogling the selection of iced-fancies with a slight flaring of his almond-shaped and walnut-coloured eyes. 'If you would be so kind as to join us, for this involves you, Missus Dobbs. You too, Mae.'

The Brownie proudly pulled up a chair beside Tommy Rawhead and the two of them swapped a (quite revolting) gurn of adoration (and might possibly have begun a game of *footsie* under the table).

Mae – head kept down, face devoid of any make-up (and Tom found it strangely unsettling to see the former member of the Carnival of Curiosities without half a ton of foundation plastered over his face) – meekly took a seat next to Tom.

'Tonight sees the return of the full moon, and with Her coming, our chance to put this unspeakable evil to bed, once and for all,' continued the were-hound.

''Ere, 'ere,' muttered Cornelius, eyeing the cupcakes like an otter, his whiskers quivering in anticipation and manful restraint.

'I have no need to remind any of you of the significance of this night's work. For if we succeed, all of the Elbi tribes of Upper Albion will be reunited with their sacred crowns (in the case of The Gentry, for first time in almost five hundred years). The possibilities that might be unveiled by such a development, could be well and truly staggering, and, if handled correctly, might very well see the dawning of a new era.

'Tom, Tommy, I give you my word that once this deplorable mess is cleared up I will not rest a day until *The Crown of Spring*, the crown of the Aelfradi, is found and returned to its people and to its soon-to-be and long-awaited king.

'I swear to each and every one of you that I will dedicate myself to seeing four Pooks sit once more upon the ancient thrones of Albion.'

Everyone sounded a heartfelt "Hooray!", a fiery fierceness kindled in their hearts (all save Tom – who offered an unenthusiastic "Hhhmmm?", and Mae – who stared silently at the were-hound with a look of stony concentration).

"Ere, 'ere,' repeated Cornelius. 'I'll eat to that,' he beamed, reaching a hand towards the nearest plate of fairy-cakes.

The Hound delivered a short sharp smack to his wrist.

'Not yet, Dandy,' he muttered.

Cornelius pulled back his hand with a mumble and a look of irked regret.

'Tonight,' continued The Hound, shooting a reproachful glance in Cornelius' direction, 'we face an enemy of justice and decency; a vile and villainous rogue who has plagued this land and tampered with the history of the Elbi people for far too long. You all know of whom I speak; Lord Manfred de Warrenne – that irredeemable swine and undead rotter! His crimes can no longer go unpunished. His reign of terror must be stopped! Tonight we shall put an end to his unmentionable unpleasantnesses once and for all!'

"Uzzah!' blustered Cornelius, heartily slapping the tabletop and reaching forth a hand.

'Not yet, Dandy,' hissed The Hound.

Cornelius stifled a sigh and reluctantly retracted his hand from the plate of cakes.

'Before we begin munching on Missus Dobbs' delicious-looking muffins,' growled The Hound, 'let us once more go over our plans for this long overdue *bat-hunt*.

'Cornelius, how went the meeting with Mr Willikins this morning?'

'Cracking,' chortled the tweedy old bruiser. 'The ring 'as been erected, an' all is well an' truly in place an' 'ot to trot, as they say. An' dear old Whelky, well, let me just say that Whelk-faced Willie the Wheeze is delighted with it all. Told me that 'is gaff is crammed full of 'ard-drinking Bucca-men, well-known goblin ne'er-do-wells, notorious nasties, an' all manner of vile an' noxious villains. All of them shelling-out their deplorable an' ill-gotten gains on Whelky's delectable an' ill-gotten wares. Plus, as we'd 'oped, de Warrenne 'as agreed for Whelky to be both stake'older an' referee.'

'Splendid,' grinned The Hound. 'Bob, how go the arrangements up at the barns?'

Bob plucked something from his beard, examined in for a moment, and then returned it, unharmed, to its tousled home before looking up and offering a tar-pit of a smile towards the were-hound.

'Ek-Boran is putting the final touches to the Glamours as we speak,' he wheezed.

'*Glamours?*' enquired Inspector Jones.

'Yes,' smiled The Hound, 'Glamours. Long Lamkin will be leading Edric's followers tonight. They are already stationed in the ruined barns that surround the courtyard where stands the make-shift "boxing-ring" – masked from prying eyes by *spells of concealment*. Once all is in place, once de Warrenne has tripped his way into our trap, Lamkin will, upon my signal of "*To me, you proud, brave banners of Albion!*", lead the charge and pounce, surrounding and ensnaring *The Wild Hunt* and their contemptible allies, *The Bucca*, in a bristling cordon of warlike and righteous spears.'

'Excuse me for asking the obvious, Mr Hound,' sniffed the Inspector, with a haunted and slightly worried look, 'but won't this witch of theirs, this *Madame Buckleberry*, be able to detect any such enchantments and instantly give the game away?'

The Hound allowed himself a wry chuckle.

'No. No she will not.' he replied. 'For while Madame Buckleberry is undoubtedly a fine and first-rate witch, compared to the powers of the Elven wizards her skills are those of a schoolgirl.'

The were-wolfhound turned and stabbed a talon onto the blackboard that stood behind him, on which was drawn a map of Castle Hill and the deserted farmstead where the proposed contest was to take place.

'So,' he began with a double tap of a claw, 'here is where Long Lamkin and the warriors of Edric's Free-Folk are stationed (determined, I may add, to honour and avenge the cherished memory of their recently-deceased lord), concealed within the barns that all but surround the *arena*. When Lamkin unleashes his hundred spears (in what will be a splendidly delightful surprise for de Warrenne and his devilish crew) all those Bucca-men who haven't the stomach for a fight but might still have the legs for flight, will no doubt flee via the obvious and only opening, along this track ... here; right into the clutches of Prince Dearlove and Mr Rawhead-and-Bloody-Bones, who will be stationed and concealed in these bushes ... here and here ... with their *Purple Frighteners* at hand.

'Inspector Jones and the D.S.C. will be at the end of this track ... here, parked in a concealed vehicle and ready to provide backup should anyone need it. Also they'll carry with them the means to cuff, truss, tie, tether and restrain the prisoners (of which I'm hoping there will be many).

'Maggs, Dame Ginty and Missus Dobbs will be working together, patrolling these hills ... here, ready to swoop down into the fray if need be or pick off any scallywag who manages to wriggle through the net.

'Cornelius and I will be, of course, at the heart of the matter along with Bob, Archie and Ned, all masquerading as Chow's retinue.

'Let me remind you all, once again,' growled The Hound, looking sternly around the room, 'de Warrenne is mine. My only other request is that Bors (my long-lost, and maltreated, brother) is captured alive, if at all possible. Bob, I'd like you to make that your priority.'

'If it can be done, it will be done, Percival,' replied the putrid Puck, 'but I can make no promises.'

'Understood,' sniffed The Hound, with a solemn nod of his head .

'And Mae ...'

Mae looked up at the were-hound, his eyes, face and voice as cold as marble.

'Yes, Mister Hound Who Hunts Nightmares?'

'... you have a great part to play in all of this, for it is down to you to keep alive the charade that Chow and the *Carnival of Curiosities* are still in existence and at the races, so to speak. We have placed a great deal of trust in you, Mae. Should you play us false in any way, then not only will you endanger the freedom of all of the Fae Folk of these islands, but you will also jeopardize any chance you might have had of a lenient sentence. However, should we come out of this victorious, should you prove yourself true, then you have my word that I, in return, will do all in my power to put in a good word for you with the right people. Do you understand me?'

'Oh yes, Mister Hound,' replied the wretched little fellow, steadily holding the were-hound's stare. 'I understand. It will be my greatest performance, I promise you.'

'Glad to hear it. We're counting on you, old chap.

'Now, everybody knows what is expected of them?

'Good.

'Any questions?

'No? Splendid. Then good luck, my friends. And here's to a great and glorious victory. Now, charge your teacups ... Missus Dobbs, would you be so kind? ... for now is the time.'

''Alle-bloody-luiah!' muttered Cornelius.

'Let us drink, my friends,' cried The Hound, the blistering light of the hunter playing in his black-rimmed eyes, 'my comrades in arms. Let us drink to the final termination, to the destruction and the end, of this unmentionable unpleasantness.'

'To the end of the unmentionable unpleasantness!' came the resounding rally.

And then everyone pounced on the plates of fancies before them with famished delight.

Well, thought Tom as he snatched up a cupcake and peeled away the casing, '*if de Warrenne and his crew were a plate of fairy-cakes, they wouldn't stand a frickin' chance!*

Tom wiped dry and stacked another plate onto the growing mountain of crockery, reflecting on the sad fact that, prince or pauper, no one escapes the dishes.

'Almost done, Mister Tom,' said Mae, which were the first words that the torch song assassin had said to him since their discussion in the Muse-aseum after the death of Dr Chow and the collapse of the *Carnival of Curiosities*.

Tom returned a smile and desperately struggled for something nice to say.

'So, how are you doing, Mae?' he asked, and instantly wished that he could have come up with something less ham-fisted and blindingly useless.

The were-cat paused and took a slow breath.

'What would you like me to say, Mister Tom? Everything is fine? I'm so happy with the way that things have turned out? Or should I tell you that my life is in ruins? Wrecked.'

'Uhm ... yes ... I mean, no ... er ... I mean ...'

'I once heard it said that the heart is the only part of the body that, once broken, can never be truly mended again.'

'I'm sorry.'

'Missus Dobbs has been most kind, though. She is a very lovely lady. And Mr Rawhead-and-Bloody-Bones, he seems very nice too. Though he has a lot to learn about fashion, Mister Tom, let me tell you. Perhaps I can teach him?'

'I hope so. You know that I'm now the sole heir to the throne of Avalon, don't you, Mae?'

'Yes, I heard. Congratulations, Mister – or should I say – Prince Tom. You must be very proud. You will make a wonderful king, I'm sure.'

'What I mean to say is that ... if you still want to come and live in *The Hidden Realm* ... then now ... it can ... definitely happen ... if you still want it to, that is.'

Mae wiped his delicate hands dry on a tea towel and looked out of the window with a face like a gravestone.

'Yes,' he said at last. 'I will live in shadow for the rest of my days.'

Tom sat on his bed, desperately fretting about the upcoming night.

What if it didn't go to plan? What if got injured? What if he were maimed ... like Edric! He couldn't imagine what it must be like to lose a hand ... or a foot. What if he were facially disfigured! What if he lost an eye? Or an ear? Or a nose! Would he be given one of those ridiculous-sounding goblin names? *Prince One-Ear-Oh-Dear Dearlove*? *Tom Iron-Hooter*? *Then* what would Crow think of him? What if he died? Murdered by a vampire or brained by a Bucca-man! Who else would even care to think about rescuing Crow from The Mound? What if someone else died? The Hound! Or Cornelius! Or any of the others! Over the last few days he'd seen more death and bloodshed than he would ever have thought possible, and he really didn't want to see any more.

He looked over to the war-putter that Archie and Ned had given him for his birthday. It lay innocently on the bed next to him, the flint head blue-black and razor-sharp; cold and uncaring, patiently waiting to have its first taste of blood.

Tom couldn't help but shiver.

Well it can bloody well wait for it, he thought.

Not long ago, the idea of weapons had filled him with romantic notions of heroic, chivalrous combat and swashbuckling duels where no one really got hurt – but the reality was nothing like that. The reality was nothing short of awful.

A gentle knock at the door pulled Tom from the sinking highway of his thoughts.

'Hello?' he said.

The door opened and Cornelius poked his head through the gap.

'All right, Tom?' smiled the old duffer. 'You got a moment?'

'Er ... yeah? Sure.'

Cornelius came and sat on the bed and set his attention on the war-club that lay between them.

'Vicious-looking thing,' he sniffed. 'Beautiful though, in its way. Not that I like weapons, you understand. Never 'ave. But sometimes, I'm sorry to 'ave to say, they become somewhat necessary. 'Ow else can decent folk protect themselves from the weak?'

'What do you mean "the weak"?' asked Tom, a little puzzled by his grandfather's words.

'Well it ain't never the strong fellows 'oo start the trouble, is it? Can't remember 'oo said it – but *save us from* the *tyranny of the weak*, an' all that.'

He slowly pulled his eyes from the putter and looked at Tom. ''Ow are you 'olding up, son? So much 'as 'appened, an' so quickly, that it feels like we 'aven't 'ad a moment to catch our breath. 'Ow you 'andling it all, Tom? Must be terrifying for you, what with all that's been going on.'

'I don't mind saying that I'm a bit scared, to be honest … especially about tonight.'

'Well, you'd be a bloody fool if you weren't, Tom, an' that's a fact.'

'But you never seem to be scared.'

The old man laughed and gently patted Tom's hand.

'Don't you believe it, son,' he chuckled. 'I've got a list as long as me arm of things that can put me in a state of abject terror.'

'Well what about The Hound? He's not scared of anything, is he?'

'Not a lot,' considered Cornelius. 'Except maybe motor-cycle covers, an' black plastic bin-bags on a blustery day. Don't know what it is exactly, but they give 'im the 'eebie-jeebies.

'You see, Tom, being brave is not about *not being scared*. In fact, it's just about the opposite. It's about being scared but still facing up to whatever it is that 'appens to frighten you. So tonight, whatever 'appens, you do what you 'ave to do, son; whatever you feel is *right*. Tommy an' the lads are there to look after you, so let them. Do your best, an' do what you *can* do. You understand me? No one can ask more. But I don't want you trying to be no 'ero, Tom. 'Eroes 'ave got a terrible 'abit of getting themselves rubbed out before their time. '

Tom nodded his head, but really the old lunatic didn't have to worry himself on that score, for Tom had every intention of sticking to the plan, and, with luck, only making an appearance when all the *unspeakable unpleasantness* had been well and truly *put to bed*.

TWENTY FIVE
Bat Trap

The moon smeared itself across the sky like a sloppy bloodstained kiss.

Tom, hidden in a copse of windswept (and damned uncomfortably spiky!) bushes overlooking the derelict farmstead at Castle Hill, drew up the hood of his purple parka and tried to wriggle some warmth into his toes. Concealed alongside him were Tommy Rawhead-and-Bloody-Bones (dressed fetchingly in a purple ball gown, complementary shawl and combat boots, and with a matching set of necklace and earrings – that from a distance looked like pearls but were in fact made from the tiny skulls of baby shrews) and five other members of *The Purple Frighteners*.

The rest of Tom's newly-acquired and hideously-attired *royal bodyguard* were stationed among the shrubbery that was dotted along the steep hillside, where they had been waiting in the damp, freezing and miserable cold for the last four hours. The best that could be said about it was the remarkable fact that the rain seemed to have eased to a misty blanket of sogginess.

Oh, it was a charmed life!

Rawhead suddenly poked an impossibly pointy elbow into Tom's astonishingly sensitive ribs, raised a finger to the ragged and open wound that passed as his mouth, and pointed down the hill and to his right with a smile of delight that would have loosened the bowels of a bronze statue of Richard the Lionheart.

Tom peered through his night-vision goggles and saw a ragged party of figures staggering along the main pathway that led to the dilapidated farmstead.

Ten, twenty, thirty, forty, forty-five, forty-six, forty-seven, he counted. Bucca-men, Goblins, a few humans, and all manner of nefarious reprobates of the very worst sort. Tom could hear their raucous chatter, accompanied here and there by the clink of a bottle and the fizz of a beer-can being popped open. They guffawed, and swapped harsh banter back and forth – a foul joke followed by the cackle of cruel laughter.

At their head could be heard the dulcet tones of Whelk-faced Willie the Wheeze Willikins.

'Thith way, gentth. Come along, thirth, thtay together now, pleathe. That'th it. Yeth indeed. Plenty of victualth of the finetht quality, for thothe who want them, when we get there ...'

The motley crew reached their destination and oozed around the specially erected *boxing ring* like a stream of sewage hitting a post, noisily jostling and contesting for the best spots from where they could observe the upcoming action from.

Willie scrambled gracelessly onto the apron of the arena, almost garrotted himself as he tried to clamber between the ropes, and then began to check the floor, ropes and ring-posts for any unexpected *embellishments* that might have been added since he'd supervised the ring's erection earlier that day.

The cries of the bookmakers and the singsong chants of the vendors of pies, grog and souvenirs soon began to cut above the drone of excited chatter, and the farmstead began to buzz and hum like a wasps' nest being stirred into activity.

Tom's heartbeat quickened and his mouth suddenly went dry.

And then the babble and hubbub stopped dead, as if someone had accidentally trodden on the volume switch, as into the courtyard seeped a stately and ungodly procession of quite sinister proportions. Twelve figures in all. And at their head, moving with a spiteful grace and an unearthly, yet debonair, elegance, was the arch-villain himself, Lord Manfred de Warrenne – dressed in a decidedly un-vampireish 1930s-style tweed jacket and plus fours, with long, handmade leather hunting boots, a knitted woollen scarf wrapped around his neck to keep out the chill (not that the undead scoundrel felt the cold, you understand) and a cloth flat cap balanced at a jaunty and rather rakish angle. All in all, the dapper little swine simply oozed exquisite tailoring and luxurious good taste.

Tom's anger rose as he made out the treacherous and backstabbing figure of Professor MacFee. He watched with growing ire as the "*Vampyre-Hunter*" theatrically removed his tall hat, put his foot on the lower rope of the ring, pulled its neighbour upwards, and then turned dramatically to de Warrenne.

De Warrenne looked triumphantly about, ignored MacFee's gesture, vaulted the ropes like a super-powered gymnast, and doffed his cap in greeting to the awaiting and, quite clearly, adoring crowd.

A roar of appreciation rose from the gathered Goblins and other assorted villains as they chanted his name, stamping their feet and clapping their hands in a warlike and thunderous anthem.

Tom couldn't help but smile to himself as he thought of the hundred spears of Edric's *Free-Folk* (now technically his *Free-Folk*, he supposed) hidden in the derelict barns that stood on all four sides of the farmstead, all but surrounding the odious and unaware mob of scoundrels (masked and completely hidden from sight, as they were, by the wonders and magic of *Puckery*). In a moment or two the hoodwinked hoodlums would be singing to an entirely different tune – and de Warrenne and his despicable crew of the damned wouldn't be looking quite so decidedly cocky.

Rawhead tapped Tom on the shoulder and pointed with his thumb towards the small track that ran its way to the farmstead from the *village* (or so it liked to call itself – but, to Tom's eyes at least, those days had long since gone) of Woodingdean. Tom followed Rawhead's pale digit and made out the slow and steady parade of a line of strange and otherworldly forms, winding their way down the snaking path.

In the forefront Tom could make out Mae, his face made-up to the nines, swaggering and shimmying his way forwards like the old trouper that he was. Behind him followed five more figures of varying heights (ranging from *small* to *frickin' enormous!*) all dressed in long *Chinese* robes of silk, and all wearing an assortment of large and wide-brimmed coolie-hats (some of which might once have been lampshades), bar one – a wide and rangy-looking fellow with a boxing-robe thrown over his shoulders, hood up, and with a long cat-like tail swishing from side-to-side from beneath said garment, as he rolled his shoulders and shot out his hands with the practised grace of the prize-fighter.

Mae reached the outskirts of the mob, waited politely for the crowd to part and a path to open, and then boldly minced his way towards the ring, to the hushed murmurs and hissed jeers of the Bucca-men.

In his wake followed the rest of the cortège:

Cornelius prowled menacingly – head down, his features masked by the shadow of his hood – and occasionally offering a low and deep-throated roar. (It had taken Missus Dobbs most of the afternoon to make the necessary alterations to the *leopard onesie* that she had managed to find in Primark – the tail weighted and stuffed with an articulated toy snake and then supported by a series of fishing-lines to make it wiggle back and forth. To finish the transformation, Mae had spent several hours applying face-paint to the whiskery old duffer's somewhat doubtful and unconvinced visage, whilst Dame Ginty had applied the necessary *Glamours* to make his *extraordinary* disguise seem believable.)

The Hound had his enormous head and pointy snout covered by a giant and veiled *Chinese-sombrero,* whilst from neck to floor he wore a long flowing robe (made partially from one of Dr Chow's old garments and partially from a near-matching curtain) which trailed to the ground (covering his decidedly un-Chow-like feet), sweeping majestically along the sodden earth around him.

And bringing up the rear – Bob Goodfellow, Ned and Archie: all three outfitted from the captured booty of Dr Chow's wardrobe; their faces hidden from view by their enormous hats. Both Ned and Archie had their hair plaited into long *Chinese pigtails* that hung down their backs. In Ned's arms he carefully carried an exquisitely enamelled and decorated wooden box, within which rested the wondrous treasure that was *The Autumn Crown.*

Mae seeped through the ropes like a cat through a half-opened window, and, with a courteous little bow, smiled sweetly at de Warrenne. Cornelius ducked into the arena and prowled to a corner of the ring, softly growling, head down and pretending to meet no one's eye. The Hound remained elegantly poised on the apron of the ring, resting his arms gracefully on the top rope, his murderous paws concealed within the long, drooping sleeves of his garment.

'Dr Chow,' purred de Warrenne, turning his attention to the imposing and stately figure. 'How splendid to finally meet you, old chap. I must say I didn't expect you to be so ... *tall*. Must be all those kippers,' he grinned.

Whelk-faced Willie hurriedly strode to the centre of the ring and looked nervously from de Warrenne to The Hound/Chow.

'Gentlemen,' he urged urgently. 'I trutht that you have brought with you the thtaketh, ath requethted?'

Mae bowed and snapped his fingers.

Ned bounded through the ropes, exquisite wooden box in arms, and stood next to Mae, head tilted forward, with only the tip of his chin visible.

Mae theatrically opened the box to reveal *The Autumn Crown* within.

De Warrenne peered over and his eyes lit up with a look of pure greed and desire.

The vampire looked over his shoulder and nodded.

There was a bustle of activity and into the ring stepped the tall and slender vampire, Okomto – former priest-prince of the great Ashanti nation. In his delicate long hands he carried a pristine metal briefcase.

De Warrenne artfully flicked open the case's two latches and flipped back the lid.

'*The Summer Crown*,' he grinned excitedly, gesturing towards the exquisite beauty of the treasure within, with a wave of his impeccably manicured hand.

Beside him, The Hound could feel Archie begin to quiver with outrage. He was aware that Ned's hands were trembling too.

Quickly, The Hound/Chow lightly clicked his talons together and Mae dutifully trotted over and listened with courtier-like patience as the towering figure of the *Chinese sorcerer* bent forward to whisper in his ear.

Mae sashayed back to the centre of the ring with a practised poise (clearly loving being the centre of so much attention – and in front of such a captivated and [as yet] non-booing audience) and bowed politely to de Warrenne.

It was then that Tom first noticed *the strange anomaly*.

His attention was taken by a shrill little gasp from the bush to his left, where the charming four-digit delight (and vice-president of *The Hidden Realm's* sewing society), Thumbscrew, was concealed. Tom almost concussed himself on a branch as he jerked upwards in fright at the ghastly sound, but he managed to stifle his yelp of pain and followed the hushed, awed and puzzled gaze of his surrounding retinue. For rolling down the hill, like a cavalry charge in slow-motion, was a thick grey mist. And from within that ghostly fog Tom thought he could hear what could best be described as the echo of a high-pitched cackle.

'So sorry, Lord de Warrenne,' purred Mae, the picture of prefect and respectful good manners, 'but Dr Chow requests to see *The Winter Crown* as well.'

'Does he indeed?' snorted the dapper little vampire, pushing back the brim of his flat cap with a finger, and eyeing *The Chow-Hound* with an enquiring arch of his perfectly shaped eyebrow. He smiled and nodded pleasantly at the sorcerer.

'Well, tell your master that he'll just have to wait. Let's see if the blighter can win this one first, shall we?'

'Oh!' replied, Mae with a practised puff of surprise. 'If you would excuse me for one moment.'

The were-cat padded his way back to the waiting Hound/Chow, raised himself on tippy-toe to whisper in the were-hound's ear, and waited for his *master's* reply, before hurriedly shimmying back to the impatiently waiting, but amused-looking, de Warrenne.

'With all due respect, Lord de Warrenne,' said Mae, meeting the vampire's disbelieving and incredulous gape with a stony-faced fortitude, 'while Dr Chow has no doubts about your honesty in such matters, he feel that it would be a gesture of *goodwill* if you would at least prove that you have brought *The Winter Crown* with you. You see, Lord de Warrenne, the venerable Dr Chow desires, so very much, to bring this *unfortunate* matter to a conclusion ... tonight.'

'Oh he does, does he,' chuckled de Warrenne, with flawless, if somewhat exasperated, good humour. 'Well, damn his eyes and send him off to bed without any supper, the naughty little tyke. Frightfully bad manners, if you ask me, old pip. Just not the done thing, I'm afraid. But here's what I'll do: if, by some miracle, your *man* does somehow manage to best *mine*, then we can talk about you chaps seeing *The Winter Crown* then, but not before. Do you understand? Now, what I suggest is that you fellows keep your eyes on the game in front of you and stick to what you can afford, for the moment. It's one crown for one crown, old cock. One at a time, and there's an end to it.'

'Then how about you feast your undead peepers over here, you bloodsucking, loathsome parasite!' screeched a voice like an uncorked fart.

As one they all turned to see (silhouetted against a billowing mist, nine salty Sea-Elves at her back – each one armed with cutlass, harpoon, trident, marlinspike, or combination of the aforementioned) the sea-witch, Cutty Sark!

TWENTY SIX
The Hag

The Hound was so surprised that he almost lost his footing.

How can this be? he wondered, astonished, astounded and flabbergasted to the very core of his being. For Cutty Sark, his old acquaintance and (until recently – unbeknownst to them all) shamed guardian of *The Winter Crown*, was believed to be dead; eaten alive by the monstrous Johnny Grendel in Petworth Park on the fateful night when she and Crow had tried to snatch *The Crown of Spring* from under the very noses of Prince Edric and his *Redcap* buddies (while they in turn were attempting to steal the blasted thing from the tomb-like prison of poor, happily unmissed, Johnny).

The old hag rolled her way forward (her newly-fashioned wooden peg leg clacking against the ground with a decidedly nautical squeak) and, with some difficulty, pulled herself up onto the apron of the ring and through the ropes, until she stood between the thunderstruck Hound and the dumbfounded de Warrenne.

She looked at the vampire like an unimpressed chaperone scrutinising an unwanted, unsuitable and lecherous suitor, and spat noisily onto the floor.

'Well, you trumped up little gobshite?' she wheezed, like a festering toothache on an Easter Sunday's morning. 'Have ye got it or nae?'

'Do excuse me, Madame,' smiled de Warrenne, oozing menacing but bemused charm, 'but just *who*, exactly, are you?'

Cutty Sark took a clunking stride forward and thrust her hands onto her hips.

'My name, ya prigged-up little ponce, is Anna Dee. Mayhap you know me better as *The Cutty Sark,* friend of The Gentry and the guardian of *The Winter Crown,*' she growled.

'Dear lord, no!' cried de Warrenne in disbelief. 'Not Nannie Dee?' he guffawed, clapping his hands together in delight. 'Not that scrumptious young filly that old Harry Ca-Nab was always mooning over? A couple of drinks and off he was – gushing over you and your skimpy attire like a lust-struck teenager. Got rather embarrassing, if truth be told. Used to upset his dear old wife something rotten, let me tell you. Well, what can I say? My god! The years *have* been quite astoundingly unkind, haven't they, you repugnant old crone.'

Cutty Sark emitted an aggressive, if somewhat mortified, warning cough.

'And you say that you're the guardian of *The Winter Crown,*' pondered de Warrenne, licking the tips of his pointy canines. 'Yes. Yes of course. I remember. Well, isn't it a pity that you were such a useless duffer in that department? Now hop along, you heinous old hag, before I decide to pluck the rest of your remaining and (quite frankly, unsightly) limbs from your withered and repulsive carcass.'

'Aye, I'll leave soon enough,' seethed Cutty. 'When ye hand over *The Winter Crown*, ya thieving wee wanker.'

'And just *why* would I do that?' scoffed the vampire, an amused look playing across his debonair features.

'Because if ye do nae hand it back, laddie, I'll have to take it from ye,' snarled the sea-witch, with a threatening smile.

'My dear old … *thing*, you seem to have misunderstood just what is happening here. Let me explain. I, and my associates, are going to play a contest with Dr Chow, and his associates, for the ownership of *The Crowns of Albion*. So, unless you have something of value to offer to the proceedings, other than your delightful personality and unprecedented standing in the eye-candy department (and my god, woman, how could you have let yourself go in such a disgraceful manner?), you can just bugger off, there's a good little hag.'

'Then how about this!' she cried, her eyes burning with outraged fury. 'Danny! Pass it over, lad.'

Danny Blackflower unshouldered a sealskin satchel and tossed it to the sea-witch.

And from that bag she pulled a crown – the most beautiful jewel that anyone had ever seen: *The Crown of Spring*.

The Aelfradi warriors at Tom's side gasped and lurched forward – and would no doubt have rushed down the hill to reclaim their lost treasure there and then, if not for a harsh and sharp reprimand from Tommy Rawhead-and-Bloody-Bones.

'Steady, boys, steady,' he hissed, his eyes blazing with a hideous longing. 'Wait a little longer. Just a little longer, and the trap is sprung.'

De Warrenne almost swooned with avarice.

The Hound did a double-take so vigorous that his veil was in danger of being shaken off, and his hat of skimming across the ring like a flying-saucer.

'Oh my dear, dear lady,' beamed de Warrenne. 'I'm afraid that you and I seem to have gotten off on the wrong foot entirely, wouldn't you say? How's this for a proposal, my dear? Once my *chap* has finished his little *set-to* with Dr Chow's *fellow*, I'll be only too happy to play you for that little trinket you have over there.'

'I'll only wager it against *The Winter Crown*, and none other, d'ya ken?' hissed Cutty Sark.

'Well, that's just swell. Oh, that suits me just fine, my dear lady. Jolly good show.

'What do you say, Chow, old cock? Shall we let the delectable Ms Dee into our little game, and thereby bring this *unfortunate matter* to its final, and logical, conclusion? You've got to admit that this is quite a turn up for the books, eh? What an absolute stroke of spiffing good fortune!'

Mae looked over to Dr Chow/Hound.

The Hound gave a slow, and he hoped inscrutable, nod of his head.

'Agreed,' smiled Mae, with a courteous bow to de Warrenne and Cutty Sark.

'Splendid!' cried de Warrenne, rubbing his hands together in glee. 'Mr Willikins, as stake-holder, I believe you have a duty to perform.'

Whelk-faced Willie stepped forward and tentatively approached the sea-witch.

'Show me *The Winter Crown* first!' demanded Cutty Sark.

De Warrenne, smiling like all his Christmases and birthdays had come at once, clicked his fingers, and seconds later *The Wild Hunt* vampire Ajit Singh was by his side with a second metal case in hand. De Warrenne flicked it open and plucked out the icy beauty that was *The Winter Crown*.

Cutty's knee buckled and she inhaled a gasp.

'Madame,' oozed Whelk-faced Willie. 'Can I jutht thay how happy I am to thee you alive and looking tho ... ravithhing. Wonderful good newth it ith, it ith indeed, indeed it ith. Now, if you would be tho kind ath to jutht hand over that wonderful crown that you have there into my thafekeeping for the fortheeable time being.'

Watching him like a cabbage-leaf eyeing a slug, Cutty slowly handed *The Crown of Spring* to Whelk-faced Willie.

Willie took the crown and reverently carried it over to a small table that was erected by the side of the ring. Then, in turn, he collected the three remaining crowns and placed them in a row: Spring, Summer, Autumn and Winter.

The fabled *Crowns of Albion!* Reunited again for the first time in millennia. Reunified for the first time since the Pooks of the four great tribes had torn them away from the tyrannical and bloody grasp of the last Oberon – Nab of the Gentry (the infamous *Snatch-hand Nab*).

The air about them seemed to glow, and sparks began to crackle between them like a soft and subtle firework display, and all who looked on were spellbound – not only by their exquisite beauty, but by the raw and naked power that radiated from them like the waking breath of a long-forgotten god.

'Tho then,' sighed Whelky, trying to tear his eyes from the glistening fortune in front of him like a miser trying to peel an unmarked stamp from the envelope of a misdirected Christmas card, 'let'th get on with it, thhall we?

'Ath cuthtom dictateth, let the challengerth now prethent their championth. Ath you were the latht here, Ms Thark, perhapth you would be tho kind ath to go firtht.'

Behind the sea-witch, Danny Blackflower made to step forward.

'No, Danny,' hissed Cutty Sark. 'This is my fight. You've done more than enough already, me old mate.'

She turned and faced Whelk-faced Willie the Wheeze.

'I'll be fighting for the honour of The Gentry,' she stated flatly, eyeing him like a hyena in a tofu factory.

De Warrenne offered a slow handclap of support.

'Oh, well played, Madame,' he beamed, obviously relishing the prospect of seeing her squashed like a bug (or, more likely, ripped limb from prosthetic limb like a frail, one-legged, old age pensioner placed in the ring with a three-hundred-and-ninety-pound maltreated and half-starved were-wolf-wolfhound). 'Very well played indeed. I do like the cut of your jib, old girl.'

The dapper little vampire turned to Dr Chow-Hound.

'*Dr Chow*?' he grinned, pleasantly.

The Hound-Chow inclined his head in the direction of the were-jaguar-cum-tweedy-old-lunatic who was currently prowling in a high state of agitation in the far corner of the ring.

Cornelius tore off his robe and pounced into the middle of the arena, hands held up before him like claws, his toy snake tail twitching violently behind him.

'My name,' he roared, ' is 'Ector Antonio Sanchez Silvio, better known to fight fans the world over as – The Mighty 'ASS!'

'I see,' smirked de Warrenne. 'How very ... *amusing*. And you're a ... were...*jaguar,* is it?'

Cornelius offered his very best ferocious growl.

'Oh for pity's sake,' giggled de Warrenne. 'Can we just put an end to this quite pathetic illusion? Take off that ridiculous onesie, Professor. You look like the brat from *Where The Wild Things Are* who's been marooned in some bizarre time-travelling tragedy. And as for you, Percival, well, I for one would have hoped that you'd have known better.'

TWENTY SEVEN
Unmasked & Undone!

'So, you've seen through our little ruse, have you, de Warrenne!' snarled The Hound, tearing off his disguise and delighting in the liberating sense of freedom and the empowering rays of the full moon's breath upon his shaggy and tousled hide. 'But never fear, you unspeakable cad, your little crime spree, I'm very happy to say, is at an end. Time, old sport, for you to pay the reckoning.'

He turned to the other members of his crew: Dandy manfully pulled back the hood (with little, tufty cat ears sewn on it) of his leopard onesie and bristled with menacing indignation; Archie, Ned and Bob, all discarded their enormous wicker hats, ripped off their long silken robes and stood poised and ready for action.

'To me,' cried The Hound, lifting his noble snout to the slate-black sky, 'you proud, brave banners of Albion! To me!'

There was a taut and agonising silence as de Warrenne looked frantically about him, anxiously scanning the hills and the skyline.

He snapped his head around to face The Hound, a look of tortured dismay cast upon his cruel and handsome features.

'Wait a minute!' he gasped. 'Oh dear, no. You don't mean … You couldn't possibly be thinking of … No … Surely not! You weren't thinking of those hundred duffers that I've got confined in these here barns around us, were you?'

The Hound's noble snout twitched uncertainly.

'What do you mean?' he hissed, a look of appalled horror slowly crawling over his face.

De Warrenne clapped his hands and barked a sharp little guffaw of delight.

'Oh Percival, Percival, Percival,' he chuckled, wiping away a tear of mirth with the knuckle of his forefinger. 'You know, one of the things that I like the best about you also happens to be your most … *destructive* flaw. You're just too trusting, old fruit. I would have thought that you'd have grown to have known better by now, but you just never seem to learn, do you? Dear old Henry must be turning in his grave. You silly old nincompoop.'

En masse, the collected gathering of Bucca-men, nasties and ne'er-do-wells pulled cosh and cudgel, knife and knuckleduster, sword and spear from sheath and pocket.

'You see, Percy, not all of dearly-departed Prince Edric's loyal and noble *"Free-Folk"* (and really, I do so love that phrase; been thinking of borrowing it myself when I become Oberon) were all that noble or loyal. Well, not to him, at any rate. You see, some of them were, *are*, members of that wonderful institution of depravity and debauchery known as the brotherhood of *The Bucca* – and were, therefore, working under the orders of their new Bucca-Boo, who, as you're only too well aware, is none other than Madame Buckleberry, who, as you very well know, works for me.'

On cue, two of the Bucca-men in the crowd pushed their way forwards to the edge of the ring and removed their hooded cloaks ... to reveal – the hulking figure of Koll and the wizened and weaselly features of the wizened and weaselly wizard, Ek-Boran-Boranaran.

'You traitor!' roared Bob Goodfellow, when he saw his one-time apprentice unmasked.

'Oh shut up, you pathetic old fool,' sighed Ek-Boran. 'The power of The Pucks has been wasted and squandered for far too long. It's way past time that you were relieved of your post, Bob. You took the wrong path, you kindly old cretin. You all did! And deep down, you know it! Now is the time to turn back the clock and right that mistake. Now is the hour to put an end to the calamitous reign of the *Goodfellows*. And I want you to know, you arrogant duffer, that I mean to make it happen.'

'Well,' gasped de Warrenne, pretending to look shocked, 'now that we all know just were we stand, I suggest that we get back to business, don't you?

'Whelky, old chap?'

Whelk-faced Willie smiled like a condemned leech hoping for a pardon.

'Yeth, Your ... Highneth?' he squelched.

'I do hope that you weren't involved in any of these disgraceful, unsporting, and decidedly un-English, shenanigans?'

'Who me, thir? No, not me, thir! Perith the thought, thir. I can athure you that I knew abtholutely nothing about thethe ungentlemanly activitieth,' cried Whelky, managing to sound both betrayed and indignant, whilst dripping like a leaking lavatory.

'Glad to hear it, old stick. Would hate to have had to *lose* you,' smiled de Warrenne, kindly.

'Now,' purred the vampire, rubbing his hands together and looking excitedly about him, 'where were we? Ah yes. So, Professor Lyons (or should I say – Professor Pussy Pyjamas? [snigger]) you're up first. I believe that you'll be wagering your *Autumn* to my *Summer*, is that correct?'

Cornelius scowled across the ring at the natty little bloodsucker with a look of mortified hatred bristling across his exotically painted face (his splendid and beloved Newgate Knocker rather wonderfully tinted with jaguar-like rosettes, and his cherished moustache tweaked and teased into the semblance of cat whiskers). *If I should some'ow live to survive this*, he thought to himself, *I swear to God that I'm going to flippin' retire!*

'Splendid!' beamed de Warrenne. 'Well I suppose that it's well past time that I introduced *my* champion. Fair's fair, and all that. Wheel him in, chaps,' he cried.

And led into the (fast becoming overcrowded) ring – a hessian sack pulled over his enormous head, his murderous paws clamped together with manacles, his ankles shackled by a short length of chain (that enabled him only the most hobbling of strides) – came The Hound's long-lost brother and fellow (and only other known) were-wolf-wolfhound, the terrifying and brutish Bors. Leading him by a silver leash around his neck was *The Wild Hunt* witch, Madame Buckleberry, at his side, silver spear in hand, was de Warrenne's firstborn *child-of-darkness,* Opchanacanough (former prince of the proud Powhatan Confederacy), and behind them walked *The Society of the Wild Hunt* "Lurchers", to wit – *The Mockney, The Russian* and *The Weeping Nut-Cupper.*

Bors lifted his hooded head, and frantically sniffed the air. He seemed to catch The Hound's scent, for he suddenly turned his grotesquely masked muzzle in his brother's direction, was stock still for an agonising second, and then exploded into a terrifying frenzy of enraged madness.

The Hound looked on in horror.

Mae leapt into Ned's arms with a high-pitched squeal of dismay.

The collected spectators collectively yelped and recoiled in fright.

Cornelius's kitten whiskers curled in consternation, as beneath his prettily patterned war-paint he turned a ghostly shade of pale.

'For those of you who haven't yet had the pleasure,' grinned de Warrenne, clearly enjoying himself immensely, 'may I introduce *The Society of the Wild Hunt's* champion – Mr Bors de Warrenne.'

Tom squinted harder through his night-vision goggles.

Something was terribly wrong.

'Where are Long Lamkin and Edric's followers?' he hissed worriedly to Tommy Rawhead-and-Bloody-Bones. 'Shouldn't they have attacked by now?'

The dumbfounded old bogeyman and child-murderer (reformed) looked nervously at him with a gesture that said (rather comfortingly) "Your guess is as good as mine, old son." and set about gnawing his fingernails.

Tom screwed the goggles back to his eye sockets and frantically swept the area around the barns.

Nothing! No sign of any movement whatsoever.

He pulled focus to The Hound.

He could only see the back of the were-hound's head, but the fact that he had removed his "Chow-disguise", and the disheartened angle of the were-hound's ears, suggested that all was not well. And just one look at the berserk and barely restrained whirlwind of fury that was being presented in the middle of the ring was enough to convince Tom that things might be rather uncomfortable down there at present. And if that wasn't enough, to the side of the enraged monster (which, Tom concluded, could only be The Hound's brother, Bors) stood de Warrenne with a gloating look of triumph etched upon his dapper features.

The vampire suddenly turned his head, looked straight to Tom's concealed position, and winked.

Tom retracted his head from the goggles as if he'd suddenly noticed a scorpion in the bottom of his teacup.

The blood froze in his veins and he felt like throwing up with fright.

'They're on to us!' he hissed.

TWENTY EIGHT
Calamity At Castle Hill

'Oh, bugger this for a lark,' sighed de Warrenne, looking around the ring with a face draped in disappointment and disillusionment. 'You've taken all of the fun out of it. Damn your eyes, you absolute rotters! Well, if you whimpering pack of spoilsports can't see fit to play fair, then why should I? Let's just be done with it, shall we.

'KILL THEM!' he roared, elegantly flying backwards into the air to land gracefully on the top rope of the ring.

And then – to use a well-worn phrase (and why break the habit now?) – all hell broke loose.

Madame Buckleberry whispered a song-like spell and the chains that shackled Bors fell to the floor like concussed serpents.

Within a heartbeat, like a missile of homicidal hatred, Bors flew at the despised and detestable figure of his doppelgänger (and infuriating rival), his brother, The Hound.

With a sharp crunch like an obese snail's shell being popped, Mae shifted into Siamese-cat form and pelted from the ring, swerving and dodging the clumsy clutches of the Bucca-men who tried to apprehend him.

Whelk-faced Willie the Wheeze heroically dived for cover under the table where *The Crowns of Albion* sat coldly watching the unravelling proceedings like stately kings.

The horde of Bucca-men surged forward to surround Bob Goodfellow, Archie, and Danny Blackflower and his Astrai crewmen. Six burly Goblins quickly drove and separated the dumbfounded Bob from the two Pharisees and formed a wary ring around the mighty Puck of The Albions, spears poised and ready to do him no good.

And, walking along the ropes like a tightrope walker, hands tucked behind his back, as if he were taking a gentle stroll on a delightful summer's morning, the arch-cad de Warrenne barked out orders like the coach of the Under Elevens rugby sevens.

'Ajit and Okomto, take half a dozen of the chaps and search the hills. There are two witches and a House-Fairy up there, scuttling about somewhere. Bring me their heads and there'll be an extra helping of jam roly-poly pudding for all of you,' he guffawed.

'MacFee, make yourself useful and sort out that waif of an Elf over there,' he demanded, pointing to Ned.

MacFee nodded, pushed back the brim of his quivering top hat with a pistol-like finger, and pulled out a crossbow.

'Not with that, you blithering idiot!' snapped de Warrenne. 'You might hit one of our fellows. Go and sort him out *mano a mano*. He's half your size, you simpering oaf.'

MacFee drew a deep breath, rolled up his sleeves, dabbed his nose with his thumb, and marched manfully towards the waiting Smack Faery, jooks up and head down.

'Lurchers!' snapped de Warrenne.

The Mockney, *The Russian* and *The Weeping Nut-Cupper* sprang to attention.

'Oh you'll love this. Saved him especially for you. Time for a little *cat-hunt*,' tittered the vampire, pirouetting on the spot and pointing at the outraged form of ~~Professor Pussy Pyjamas~~ Cornelius *Dandy* Lyons.

The Wild Hunt henchmen sprang forward like greyhounds towards the Tigger-like form of the bristling-whiskered ex-Regency pug. Cornelius leapt over the ropes and dashed towards more open ground, determined to give himself a fighting chance by having more room to work in.

'Madame Buckleberry, would you be so kind as to rid me of that turbulent (and hideously revolting) hag?' he enquired politely, waving a dismissive finger in the direction of the sea-witch, Cutty Sark.

A cruel smile played across Madame Buckleberry's handsome face as she eyed the peg-legged Cutty contemptuously. Around and around she began to spin, whispering singsong enchantments, while the air around her began to crackle with the promise of a thunderstorm. She clapped her hands together and then pushed them out as if she was playing pat-a-cake with an imaginary friend. The sea-witch was sent tumbling through the ropes as if she'd been shoved by a giant. Madame Buckleberry followed after her, a savage and forbidding expression warped onto her comely face.

'Koll, old chap?' sniffed de Warrenne, standing on tip-toe to see if he could see the hulking Goblin. 'Where the devil are you?'

The burly Bucca-man waved his long arms from the edge of the ring – where he'd been doing his frustratingly inadequate best to catch the pesky little Siamese moggy that was squealing all over the place, and irritatingly getting under everybody's feet.

'Ah, there you are, dear boy. If you've got a moment, could you take a dozen of the lads over to those bushes on that hill? There's a party of Aelfradi warriors hiding up there. Now's your chance to prove to one and all that you Bucca-men have got the beating of those dreadfully snooty Avalon types, once and for all. Prince Tom, good old Johnny Spiritweather's boy, is up there with them (bless his still-beating heart). Do me a favour, old cock, and bring him back alive; ruffled, ruffed-up and barely breathing will be just fine. My advice would be not to push him too far though. Understood? Cracking. Oh, and Koll, once you've done that, there's a car-load of coppers at the end of the track. Do your worst. But do be careful – they've got a Troll with them.'

Koll grinned unpleasantly, called to him his twelve filthiest fighters, and off they set, filled with delight at the opportunity to stuff and slaughter their hated rivals. Trophies would be taken, reputations enhanced. Payback time for the Bucca-men, so cruelly crippled all those years ago by the Avalon prince, Johnny Grendel; for up there, in the hills, was his son. Retribution and redemption were at long last at hand.

'Oh thanks awfully, old chap. You will be careful now, won't you?' cried de Warrenne, waving Koll off like he was about to walk to school on his own for the first time.

'Opchanacanough, you stay at hand, that's the ticket – just in case we need to even the score up here and there. You are such a dear boy.'

The *Powhattan prince of darkness* showed his fangs and then leapt onto the opposing ring rope, prowling in stately agitation along them, whilst twirling a matching set of silver-coated tomahawks skilfully in his hands.

'We've got to do something!' gasped Tom, turning with a look of despair to Tommy and *The Purple Frighteners*, who were quickly gathering around him, wondering what to do.

'Thirteen Bucca-men heading this way, Tommy,' grinned an enchanting member of Tom's newly-formed bodyguard – a delightful chap known by the enthralling moniker of *Earwiggy*. 'I'll ready the lads, shall I? Beautiful chance to collect some *trophies*, I reckon,' beamed the charming old psychopath, distractedly fondling an earlobe (not his own, you understand – for his own ears had long since been ... *misplaced* – but one of the hundred or so that made up the eye-wateringly disconcerting *periwig* that perched at an unsettlingly peculiar angle on top of his unsettlingly peculiar head).

Tommy Rawhead nodded, picked up his kingfisher-headed cane and grinned like a conga eel after feasting on a bowl of overripe raspberries.

'Then let us rush forth to meet our enemies, brothers!' he cried, his eyes glistening like freshly-lanced buttock boils. 'Let us show these Goblin curs how real Elves sell their lives! Our names will be sung in the long halls of *The Hidden Realm* for a thousand years! And yours, Prince Adamsbane – *Tomas Grendel-Slayer, The Pook Who Never Was* – will be cheered throughout *The Nine Realms* for all eternity. Oh, how you are blessed, young warrior, to have the opportunity to end your short life in such a heroic and bloody fashion. Onward, my brothers! Let us unleash the true worth of *The Nightmare* upon our faithless foes!'

'No no no no no no no! Wait a minute!' hissed Tom, desperately trying to swing things back into the *"let's all do our very best to try and stay alive"* school of thought. 'Surely there's a way that we can turn this around?'

'But how, my prince?' asked Bloody-Bones. 'Look yonder – our friends battle against impossible odds; out-thought, outmanoeuvred, outnumbered. And our trump card, The Hound Who Hunts Nightmares, appears to be ... well, well-and-truly trumped, I'd say,' he stated, pointing down towards the faraway ring where

The Hound was locked in mortal combat with his bigger, older and psychotically deranged brother.

Tom all but dashed his hands on the floor in frustration. Why oh why did everybody think his life was so frickin' inconsequential! He'd only just got used to the heart-warming and utterly splendid idea that he was actually going to survive beyond his sixteenth birthday, and already some callous and demented bastard (this time, his old midnight debating buddy, Rawhead-and-Bloody-Bones) was already deciding how best to throw that future away. Well it wasn't fair! He wanted to live! He wanted to see his friends live; The Hound, Cornelius, Dame Ginty and Maggs, Ned and Archie, and all the rest of them! He wanted to see his Mum. He wanted to say to her all the things that he should have said to her but never seemed to get round to saying. He wanted to see Crow again. God, did he want to see Crow again! If he survived this, he was going to get her out of The Mound if he had to dig through its steel walls with his bare hands! He wanted to get to know Inspector Jones better, and understand his mystifying passion for *Prog-Rock*. And Hettie. He wanted to have a conversation with Constable Tuggnutter, maybe even find out what his first name was, if he had one that is ... But hang on! Wait just one minute ...

'Lads!' he gasped, almost in tears. 'I think I've got a plan.'

The Hound vaulted the ropes, ducked under and rolled around his brother's murderous attack, and managed to grab both Ned and MacFee by the scruff of their jackets. Like a discus thrower with double discuses, he hurled *The Smack Faery* and the treacherous *Vampyre Slayer* from the ring. He had no wish to see anyone come to harm because they happened to get caught in the crossfire (so to speak) between he and his psychotic sibling.

Now he and Bors were alone in the ring (save, of course, for the two despicable bloodsuckers currently stalking along the top ropes like a devilish circus act). Time to put an end to this deplorable charade.

The Hound turned, drew breath and faced his long-lost brother.

Archie was surrounded by a hostile sea of Goblins, all armed to the teeth and thirsting for blood.

Entrapped beside him were the nine Astrai fighting-Elves who had arrived with Cutty – the elusive Sea-Elves, the fabled Red Clan (who, as a point of interest, were closely related to the Pharisees, and were believed, by some historians, to be an offshoot of the Southern Elbi).

''Ow do, Danny,' grinned Archie, fiercely waving his war-putter and managing to keep the ferocious and bloodthirsty *Bucca* thugs at bay.

'Archie,' replied Danny Blackflower, with a curt nod of his head, vigorously flicking a ragged-looking cutlass back and forth with murderous intent. 'Would say that it's good to see you, old friend, but, under the circumstances ...'

'Likewize.'

'So sorry to hear about your dad, Archie. Really wanted to make it to his funeral, but, well, we had problems of our own.'

'Underztood, Danny. It was a fine celebration an' you waz mizzed, my friend, make no miztake about it.'

'Well let's just see if we can't make your old dad proud now, shall we?' snarled Danny. And together they launched themselves at the seething and hysterical mob of Goblin hooligans (Gobligans? or perhaps – Hooliblins?) before them.

Bob Goodfellow looked slowly at the face of each and every Goblin and Fae-world nasty that surrounded him.

'You ought to be ashamed of yourselves,' he tutted. 'Sucking up to these enemies of our people like this.'

'No!' barked a shrill and weaselly voice, and into the circle sprung the wizard Ek-Boran-Boranaran. 'It is you who should be ashamed, my old *master*, for it is *you* and your line who have shamed *us*. Best if your days were over, for you have betrayed *The Children of the Light* for far too long. Prepare to die.'

The small wizened Goblin began to whirl around and around, dancing and jigging in jagged little circles, whispering words of dark and ancient magic that seemed to make the very wind recoil in horror.

Bob dipped slowly to the ground, and, with a whisper of apology, plucked a handful of grass.

Ek-Boran stuck his hands in his pockets and suddenly cast two fistfuls of dust towards his old mentor.

Bob blew the grass from his hands like a lover's farewell kiss.

Dust and grass collided mid-air, and, to those around them, the chill night suddenly grew uncomfortably warm.

Bob and Ek-Boran stretched their arms and spread their fingers, as if trying to manipulate the very matter of existence, popping and creaking with strained expressions, like two decrepit and arthritic Go-Go dancers trying to relive their days of glory.

Ned sailed through the air and landed gracefully on his feet like a golden polecat.

Beside him Professor Marvin MacFee hit the deck like a black velvet squid, but, to his infinite surprise, somehow managed to roll, unharmed, to his feet.

The Professor quickly checked himself for injury, amazed that he had somehow seemed to have escaped his rather humiliating ejection unscathed. (To be honest, it wasn't the first time that he'd been humiliatingly ejected; though in the past he tended to have been a lot drunker, and not thrown quite so high and far, nor indeed by a seven-and-a-half foot tall were-wolf-wolfhound of legendary repute.) It was then he noticed, with an anger-inducing dismay, his crumpled top hat.

'All right, *Fairy Boy*, that's it!' he growled, like the hard-bitten sheriff of a Wild West boom-town about to have the final showdown with a troublesome cowboy in the roughest saloon around. 'Let's get it over with. I'll try and make this as painless for you as I can, son.'

Cornelius sprinted as fast as he could for thirty seconds, pausing only to tear the articulated snake toy *tail* from his onesie – an act he soon regretted, for there was quite a chill in the air. However, he had more pressing matters to worry about than the night's frosty kiss upon the seat of his stripy long johns. He skidded to a halt, turned, and watched as the three *Wild Hunt* henchmen pounded menacingly towards him.

'Ow could it come to this? the tweedy old codger couldn't help but think to himself, almost weeping at the injustice and humiliation of it all. Here he was, Cornelius *Dandy* Lions – once the pride of The Fancy, the idol of the Swell Mob, famed for his flash and dapper clothing and his sharp sense of fashion – about to meet his doom dolled up like an understudy for a pantomime of Postman Pat, with his face painted like Bagpuss at a toddler's carnival parade. *'Owever would 'e live it down?* he wondered. *That is*, he suddenly considered, *in the unlikely scenario that 'e did live to tell the tale.*

'Ah well, me old mucker,' he muttered to himself, as *The Wild Hunt* goons slowed down to an ominous walk, and spread out in front of him, 'if you're going to go out, you might as well go out in style.'

He wiped his whiskers with a gnarled knuckle of his cast-iron fist and glared at the cautiously approaching hoodlums.

''Ello again, gents,' he growled, with a carefree air. '*Round Two* it is then?'

Madame Buckleberry spun through the air, her hair fluttering in an unperceived breeze, sneering with cruel intent and throwing her hands out like a baseball pitcher having a paddy.

'*Iron, steel and stone;*' she chanted, '*break her ugly bones!*
'*Hammer, slash and pound; grind her to the ground!*'

It was all that Cutty Sark could do, weakened by her recent ordeals as she was, to curl up on the floor with her head tucked between her elbows in a futile attempt to defend herself from the incessant, violent and hurtful blows of *The Wild Hunt* witch's powerful magic.

'Right,' said Tom. 'Listen up.'

He looked around at the circle of pale and frightful faces of his *Purple Frighteners*, as they huddled around him and beamed down with expressions of eager-to-please zeal and suicidal enthusiasm.

'What we need to do is to somehow get to Bob Goodfellow and then get him into a position where he can unlock whatever enchantment it is that is keeping Long Lamkin and Prince Edric's *Free-Folk* out of the fray. If we can free them, and so unleash their hundred spears into the fight, then we'll turn the tide, save our friends and win the day,' announced Tom, dramatically.

'It is a ... splendid *idea*, Prince Tomas,' said Tommy Rawhead, looking pleased that Tom had actually come up with something that sounded halfway like *princely* intelligence (God help us!), but also equally sounding more than a little unconvinced. 'But how can we get to The Goodfellow in time? *The Bucca* war-party is almost upon us and, even if we manage to fight our way through them and reach the farm, we will still be hopelessly outnumbered?'

'Not necessarily. Here's the plan: Tommy, you and me, along with Mouse' (Mouse being the largest, burliest and most dangerous-looking member of *The Purple Frighteners* by a long shot – oh, Tom knew how to pick his teammates, never you fear!) 'are going to make it down to Inspector Jones and The Department of Special Cases, while the rest of the lads hold off these pesky Goblins and buy us the time to reach them.'

'So you, me and the Mouse are going to ... run away?'

'No, no, no,' smiled Tom, slowly shaking his head. 'Not *run away*, Tommy. We're going to get help that will help us *win the day*,' he explained, kindly.

'I see,' replied Rawhead, sounding somewhat sceptical. 'And the rest of the lads are going to stay here and fight Koll's war-band?'

'You mean – *hold them off*. Exactly. Shouldn't be too hard, eleven Aelfradi are worth double their number of Bucca-men any day of the week.'

The Purple Frighteners looked very pleased with themselves, and slapped backs and punched shoulders and vocalised their heartfelt agreement on the subject.

'As you wish, my prince. We are here to serve,' growled Rawhead, looking proudly at his team, but still somewhat unconvinced (or, more probably, Tom decided, miffed that he would be missing out on a good fight and the chance to lop fleshy things from his gallant opponents). 'But I still don't quite understand how –'

'Just trust me, Tommy!' cut in Tom, trying his best to sound commanding. 'There isn't time to explain everything.'

'Of course. You are my prince, my prince. You have my undying loyalty.'

'But listen,' continued Tom, changing his tone to one of parental concern. 'I don't want any of you lads getting yourselves killed. You're no use to me dead, and if any of you do get yourself killed, then you'll have the full wrath of *The Grendel Slayer* on your ungodly heads. Do I make myself understood?'

The chaps looked at the floor and shuffled their feet. Tom was convinced that he might have heard the odd sniff here and there.

'Now, I've got a brand new shiny fifty-pound note at home, and when this night is over I'm going to buy each and every one of you a bottle of beer and a bag of crisps. (Of course I won't be able to do it myself, due to the licensing laws, but I'm sure that we can find someone to run along to the off-licence on my account). Are you with me, warriors of *The Hidden Realm*?'

'AYE!' they roared.

'Then to arms, my brave brothers!' cried Tom, standing up and pumping his fist into the night sky – so that, by chance more than design (but what the heck), it was framed, heroically, against the blood-red moon. 'Imitate the action of the tiger!' he cried, suddenly overcome with a zealous fervour of his own (princely stuff – must be genetic, you know). 'Stiffen the sinews, guzzle their blood! Disguise foul nature with ... even fouler-favoured rage; lend the eye a ... er ... an even more terrible aspect and teach the buggers how to war. And you, you good bogeymen, whose limbs were made in Avalon, show us the mettle of your ... *pasture*(?); let us swear that you are worth your breeding; which I for one doubt not [God help us all!]; For there is none of you so mean and base, [well that might be pushing it a bit] that hath not murderous bloodshed in your eyes [how true]. I see you stand like wish-hounds in the slips, straining upon the start. The game's afoot; Follow your spirit, and upon this charge cry "God for Tomas, Avalon and ... urm ... The Hound! On you noble horrors and unleash The Nightmare!'

The Purple Frighteners gleefully howled their blood-curdling battle-cries and, whooping like the practised pack of bogeymen that they were, set forth to serve a sound trouncing to the fast approaching Bucca-men.

Tom pulled the mountainous Mouse and the murderous Rawhead to one side, told them to stick close by at all costs, and dashed off across the hillside to where (he hoped) Inspector Jones and the D.S.C. awaited in their lovely warm (and fast) car; feverishly praying that they would make it there alive, and silently giving thanks to his old English teacher and a rare and cherished afternoon at school watching videos of Henry V.

The Hound blocked a savage (but wild) roundhouse swipe of Bors' lethal claws, by jabbing his elbow into his brother's wrist and following it immediately by extending his arm like a piston and delivering a perfectly placed hammer-blow to the tip of the were-hound's nose.

Bors' yelp of rage and frustration was cut swiftly cut short by a smart right hand lead to the jaw, as The Hound (Percival that is) compassed to his right and out of distance of his brother's clumsy riposte.

Percival fought on the defensive, using the size of the ring to outmanoeuvre and frustrate Bors with fancy and fast-flowing footwork (when most people talk about "footwork" what they actually mean is "leg-work", The Hound, however, knew the subtle and, in this particular case, life-saving difference). Apart from the canicidal and fratricidal were-wolf-wolfhound trying to rip him into tiny pieces, his other problem, of course, was the two vampires running along the top ropes aiming cowardly and sneaky kicks and blows at him if he strayed too near them, along with a constant stream of biased cries of encouragement offered to Bors, and useless (though under the circumstances perhaps understandable) sneers of derision and quite unnecessary and ungentlemanly suggestions directed towards he (The Hound), an act that The Hound had every intention of making the vulgar little scoundrels pay for.

However, he knew that he couldn't keep up his defensive strategy indefinitely, for two reasons:

1. The longer the fight went on the more chance that he would make a mistake or Bors would get lucky or, even worse, adjust his tactics. Although his brother was bigger and heavier than he, possibly stronger, almost as quick, and ten times more savage, The Hound had one massive advantage over him: he had been trained by some of the greatest martial artists that the world had ever seen, (the Renaissance master-at-arms, *Vincentio Saviolo*; the Cheyenne warrior, *Stands Alone* [though The Hound liked to think that he'd been able to export some wonderful insights into the art of arms to his adopted people – a thought that they seemed to have reciprocated, for did they not bestow upon him the great honour of naming their most famous war-society after him?]; the *Charlemonts* [both Joseph and his son Charles] professors in the art of Savate; and not forgetting the terror of the Regency prize-ring himself [one of the most scientific and savage pugilists to ever grace the squared ring], *Cornelius Lyons* – to name but a few) while his brother, though gifted with all the physical attributes to make him a battler of the first and highest order, had had none of this education and thus fought purely on instinct, savagery and brutality.

2. If he didn't hurry up and *put* his brother *away* (to borrow a phrase from Cornelius) it was more than likely that all of his dear friends and comrades would be slaughtered. Not only that, de Warrenne would triumph and, unopposed, would actually be crowned as The Oberon of Albion. This The Hound could not let happen. But just how the devil was he going to turn the tables on the despicable and odious cad? Once again he had been outmanoeuvred, out-thought and, quite possibly, outfought!

Tom tore along the hillside, Rawhead and Mouse struggling to keep apace with him. Behind him he could hear the sounds of a hard-fought scuffle being painfully contested, and he winced as he thought that he had so easily put other peoples' lives in danger. But what else could be done? If they managed to reach Inspector Jones and the D.S.C. in time, then surely more lives would be saved than lost.

MacFee thumbed his nose and shot out a businesslike left jab to the face of the infuriatingly handsome little fellow dressed up like a musical hero of his (MacFee's) youth.

Ned Leppelin weaved under the blow, trapped the *Vampyre Hunter's* arm at wrist and elbow (a punch is never correctly finished until the hand has been brought back to a defensive position), snapping said arm with a stomach-turning crack, and sent the Professor crashing to the floor with a side kick that swept away his over-weighted (and over-extended) lead leg.

MacFee hit the floor clutching his shattered limb and whimpering in pain.

'Sweet Jesus!' he snivelled, his face screwed up in agony. 'What in Blue Jiminy did you do that for?'

Cornelius soon began to enjoy himself.

These modern fellows, he thought to himself with a regretful shake of his head, *just didn't know 'ow to 'andle themselves.* He almost felt sorry for them. *All thunder an' no lightning. Still, shouldn't be too 'ard on them. Weren't their fault; there being nobody to pass on the finer points of the Art to them these days, an' even if there were, the canvas (so to speak) for them to develop an' refine their skills on 'ad long since gone. Everything,* he supposed, *'as its day.*

As he settled himself into the rhythm of things, he began, as was his wont on such occasions, to hum a little ditty.

"*Arry, 'Arry, 'Arry, 'Arry ...*' [straight left hand to jaw of wide-open *Mockney* {shocking technique!}. *Just what did the poor lad think 'e was doing?*] '*you 'ave got a chance ...*' [side-step and roll under lazy hook from *The Russian*] '*to*' [shovel-hook to short ribs] '*marry ...*' [pause for all to hear "*Oomph!*" effect] '*A nice ...*' [straight left knife-punch to throat, with a left foot pass {trigger-stepped, of course}] '*little ...*' [right hand corkscrew to nose] ' *widow ...*' [observe blighter sink to floor like a dropped anchor] '*with a ...*' [pivot and shimmy to avoid *The Weeping Nut-Cupper's* over-zealous attempt at a *take-down,* tripping the cack-handed hoodlum as he passed] '*nice ...*' [lead left hand to *The Mockney's* already claret-leaking schnozzle] '*lit-,*' [repeat] '*-tle*' [repeat] '*pub ...*' [repeat], '*plenty...*' [turn last jab into hook to temple, delivered with the heel of the hand] '*of ...*' [curl fingers and grab a fistful of the blond bombshell's woefully long fringe and turn head] '*baccy,*' [right elbow to left cheek] '*beer,*' [in same movement, bring right hand back, pivoting at the elbow, and deliver backhand hammer-blow to right cheek] '*an' plenty of ...*' [head-butt to bridge of nose] '*grub.*' [Observe flaxen-haired henchman topple like a starched plank.]

'*I could ...*' [block straight punch {woeful delivery; all arm and no turn of hip nor shoulder! *Just 'oo teaches these Muppets?*} from *Weeping Nut-Cupper*] '*come round ...*' [punish the uneducated, though admirably enthusiastic, duffer for holding his chin too high with light tap on Adam's apple] '*to see you ...*' [uppercut to *the mark*] '*to keep you company ...*' [Step back and admire work as *Nut-Cupper* gasps like a tickled trout in a bowl of treacle] '*Wouldn't it be nice ...*' [wait for poor chap to get his breath back, whilst artfully twirling ends of moustache, then parry his intended ankle-kick with sole of boot] '*for you and ...*' [block reprehensible knee-strike to groin, by sinking body weight behind sharp pointy elbow and into the inexcusable duffer's thigh] '*er ...*' [lift arm straight up from the elbow-block and push head back at chin {still held distressingly high, and not a sign of an adjustment!} with heel of the palm] '*an' ...*' [listen with slight grimace as teeth crack like a gunshot] '*wouldn't it be nice ...*' [step in and deliver reprehensible knee-strike of one's own between legs of stumbling and off-balanced amateur] '*for ...*' [retreat and watch in horrified sympathy as *Weeping Nut-Cupper* seeps boss-eyed to the floor, cupping genitals and weeping softly for a nurse, who is in no danger of showing up in the foreseeable future] '*... me.*'

Something soft and leathery flickered against the side of the hood of Tom's parka.

Tom frantically tore down said hood and wailed in horror, as he thudded to an aghast halt.

There, before him, stood *The Wild Hunt* vampire, Ajit Singh – naked as the day he was born.

'You!' hissed the vampire, the look of evil delight in his shark-like eyes suddenly morphing into one of surprised and nervous apprehension.

Well, he wasn't the only one wearing a look of surprised and nervous apprehension, let me assure you! But, judging by the look of trepidation on Ajit Singh's face, Tom suddenly wondered if the hateful bloodsucker was remembering their last encounter – when Tom had (apparently) morphed into a monstrous Half-Grendel and battered the unliving daylights out of the despicable swine – and having second thoughts about the whole unseemly matter?

With a speed of thought that few thought him capable of (but really, Tom found that coming face to face with a stark-naked vampire in the middle of the Sussex countryside on the night of a full and blood-red moon sharpened the wits most wonderfully) Tom pretended to shudder and bubble as if he was on the edge of another monster-shape-shifting 'episode'.

Ajit flinched and recoiled a little in uncertain consternation, and, in his moment of hesitation, Rawhead and Mouse were on him like terriers, wrestling him to the floor and battering him with clubs and sticks, knees and feet, fists, heads, elbows and teeth.

'On, Prince Dearlove! On!' barked Tommy Rawhead-and-Bloody-Bones. 'We have him. We have him!' he cried, a look of soon-to-be blood-letting glinting in his hideous eyes.

Mouse straddled and pinned the vampire to the floor with weighty bulk and snake-like sinewy muscle, while Tommy stood poised with his kingfisher-headed spear over the undead Sikh's heart.

'NO!!' screamed Ajit, writhing like a netted alligator.

'Fly, Tomas, fly!' hissed Tommy.

Tom didn't have to be asked twice. He put his head down and sprinted so hard he thought his lungs would burst from his chest.

Inspector Jones nibbled on another Hobnob and worriedly checked his watch again.

'Shouldn't Mr Hound have sent us the signal by now?' asked Hettie, leaning back to look out of the rear window of the D.S.C's. sleek grey Alfa Romeo and at the strange and blood-red moon.

Constable Tuggnutter mumbled something unintelligible in possible agreement.

'He was very explicit that we shouldn't stir until he gave us the call,' replied Jones, hurriedly glancing at the mobile phone on the dashboard to double-check that they still had a signal. 'I'm sure that these things always take a little longer than you expect,' he added, trying hard to convince himself as much as the others.

'NAAAAAAAAAAAAAAAAAAAAAAAAAAAAAAAARRRRGGHHHHH!!!!!!!!'

Hobnobs flew in all directions, as the scream of terror (so terrible and horrendous as to be almost unearthly) hung like the waking moment of a nightmare in the bloodstained sky.

'WHAT THE FLIPPIN' HECK WAS THAT!' cried Hettie, almost reopening the wound on her forehead as she flinched in horror and cracked her noggin on the roof of the car.

Jones, Clem and the Constable all found themselves clinging to one another in a primordial dread.

Tuggnutter mumbled something and pointed a finger like a squashed haggis towards the hills to the left of the car.

Inspector Jones and Sergeant Clem followed the line of his digit and saw, to their utter dismay, a ghostly apparition tearing towards them at breakneck speed, quivering like a demon released from the pits of Perdition, with ghastly disc-like eyes that caught the light of the blood-red moon and sent it back like glistening hell-fire. Something long, dark and hideous flapped violently from its shoulders like the wings of a deformed bat. And as it shuddered towards them it screeched horribly like the very souls of the damned.

'What in the name of God?!' gasped Inspector Jones, squinting through the windscreen to try and make out just what the heck was coming their way, whilst hastily fumbling with an unsteady hand at the ignition key.

Constable Tuggnutter turned to him, put a calming hand on the Inspector's arm and smiled.

'It's Tom,' he said.

TWENTY NINE
The Reckoning

Whelk-faced Willie peered out from under the table at the carnage all around him and winced with a sorrowful shake of his head. He looked on with regret as he watched young Archie Swapper and the Astrai boys battle valiantly against the overwhelming horde of Bucca-men. He glanced, with a passing professional interest, at Puck Goodfellow locked in mortal combat with his old friend and apprentice Ek-Boran Boranaran, neither one seemingly able to get the upper hand.

Oh, well, sighed Whelky. *What a pity it would be to wathte thuch a golden, and, quite frankly, unique, opportunity. Indeed it would. It would indeed.*

With a quick look up towards the ring-ropes, just to make sure that that nice Lord de Warrenne fellow and his erstwhile colleague (the sour-faced, but undoubtedly charming, Mr Opchanacanough) still had their attention firmly fixed on the fascinating little tear-up that was currently being contested between his dear friend, Mr Hound, and this remarkable new *fellow*, Mr Bors de Warrenne (*And wasn't he an unexpected turn up for the books ... and quite the prospect, by the looks of things.*), Whelky stealthily drew from the inside pocket of his suit a large, discreet and nondescript holdall.

'Hello, my little beautieth,' he gushed, his eyes almost popping from his head, like a slug who's been offered his pick of the winners at the All England Cabbage-Growers' Convention, as he gazed down in enraptured wonder at the glittering and priceless crowns of the Elbi Kings. 'Let'th juthth let Uncle Whelky make thure that you're kept thafe from harm, tthall we?'

He reached out a tentative and slimy finger to touch a crown (just one, to begin with, he wasn't greedy ... well that wasn't strictly true ... perhaps some might say he was, but that was to misunderstand him; no, he wasn't *greedy*, he was a ... what was the word now? ah yes ... a *connoisseur*; a connoisseur of expensive ... *stuff*); just, you understand, to see what it felt like to hold such unbelievable beauty in one's hands – such power, such history, such wealth! Why, each one alone would be worth a Pook's ransom!

'Hello, Brother Whelky,' whispered a voice like a semi-submerged sneeze.

Whelk-faced Willie guilty shot his head around, like a rat caught contemplating a cheeseboard, sending a long globule of snot flying from his perpetually dripping hooter to land, to Whelky's mortified dismay, in the eye of the speaker.

'Oh ... er... hello, Peachy,' replied Whelky, as calmly and innocently as he knew how – a smile of innocent terror strapped across his wilting visage like an arthritic limpet struggling to cling to a melting iceberg. 'Fanthy theeing you here.

And you too, Danny. How'th your mum thethe dayth? Do thend her my regardth won't you–EEK!'

A rather impressive meat-cleaver gently rolled around Whelky's rather gently wibbling throat.

'And just what are you up to, Uncle?' grunted Danny, menacingly.

'Nothing, Danny. Whyever do you athk?' squeaked Whelky, somehow managing to sound both curious and offended.

'Well, Whelky, old mate,' beamed Peachy, wiping The Wheeze's snot from his crocodilian eyes, his pasty face lighting up in delight at the sight of the crowns laid out on the table before them, 'it looks suspiciously to us like we might have caught you in the despicable act of taking what isn't yours to take. Would that be a fair assessment of the situation, Brother Willikins?'

'Not a word of it, Peachy! On my thithterth grave!' gasped Whelk-faced Willie the Wheeze, his voice squelching with affront. 'Very hurtful, I mutht thay, Brother Peachy. Very hurtful. No ... no, what I wath actually contemplating wath ... wath taking thethe prethious relicth, thethe pritheleth jewelth and artifactth that are of thuch hithtorical and cultural importanthe to our proud and noble people, out of harmth way in cathe they got ... damaged ... in all thith madnethth and mayhem, that'th all.'

'Well that is most considerate of you, Brother Whelky,' smiled Peachy, with a petrifying wink. 'What a wonderful act of kindness and dedication to *The Cause*. But I think that it would be more ... appropriate ... for me and Brother Danny to take over in the accomplishment of that most thoughtful and selfless of gestures, don't you? For the good of *The Brotherhood*, you understand. Here? You are up to date with your subscription, aren't you, Whelky?'

Danny pressed the meat-cleaver tighter to Whelk-faced Willie's throat.

Whelky was just about to explain how business had been a little slack recently, when the night was suddenly torn asunder by a scream akin to Mick Jagger being scalped.

'NAAAAAAAAAAAAAAAAAAAAAAAAAAAAAAARRRRGGHHHHH!!!!!!!!'

'What the frickin' hell was that, Danny?' hissed Peachy, looking round in terror.

'The Devil only knows, Brother Peachy ... but it seems that I might have just done a very regretful thing,' gruffed the sinewy Goblin, looking appalled and somewhat embarrassed by his socially awkward *faux pas*.

'Whatever is it, Brother Danny?' enquired Peachy, his head snapping back round to address his dear companion. 'Oh my word, Danny, what have you done!' he hissed, his toothy, alligator-smile for once absent.

'That horrible noise made me jump!" grunted Brother Danny, defensively. 'I didn't mean to do it! Honest. My hand slipped!"

For at Brother Danny's feet lay the writhing form of Whelk-faced Willie the Wheeze Willikins – the south-side snotter, the mollusc-mouthed mucous muncher, the lisping Lothario of the Lowland Ladies, landlord of the Concealed

Arms and co-founder of the notorious *Underground Bridge Club* – his throat slit from ear to ear and spurting blood in all directions.

'Oh dear, oh dear, oh dear,' sighed Peachy, shaking his head, a toothy and sympathetic smile slowly creaking back into place. 'Now that is a shame. Such a shame. Oh well, can't be helped. Accidents will happen. Brother Danny,' he continued, as he began hastily stuffing *The Crowns of Albion* into poor Whelky's large, discreet and nondescript holdall, 'I suggest that we *liberate* these treasures, for the good of *The Brotherhood,* you understand, and make ourselves ... unavailable.'

It was a suggestion that Brother Danny was obviously in complete concurrence with, for the two of them fled the scene faster than a pair of murdering and double-crossing *tea leaves* who have just stolen the long-sought-after-and-cherished-objects-of-desire of a violent gang of criminal vampires, from right under their undead nose.

'Oh come on, Bors!' groaned de Warrenne in frustration. 'Stop messing about and just finish the little runt.'

Bors, down on one knee and staring hot murder towards his little brother (who was, no doubt about it, besting him in all and every department), wiped the blood from his muzzle on the back of his bloodstained paw. His face was battered, bruised and swollen, his ribs discoloured and one eye half-closed.

On the other side of the ring, The Hound looked down at him and silently begged that the brute would come to his senses and give up – a wish that he didn't hold out much hope for. He himself was covered in blood; cut and slashed by Bors' terrible talons and, on one occasion, by his ferocious fangs. While The Hound had restrained himself and refused to use anything that might prove lethal to his opponent, his older brother had shown no such qualms about using the full and fearsome range of his terrifying arsenal. The Hound had hoped that he would be able to cudgel his brother insensible but, alas, Bors had proved himself to be even tougher than he had feared.

A cry, somewhat akin to Freddie Mercury having his moustache ripped off, suddenly sliced through the blood-soaked sky.

'NAAAAAAAAAAAAAAAAAAAAAAAAAAAAAAARRRRGGHHHHH!!!!!!!!'

De Warrenne lifted his head towards the direction of the hideous scream, and his jovial and dapper features morphed into a frozen mask of infuriated dismay, for he knew that voice and he knew, of old, that sound – and somewhere deep inside, whatever was left of his immortal soul cried out in fear and sorrow. Ajit Singh, his youngest (and, though he would never openly admit it, favourite) *son-in-darkness,* was in mortal peril!

'Opchanacanough!' he hissed, his voice as solemn as a grave. 'Ajit is in trouble. Find him!'

The Powhattan turned his handsome features towards the moon and clapped his hands. As his clothes crumbled onto the apron of the ring, a huge bat flew high into the slate-black sky and towards the hills where the terrible scream had come from.

At that moment De Warrenne just happened to look over his shoulder towards the table where *The Crowns of Albion* should have been displayed, and almost fell off the ropes.

The table was empty!

A dark cloud of fury passed across the vampire's debonair features.

He turned to Bors.

'Finish it!' he roared. 'Or I'll kill you both myself.'

And then, with murderous hatred in his undead heart, he leapt from the ring-ropes and down towards the empty table.

Madame Buckleberry stood over the cringing, curled and prone figure of Cutty Sark, chanting dark rhymes of long-banished and hateful magic, and throwing her hands towards the sea-hag as if she was casting stones.

'*Slash and stab and pound,*' she chanted, her voice a sweet and singsong cackle of malice, '*grind her to the ground!*'

Blood seeped through the cuts and scratches on the back and sleeves of the sea-witch's oil-skin jacket, and the old crone could be heard grunting through gritted teeth.

A cry like the damned in Hell suddenly cut through the night, as if someone had been caught stealing the last tiramisu from Pavarotti's rider.

'NAAAAAAAAAAAAAAAAAAAAAAAAAAAAAARRRRGGHHHHH!!!!!!!!'

Madame Buckleberry stopped her chant and looked towards the hills with a look of dread.

Cutty Sark suddenly snapped her head around and glowered at the young, and almost beautiful, sorceress.

'Och, why don't ye just put a wee sock in it, ya horse-faced and intolerable bucketful of sour shite!' she sneered. And, springing upwards with an almighty hop, and holding her unfastened wooden-leg like a war-club, she brained the flabbergasted and distracted Madame Buckleberry with it, sending *The Wild Hunt* enchantress crashing to the floor and into a long and, one hopes, fretful sleep.

Ned dragged the incessantly whimpering Professor MacFee to where Professor Lyons had cuffed and trussed the battered and bruised *Wild Hunt* henchman.

'So run that by me again, son,' quizzed Cornelius, raising a sceptical eyebrow.

The Mockney peered up at him through two blackened eyes, claret dripping from his broken nose, and spat blood violently onto the floor.

'My dame is Tony Doyle,' he stated, in a strong accent devoid of any *Mockneyism* but brimming with the musical twang of the North Americas, 'American Indelligence.'

The old fellow raised a quizzical eyebrow, but didn't say anything.

Tony Doyle, if that was indeed his name, sighed and shook his head.

'Special *Agent* Tony Doyle of the Federal Bureau for Paradormal Invesdigation,' he said again. 'Dear God, I dhink you broke my dose!'

'An' you?' asked Cornelius, turning to the still gasping and swollen-necked *Russian*.

'Karol Lesnevich ... *Brotherhood ... of ... the ... Jaeger*,' he managed to wheeze, gulping painfully, and with some difficulty, between each word.

Cornelius twirled the tip of his dyed and jaguar-rosetted moustache in interest. The secretive and mysterious *Jaeger Brotherhood* were a near-legendary and ancient organization dedicated to the destruction of the powerful and ferocious *Vampire Families* of Eastern Europe. Would it really be a surprise if they had infiltrated *The Society of the Wild Hunt* – what with de Warrenne's past associations and history?

'An' what about you, son?' frowned Cornelius, puckering his lips in curiosity and tapping the toe of his onesie-covered foot against the upturned sole of the curled and doubled-up *Weeping Nut-Cupper's* boot. 'No, 'ang on, let me guess – MI Unseen?'

The Weeping Nut-Cupper slowly shook his head, his face ashen, his bloodshot and swollen eyes still watering, and his mouth firmly set in an agonized grimace.

'I...PISS,' he rasped. 'Special ... Agent ... Patrick ... Windsor.'

'Is that so?' sniffed Cornelius, casting a misgiving glance in Ned's direction. 'Got any proof of that, son?'

Special Agent Patrick Windsor rolled onto his back with a gasp and looked up at the sky.

'Go ... to ... Hell, you ... miserable ... bastard!' he whimpered.

Cornelius looked down at the tormented poor chap, sucked his teeth and nodded his head in understanding sympathy.

'Anyone else?' he grunted, shooting a quizzical scowl towards MacFee.

MacFee obviously contemplated putting his arm up and trying to talk his way out of his unfortunate predicament, but one look at Cornelius' face convinced him that it wouldn't be wise to try.

Cornelius suddenly lifted his head to the skies, for he thought he heard the unmistakable low, cutting buzz of a helicopter rolling across the valley.

'Dandy!' cried Ned. 'Look. Over there!'

Cornelius tore his eyes from the heavens, followed Ned's outstretched hand and saw two shadowy and decidedly shifty-looking figures making their way up the hillside and about to disappear behind a little copse of bushes. One of said suspicious figures had a large, clearly weighty and gently-clinking bag of what could only be ill-gotten swag slung across his shoulder.

De Warrenne landed by the empty table like a meteor.

'Where are my bloody Crowns?!!' he meeped, casting his head from side to side and looking like he might be close to tears.

219

He noticed the prostrate and leaking form of Whelk-faced Willie the Wheeze Willikins lying close by on the ground, and shuddered over to him like a grief-blinded bullet.

In one lightning-fast action he grabbed Whelky by the labels of his jacket and hoisted him up, face height, with one hand.

'WHERE ARE MY CROWNS!' he roared. 'Oh, for Heaven's sake, you wretched little blighter, stop playing possum and tell me what happened here or I *will* cut your throat!'

Whelk-faced Willie the Wheeze peeled open an eye and offered the vampire a warm, if slimy, leer of greeting.

'Lord de Warrenne,' he beamed, 'what a lovely pleathure to thee you, Thire. It ith indeed, indeed it ith.'

De Warrenne took a deep and infuriated breath.

'WHAT! HAPPENED! TO! THE! CROWNS?' he barked, politely.

Whelky carefully removed the steel collar from around his neck (covered, as it was, with a thin and [pasty] flesh-coloured sack, filled with theatrical blood – you'd be surprised [or perhaps you wouldn't] just how many people had tried to slit The Wheeze's throat over the years, and so, in consequence, Whelky always saw it as a necessary precaution to be suitably prepared).

'Thome bigger boyth took it,' he replied, unable, even at such a precarious point in his long and, quite frankly, disreputable life (where that life, quite literally, hung in the fingertips of an irate, ruthless and terrifyingly powerful vampire), to break the unspoken rule of *not snitching* and not dropping a fellow felon (alleged) in it.

'And which way might these *bigger boys* have gone?' enquired de Warrenne, pleasantly, drawing Whelky's mollusc-like mush to his own (not that de Warrenne's face was in any way mollusc-like, you understand).

'I tried to thtop them, Thire,' lied Willie, bringing the noble tears of the loyal servant (who, through no fault of his own, has let down a beloved and cherished master) to his rheumy eyeballs, 'but I'm an old fellow, a mere thhadow of my former thelf ... worthlethth and uthlethth old fool that I am,' he wept, dejectedly.

'WHICH WAY!'

'That way,' said Whelky, with cast-iron certainty, as he pointed a finger dramatically towards the hills (though, truth be told, he had absolutely no idea which direction Peachy and Danny had scarpered in, but it seemed a lot quicker to at least say something positive rather than have to (quite literally) hang around any longer than was absolutely (and to be honest, quite painfully) necessary and try to explain to the (quite clearly, and understandably, upset) monstrous bloodsucker that he'd been a bit preoccupied at the time of their exit.

De Warrenne squinted into Whelky's squelchy eyes with a look that threatened untold *unpleasantness* if he was to discover that he was being deceived in any way.

Whelky blessed the vampire with his most trustworthy and endearing smile, and then found himself sailing upward and across the night sky as de Warrenne hurled him away like an unwanted baseball and hastily followed on the trail of the thieves.

Whelky watched in wonder as the blood-red moon grew closer and closer, marvelling, momentarily, at Her beauty, and thinking how he'd never had the opportunity to examine Her quite so closely before. Then gravity took a hold and he began his long descent.

'Oh thhit!' he whimpered.

The sleek, grey Alfa Romeo skidded awkwardly along the narrow and bumpy track and towards the unruly melee that swarmed in and around the derelict farmstead. Inspector Jones had his foot to the floor, one hand stuck to the horn and all lights blinking, as they sped onwards – the rarely used siren heralding their arrival like a screeching Banshee with a touch of tonsillitis.

'We've got to get to Bob, so he can free Lamkin and Prince Edric's followers!' repeated Tom for the umpteenth time, peering frantically out of the window with dismay as he sighted a posse of Bucca-men splintering off from the fray with the clear intent of intercepting the Alfa Romeo.

To his left he saw the unmistakable sight of *The Purple Frighteners* streaming and whooping (like the ferocious old nightmares that they were) down the hill and onwards towards their enemies. They'd made short work of the Bucca-men, who were, after all, little more than gangland heavies, while the Aelfradi were bloodied warriors and first-rate bogeymen (and three bogeywomen) to an Elf. Their biggest hurdle had been Koll – who had managed to take down four of *The Frighteners* before being overpowered – but even with him out of the way, their appetite for bloodshed had not been sated.

Five Bucca-men hit the Alfa like a troop of out-of-control baboons in a drive-through safari. One villainous-looking thug hopped forward and smashed the front passenger window with a crowbar. Constable Tuggnutter lost his temper (the hours he put into keeping the D.S.C. motor in pristine and tip-top condition didn't bear thinking about [like all Trolls, Tuggnutter was fascinated with all things mechanical]) and, with a heartfelt howl of despair, he ripped off the door, leapt out of the now pootling to a standstill vehicle, and wrapped said car door around the inconsiderate vandal like a coat.

Tom crawled over the seats, dived through the doorless opening (brand spanking new battle-putter clutched nervously in hand) and shimmied his way towards the cordon of jostling and jeering Bucca-men currently surrounding the wizardly duel between Bob and Ek-Boran.

Not having the stomach to hit anyone on the head with a war-club, Tom restricted himself to hacking at the ankles of any one who obstructed his desperate dash.

Cornelius and Ned sprinted to the little copse of bushes just in time to see de Warrenne hurl the severed head of Brother Danny at the quivering and cornered Brother Peachy. As Peachy instinctively dropped the holdall containing *The*

Crowns of Albion to catch dear departed Danny's hurtling noddle, de Warrenne erupted forward like an exploding warhead, leaping on the shrieking Bucca-man like a tweed-camouflaged tiger, sinking his murderous fangs into the neck of poor Brother Peachy. Slivers of pale, leathery flesh flew in all directions as the vampire tore and savaged his hapless prey.

In that moment, while the vile vampire's attention was taken, Ned darted in, hooked de Warrenne's foot away with the head of his putter, snatched up the dropped holdall, and sprinted towards the horizon as if all the demons of Hell were behind him (or at least one of them).

De Warrenne regained his balance, turned his head, hissed with outraged fury, and sprang forwards after the fast disappearing *Smack Faery* with a roar ... and leapt straight into the best right hand that Cornelius had ever thrown.

With a frightful crack, de Warrenne's head span around two-hundred-and-thirty-three degrees and his eyes rolled upwards into the back of his head.

Cornelius skipped forward and put every ounce of his not inconsiderable bulk into an uppercut to the solar plexus.

The vampire gasped and began a slow descent to the floor.

As Cornelius followed up with a hefty stamp of his paw-like (and sadly un-lethal) jaguar-onesie slippers, de Warrenne suddenly lashed out a hand and caught the old codger's foot in a vice-like grip. Then, slowly, the vampire shuddered and twisted his dapper and undead head back into a workable position, to the accompaniment of an eye-watering cacophony of clicks, clunks and cracks.

'Is that all you've got, Professor?' he grinned, sending the old fellow tumbling through the air with a flick of the wrist. 'Well, I must say, after all that I'd heard, I'm a trifle underwhelmed, old chap.'

Only ten yards separated Tom and the ring of Bucca-men surrounding the battling wizards.

A blanket of darkness suddenly dropped before him, and there, ogling him with a terrifying and sour-faced sneer, was *The Wild Hunt* vampire, Opchanacanough – disconcertingly naked and disconcertingly barring his way.

Tom tried to swerve past the undead swine, aiming a wild hack at the vampire's kneecap as he shimmied and side-stepped.

With a speed that can only be described as *otherworldly*, Opchanacanough effortlessly caught the haft of Tom's weapon with one hand and contemptuously slapped him to the floor with the other.

Blood gushed from Tom's torn, battered and instantly swelling lips.

The vampire stalked forward, laughing at him like a school bully crushing the hopes of an irritating little oik who has ideas above his station.

Deep down inside Tom felt an unbearable anger and sense of injustice bubbling up inside him.

Not now! he wept inwardly, and he could feel tears of frustration welling up in his eyes. *Not now! I was so close! It's just not fair! IT'S NOT FAIR!*

The vampire shot out a hand and hoisted Tom to his feet, pulling him towards him like a loving parent trying to comfort a weeping child.

Tom tried to scream but Opchanacanough covered his mouth with a frozen hand, bared his fangs, his mouth stretching and warping like a milked viper, and stooped his head forward for the kill.

There was a sudden grey flash of movement behind them. Warring Elves and Goblins hastily parted like the Red Sea. And through the gap charged Bess, a small saddle strapped to her back, and in that saddle (occasionally) bounced Missus Dobbs, bobbing up and down and from one side to the other like a rodeo superstar. Over her shoulders she wore a strange and bulky rucksack, in one hand she carried a hefty, copper-bottomed frying pan, and upon her face she wore a gurn of deranged and terrifying concentration.

Bess bounded past Opchanacanough and raked her teeth across his bare buttocks.

The shocked and indignant Powhattan prince looked around just in time to be twatted across the face with Missus Dobbs' hefty copper-bottomed cooking utensil.

The House-Fairy gurgled demonically as she and Bess surged onwards towards the duelling warlocks.

'Good luck with that, Ducky,' chortled the demented little tea-poisoner over her shoulder, as Bess vaulted the last Bucca-man in her way and Opchanacanough gaped after them with an expression of outraged confusion on his comely and incensed features.

But only for a moment.

For he soon turned his attention back towards the irksome – and soon-to-be dispatched – child (currently quivering and quaking in his tomb-like grasp) and got the shock of his un-life.

All that remained of Tomas Dearlove offered an apologetic and almost embarrassed grin to the startled vampire. The Powhattan gasped and tried to recoil in horror, but it was not to be. *Tommy Half-Grendel*, gibbering like a shaved and unhinged orang-utan after his ninth double espresso, tossed him into the air like a rag-doll and began to thrash him back and forth like a toddler having a tantrum and taking it out on his least-favourite teddy bear.

Surrounding Bucca-men, hardened and ruthless Goblins one and all, began to squeal and flee in terror.

(An independent observer might have noted that the one good thing that could be said about the unfortunate matter was that at least the humongous purple parka now not only fitted Tom, but also quite suited him.)

As Bess sailed through the air, Missus Dobbs gathered both feet onto the saddle and pushed upwards.

Launching herself skyward like the missile from a trebuchet, she came crashing to the ground with a well-aimed swipe of her hefty copper-bottomed frying pan to the back of Ek-Boran-Boranaran's wizardly noggin.

The Goblin warlock crumpled like a miss-hit tent peg.

Almost before he hit to the floor, wild grasses were beginning to grow around and over him, pinning him to the floor and ensnaring him in ropes of twisting and winding vegetation.

Bob turned his attention towards the derelict barns that surrounded them and whispered an unlocking enchantment.

A slow and deep rumble, like a heavy chain hitting the bottom of the ocean, echoed around the farmstead. There was chorus of blood-curdling whoops and battle-cries and, with a roar like a tidal wave finally breaching a flimsy sea-defence, one hundred spears (well, ninety-eight if we deduct the treacherous Koll and Ek-Boran) surged forward, their proud, brave banners piercing the sky.

The dismayed Bucca-men cried and yelped in dismay, for the tide had turned, the battle was all but over. They were surrounded, outnumbered and undone.

Whelk-faced Willie hit the deck with a bone-cracking crunch.

'That hurt!' he managed to rasp, rubbing his back and silently thanking his stars that he always wore a padded mattress sewn into the back of his jacket (you'd be surprised [or perhaps you wouldn't] just how many people had tried to throw him from death-defying heights over the years, and so, in consequence, Whelky had always thought it prudent to take some precautions).

Massaging his hips, he managed to stagger to his feet and take in, and make sense of, his new and somewhat unexpected surroundings.

'Oh thhit, thhit, thhit, thhit, thhit, thhit!' he snivelled.

For poor Whelky, directed, no doubt, by some unknown hand of kindness, had had the rollicking good fortune to land in the middle of a boxing ring where two bloodied and battling were-wolf-wolfhounds were in the process of knocking seven shades of hell out of each other. *Oh what thumping good luck, Whelky, my boy*, he managed to think to himself. *Way to go, old thon!*

Bors looked at the crinkly new arrival like an alcoholic just noticing an unopened bottle of Scotch in his cupboard, and made to take a step towards him.

'Aaargh! Nithe boy,' cringed Whelky, as he slowly backed away.

'Leave him be, Brother,' growled the familiar clipped and impossibly deep tones of The Hound.

Whelky could have kissed him.

Bors re-focused his attention back to his brother and scowled at him through the bruised, swollen and bloodied slit of the one eye that wasn't completely closed.

'NO!' he roared.

The Hound was somewhat startled to discover that his brother had the power of speech, and, despite all that had happened, felt an emotional lump rise in his throat.

'NO!' snarled Bors, and the words sounded strange and clumsy on his lips. 'THIS WRONG! WE FIGHT LIKE WHEN WE WAS *RIGHT!*'

There was a seven second cacophony of cracks and snapping pops and there before them stood the snarling Bors in monstrous and bloodied dog-form.

During the pause in action, while Bors shape-shifted from one terrifying form to another, Inspector Jones had clambered through the ropes to stand by The Hound's side, an assault-rifle raised at his shoulder and pointed at the snarling and slavering *Wild Hunt* wolfhound.

Bors lifted his massive snout, sniffed the air, scented the silver bullets with which the rifle was loaded, and then turned and vaulted the ropes in a single bound.

Inspector Jones carefully took aim.

The Hound gently grabbed hold of the nuzzle and bent it like a banana.

'Don't,' he whispered. 'Please.'

De Warrenne was surrounded by twenty or more infuriated foes: Elves from all the measly tribes of Albion, Goblins from the nine clans, that insufferable NARG (*Not A Real Gentleman*, for those of you who haven't had the dubious pleasure of spending time with the pearls of humanity who inhabit the world of Britain's glittering *social elite*) Cornelius Lyons, and even a Troll (glowering at him through homemade glasses with lenses like milk-bottles, and menacingly hefting a sixteen-pound sledgehammer in his hands like it was a feather duster).

The Hound joyfully strolled through the heavily-armed ring of *Free-Folk* (Inspector Jones and Ned Leppelin at his side) with Whelk-faced Willie's holdall (wherein lay *The Crowns of Albion*) slung jauntily over his shoulder. He tipped a wink – that said *"Everything all right your end, my dear, dear friend?"* – towards Dandy, and then nodded an unconcerned greeting in the direction of the seething vampire.

'Well, there's an end to it,' he smiled. 'You little jaunt is over, de Warrenne. Game, set and match, I'd say, wouldn't you?'

'Oh, well played, Percival,' grinned de Warrenne, doing a remarkably good job of masking his disappointment and doing his utmost to be the good sport. 'Very well played indeed, old fruit. I must admit that I didn't think that you had it in you, dear boy. Would love to stand around and chat, old cock, but I don't think that I could bear to have to look at your pompous and shockingly gloating face for a moment longer. I must say, though, it's been an absolute blast. Toodle-pip, old chum. I do hope that we'll meet again. In fact … I just know it.'

The vampire clicked his fingers and where, just a fraction of a second before, there had stood a dapper and impeccably-tailored dandy (who bore more than a passing resemblance to the actor David Niven) there now flapped an enormous bat, majestically thrashing its leathery wings and beginning to take to the skies.

'Away you go, boys,' sniffed Cornelius, and a hail of sharpened arrow-shafts launched into the air above de Warrenne's head.

The bat fluttered groundwards rather rapidly, and transformed back into the frowning, but still smiling and dapper, de Warrenne.

'Oh it's like that, is it? I see. Bad form, dear boy. Never mind, there's more than one way to skin a bat.'

And as he spoke he began to fade like an over-developing photograph, a swirling spiral of mist rising upwards, until all that remained (like the Cheshire Cat) was a smug and rather self-satisfied grin.

'Oh, Missus Dobbs,' sighed The Hound, examining and flicking a grain of grit from beneath a claw with his thumbnail, 'would you be so kind?'

'Be my pleasure, Ducky,' gurned the House-Fairy, removing from her rucksack a portable vacuum cleaner and gleefully Hoovering up the spiralling column of smoke.

The remnants of de Warrenne's arrogant smile morphed into one of pure terror, and perhaps the distant rumble of a scream could be heard.

Missus Dobbs banged a rubber stopper over the end of the nozzle and then wiped her hands together with a stern nod of her head in satisfaction of a job well done.

'And good riddance to bad rubbish,' she sniffed.

THIRTY
Oh Proud Brave Banners

Tom woke up to find himself lying on his back, in what appeared to be a large, derelict barn. He lifted his head and was surprised to discover that he was stretched out on a camp bed, and in a distressing state of nakedness, save for his purple parka (which was resting over him like a hideous blanket).

There was a soft groan to his left and Tom quickly sat up and looked over to see that there were at least a dozen other camp beds arranged in two rows, all filled with bruised and battered veterans of the recent battle. He could make out the figures of Ginty, Bob, Maggs and Missus Dobbs tending to their needs. And there, in the doorway of the tent, still dressed in his bespoke jaguar-onesie (though it should be noted that said garment was looking decidedly ragged, torn, and stained with blotches of grass, mud and blood), looking like *Garfield* after he'd taken a wrong turn and accidentally had to battle his way through an episode of the *Teenage Ninja Mutant Turtles*, stood Cornelius.

The old fellow padded over towards him on soft cat-slippers and sat beside him on the bed. Tom tried not to laugh at the ludicrous cat mask painted onto the old fellow's smiling features.

"Ow you doing, Tom?' beamed Cornelius, warmly. 'Looks like you 'ad another one of your … *episodes*.'

Tom's smile migrated southward. He flopped back on the camp bed, covered his face with his hands and silently sobbed.

'Oh no,' he groaned, closing his eyes and desperately trying to recall what the last thing that he could actually remember was.

He could recall running towards the battling wizards, Bob Goodfellow and Ek-Boran-Boranaran; he could recollect being stopped and assailed by the terrifying Opchanacanough, and he could most definitely remember (with a startling clarity that made him suddenly shudder violently with terror) the sight of the vampire's gaping maw and viper-like fangs, and he thought he had a vague memory of seeing Missus Dobbs and Bess … but beyond that – nothing.

He opened his fingers and peered through them at the old man.

'What happened?'

'Well,' grinned the demented old charmer, 'from what we can piece together, you did your usual trick of pummelling the unliving daylights out of one of them there despicable *Wild 'Unt* bloodsucking parasites.'

Tom dragged his fingers down his face, contorting his features into something resembling Munch's "*The Scream*".

'Don't worry, son, 'e's *alive* (so to speak) to tell the tale,' chuckled Cornelius, 'though I doubt that 'e'll forget about it in an 'urry (no matter 'ow 'ard 'e might try). Apparently, Ginty an' Maggs managed to calm you down an' get 'im to safety just after they'd arrived with six Bucca-men trussed in a line and with another *Wild 'Unt* vampire being dragged along by 'is ankles by Nipper an' Snapper. I 'eard that 'e was equally 'appy to 'and 'imself over,' chortled the old codger. 'An' I can't say that I blame 'im,' he added.

'I take it we won, then?' asked Tom, though by his surroundings he already knew the answer, he just wanted to change the subject.

'Didn't we just!' cooed Cornelius, rubbing his hands gleefully together. 'De Warrenne's corked an' bottled, so to speak, one vampire *switched off*, two more incarcerated, Madame Buckleberry gagged an' in chains, an' the rest of *The Wild 'Unt's 'enchmen* making all sorts of wild an' wonderful claims to keep themselves from going down. Got *The Bucca* too. (Oh, I don't doubt that maybe we lost one or two of the rascals 'ere an' there, if they managed to scarper before things got too 'ot, mind.) But they're done, Tom. Finished.'

'That's great news,' replied Tom, an overwhelming feeling of relief that it might finally all be over seeping through his limbs like hot soup on a chilly day. Then he had a worrying thought. 'Any casualties?' he asked.

Cornelius looked up and towards the other beds.

'A few split 'eads an' broken bones,' he muttered. 'The worst of them are in 'ere.'

'So no fatalities. That's great!' sighed Tom, his spirits lifting even higher.

'Didn't say that, son. A few were lost on either side, I'm sorry to say.'

Tom sat up again.

'Show me,' he said.

They were set out, in two neat rows, in the field that ran behind the derelict barns. Tom slowly walked between the lines, his bare feet soaked by the wet grass and his thin shins sticking out from the hem of his flapping purple parka like weedy pipe cleaners.

The first row was made up of seven Bucca-men, including the mutilated corpse of Brother Peachy and the decapitated form of Brother Danny. Beside them was a bucket full of ashes with a pair of tulwars rested on top it (which Tom reasoned must be the unearthly remains of Ajit Singh).

Running in a parallel line were the bodies of two Astrai and one of Prince Edric's followers (none of whom Tom recognised). Next to them, Tom was deeply shocked to see, lay the beaten and bloodied body of the Aelfradi warrior and *Purple Frightener*, Inkcap.

Tom felt sick, and somehow couldn't help but feel more than a little responsible for the poor fellow's demise.

At the end of the row, next to Inkcap, was a blanket with a tiny mound in the middle of it. Intrigued despite his misgivings, Tom knelt down and pulled away the blanket to uncover the squashed and lifeless remains of a Siamese cat, obviously trampled underfoot in the course of the melee.

Tom had never really liked Mae, had always found him spiteful, sneery and somewhat condescending, but he never in a million years would have wished this upon him. This is what happened when people were forced to make war and choose sides; to fight because someone was so stupid or arrogant or greedy that they didn't think or even care about the consequences. It was the innocent who got hurt and punished. Always the innocent. And Mae *was* an innocent. He'd had no desire to be involved in any of this, just the rotten bad luck to get caught up in things that he had no concern for.

Tom couldn't help but burst into tears.

Cornelius let him be for a moment and then put a comforting, bruised and scuffed, hand on his shoulder and gave him a hug.

'Come on, Tom. 'Is Nibbs is just about ready to wind things up. An' 'e very much wants you to be there.'

As Tom and Cornelius plodded towards the ring, where The Hound was about to give his address to the victorious warriors, they happened to walk past Archie Swapper and Sergeant Hettie Clem.

'Oh my God! Are you all right, Archie?' gasped the Gothy sergeant, rushing forward and reaching a concerned finger towards the bloodied bandage around Archie's forehead.

'Oh, er ... er ... Mz Clem, er ... I mean, 'Ettie,' fumbled the changeling. (He might just have played a hero's part in a hard-fought and ghastly battle, fearlessly overcome overwhelming odds and terrifying foes, but Tom couldn't help but think that he looked rather nervous and awkwardly unsettled when confronted by the beautiful and ravishing police officer.) 'Juzt a zcratch really. Nothing to worry 'bout. Lookz like you an' me ... well, lookz like we'll be 'aving matching zcarz, I reckon.'

Hettie smiled and her cheeks blushed a little.

'Well if that isn't a sign then I don't know what is.' she sighed, reaching forward and pulling the dumbstruck Pharisee prince towards her. They collided into each other's arms and kissed.

Perhaps the magic of the moment might have been ruined by a pale and gangly lad, dressed in a horrendous purple parka, making loud and uncouth gagging noises as he waddled past (though he was secretly delighted) but, if so, they seemed not to notice.

Cornelius gave Tom a gentle clip around the back of the head and then shoved him onwards with a wry chuckle.

The Hound stood, centre stage, looking over the victorious army gathered before him.

'*Children of the Light,*' he roared, looking over the jostling throng like a proud headmaster giving a congratulatory speech at a morning assembly held for all the sixth-formers who had managed to get into university, 'this night you have won a great victory. A terrible foe has been humbled and, with his defeat, a new dawn, a new age, awaits the Fae Folk of Albion. The bards will sing of your deeds until the end of days. And your names shall stride proudly in memory besides the great heroes of your noble people.

'I see the proud and bold banners of the Elbi before me: the Coiled Adder of the Aelfradi; the Fighting Hare of the Pharisees; the Golden Owl of the Ellyllon; the Silver Capercaillie of The Gentry. I see the flags of their brothers The Sith and Sidhe. I see the Heron of the Ferrisyn; the Green-sprite of the Oakmen. I see the standards of the nine fabled Goblin Clans. With them stands the Red Porpoise of the Astrai. Behold the Slaughtered Goat, spit-roasted on a hammer between two golden bridges, of the Troll folk. I see the noble banner of Prince Edric fluttering in the night – the rampant White Stag with a blood-red crown; how proud he would have been of you all. How you have kept his dream alive – *The Children of the Light* united as one against their common enemy. And I see the ... defecating ... purple baboon(?) ... (Tom, are you quite sure about this?) ... of Prince Dearlove!'

A roar went up from the crowd like a blazing flame – 'THE HALF-GRENDEL! HALF-GRENDEL! HALF-GRENDEL!' And Tom, standing at The Hound's side, felt tears welling up in his eyes again.

'For the first time in five hundred years,' continued The Hound, 'all four crowns of the Elbi can be returned to where they belong.

'Dame Ginty, I entrust to your safekeeping *The Autumn Crown*. Take with you a guard, and return the crown to Pook Nudd at once.'

Dame Ginty came forward and accepted the offered crown with a sultry pout.

The gathering broke into wild applause; cheers of support filled the air (along, it should be noted, with some wolf-whistles and some decidedly inappropriate suggestions).

'Cutty Sark, our dear, dear friend – who we all thought dead but who is now ... not – please step forward and take *The Winter Crown*. Return your long-lost charge to *The Seelie Court*. Your honour is restored. Your quest is at an end. And what an extraordinary adventure you have had, dear Cutty – devoured by a wild and rampant monster, you raged, helpless in the belly of the beast, wounded, mutilated, but never defeated. Escaping from the most cruel and repulsive of prisons with your last ounce of cunning, turning yourself, with your last desperate sprinkling of magic, into an out-of-date Jalfrezi curry ... and waiting for nature to take its course.'

A collective groan seeped across the crowd as the harsh reality of that particular nugget of information was digested.

Cutty Sark rolled forward like a slow handclap and took *The Winter Crown*, tears streaming down her battered cheeks, and, for a fraction of a moment, Tom saw her face light up and her grimacing features lifted, and he thought he glimpsed a flash of that young and bonnie lass who had had her life destroyed by de Warrenne and his callous chum (Harry Ca-Nab – The Devil's Huntsman) so many years ago.

'CUTTY, CUTTY, CUTTY!' came the call. 'SARK, SARK, SARK!' came the response.

'Step forward, Archie Albi. Step forward and take your father's crown. Your people can now return home, safe in the knowledge that their new king is not only a great warrior but also a wise leader. Hail to the Pook of the Pharisees! Long live Pook Archie!'

'HAIL TO POOK ARCHIE! THE SILVER SPEAR! HUZZAH!'

Well, thought Tom, *this is turning out to be just like the Academy Awards. And here I am without a tuxedo!*

He waited with modest excitement for the next announcement to be made, desperately trying to master the smug smile that was in danger of cracking his face in two.

'And it gives me great pleasure,' grinned The Hound, lifting his noble snout to the moon, 'to be able to return *The Crown of Spring* to the Aelfradi after so many anguished years. Step forward – (so sorry, could you just move a little out of the way, Tom, you're blocking everybody's view, there's a good chap) – Tommy Rawhead-and-Bloody-Bones, President of the Council of Avalon. It is into your noble hands that I must place this charge, for it is you who will hold it safe until the day that Prince Tomas can take his place and become the long-awaited *Pook of Shadows.*'

'BLOODY-BONES! BLOODY-BONES!' came the cry, as Bloody-Bones raised *The Crown of Spring* high into the morning sky.

The crowd had dispersed. The Fae Folk had departed, starting the long arduous journeys to their respective homelands with a new hope kindled in their hearts. Bob Goodfellow, Tommy Rawhead and *The Purple Frighteners* were making their way back to *The Hidden Realm* with the *Crown of Spring* and their prisoner, the wizard, Ek-Boran-Boranaran. Inspector Jones and the D.S.C. had rounded up the remaining felons and, along with Archie, Ned, Maggs and Ginty, were escorting them along the long winding track towards the police wagons that were waiting for them, ready to cart the nefarious baddies and Bucca-men to The Mound.

All the prisoners, that is, bar one.

The Hound tapped his talons lightly on the handle of the vacuum cleaner that imprisoned the arch-cad, de Warrenne. He would be escorting this particular prize catch to The Mound himself.

Time, he thought, allowing himself a contented smile of satisfaction, *now that this appalling adventure is well and truly at an end, for a much deserved holiday.*

He was just about to jog along and catch up with Tom and Dandy (who were making their way out of the valley of Castle Hill and towards the car park on Warren Way, where Old Nancy awaited them) when the hackles on the back of his neck suddenly bristled in alarm.

'A most excellent night's vork, Herr Hund,' came a voice like an assassin's recently-whetted blade.

231

The Hound spun around to see, to his amazement, the tall and gaunt figure of the Nachzehrer vampire, Victor Bertrand!

Even more of a surprise was the appearance of the six MI Unseen agents beside him (armed to the teeth with God only knew what new and terrifying military technology – but he could almost taste the bitter tang of pure silver emanating from their weaponry), led, The Hound was almost beside himself with joy to see (not), by the mysterious and unsettlingly dangerous form of Captain Montgomery Phelps.

'I think that it would be for the best if *I* took the *prisoner* from here, *sir*,' smiled Phelps, his cold eyes flicking toward the portable Hoover.

'That is most very kind of you, Captain,' replied The Hound, as calmly as he could, 'but de Warrenne is my prisoner. I feel it my responsibility, nay, my duty, to deliver him in person.'

Phelps smiled sadly and shook his head.

'You can hand him over to me, and that will be an end to it,' replied the Captain, weighing up the were-hound with his lifeless sapphire-blue eyes, 'or you can make a nuisance and wind up in a cell yourself,' he said, suddenly grinning (as if there wasn't anything in the world that would give him more pleasure), '*sir*,' he added with a contemptuous smirk.

'Justice muzt be done, Herr Hund,' hissed the Nachzehrer, watching the were-hound with peepers like pitiless pools of despair.

The Hound looked from the MI Unseen *super-soldier*, to the razor-cheeked and deathly features of Bertrand, and then to the heavily-armed (and clearly on a hair-trigger) agents, currently fanning out to surround him, and sighed.

What did it really matter, he thought, *de Warrenne was going to The Mound, and that was all that mattered. Wasn't it?*

He curled his talons around the handle of the vacuum-cleaner, thought for one millisecond about braining Phelps with it, and then handed it over to the upturned and waiting palm of the smug and arrogantly unpleasant blue-eyed little bastard.

THIRTY ONE
A Half-Remembered Ditty

It wasn't until almost three weeks later that Bob Goodfellow made his return to Upper Albion to supervise the preparations for the upcoming coronation of Archie Swapper, and to visit his dear friends at One Punch Cottage.

They spent the early afternoon sitting in The Study together, enjoying a pot of tea and a tin of Marks and Spencer's assorted *luxury* chocolate biscuits, swapping tales, putting the world to rights, and generally enjoying the contented feeling of a job well done.

'So,' said Tom, licking chocolate from his lips, 'one thing that I don't understand is why de Warrenne didn't try to assemble *The Crown of Albion* and use it against us when everybody's attention was elsewhere?'

'Wouldn't have worked,' grunted Bob, struggling to open the bright-green foil covering of a chocolate teacake with his near nailless and grimy fingers.

'Yes, we must presume that for the Crowns to have been successfully reunited, a spell, or some such thing, would be needed, and, powerful though de Warrenne undoubtedly is, it is our good fortune that the rascal just doesn't possess that kind of magic,' speculated The Hound, taking a moment to savour the myriad of flavours of a dunked plain chocolate shortbread.

'An' 'is sorcerers – the 'ateful witch, Madame Buckleberry, an' the treacherous sod, Ek-Boran Boranaran – both 'ad their 'ands well an' truly full, by all accounts,' clucked Cornelius, wiggling his fingers in delight as he scanned over the contents of the biscuit tin.

'And even if they hadn't,' grumbled Bob, finally managing to tease open a corner of the wrapper, his face contorted into a perfect picture of frustrated concentration, 'it still wouldn't have worked.'

Tom, The Hound and Cornelius stopped their respective self-satisfied munching and looked at the old Puck with perplexed interest.

'Whyever not, Bob?' asked The Hound.

'Load of old cobblers, that's why,' squinted the old ragamuffin, his tongue protruding from the corner of his grisly mouth like a questing mole.

'What exactly are you saying, Bob?' quizzed Cornelius, a confused frown settling onto his face.

'This whole *Crowns of Albion* nonsense,' grunted Bob, beginning to lose patience with the infuriating biscuit in hand, 'it's just a half-remembered ditty, that's all. A misheard story that has been around for so long, retold and reshaped so many times, that the truth of the matter has been long lost.'

'Are you saying that the legend isn't true?' gasped Tom. 'I mean, do you really mean to tell us that the whole – "*who so ever reunites The Crowns of Albion will have dominion over all of the supernatural beings of Britain"* is a big fat stinky lie!'

'No, not a lie ... *exactly,*' sighed Bob, finally giving up on trying to unpeel the biscuit wrapper with his fingers and just going in with his teeth. 'It *was* true ... once.'

'Once?' enquired The Hound, his snout buried between the rippling steeple of his fidgeting talons.

'It used to work, is what I'm saying,' croaked old Bob, spitting out a splinter of bright-green tinfoil and getting it snagged in his unkempt beard. Something jiggled and rustled within his facial-furniture and tugged the slither of tinfoil into the unexplored jungle of his whiskers. 'You see, way back, when the Crown was dismantled, it wasn't divided into four parts as everybody seems to think.'

'It wasn't?' scowled Cornelius, crumbs dangling on the end of his own whiskers like a row of miniature Christmas-tree lights, as his jaw slowly creaked downwards like a flabbergasted portcullis.

'No!' guffawed Bob. 'There were *five* pieces to it. And the one that mattered, well, if it's magic that matters to you, that is – the piece that had all the power encased within – well, that was what was known as *The Puck Stone.*'

'The *Puck Stone,*' repeated The Hound, emotionlessly.

'That's right,' replied Bob, looking very pleased with himself as he took a munch on his, now de-foiled, biscuit.

'And just what, *exactly*, became of this ... *Puck Stone*?' enquired the were-hound, politely.

'It was thrown away, of course.'

'*Thrown away*?'

'Of course it was. As I'm sure you'd readily agree, Percival, it would be far too dangerous to have an object that powerful out and about in the world.'

The Hound looked genuinely dumbfounded.

'So what happened to it?' asked Tom.

'Well, like I said, Prince Tomas,' chortled old Bob, clearly enjoying himself, 'when *The Crown of Albion* was split, the Council of Pucks (back in the day when we had one, you understand) decided, in their wisdom, to get rid of the damned thing that had caused all the problems in the first place.'

'Go on,' sniffed Cornelius, cracking a milk chocolate-coated ginger snap in two.

'So, the High Puck at the time, the great *Ginjen Peganel*, took it away and hid it. Hid it so well that none would ever find it. And, before you ask as to where it is, no one will ever know, for the secret died with Ginjen Peganel thousands of years ago,' smiled Bob, contentedly.

'SO WHY THE FLIPPIN' 'ECK DIDN'T YOU SAY SOMETHING BEFORE'AND?' blasted Cornelius, showering The Puck in a gale of biscuit crumbs.

'Been trying to for months,' chuckled Bob, for some reason looking extremely pleased with himself, 'but none of you would listen to me – all of you so engrossed in what you wanted to believe – so eventually I gave up trying. Probably all for the good, if you ask me. Kept you all focused on one thing, and, in the end, it finally got a lot of problems sorted out for the best. Well, that's the way I see it anyway.'

'You mean to say that all those people died for nothing!' gasped Tom, suddenly feeling his heartbeat thudding in his throat and temples.

'I would hardly say "for *nothing*", Tom,' huffed The Hound, puffing his cheeks out and giving The Puck a long hard stare. 'No, perhaps Bob is correct. As he says, the legend of *The Crowns of Albion has* been the focus of a truly terrible evil for nigh on five hundred years. If de Warrenne had not believed in its power then he would not have invested so much of his considerable talent upon it, and then I can only begin to dread what other vile atrocities he might have committed over the centuries.

'And with the recent turn of events, not only have The Gentry had their long-lost symbol of sovereignty returned to them (an act that offers untold possibilities for their future) but also the line to the crown of the Aelfradi now lies unopposed.' The Hound paused briefly to offer Tom a comforting half-smile. 'And most importantly of all, the Fae Folk of these isles have, for the first time in generations, a glimmer of hope for the future. No, Tom, we must not say that it was all in vain.'

At that moment the candlestick phone burst into life with a shrill ring.

The Hound seeped back into his armchair and let out a long and drawn-out breath.

'Dandy,' he sighed, 'would you mind answering the phone, dear chap. I fear that I find myself somewhat fatigued. If it's for me, would you be so kind as to tell them that I am out and take a message.'

'On it, 'Aitch,' said Cornelius, launching himself from his armchair, though still unable to take his disbelieving orbs off Bob.

'Lyons an' 'Ound Detective Agency,' he rumbled into the mouth piece of the antique phone. 'Oh, 'ello, 'Owie. 'Ow's things? I reckon you must be near to overflowing, what with the recent influx you've 'ad ... Ha ha. Yes, best place for 'em, no doubt about it ... Is that right? .... Can't say it's a surprise ... No, I'm sorry, 'e's not in at the moment ... Course I will ... Yeah, all right, I'll pass it on.'

Cornelius carefully placed the earpiece back onto its stand, and then stood looking at the back of The Hound's armchair, thoughtfully chewing his lips, with his thumbs wedged into his waistcoat pockets.

'That was Governor Butterworth,' he sniffed at last.

'Was it indeed,' replied The Hound, rubbing the bridge of his snout between thumb and forefinger. 'And what did Governor Butterworth want?'

'Wanted to let us know that de Warrenne is being 'anded over to *The Council of the Twelve* (that's the 'igh court of the twelve vampire *Families*, Tom) tomorrow morning.'

The Hound wiped his hand along the length of his muzzle and looked sternly at the floor. 'Well, I suppose that we all knew that that was on the cards,' he sighed, with a twitch of his thin black lips.

''E also wanted to tell you that de Warrenne 'as a last request, so to speak.'

'Does he indeed? And just what, pray tell, does the despicable bounder want?' enquired the were-hound, turning his head around to look at his old friend.

Cornelius held his enquiring gaze and arched an eyebrow.

'You,' he replied.

THIRTY TWO
Last Request

Agent Fowler escorted The Hound down a clinically clean and soulless corridor to a heavy metal door marked *"Interview Room 1"*.

'He's in there, Mr Hound,' said the extremely likeable MI Unseen warder, offering him a friendly but uncertain smile. 'If you need anything just press the panic-button on the side of the table. It'll be to your right … the panic-button, that is.'

The Hound thanked her, rolled down the enormous collar of his knee-length tweed overcoat, turned the handle and slowly pushed open the door.

He had arrived at The Mound as soon as he could. He wasn't quite sure why it had mattered to him so much to fulfil the despicable little bloodsucker's request but, for some reason, it had. Perhaps it was the knowledge that once de Warrenne was handed over to face the "justice" of *The Families,* that would be the end of him. Perhaps he just needed to speak, one last time, to somebody, anybody, who was connected to his fast-vanishing past. (And perhaps de Warrenne could answer some of the many questions that The Hound had about that past.) Or perhaps he simply wanted to have one final gloat over a defeated and bitter enemy.

Cornelius had driven him over and was currently punishing the vending machine in one of The Mound's waiting-rooms. Tom had come with them too, delighted to have the unexpected opportunity to visit Crow again. And once more the were-hound found himself wondering just how he was going to be able to get the young Half-Elfling out of her current pickle.

He stepped into the room.

Interview Room 1 was divided in half by a thick wall of reinforced glass. Two tables (bolted down, quite naturally) were pressed together on adjacent sides of that glass wall, a chair in front of each of them. On each of the tables stood a large telephone (the base of both, of course, bolted to the tabletop). The side that The Hound had entered was painted a stark and utilitarian white, while the other side of the divide was a seamless box of steel – floor, walls and ceiling.

On that other side sat Lord Manfred de Warrenne – scion of the renegade *House of Alexios*, the so called *King of the Wild Hunt,* and one-time impersonator of the Elven bogeyman *Ter-Tung-Hoppity* (known to modern human society as *Spring-heeled Jack*). He was dressed in a boiler suit of the most horrendous shade of mauve imaginable. Still, to give him his due (and damn the infuriatingly debonair swine's undead eyes for it!), the elegant little parasite managed to wear the revolting garment in such a manner that it looked rather stylish.

The vampire looked up and greeted The Hound's arrival with a cheeky wink and a smile.

The Hound casually pulled the chair from under the table, sat down, leant back into it and regarded the dapper little scoundrel with a look that he very much hoped was devoid of any emotion whatsoever.

De Warrenne pointed a finger at the telephone on his side of the divide and returned a chirpy look that said *"Shall we?"*.

The Hound took a deep sniff and slowly picked up the phone.

'Hello Percival, old chum,' said de Warrenne, cheerfully. 'Thanks awfully for taking the time to come and see me.'

'What do you want, de Warrenne?'

'Well, I was hoping that you'd smash down these prison walls for me, smuggle me out of the wretched place inside your coat pocket, and then send me on my merry way with a couple of vestal virgins and a suitcase full of used twenties,' chuckled the vampire. 'But by the look on your face, I very much doubt that that's going to happen, I'm disappointed to say.

'Percy, my dear boy, you're such a stick-in-the-mud these days. Just what happened to make you such a *square,* I'll never understand. I mean, dear old Henry was positively off the scale! Whoosh and wham-bam! The laughs we used to have, let me tell you ... No? Oh well, I guess I'll just have to settle for a good old heart to undead-heart then.'

'About?'

'Oh, this and that. *Stuff.* You know – things that I really should get off my chest.'

'Before you're extradited to *The Council of the Twelve,*' sighed the were-hound, trying to sound unconcerned.

'Well you certainly know how to poop a party, don't you! My God, man, don't waste any time, will you!' chortled de Warrenne. 'Yes, tomorrow I'm to be handed over to the narrow-minded little fuckers for a *trial.*' He laughed and shook his head. 'If that's what you want to call it, that is?'

'What's the matter, de Warrenne? Afraid that you aren't going to get the justice you deserve?'

'Oh I know exactly what I'll be getting, don't you worry, old stick. A stake through the heart and my head on a spike, that's what. Open and shut case, I suppose. So, unless you could recommend any good lawyers? No? Hhhmm. Never mind. Between you and me, old fruit, I suspect that it wouldn't do me much good anyway.'

The Hound held the vampire's eye and shook his head somberly in agreement. They both knew very well that whatever trial de Warrenne was to be given would be an utter sham. In the eyes of *The Families*, de Warrenne was already as good as dead (well, technically he was already dead, but you get the drift).

'Any word on Bors?' asked de Warrenne, breaking the heavy silence.

'Alas no. I've searched for him but, sadly, been unable to pick up his trail, and, as yet (I'm very relieved to say) no ... *untoward incidents* have been reported.'

The vampire chewed his lip and looked thoughtful.

'You will do your best to look out for him, won't you, old chap? I know that I'm in no position to ask anything of you ... but, well, I'd never forgive myself if anything rotten were to happen to him.'

The Hound nodded.

'I'll do all that I can,' he replied.

'Course you will,' smiled the vampire. 'Blood thicker than water, and all that.'

There was another long silence as de Warrenne examined the were-hound's face, as if he were trying to read his thoughts.

The Hound wondered if he should tell the hateful little cad that his whole quest for *The Crowns of Albion* had been a complete non-starter, a total farce, but decided against it. What was the point? It was over. Let it be over.

The vampire sucked his teeth and leaned in a little closer towards the thick glass divide.

'Now listen to me, Percival, there's something that I very much want to say to you.'

'I'm all ears.'

'I want you to be careful, you big, thick-skulled, over-trusting buffoon. The world is changing fast, and I'm sorry to say that *you*, like *I*, like all of us *"monsters"*, in fact, are ... shall we say ... *surplus to requirement*. And it's not just us "man-eating" types; soon enough it'll be any*thing* and any*body* who isn't quite *"right"*. Oh no doubt at first they'll try to embrace our *"afflictions"* and try to *"fix"* them. But if they can't, well, *God help us all*, is what I say.'

'Ah!' huffed The Hound, dismissively. 'The mysterious – *"They"*.'

'Don't be a klutz, Percy. You know very well whom I'm talking about. We're different, you see. We don't conform to the norm, old pip. And if there's one thing that weak, ambitious idiots in positions of authority detest and despise more than anything else it's that which they can't control, let alone understand.'

'Is that so?'

'It's not the first time that they've tried this sort of thing, and you know it, Percival. But now they've got the technology to be able to pull it off. And now that they've finally managed to position the populace into a position of willing slavery (chained by their own stupidity and greed) it's just a case of weeding out those who won't kowtow to the way that *they* want the world to be.

'If you're not careful, old cock, I'm afraid to say that you'll soon find yourself stretched out in some ghastly laboratory with wires poking into you and bits being lopped off. Just so that *they* can try to *understand* what makes *you* tick. Just so that *they* can find a way to make *you* fit into their blinkered view of the world. And if *they* can't coerce you or, worse still, comprehend you, then it'll be ...' the vampire curled the fingers of his left hand into a pistol shape, put the nozzle to his temple and mimed a shot being fired, *'good night sweet nurse and don't bother to thank me for all my good deeds, or the countless "enemies of humanity" that I've murdered and sent to their graves on your account.*

'The times they-are-a-changing, Percival, old fellow. And you're *old school*, I'm afraid to say. At best – an embarrassment. No, old nubber, I hate to say it, but your days, as much as mine, are well and truly numbered.'

'Well that's all most edifying, de Warrenne,' sighed The Hound, turning up his coat collar and making to stand up. 'I would like to say that it's been an absolute pleasure seeing you again, old hen. But, now, if you don't mind, I'd best be heading off: things to do, people to see, horrible and wicked man-eating monsters to apprehend –'

'Oh sit down and don't be such a sulky puss, you overgrown Womble. Listen; they're coming for you, Percy, mark my words, boy, they've got your card marked. Maybe not today, maybe not tomorrow, but one day it'll happen, just as I'm telling you.'

The Hound gave the vampire a hard stare.

'Even if we suppose, just for one moment, that you *are* right,' sneered the were-wolf-wolfhound (though he had a terribly anxious [and fast becoming worryingly familiar] feeling wriggling in the pit of his stomach that the odious little swine might just be – hadn't dear old Lettice said pretty much the very same thing to him only a matter of days ago!), 'what would you have me do; run off and live the remains of my days in some ever-diminishing wilderness?'

'You've done it before.'

The Hound puffed out his cheeks and turned his head dismissively.

'But there's a better option, old stick. Much better,' said de Warrenne, and though he wore, as ever, his chipper and near-mocking smile, his voice was deadly serious.

'Humour me,' scoffed The Hound, with a contemptuous curl of his lip.

'Oh, I mean to. Now, make yourself comfortable and, just this once, shut up and listen to your dear old Uncle Manny, for I'm going to give you a bit of a history lesson, old boy. So, do yourself a favour and pay close attention, because what I'm about to tell you is going to knock your furry little socks off.'

240

THIRTY THREE
The King Of Avalon

De Warrenne lent back in his chair, cradled the handset of the telephone between his shoulder and chin, and regarded the were-wolfhound with a peculiar smile.

'Do you know,' he began at last, putting a slender and immaculately manicured hand back to the receiver and lifting it to his lips, 'my old stomping buddy, dear old Harry Ca Nab (reprobate and rapscallion that he was), was a veritable mine of old stories and long-forgotten histories. You see The Grabbers, Harry's people, grasped onto the past so tightly that they remembered all the things that others had chosen to forget. I suppose that's what happens when you feel that you've had your privilege and prestige unfairly ripped from under you; you tend to wistfully cling on to the way things were – stuck in the past, remembering all that you have lost, while dreaming about the future and your moment of revenge and, in the meanwhile, ignoring the present and forgetting about the here-and-now. Ah well – *the Offender writes in sand and the Offended in stone*, as they say. But the upshot of it all was that Harry had a wealth of, shall we say, *overlooked history* at his fingertips. Should have written it all down. Would have liked to have written a book, now that I think on it. Oh well, too late now, I suppose.

'Anyway, here's one of Harry's very best – for you, old chap. Think on it as a parting gift.'

The Hound kept his eyes locked on the vampire, drew a deep breath and rested the mouthpiece of the phone against his muzzle as he buried his snout into the lapels of his tweed overcoat.

'Tell me,' smiled de Warrenne, smoothing his dapper little moustache with the thumb of his left hand, 'what do you know about the history of The Pucks?'

The Hound pricked up an ear and lifted his great black nose from within the folds of his coat.

'The ancient order of Elbi wizardry?' he asked. 'What about them?'

'Clever chaps ... generally speaking,' sniffed the debonair little bounder. 'Knew a thing or two, let me tell you. You see, back in the day, they understood the duality of the nature of existence. They believed, for example, that life without death had no meaning (well, I could bring them up on that one, but they're entitled to their opinion, I suppose): they understood that happiness without hardship is devalued, that reward without endeavour is diminished, and they believed that *good* (for want of a better word) could not flourish without being offset by the existence of *evil*. That's why, way, way, way back in the dim passage of time, the position of *High Puck* was in fact held simultaneously by *two* sorcerers: *The Goodfellow* (like your dear friend, the odorous and unwashed little urchin, Bob) and, as a counterbalance to him or her, the other half of the *agreement,* so to speak, their counterpart; known, quite obviously, as – *The Badfellow.*'

The Hound raised an eyebrow. It wasn't exactly a groundbreaking revelation, for it wasn't the first time that he'd heard that particular rumour whispered over the years. He briefly considered stopping de Warrenne there and then but thought better of it. It would be, after all, interesting to hear more on the subject.

'For some reason,' continued de Warrenne, holding the were-hound's eye, 'it was a tradition that the Elbi chose to abandon. Can't see why myself, but there you go, who am I to judge? Want to know who the last of *The Badfellows* was?' grinned the vampire.

'Enlighten me,' scowled the were-wolf-wolfhound.

'Ashdread Adamsbane.'

'King *Corpse-Hand*?' snapped The Hound in surprise.

'That's right, old stick. *The White Wyrm of Avalon. The Puck-Pook* of the Aelfradi,' chuckled de Warrenne.

'Incredible! Are you sure?'

'According to Harry – yes … and I believe him. You see, I met old Ashdread once, long time ago now, you understand.'

'Preposterous!' snapped The Hound, contemptuously. 'Ashdread Adamsbane first took the throne of the Aelfradi nigh on two thousand years ago. He was long in his grave before even *you* were born.'

'Was he?' chortled de Warrenne. 'Was he indeed? Remind me again, Percival, just how did he die?'

'His death remains a mystery, and you know it, de Warrenne. One of the great mysteries of the Elbi people.'

'Well if you'll shut up and listen, Percival, my dear fellow, I might just be able to unravel that *great mystery* for you.'

The Hound rumbled deep in his throat, but stayed schtum. What harm would it do to listen to the demented little bloodsucker one last time? And besides, despite all his misgivings, he found himself intrigued.

'You see,' continued the elegant little cad, 'when old Ashdread managed to wrest the throne from the Grimtooths, it sent a shudder of terror throughout the whole of *Faeryland*. I mean, really, the most gifted and talented warlock in all the isles was now the king of the most aggressive and pugnacious tribe of *The Albions*. Oh, they feared him, you see, for he had become the most powerful and the most dangerous individual that the *Fae World* had seen since the disastrous days of the Oberons. And you know what people are like, old hen, they just can't help but get jealous. And thus the decision was inevitably taken (by the envious types, of course) to knock this upstart Puck-Pook off his newfound perch, because it just wasn't cricket, old bean, to have all that wealth and power in the hands of one chap. And they feared, once more, the rise of tyranny in these fair lands.

'But the problem was this – just how were they going to do it? I mean, no wizard in the land could hope to stand up to *The White Wyrm*, for he was more powerful than all the rest of the Puckery put together. And as to physically putting him in his place? Well, they didn't dare. Ashdread was the Pook of the Aelfradi, the mightiest and most warlike of the Elven Kingdoms; not all the tribes of *Upper Albion* united together could hope to defeat them in battle. No, they knew that it just wasn't going to wash, and so they came up with a plan (quite despicable really, if you ask my opinion), a plan to assassinate poor old Ashdread. But just who was going to have a snowball's chance in Hell of doing such a thing?

'And then they hit upon an idea so crazy, so preposterous that it sounds paramount to idiocy, but there you go, desperate times call for desperate measures. Somehow they managed to persuade/bribe/blackmail an ancient war-goddess to do their dirty work for them. An old, little remembered and uncared for deity, whose time was over and whose glory days were well and truly gone. Well, you know Gods, Percival, as well as I do, pretentious little blighters. Nobody likes them at the best of times. They only get listened to because everybody's afraid of them or they want something from them. So there she was, down on her luck and in desperate need of some attention; the bloodthirsty old harridan herself, *The Phantom Queen*, the gore-drenched goddess of war, murder and mayhem – *The Morrigan!*

'Well, to cut a long story short, Percy, she sought out poor old Ashdread, and the two of them battled for seven days and seven nights (according to Harry, but he did like to embellish things a little), locked in mortal (or should that be immortal?) combat; The Morrigan (weakened from her years of neglect) and the vastly powerful (but mere-mortal) Adamsbane. And do you know what, Percy, old chum?'

'Surprise me.'

'Oh I mean to, old boy. I mean to,' tittered de Warrenne. 'The hateful old nightmare (The Morrigan that is, not Ashdread – though, no doubt about it, he was a hateful old nightmare himself, by all accounts) triumphed ... sort of.'

'Sort of?'

'Well yes – and here's the interesting thing: for while she undoubtedly managed to overcome her infuriating worm of an opponent, it wasn't without a price. You see, old *Corpse-Hand* had become so mighty a warlock that it cost The Morrigan dear to defeat him. My, how it cost her. She became so weakened by her exertions that she only managed to retain a fraction of her old powers. So enfeebled that she went a little scatty, if truth be told. She still hangs around to this very day – a shambling, dizzy-headed parody of herself – bimbling along, only half-remembering who she really is and what she was. Sad really. She was a good friend of old Harry Ca Nab, in fact. Between me and you, old fruit, I think that they had a bit of a *thing* going on there for a while. Ugly as sin was old Harry, but for some reason the ladies couldn't get enough of him. Got him into all sorts of trouble, let me tell you, couldn't keep himself to himself, if you follow me. Made one feel sorry for the wives.

'Anyway, I do believe that she's a good friend of yours too,' smirked de Warrenne, shooting a cheeky and knowing wink at the were-hound.

The Hound leaned in towards the glass divide and carefully tilted the receiver to his lips.

"*Impossible!*" is what he wanted to say, but as de Warrenne's words sunk in the more it made sense. The description of The Morrigan (in certain old texts) certainly fitted that of Old Maggs, and she was certainly older than any witch should be, for she had been ancient when The Hound had first met her, way back in the early 1600s.

The were-hound's jaw slowly sunk open in amazement.

Old Maggs was The Morrigan! Unbelievable!

'Oh don't look so flabbergasted, old chap,' sniggered the vampire, with a rueful shake of his head. 'I've barely begun to get started yet.'

'There's more?'

'Hell yes! I should cocoa. You just hold onto your hat, old cock. You see, though your chum The Morrigan had managed to defeat Ashdread, for some reason she wasn't able to kill him outright. Maybe she was weakened too much by her exertions. Perhaps old *Corpse-Hand* was just too strong. Who knows? So she did what she could, and cursed the wretched little blighter. Turned him into a monstrous dog.'

'*Dog?*'

'Correct. You've heard, no doubt, of *The Billy Shuck*?'

'You mean the legendary faery-hound who once led Herne the Hunter's pack on the nights of the Wild Hu...'

'That's the fellow. Gave me part of the idea, you know, for *The Society of the Wild Hunt*, that is. Big brute, size of a bull, paws bigger than a man's hands. Ugly-looking fellow too: yellow shaggy hide, with one blood-red ear and eyes like the Devil's haemorrhoids. Used to give me the heebie-jeebies just looking at the ghastly bastard. Mind you, if you did look into his eyes (and could somehow manage to keep your dinner down) you could see that there was *someone* at home in there, if you follow me ... and someone that you hoped never got the opportunity to *get out*! Maybe the centuries spent trapped inside the body of a hound had driven him quite mad (that's if the frightful bugger wasn't off his trolley in the first place, mind). Perhaps the untold years living life as a dog had made him forget just who and what he had once been? Wouldn't even like to hazard a guess on that one.'

'You're telling me that you met *The Billy Shuck*!' wheezed The Hound, almost sinking from his chair in disbelief. 'And that he was, in actual fact, the founding member of the Adamsbane dynasty, who'd been cursed into canine form by a spiteful old war-goddess, who, it just so happens, turns out to be my dear friend, Maggs? Are you out of your depraved and demented little mind, de Warrenne!'

'Perhaps,' chuckled the vampire, 'but this is the absolute truth, old hen, I promise you. You see, Harry Ca Nab had won *The Billy Shuck* in a card game with Herne, just before he (Herne the Hunter) retired. Harry was always fascinated with dogs, especially exotically unusual and supernatural ones. Shocking loser, I have to say (Herne the Hunter, that is). Frightful bad form. Still, he was an even worse card player! (Most of these demi-deity types are, for some reason; which makes me wonder why the horn-headed old honker was so bloody addicted to the gaming tables in the first place.) Mind you, Old Harry wasn't above fixing the deck, if you follow me. Though I have to say that to this day I'm still not convinced that Herne wasn't pulling a fast one on Harry, for *The Billy Shuck* was about as friendly as a rabid ferret. Plus the horrible old brute was on his last legs and looked like he was set to expire at any minute.'

De Warrenne suddenly sniggered and shook his head.

'What's so funny, de Warrenne?'

'Oh, nothing really. Was just thinking that the frightful old fiend can't have been as decrepit as he was making out, because, damn his ungodly eyes, the randy blighter managed to mate with one of my bitches ... I say? What's the matter, Percy, old chum, you look positively all at sea? Oh I say. Oh no! Please no. Please tell me that you haven't worked out my little surprise! Oh damn and blast it,' he clucked, throwing a theatrical hand over his mouth. 'I was so looking forward to saying it out loud.'

The Hound was shaking his head furiously.

'No,' he whispered.

'Oh, bugger it, I'm going to say it anyway. Nothing left to lose, after all, what?'

'No.'

'Yes, Percy. Yes! You're just going to have to learn to live with it. I suppose that it does make sense of your rather *unique* and peculiar mutation, wouldn't you say?'

The Hound was studying the vampire's face, desperately looking for some sign that the vile little bounder was telling a lie, just trying to upset him one last time before his hateful days ran out. But de Warrenne's face showed no signs of deceit, just a delighted certainty.

'Yes, it's true, dear boy. You, and of course dear old Bors, are the sons of Ashdread Adamsbane. Which makes you both, I very much believe, the rightful heirs to the throne of the Aelfradi.

'Now Bors, bless his heart, is an absolute mindless *monster* (in every sense of the word), no one in their right mind is going to stick *The Crown of Spring* upon his bloodthirsty and depraved head. Oh no, no, no, it just wouldn't do. Which leaves you, old chap; a little pompous for some, perhaps, but educated, refined, and quite the hero. Oh yes, you'll do very nicely indeed.

'You see, dark days lie before the Elbi, Percival, old chum. And what they need is a strong leader to see them through that darkness. Now I'm sure that young Tomas Dearlove is a lovely fellow, but, well, he's a little wet behind the ears and, to be honest, I'm not too sure that he's up to the task. What the Aelfradi need is a fighter, you see, a warrior; someone who understands both sides of the game and how to play it. I say, I should bow down before you, I suppose – Pook Percival the First, *the long-lost King of Avalon* – but to be honest, I just can't be arsed.'

'Are you playing me for a fool, de Warrenne?' growled The Hound.

'Not a bit of it, *Your Highness*,' chortled the vampire. 'If you don't believe me why don't you ask your old chum, Bobby Goodfellow, I'm sure that he can set you straight. And if you don't believe him, then how about a little chat with your dear pal, Maggs? Might do her the world of good. You never know, it might even bring her back to her senses. Wouldn't that be a wondrous thing! Can you imagine? I'm almost sorry to have to miss it.'

The dapper little vampire leant back in his chair, lanced The Hound with a weighty stare, and then pressed a button to the right of him.

'Well, that's me done, old boy. I do wish I could stick around and see how things play out, but alas, it's out of my hands now. Time's up, I'm afraid.'

He stood up and smiled one last time at the were-hound.

'I'd have made a grand Oberon, you know,' he said, with one last cluck and a cheeky wink.

He gently put the phone down. It made a soft click, like a full-stop.

And then Lord Manfred de Warrenne turned to face the slowly opening doorway that was appearing in the back wall of the steel cell, and headed towards it with a carefree and jaunty saunter, as if he were strolling along an Edwardian seaside promenade on a long-remembered and beautiful summer's afternoon.

THIRTY FOUR
The Prisoners

The Hound slumped back in the chair and stared at his own faint reflection in the glass divide for what could have been one minute, could have been five. He let the phone slowly slip from his face and rest across his knee as he tried to galvanise his jaw-muscles into closing the open draw-bridge of disbelief currently disappearing within the lapels of his overcoat.

Speechless and in a state of bewildered incredulity, he replaced the receiver, slowly pushed himself from his seat, walked to the heavy metal door, pushed it open and came, to his enormous surprise, nose to nose with the barrels of six extremely nasty-looking assault rifles, all pointed threateningly towards him in the unfriendliest of manners and all strongly reeking of silver ammunition.

Behind the flowering line of heavily-armed and armoured MI Unseen agents could be seen the self-satisfied and smiling features of MI Unseen's Director of Operations, the impeccably (if rather unimaginatively) dressed, Colonel Sebastian Sinjon Sin-John. Beside him, bristling like an attack dog itching for the command, stood the smugly grinning form of Captain Montgomery Phelps, head of the mysterious *Achilles Project XIII*.

'Ah, Hound,' beamed Sinjon Sin-John, 'thought you'd got lost in there.'

'And just what is the meaning of *this*?' demanded the were-hound, tapping the nearest gun nozzle off target with the tip of a claw.

'I'm most delighted to say,' grinned Sinjon Sin-John, 'that I'm placing you under arrest for crimes against the State.'

'Preposterous!' blustered The Hound, piercing the colonel with a look like a righteous javelin. 'I demand to see Governor Butterworth, immediately.'

'It is with much regret,' purred the Colonel, with a tone dripping with anything but regret, 'that Governor Butterworth has been *relieved* of his duties. Until his replacement can be found, The Mound – in fact every facet of The Agency – is now under my complete control.'

'I see,' sighed The Hound. And he did. All the warnings that he'd so recently been given had come home to roost – and a lot quicker than he could ever have anticipated! 'And what exactly, may I ask, is the charge?'

'Let me see,' smiled Sinjon Sin-John, lifting his nose to the sky and all but rubbing his hands, 'where to begin? How about we start with – deliberately withholding information that would have prevented the escalating hostilities between the Della Morte and the Nachzehrer families.'

'Indeed? Yes, I couldn't help but notice that *The Agency* seems to have become uncomfortably *cosy* with the Nachzehrers recently,' sneered the were-hound, contemptuously.

'Purely business. Now, where was I? Oh yes. You are also accused of corrupting an agent of the Crown into committing murder on your behalf.'

The Hound looked at the Colonel in disbelief.

'You don't mean Crow?' he gasped, close to laughter.

'Agent AP9-15. Yes, I do.'

'You're out of your mind, you pathetic little fool,' growled the were-hound – possibly not the best of things to say under the circumstances but he'd had an altogether quite taxing day.

'And finally, for the moment,' continued Colonel SinJon Sin-John, choosing to ignore The Hound's outburst, '– though I have no doubt that with a little gentle digging we'll uncover even more of your ghastly and treacherous delinquencies – you are also charged with wilfully assisting a known murderer (a monster who has already cost The Agency eighteen lives, and the lives of God alone knows how many innocent civilians!) to escape, when it was in the power of a British police officer to stop that killer. A killer who, it turns out, just happens to be your own brother!'

The Hound had to admit that they had him on that one.

'And where, pray tell, *is* Inspector Jones right now?' he asked, trying to deflect that particular line of enquiry. 'I suggest that you need to have a long and detailed talk with the Inspector.'

'Oh I have already. Inspector Jones, along with the rest of the Sussex Police's *Department of Special Cases*, has been suspended from duty, pending an ongoing investigation into his rather maverick and, dare one say, unprofessional behaviour.'

'And where, may I ask, is Professor Lyons? Before we go any further with this ridiculous charade I demand to see him,' demanded the were-hound, with a sinking heart, for he had the uncomfortable feeling that he knew where this was all heading.

'*Professor* Lyons has been detained,' smiled SinJon Sin-John. 'As has young Mr Dearlove.'

'Tom? What the devil has he got to do with any of this?'

'That is what I mean to find out,' grinned the Colonel.

'But he's but a child!' pleaded The Hound.

'And that is why he is currently being detained in The Mound's juvenile facility – until the depth of his guilt and association can be satisfactorily ascertained.'

'Are you mad, Colonel? Young Tomas Dearlove is the Crown Prince of the Aelfradi. If he is incarcerated in The Mound you might very well start a war!'

Colonel SinJon Sin-John took a step towards the were-wolf-wolfhound and looked up at him through the thicket of assault-rifles trained on the outraged were-hound. A look of cold-blooded delight danced excitedly in his eyes.

'Oh dear,' he hissed, without the least flicker of an emotion in his voice. 'Now wouldn't that just be a terrible shame?'

The worst part about being locked up in a cell, Tom had decided very quickly, was the ticking clock hanging high on the wall, way out of reach. Time dragged horrifically. And even though his small room was furnished with a TV and PlayStation, the hours painfully dragged their heels.

Tick-tock-tick-tock-tick-tock-tick.

Tom had been picked up yesterday, after he'd left Cornelius struggling with the wonders of trying to coax a mocha out of the vending machine in the visitors' waiting-room. He had just entered through the doors of the Visiting Room to go and see Crow, when his way had been barred by the joyous and piggy features of the *delightful* Agent Charmers, who had requested that he come with her and wait for *Miss Crow* in a private room.

She'd led him through a baffling maze of corridors to a small chamber and told him to wait there. As soon as he'd stepped in, a glass door had closed behind him and the smiling features of Colonel Sinjon Sin-John had appeared from the other side of the door and joyfully informed him (via the intercom) that he was under arrest and would be held in this very cell until further notice. And no, he could not make a phone call.

And that had been that. Trapped like a rat in a box.

His attempts at calling for help, or at least an answer as to *why he was being held here*, had been ignored (assuming, that is, that he could even be heard through the glass door).

Food and drink had appeared in a hatch on the side of the wall at dinnertime and first thing this morning, but he'd had no visitors or contact with another soul for twenty-four hours (and eleven minutes and twenty-nine seconds, to be exact) until Agent Charmers reappeared with two burly guards at her side, both armed with batons.

'Prisoner Dearlove,' she sneered, 'come with me. It's time for your daily exercise. Put this on.'

She threw a monstrous mauve boiler suit on the floor in front of him.

Tom looked at it in horror, but, after a moment of wondering what he'd done in a past life to be subjected to such a wide variety of horrendous fashion statements, did as he was told.

Agent Charmers led him along a soulless white corridor (the two guards flanking him and painfully rapping him on the head with their batons if he made any attempts to ask questions) to a wide door that had the words "*Recreation Hall*" written above it.

'You've got an hour of … *recreation*,' sneered Agent Charmers, looking like a warthog with a mouth ulcer sucking on a pineapple. 'Don't abuse this privilege and it won't be taken away from you. Do you understand me, Prisoner Dearlove?'

Tom looked in trepidation from one baton-wielding guard to the other and decided that a nod would be the least painful answer.

'Hhhmm,' growled Agent Charmers, scrutinising him like he was a cockroach in a colander. 'If there's a hint of trouble from you, boy, it's solitary confinement for the rest of your miserable existence! Do I make myself clear, Prisoner Dearlove?

Tom nodded meekly, and silently decided that someday, somehow, he was going to make her pay for her unnecessarily unpleasant manner.

'Good. Off you go then. You've got an hour. Do you understand me, Prisoner Dearlove?'

'Yes, an houAAAGGHH!' yelped Tom, as one of the guards rapped him on the head with a baton.

'Did I tell you speak, Prisoner Dearlove?' rasped Agent Charmers indignantly, thrusting her foul face into his, and looking like she was in danger of popping an eyeball from its socket.

Tom, ever the quick learner, shook his head.

'Good. Then get your sorry hide in there before I change my mind!' she barked.

Tom hastily made for the door, pushed it open and entered into the large sports hall beyond.

There were fourteen individuals scattered around the hall, all of them, it would appear, *minors*. A small group of tough-looking kids were noisily kicking a football about, others aimlessly mooched around on their own, while the rest huddled together in groups of twos or threes.

And then he saw her. Crow!

His heart skipped a beat. She turned around, as had everybody else (to see who the new face was), and almost choked in surprise when she saw him.

She rushed over to him – to the jeering sneers from the group of apprentice toughs with the football – threw her arms around him and planted a kiss on his cheek. (Tom decided that that almost made the whole *being-detained-and-imprisoned-without-any-idea-of-what-was-going-on*-thing worth it.)

'Tom! What are you doing here? Visiting times aren't till the afternoon.'

Then she took a step back and clocked his delightful mauve attire.

'Oh my God,' she hissed. 'No!'

Tom nodded his head and shrugged his shoulders.

They sat, shoulder to shoulder, with their backs against the wall.

'So, just how are you going to get me out of here now then, genius?' she chuckled. ' Why? How? And just what in Heaven's name have you done to be in here, Tom?'

'I honestly don't know,' replied Tom. 'They haven't told me yet. But I came here with The Hound and Cornelius, so I reckon that they must have been locked up too.'

'Wow. The Hound in The Mound,' she whispered. 'So what's been going on in the outside world for this to happen?'

Tom told her about the battle at Castle Hill and the capture of de Warrenne and the destruction of *The Society of the Wild Hunt*, and they talked and chatted excitedly about what that might mean and what might happen now that the Elbi had their stolen crowns returned to them. And then Tom told her that Cutty Sark was alive and Crow burst into tears and buried her face into his shoulder.

'Wait a minute!' she gasped, lifting her head up and wiping the tears from her eyes with the back of her hideous mauve sleeve. 'That means that you're the Pook of Avalon! Well, well, well. Never thought I'd be rubbing shoulders with royalty, especially in this joint.'

'Don't,' groaned Tom. 'Please. Could we just forget about that for the moment? What we need to concentrate on is ...' he looked about the room and whispered the rest of his sentence, '... finding a way to get out of here.'

Crow considered him carefully and then laughed.

'How?' she shrugged. 'Nobody's ever escaped from The Mound. Ever!'

'Nothing's impossible, surely?'

'Listen Tom; we're on Level One, one floor below ground level; it's here where they keep the juveniles and those prisoners who are deemed to be *non-dangerous.*'

'So that means we've got the best chance of getting out, doesn't it?' he replied, wondering how it was that MI Unseen weren't aware of his most definitely dangerous alter-ego – *Tommy Half-Grendel*?

'Let me get this right, Tom,' smiled Crow. 'What you're suggesting is that we dig our way through the steel walls, fight off the heavily-armed and highly-trained guards, and then tip-toe our way through the minefield that surrounds The Mound?'

'There has to be another way out though ... doesn't there?'

'Below us,' continued Crow, 'on Level Two, they house the human detainees (that's where Professor Lyons will be being held). Below them, in Level Three, they keep the Fae Folk prisoners. Level Four – *spirits and monsters* (that'll be where they'll be keeping The Hound). And then there's Level Five ...'

'What's in Level Five?' asked Tom, though he didn't like the ominous way in which she said it.

'No one's too sure,' she whispered, 'but the rumour is that they've got a Prince of Hell imprisoned down there.'

'Nah,' scoffed one of the football players, screeching to a halt and artfully tucking the ball under his arm. 'I heard that it's an Aztec War God.'

And then everybody began to gather around them to offer their own personal theory on the nightmare that inhabited Level Five.

The remainder of the hour flew by as Tom got to meet his fellow junior jailbirds, but he deeply regretted the fact that he wasn't able to talk to Crow on her own any longer.

Oh well, there was always tomorrow.

Cornelius gave a hard stare to the *Muscle Mary* serving up the slop that passed as breakfast in this place. The gym-monkey, a shaven-headed scowler (who excitedly told anyone who was bothered to listen all about his dangerous were-dog curse), sniffed and dribbled a second spoonful of porridge into Cornelius' bowl.

Cornelius offered an over-polite nod of thanks, pocketed another banana and an oatcake into his horrendous mauve boiler suit, and carried his tray to find somewhere to sit.

The canteen was full of The Mound's *human* detainees; witches and warlocks, would-be *dark-druids*, dealers and dabblers in the occult, thieves and murderers with a paranormal leaning, and those afflicted by unnatural spells and supernatural curses.

'Morning gents, mind if I join you?' he asked, as he approached the table where sat "The Pack" (the members of The Hound's self-help group for were-canines learning to live with the *wild-child* within) – Aussie Joe, Dr Malik, Professor N'Gugi, Billy Blue-Feather, and the hulking and silent figure of Vladimir Chapman.

'Be delighted, Prof,' smiled Aussie Joe, offering Cornelius a welcoming smile and shuffling along to make space for the old codger's sizeable frame. 'Always room for one more, ain't that right, fellas?'

'Any friend of Mr Hound's is a friend of ours,' smiled Clarence N'Gugi, carefully plucking off his glasses and cautiously attending to the sticking-plaster (which seemed to be the only thing holding that was holding them together).

'May I ask how you are finding your stay at *Hotel Mound*, Professor Lyons?' asked Faisil Malik, 'I do hope that the room is to your liking.'

Cornelius chuckled.

'Well, to tell the truth, boys, I've known worse. You should 'ave seen some of the 'ell 'oles that I've 'ad the misfortune to 'ave been a guest of in my time. Must say that the grub's not up to much, and the portions, well, let's just say that they're a little on the stingy side – but, other than that, it's been an absolutely delightful four days. Couldn't 'ave wished for better. Now, if you'd be so kind as to collect my bags for me, I'll finish me breakfast an' settle up the bill on me way out.'

'Any news of Mr Hound?' asked Billy, lifting up a slice of drooping toast and then thinking better of it.

'Not a dicky bird, Billy.'

'Maybe we can help you out on that one, Professor.'

'An' 'ow's that then, Joe?'

'Well it's three days before the next full moon, so me and the fellas will be getting shunted down to Level Four later this afternoon for safekeeping.'

'That's where they will be keeping Mr Hound,' added Clarence, unhappily.

'We'll be back here in about a week, when they're happy that all of the "juices" are out of our system, if you follow me, Professor,' smiled Joe. 'Maybe we'll get a chance to see Mr Hound when we're down there. Maybe pass a message on to him, if we can. I have to say it's unlikely, but we'll do our best, won't we, boys.'

'Oh yes, Professor Lyons,' smiled Faisil. 'If it can be done, then it will be done, and let me tell you that we are the very chaps to do it.'

'Amen,' sighed Clarence, tentatively perching his glasses back onto the end of his nose and testing his handiwork with a nasal wiggle.

'Thanks, boys,' smiled Cornelius. 'Appreciate it. Well, if you do see 'im, or you do get the chance to get a message to 'im, then tell 'im that I'm fine. Tell 'im that I ain't seen, nor been able to speak, to anyone, though. An' tell 'im that I 'aven't seen 'ide nor 'air of Tom, neither.'

The Pack shook their heads and muttered in sympathy.

'We'll do our best, Professor,' said Billy Blue-Feather, glumly scrutinising the attempt at toast that was wilting like a swooning slug over the sides of his plate.

Cornelius nodded and in turn looked down miserably at the bowl of soup-like porridge in front of him. Oh how he longed for one of Missus Dobbs' breakfasts! And for the umpteenth time, he hoped that she was all right. He didn't doubt that Sinjon Sin-John would have targeted One Punch Cottage – and all their other known friends and associates, to boot. He just hoped that they'd had the good sense and good fortune to be able to make themselves scarce and avoid the pinch.

And what about young Tom? Where was he? How was he? And just what would become of him?

And His Nibbs? Had their luck finally run out? Was this to be the end of it? For here they were, buried alive – head-first without a shovel. And try as he might, Cornelius *Dandy* Lyons – legend of the Golden Age of the Regency Prize-Ring, a one-time Prince of Fairyland, and paranormal investigator extraordinaire – just couldn't see a way out of it.

THIRTY FIVE
What Strange Game Is This?

The Hound paced restlessly around his steel cell, swinging his arms, rolling his shoulders and twisting his neck – in an attempt to banish the numb feeling of inactivity from his limbs.

Outside it was a full moon. He could feel Her call like a distant lover and he longed for Her touch upon his skin. It was like an itch that he couldn't reach. A terrible itch. He'd shifted between dog-form and were-form a dozen times or more since She'd risen, to try and stretch his bones and scratch that itch.

Oh, what he wouldn't have done to have his beloved hurdy-gurdy here to while away the hours! What he wouldn't do for a cheese-and-onion toastie with a smidge of horseradish, a splash of Worcester Sauce and a sprig of parsley. And oh, for a cup of Lapsang Souchong!

He pricked his ears.

Something was different. Something was wrong.

He realised that what had suddenly changed was that the constant low hum of electricity (that rattled incessantly throughout The Mound like an old man's dying breath) had stopped, and that the lights from the hallway (his own cell's stark lighting having been switched off hours ago) had gone off.

The door to his cell gave a little clunk and slowly swung open to reveal an empty hall in total blackness.

'Guard?' he called out. 'Guard?' But there was no answer.

What strange game was this?

And then the thought hit him, and it wasn't at all an unexpected one. They were going to kill him. The cowardly swine!

Well, he would sell his life dearly. By God, wouldn't he just!

There would be no holds barred this time. He'd give them everything he'd got, and damn them to Hell for the privilege.

Crow lay on her bed staring at the ceiling, half-listening to the pop song that wafted from the TV. She found that she enjoyed the songs more if she didn't watch the facile videos that the music channels pumped out all day.

She was thinking hard about Tom. And Sparrow.

He'd come to see her again, shortly after Tom's visit, and she'd listened to his empty-headed banter for a while (*I mean, God help us, but when did he get so full of himself?*) before asking him outright if he'd killed Prince Edric. He'd denied it of course, but the look on his face said otherwise. And then he'd got angry with her. Him! Angry at her! The barefaced cheek of it! Accused her of becoming "*tainted*" (whatever that meant). Accused her of letting down The

Agency and turning her back on everything that they had believed in and worked so hard for. How dare he? She hated him!

Suddenly the song fizzled out mid-beat as the TV screen clicked and slowly faded to blackness, and she found herself lying in a rather uncomfortable darkness.

She rolled her feet off the bed and sat up.

Something was wrong.

The lights in the hallway were off.

A power-cut? Surely not. But if it was ... then it might just offer the truly unexpected but wondrous possibility for an escape. *Got to be worth a try. I mean, anything's better than being stuck in here for ever. Right?*

She shuddered over to the door and turned the handle. To her delight, and absolute surprise, it was unlocked!

She waited for a few minutes before making a move, just in case it was a trick and the guards were looking for an excuse to punish somebody, anybody who dared leave their cell. She'd learnt the hard way that you couldn't trust anybody in here. Except Tom. Tom! She'd have to find his cell. He'd be in the Boy's Corridor, but it shouldn't be too hard to find him.

Crow pressed her ear to the crack in the door.

Nothing.

Slowly she pushed the door ajar and peeked through the gap. She could barely see anything but, as far as she could tell, the place seemed completely deserted.

Oh well, here goes.

She slipped through the doorway like a shadow at midnight (her senses and every fibre of her body tingling on high alert) and cautiously made her way down the corridor.

She saw something move in the hallway before her and she quickly and silently crouched down. There was somebody standing at the door to the Boy's Corridor, their back to her, looking through the window.

Wait a minute. She recognised that coat. It must be the only one in existence – a hideous purple monstrosity, hanging like a tent on a flag-pole. Tom!

She tip-toed up behind him, almost weeping with relief and excitement, and was about to tap him on the shoulder when he turned around.

Except that it wasn't Tom.

A pair of eyes (like a brace of blood-soaked nightmares set deep into a hideous face, somewhat akin to a miffed hatchet) glowered at her in delight – like a half-starved albino weasel turning to find that a newly-hatched duckling has imprinted on him. Crow let out a scream, for she knew that face (and it still gave her bad dreams) for it belonged to one of the *Redcap* warriors who had abducted her and Nanny Nannie on the night they'd tried to steal *The Crown of Spring* – the infamous bogeyman and legendary man-murderer ... Long Lamkin!

Tom awoke with the sudden realisation that something was amiss.

He tried to flick the light on, but it didn't seem to be working. Then he noticed that the door to his cell was open. That was strange. Just what the heck was going on?

He crawled out of bed and sleepily pulled on his hideous mauve boiler suit.

There was a soft shuffle of feet and a harsh rattle of whispers outside the door.

He suddenly felt very, very afraid.

'Hello?' he offered, hesitantly.

Nothing.

He looked around for anything that might be used as a weapon, but of course there was nothing in his room that might be of any use that wasn't bolted down.

Tentatively he walked forwards, slipped his head through the doorway and peered into the corridor.

Something soft and dark was thrown over his head. He tried to scream but his mouth was stuffed with material and his cry was cut off by a sharp blow to the back of the neck that instantly rendered him unconscious.

The Hound crouched down, ready to launch himself at the first thing that dared to come through the door.

He could hear the scrabbling of feet rushing down the corridor.

And then a large snout tentatively appeared around the edge of the doorway, followed by large tawny eyes and a set of pointy ears.

The were-hound instantly recognised Aussie Joe – now in his were-dingo form. Several more heads joined Joe's; the mottled snout of Professor Clarence N'Gugi, the red muzzle of Dr Faisil Malik and the massive shaggy grey head of Makkapetew. Behind them lurked the huge and hulking were-wolf form of Vladimir Chapman.

Come, they called, and though they didn't speak he could hear their every thought. *Come! The Moon. We hunt. This night is ours! This night we will be free!*

Suddenly there was nothing in the world that The Hound desired more than to run with his brothers, free and unburdened from the restraints of this world, free and wild under the splendour of Her skies.

There was a low, menacing and blood-curdling roar from something huge and terrifying at the far end of the corridor. As one, The Pack lifted their heads, their ears pricked forward, and the joy of the hunt sparkled like blood from a fresh kill in their eyes. They threw back their heads and howled back their acceptance of the challenge, their tails stiff and bristling. And then they tore towards whatever poor monster it was that had dared to rear its head in their presence.

The Hound, mid-howl, almost joined them, but something stopped him.

The sounds of snarling and snapping and the terrible yowls of pain thundered down the hallway.

If all of the cells of had been opened ... he suddenly realised, his blood running cold with the thought, *if all of the guards had vanished, that meant that all manner of murderous nightmare would be rampaging through the long corridors of The Mound!*

He instantly knew that he had to get to Cornelius, and Tom (if he was here), before it was too late!

THIRTY SIX
The Enchanted Kingdom

Tom was gently dumped onto soft and damp ground. He had regained consciousness almost an hour ago, awakening to find himself with a hood over his head and slung across someone's (or something's) shoulder, as they travelled at a very bumpy and urgent pace. The incessant jarring and jolting, coupled with having a bag over his head, had made him feel a little woozy, and it was almost a relief when the hood was finally pulled from him, even though he dreaded to think what terrible fate now awaited him.

He waited for his eyes to adjust to the light, his vision somewhat blurred and his head rather groggy from both the blow to the back of his neck and the rather challenging journey that he'd just endured. A hand (decidedly deficient in digits) reached forth and tenderly hoisted him to his feet.

'Thumbscrew!' gasped Tom, close to vomiting (for many reasons).

The demented old horror beamed proudly up at him with a face like a sun-starved buttock slashed with blunt razor-blades. And as Tom turned he saw all his old chums from his personal bodyguard, *The Purple Frighteners*, surrounding him and smiling kindly at him with their own peculiar version of parental concern.

Tom turned his head and threw up.

'Prince Tomas,' oozed a familiar voice like a garrotter's chilled cheese-wire slicing through a windpipe, and Tom looked up to see Tommy Rawhead-and-Bloody-Bones gurning at him with a smile like a warmed-up corpse at a christening. 'Please forgive the rather rough and harsh treatment that we have had to subject you to, Your Majesty.' he rasped apologetically. 'But it seemed the quickest and easiest way to get you out of there. The frightful place was literally crawling with bloodthirsty and ravenous monsters, and we feared that if we spent time explaining our plan to you then we might all have been ripped limb from limb – our heads torn from our shoulders, our hearts torn and savaged from our blood-spurting bodies, our brains sucked through the eye-sockets of our ruptured skulls – before we had made ourselves understood.'

Tom held up a hand in thanks and noisily heaved again.

'Were it not for the good fortune of Long Lamkin (who has offered his services and joined our proud brotherhood as a replacement for the sadly lamented Inkcap) we might have missed you altogether.'

Tom looked over and saw the gruesome figure of the tall and spindly Lamkin, who curled his fingers and offered a jaunty wave of hello. But Tom's attention was suddenly focused elsewhere, for standing next to him was Crow, looking pale and mildly terrified it must be admitted, but alive and safe, and free from The Mound.

He ran over to her and threw his arms around her. And then, overcome with emotions, he kissed her, or at least he tried to because she jerked her head violently away.

'Oh ... er ... I'm sorry ... I didn't mean ...' he fumbled awkwardly.

'No, it's fine, Tom, in fact it's wonderful, but you might want to have a bit of a clean-up first,' she grimaced, wiggling her fingers in the direction of Tom's puke-encased chin.

'Oh God! I am so sorry,' he gasped, mortified beyond his wildest dreams, hastily wiping his mouth clean on the sleeve of his horrendous puke-coloured mauve boiler suit.

But Crow just smiled again and hugged him all the harder.

'So was it you who shut down The Mound's power supply?' Tom asked Bloody-Bones, after he and Crow had managed to draw themselves apart.

'No, it was not,' replied Rawhead-and-Bloody-Bones, looking worryingly puzzled. 'That was just a strange stroke of fortune. I reasoned that you must be being held in The Mound as soon as Missus Dobbs had informed me of your disappearance. For no one had seen you since your visit to that ghastly institution. Emissaries were sent to MI Unseen and the Humans' government, but were told that they had no knowledge of your whereabouts. I chose not to believe them. Henceforth we have kept a vigil, night and day; watching the comings and goings at The Mound, waiting and praying for a chance to find you and free you, my prince. And then, earlier this evening, a most remarkable thing happened – all of the guards left the building and were transported from the site. Sometime later the power went off – and so, in went we.'

'That's odd,' said Tom. 'What about Cornelius and The Hound?' he asked, suddenly looking around. 'Where are they?'

'We did not have the time nor the resources to look for them, Prince Half-Grendel,' replied Bloody-Bones, with a regretful shake of his head. 'I am sorry. No doubt they were being held within the lower levels, but by the time we found you the place was on the verge of being overrun by all manner of deadly creatures that were rising from the deep, and we dared not take the chance of searching for them and risk not being able to get you out.'

'Smash and grab,' grunted the delightful Earwiggy, nodding his head sagely and fondling a lobe.

'But we've got to go back and get them out of there!' cried Tom.

Bloody-Bones solemnly shook his head.

'We cannot risk it, Tomas. Come, Prince Spirit-Lyon, we must tarry here no longer. Who knows what follows us?'

'But we can't just leave them!'

'We must. When you are safely in the realm of Avalon then we will make plans to find them.'

'No!' he said, trying to sound as princely and commanding as he could. 'I'm going back to find them.'

'No, you are not, Your Highness,' said the goblin, sternly.

Tom looked sternly back at the frightful old nightmare.

'I don't care what you say,' snapped Tom, 'I'm going back to get them.'

'They are my friends too, Prince Tomas, but I have made a promise to them both that I would protect you. I will not break that promise. I will not endanger you any further.'

'But ... !'

'Tom,' said Crow, putting a hand on his shoulder. 'By the time we left there it was like a zoo at feeding time. We'd never get back in. But if there's anyone who's going to be able to survive in there it'll be The Hound and your granddad.'

'But ... But we've got to do ... something!'

Bloody-Bones sighed.

'All right,' he said at last, 'Enough. This is what will happen, Prince Grendel-weather. Myself, Mouse, Earwiggy and Thumbscrew will escort you and Crow to *The Hidden Realm*. The rest of the lads will head back to The Mound and search for any sign of Cornelius and The Hound.'

'But ...!'

'It is my last and only offer, Prince Tomas.'

Tom reluctantly agreed, even though he felt like he was betraying his friends by not going himself.

Bloody-Bones turned and nodded to the lads and, like the purple parka-clad collection of horrendous old monstrosities that they were, they slipped into the morning mist and vanished like a ghostly dream.

Tom watched them disappear. He felt terrible about sending others to do his dirty work, but what could he do? Was this what it actually meant to be royalty, that you never actually got to do anything yourself, just got other people to do things for you? He didn't think that he liked that. And then he recognised his surroundings, and he suddenly realised that they were standing at the top of Chanklebury Ring.

It took them less than ten minutes to make their way down to the ancient, gnarled and giant tree that stood at the bottom of the hill, standing like a sentry on tippy-toe. Its ginormous roots cascaded like a living waterfall down the hollowed side of the slope, forming the bars of a cage straight out of a particularly unpleasant fairy tale. It was (Tom knew because Cornelius had told him) a portal between *The Two Albions,* an old and forgotten entrance to *The Hidden Realm,* the land of the Aelfradi – Avalon.

'Your kingdom awaits you, my prince,' smiled Rawhead-and-Bloody-Bones, opening the palms of his hands and gesturing towards the entrance.

Tom took hold of Crow's hand, and together they threaded themselves through the roots and made their way into the dark and musty-smelling passageway that led to the enchanted kingdom.

EPILOGUE
The Forgotten Thing

It had been a long and arduous journey, but now she was here, standing at the very edge of it. It called to her. She could smell its tears. It was where she was meant to be. Where it had all begun (or maybe it had all ended) so many years ago.

When the carnage was finally over and The Mound had fallen into a hushed and appalled silence, she had crept from her pool and feasted upon the flesh of what had been slain. And it had made her strong. Then, like a scampering newt, she had scuttled from shadow to shadow, up and up and up and out – into the open air. Oh, she had raised her hands into the sky and twirled and jigged and danced beneath the moon like a little girl.

How long since she had breathed the crisp cold air of freedom?

How long since she had felt the kiss of the Goddess tickling her skin?

How long since she had heard the music of the wild things singing to the night?

Carefully, carefully, past the stupid, mutilated corpses of the unthinking things who had unwittingly stepped upon the mines that surrounded the prison (and so thrown away forever their chance of freedom). She had picked her way through the splattered remains of those who had all too hastily sped to their doom, or been caught fleeing from greater horrors than they (or all too lustily pursued lesser ones).

Through the dead fields she had crawled, over the hills, until, at last, she had come to the dark and cold fresh waters of a river.

And she had sat by its banks and listened to its song and sobbed tears of pure joy.

And then she had followed the lines. Then she had followed her memories. Delighting in the babbling of the waters, as they told her their secrets, their stories, their tragedies. They swirled with life and death, with flashing fishes and wriggling worms. On and on she had travelled, sleeping by day and scampering by night, like a salmon returning to the place of its birth, until the sky had blinked its night eye shut and she had come to the place. The place where it all began (or maybe it was the place where it had all ended). The place where everything had changed.

It was a small lake, unspectacular, hidden high in the hills, unremembered and unknown. Its waters were silent and black and still and deep. As deep as the pits of Hell. So old it was, that not even the Goblins knew its true name. *"The First"* they had called it – *"the womb of the world"*.

And in that water lived an old knucker; ancient and wise and mean and bitter. And along with the knucker, it lay – *the forgotten thing*.

She had put it there, oh so long ago. And everybody had forgotten. But not her, no. And that should have been an end to it, but *he* had tricked her, hadn't he? *He* had cursed her! Made her forget everything. She had forgotten her friends. She had forgotten her family. Maybe she had even forgotten how to die – because here she was, still alive, and that, she knew, just should not be. No. Not after all these years. So many, many, many years. Where do they all go? Why couldn't she remember them? But the one thing that she could remember, the one thing that she kept inside her like the last heartbeat of a life, was where the *forgotten thing* lay hidden.

She slipped into the blackness of the lake like a knife; like a kingfisher hunting to take a life. Into the water with barely a splash (don't wake the knucker or he'll taste your flesh). Way down at the bottom, under the silt, in the deepest hole, in the dimmest pit – carved from a dragon's eye, from a dead God's bones, lay the wild, dark magic of the lost *Puck Stone*.

Down she swam, deeper and deeper, into the cold and into the darkness, deeper and deeper, past the sleeping dragon, deeper and deeper and downwards she dived – until she came to the bottom of the world. Nimbly her hands sifted through the mud and the sand and the silt, one eye kept fast upon the slumbering wyrm, searching for what was lost, for the thing that was forgotten.

'Oh, sssome callss me Ginny,
ssssome callss me Jenny,
and there'ssss ssssome,
(and theyss can rot in Hell)
as callsss me
Peganel.'

www.caractacusplume.com

The Hound Who Hunts Nightmares

The Case Of The Lost Crowns Of Albion

Silvatici Books

silvatici@outlook.com

Printed in Poland
by Amazon Fulfillment
Poland Sp. z o.o., Wrocław